Dear Reader,

Welcome to another exciting month of Duets—romantic stories guaranteed to make you smile!

In Duets #25 Kristin Gabriel's *The Bachelor Trap* is the first book in a new miniseries called CAFÉ ROMEO, about a coffeehouse that also doubles as a dating service. *What better place to find both lattes and love!* Talented Kristin received a RITA Award this year from the Romance Writers of America for her Love & Laughter novel *Monday Man*. Popular Carrie Alexander also kicks off a trilogy, called THE COWGIRL CLUB, about three lifelong female friends who love horses and—what else?—cowboys! You'll have a galloping good time reading Grace's story in *Custom-Built Cowboy*.

In Duets #26 we return to the BEST OF THE WEST with fan favorite Cathie Linz. This time, in *The Lawman Gets Lucky,* charming Reno Best is the sheriff hero who comes undone when he encounters gorgeous new schoolteacher Annie Benton. *The West will never be the same!* New author Isabel Sharpe delivers the sharply funny *Beauty and the Bet,* another book in the MAKEOVER MADNESS miniseries. Beautiful Heather Brannen makes herself over as a plain Jane in order to best ladies' man Jack Fortunato. But she's sure surprised when Jack falls hard for the plain "Marsha," and Heather is jealous of herself!

I hope you enjoy all our books this month and every month!

Happy reading!

Birgit Davis-Todd
Senior Editor, Harlequin Duets

Harlequin Books
225 Duncan Mill Rd.
Don Mills, Ontario
M3B 3K9 Canada

The Bachelor Trap

"You want me to protect you from a chef?" Jake asked incredulously.

"This isn't funny. I think the man is unbalanced. He's been stalking me for the last three weeks," Nina countered.

"Maybe his puffy white hat is too big." Jake settled back in his seat. "I think I can handle a chef—on one condition."

Oh, no. "What exactly do you want from me?"

"A review." Jake sat up and looked at her. "I want the works. I guarantee it'll be a good experience for you."

The man certainly wasn't modest. But what exactly was he asking for—a publicity quote on his sexual prowess? She could picture it now: *The Jackhammer lives up to his name.*

Nina swallowed. "I'm sorry, Jake, but I'm not that type of girl. Even if I was, I wouldn't know where to start. I've never reviewed a lover before...."

Jake just stared at her. "I was talking about a review of Café Romeo—not me." Then he grinned. "But if you'd like to sample the Callahan charm, I'm game. I haven't had any complaints so far."

For more, turn to page 9

Caught in the act!

When the closet door opened, her eyes were closed. For a few blissful seconds she'd forgotten herself, but when Shane said "Grace?" with a horrified, quizzical, absolute dumbfoundedness, it all came rushing back: She was in his closet in the middle of the night, wearing fuzzy green slippers and a cartoon nightshirt, plus his cowboy hat, bandanna and jacket.

"What are you doing?"

She scrunched up her face. Gestured with the flapping sleeves. "Trying on your jacket?" she squeaked.

Shane gave a short, disbelieving laugh. "In the closet with the door closed? Why?"

"Because I didn't want to wake you," she said, squinting at his face. "Which makes perfect sense, doesn't it?" she asked hopefully.

"It makes perfect Grace Farrow turn-the-world-upside-down sense," he said, his gaze sliding over the jacket to her nightshirt and exposed bare legs. Suddenly he looked wide awake. Grace tried not to grin. Must be the sight of her fuzzy-wuzzy slippers packed quite a wallop.

For more, turn to page 197

If you purchased this book without a cover you should be aware
that this book is stolen property. It was reported as "unsold and
destroyed" to the publisher, and neither the author nor the
publisher has received any payment for this "stripped book."

HARLEQUIN DUETS

ISBN 0-373-44091-X

THE BACHELOR TRAP
Copyright © 2000 by Kristin Eckhardt

CUSTOM-BUILT COWBOY
Copyright © 2000 by Carrie Antilla

All rights reserved. Except for use in any review, the reproduction or
utilization of this work in whole or in part in any form by any electronic,
mechanical or other means, now known or hereafter invented, including
xerography, photocopying and recording, or in any information storage
or retrieval system, is forbidden without the written permission of the
publisher, Harlequin Enterprises Limited, 225 Duncan Mill Road,
Don Mills, Ontario, Canada M3B 3K9.

All characters in this book have no existence outside the imagination of
the author and have no relation whatsoever to anyone bearing the same
name or names. They are not even distantly inspired by any individual
known or unknown to the author, and all incidents are pure invention.

This edition published by arrangement with Harlequin Books S.A.

® and TM are trademarks of the publisher. Trademarks indicated with
® are registered in the United States Patent and Trademark Office, the
Canadian Trade Marks Office and in other countries.

Visit us at www.romance.net

Printed in U.S.A.

KRISTIN GABRIEL

The Bachelor Trap

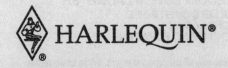

HARLEQUIN®

TORONTO • NEW YORK • LONDON
AMSTERDAM • PARIS • SYDNEY • HAMBURG
STOCKHOLM • ATHENS • TOKYO • MILAN • MADRID
PRAGUE • WARSAW • BUDAPEST • AUCKLAND

Dear Reader,

People are always asking me how I come up with my stories. Well, I can honestly say that the idea for CAFÉ ROMEO came from watching CNN. There really is a coffeehouse in the world that doubles as a dating service! What better place to find both lattes and love? However, as a writer, I couldn't help doing a little embellishing. At Café Romeo, you can also find a storyteller who reads coffee grounds and plans to test her matchmaking talents by setting a bachelor trap for each of her three nephews.

The first bachelor at risk is ex-boxer Jake Callahan, who meets his match in food critic Nina Walker. That's when he discovers he's in for the fight of his life! And he's not alone. Don't miss the romantic misadventures of Sophie's two other nephews, Trace and Noah, in Duets #27, *Bachelor by Design,* available in May 2000, and Duets #29, *Beauty and the Bachelor,* on the shelves in June 2000.

Happy reading,

Kristin Gabriel

Books by Kristin Gabriel
HARLEQUIN DUETS
7—ANNIE, GET YOUR GROOM

HARLEQUIN LOVE & LAUGHTER
40—BULLETS OVER BOISE
56—MONDAY MAN
62—SEND ME NO FLOWERS

Don't miss any of our special offers. Write to us at the following address for information on our newest releases.

Harlequin Reader Service
U.S.: 3010 Walden Ave., P.O. Box 1325, Buffalo, NY 14269
Canadian: P.O. Box 609, Fort Erie, Ont. L2A 5X3

To Malle Vallik, for making it all possible.

Prologue

"ARE YOU dead yet?"

Sixty-year-old Sophie Callahan cracked open one eye to see the lined face of her best friend, Hannah Baker, hovering above her bed. "Do I look dead?"

"Almost."

"Good." Sophie sat up in bed as the macabre strains of a funeral dirge filled the air. The spicy aroma of incense mingled with the minty scent of her arthritis salve. "I thought I might have overdone it with the makeup."

"No, it's very realistic." Hannah looked over at the stereo in the corner. "The music is a nice touch."

"I wanted to set the mood."

"So far everything is going smoothly," Hannah assured her. "I've got your visitors settled in the parlor with my homemade peanut brittle. I added some extra salt to the recipe for good measure."

Sophie looked up. "What about the coffee? Please don't tell me you forgot the coffee."

Hannah sniffed. "Of course not. I brewed up a pot of the Jamaican almond blend, just as you instructed."

Sophie breathed a sigh of relief. "Good. We can't

trust something this important to those inferior Colombian blends.''

"If you're ready, I'll send them in."

Sophie reclined against the pillows, crossed her arms in an X over her chest, then closed her eyes. "I'm ready." She lay still as a corpse as Hannah walked from the room. Sophie's days as a fortune teller in the carnival were long over, but she still enjoyed putting on a show. A tingle of excitement raced through her when she heard the heavy tread of footsteps out in the hallway. *Her nephews.* She bit back a smile. This was almost too easy.

The door creaked open. "Aunt Sophie?"

She moaned softly, turning her head toward the sound of the deep, masculine voice. Opening her eyes, she saw the three Callahan men towering over her bed.

"It's me…Jake," whispered the one standing closest to her. He sat down on the edge of the bed, clasping her small, wrinkled hand in his big, warm one. Worry clouded his midnight blue eyes. "Trace and Noah are here too."

At twenty-eight, Jake, her oldest nephew, still looked more like a powerful boxer than a business manager. But the gifted athlete had hung up his boxing gloves one fateful night five years ago and never looked back. Now he kept his emotions as tightly locked up as his heart.

"You should be in the hospital, Aunt Sophie," Jake said in his no-nonsense voice. "If you don't go willingly, I'm going to pick you up and carry you there.''

Trace Callahan, the black sheep of the Callahan clan, stepped forward. He wore a chambray shirt with the sleeves cut off, revealing his finely honed biceps and a tattoo of a coiled snake. He'd gone from juvenile delinquent to successful building contractor. With Sophie's guidance, of course. ''Maybe you've got food poisoning. Has Hannah been cooking again?''

Noah stepped up beside him. ''Her peanut brittle could make anybody sick. At least go see a doctor. Or let us hire a full-time nurse. I know one or two with great bedside manners.''

Sophie didn't doubt it for a moment. Her youngest nephew was a playboy who had been breaking hearts since he was fifteen years old. A crack insurance investigator, Noah's personal specialty was the kiss-and-run.

Her gaze drifted to the salsa spot on the ceiling—a small memento of the last party she'd thrown for her old carnival pals. Time to get down to business. *''I, Madame Sophia, have seen the future.''*

All three men groaned. Jake gently squeezed her hand. ''Aunt Sophie, you're ill. This really isn't the time to start up with that nonsense.''

As a fortune teller, she was used to skeptics. So she ignored him. ''I see my three nephews,'' she continued in an unnaturally deep voice, ''who have been like sons to me. They are successful men. Powerful men. Lonely men.''

"Not again," Jake muttered under his breath.

"If only they had visited my coffeehouse." She breathed a mournful sigh. "Madame Sophia brews up perfect coffee and perfect couples at Café Romeo."

Noah leaned toward Jake. "That's sounds like an advertising slogan."

"It is," Jake muttered, his eyes narrowing on his aunt. "I heard it on the radio this morning."

Sophie coughed weakly to get their attention. "But, alas, now it is too late. They shall remain bachelors…forever."

"Must be fate," Jake chimed in, sounding much too cheerful about it.

She opened her eyes and glowered at him. "It's sheer stubbornness, Jake Callahan. If you'd just let me read your coffee grounds, you'd live happily ever after."

"I'll only be happy when you're feeling better, Aunt Sophie. I don't want to lose you." Jake leaned over to kiss her cheek. As soon as his lips touched her, she knew the scam was over.

He straightened, wiping his fingers over his mouth. "What the hell…?"

"It's makeup," Trace proclaimed, running his index finger over her forehead, then holding it up to show them the white greasepaint smeared across his fingertip. "This is another one of her tricks."

Noah grinned. "Good one, Aunt Sophie. You really had us going there."

"Don't encourage her."

A muscle twitched in Jake's jaw, but otherwise he

remained calm. He hadn't displayed a sign of his explosive temper in exactly five years and three months. Sophie rolled her eyes, preparing herself for another one of his lectures.

"Aunt Sophie, you have more to worry about than our romantic futures," Jake began. "Café Romeo is in serious financial trouble."

She scowled as she struggled to sit up in bed. "Don't try to change the subject, young man. You need a relationship in your life, and I don't mean with an adding machine."

Noah laughed until Trace jabbed him in the stomach with his elbow. But it was too late. Sophie turned her attention to Jake's younger brothers. "You all need some romance in your life."

"Don't worry about me, Aunt Sophie." Noah grinned. "I have plenty of women in my life."

Trace folded his burly arms across his chest. "Me, too."

Sophie pressed her lips together. She hadn't intended to argue with them today. Especially since they were every bit as pigheaded as their father. And as clueless about women. If her little brother had listened to her advice thirty years ago, he wouldn't have married the woman who had eventually abandoned him and their three young sons. Sophie had no intention of letting history repeat itself.

As Madame Sophia, she read the romantic futures of her customers in their coffee grounds. Her predictions weren't always entirely accurate, but love was an inaccurate business. Her nephews might scoff at her skills, but she'd had some successes at Café Romeo, the only coffeehouse in St. Louis that also doubled as a matchmaking service.

She gave it one last shot. "I know I could find the perfect woman for each one of you."

"That's what scares us." Jake stood up, letting go of her hand. "Give it up, Madame Sophia. We know you too well to fall into one of your bachelor traps. Save your séances for your customers."

"Séances are for charlatans," Sophie said with a sniff. "I read coffee grounds. It's a gift."

"I'd rather have a new radial-arm saw," Trace quipped, giving his aunt a quick peck on the cheek before he walked out the door.

Noah moved to follow him, but not before planting a kiss on the top of her head. "Goodbye, you old shyster. Better luck next time."

She watched her youngest nephew walk from the room. He was as playful as his oldest brother was serious. Too playful in her opinion. It was time for Noah to settle down. It was time for all her boys to settle down. Provided they found the right women.

Jake moved toward the door. "I'll see you at Café Romeo on Monday morning, Aunt Sophie. We can't hold off those loan payments much longer. I'll go over all the accounts again this weekend and draw up a new balance sheet."

She rolled her eyes. Her gorgeous nephew was planning to cuddle up to a balance sheet on Saturday night. If any man needed a woman in his life, it was Jake Callahan.

Lucky for him she could handle that little detail.

Several tense minutes later, Hannah peeked her head around the door. "The coast is clear. Your nephews just left."

Sophie clutched the bedcovers. "Did it work?"

Hannah jumped into the room, pumping one gnarled fist in the air. "We got 'em!"

Sophie leapt out of bed and did a victory dance over the hardwood floor. She sashayed over to the stereo and switched the music to Van Halen, undulating to the beat until her bad hip began to ache. Then she collapsed into a beanbag chair. "This is the best day of my life."

Hannah cackled. "Those boys didn't suspect a thing. They were so happy you weren't on your deathbed, they just walked out the door without a second thought."

Sophie rubbed her hands together. "Well, don't keep me in suspense."

Hannah slipped out of the room. A few moments later, she returned carrying a small serving tray with three coffee cups on it.

Sophie smiled at the sight of the soggy coffee grounds settled in the bottoms of the three cups. This would teach those boys to underestimate her. They'd been keeping their coffee grounds out of her reach for the last decade. Until now. "Which one is which?"

Hannah's grin faltered. "What?"

"The coffee cups, Hannah. I can't read the grounds correctly if I don't know which cup belongs to which nephew."

"Oh, dear." Hannah frowned at the coffee cups before her.

Sophie closed her eyes with a groan. "Don't tell me you didn't keep track."

"Now don't panic. I'm sure I can remember."

Sophie nibbled her lower lip. Hannah was a wonderful friend and a good housekeeper, but she didn't have the best memory. Just last week she'd forgotten to add bananas to the banana bread.

"Let me think," Hannah murmured. "Jake had the red cup...Trace had the blue cup...and Noah had the green cup."

"Are you sure?" Sophie asked anxiously. "Because red is Noah's favorite color."

"Now that you mention it, I believe Noah did have the red cup. Which means Jake had the blue cup and Trace had the green cup."

"I thought you said Trace had the blue cup."

"Did I?" Hannah stared thoughtfully at the ceiling. "Yes, I believe Trace did have the blue cup."

"So Jake had the green cup?"

"No, Jake had the yellow cup."

Sophie sagged onto the bed. "There is no yellow cup."

"Oh, that's right." Hannah glanced down at the tray. "The yellow cup broke this morning. We'll have to replace it."

"Think, Hannah. Think very hard. Because if I mix up these cups," she said with a shudder, "I don't even want to think about the potentially catastrophic consequences."

Hannah took a deep breath. "Noah had the red cup." She carefully set it to one side. "Trace has the blue cup." She placed it next to the red cup. "And this one," she picked up the green cup, "belongs to Jake."

Sophie reverently took the green cup from her hand. "You're sure?"

"Positive," Hannah affirmed. "Really. I'm almost completely positive."

But Sophie barely heard her as she closely examined the damp coffee grounds in the bottom of the green coffee cup. After several silent moments, a triumphant smile curved her lips. *"Jake Callahan, I see romance in your future."*

NINA WALKER didn't normally accompany her trash into the Dumpster, but tonight was an exception. As soon as she saw the long black hearse pull into the parking lot of her apartment complex, she scaled the steel side of that Dumpster like a champion hurdler.

Still clutching her neatly sealed kitchen trash bag to her chest, she crouched low, holding her breath and trying not to think about what else might be in the Dumpster with her. Especially not any furry rodents who might consider her the latest dish in their rubbish buffet. After a long moment, she peeked over the rusty rim of her hiding place and watched the hearse make a slow circle around the parking lot. The name on the vanity license plate confirmed her worst fears.

It was him.

She took a deep, calming breath, realizing her mistake a second too late. The putrid stench of rotting meat, soiled diapers and sour milk invaded her nose and throat, burning her lungs. She coughed and gagged as her foot slid into something soft and warm and slimy.

Only the thought of the man behind the wheel of that hearse kept her from leaping back out of the

Dumpster. Bo "The Bonecrusher" Bonham wanted to crush her. A former pro wrestler turned chef, The Bonecrusher hadn't appreciated her review of his cooking talents in her latest "Nina's Nibbles" column. Could she help it if his pasta tasted like paste and his carob cake resembled cardboard?

Some people just couldn't handle a little criticism. Most of them, however, responded with a nasty phone call or a terse letter to the editor. Not The Bonecrusher. He'd walked right up to her desk at the *St. Louis Post-Dispatch* and snapped a turkey-leg bone in half with his bare hands.

"You're next," he'd growled, then he'd thrown the bone fragments into her in-box and walked away.

It had been their first and only confrontation—until tonight. Still, Karla Ruskin, a part-time stringer for the *Dispatch* and a wrestling fanatic, picked up the story and made it an ongoing saga in her articles. Karla had even bestowed Nina with a wrestling moniker: The Nibbler. Not exactly a name to induce terror in others. Giggles, maybe, but not fear.

Thanks to Karla's inflammatory reporting style, The Nibbler versus The Bonecrusher had been the hot topic in the "Letters to the Editor" section for the last month. Nina had received some personal hate mail, too, from some of The Bonecrusher's more devoted and demented fans.

No doubt Karla's latest story would only add to the uproar. She'd reported that The Nibbler and The Bonecrusher were preparing for Round 2 at the Reviewers' Choice chefs' competition in Chicago. Nina was slated to be one of the judges—and The Bone-crusher one of the contestants.

Just the thought of it made her stomach hurt.

Her back hurt, too, from crouching in the Dumpster, and her lungs ached from trying to hold her breath for so long. The noxious fumes brought tears to her eyes. She blinked them back, then blinked again at the sudden glare of bright headlights shining on the Dumpster.

He'd found her.

Her heart dropped to her toes as the driver's door of the hearse opened and three hundred pounds of solid muscle stepped out onto the asphalt.

She was going to die in a Dumpster.

Just one more humiliation heaped upon a lifetime of humiliations. Her entire, insignificant life flashed before her eyes. She'd been the only Walker not to make valedictorian in high school. The only Walker not to qualify for Mensa. The only Walker not to graduate from an Ivy League university. Her parents thought she was still trying to find herself. Her older, overachieving brother and sister thought she was adopted.

She swallowed hard, realizing she might never see her family again. She did love them, despite their never-ending string of successes.

The sound of heavy footsteps made her breathing hitch. Through a small, corroded hole in the side of the Dumpster, she could see a massive pair of ostrich-skin cowboy boots moving toward her. The tiny hairs on the back of her neck prickled as she hunched lower in the Dumpster.

"Good evening, Miss Walker." The deep rumble of his voice sent shivers down her spine. It was too easy to remember the sound of splintering turkey bone. Too easy to envision him snapping her in two.

He chuckled low. "Now what's a nice girl like you doing in a place like this?"

She swallowed hard, looking frantically around her for some kind of weapon. She grabbed an empty Spam can, the sharp, ragged metal lid protruding from one end. Then she sank farther into the shadows, waiting for him to make the first move.

"If you're smart, you'll stay there," he growled. "At least for the next couple of weeks. We both know it's right where you belong—with the rest of the garbage."

The next moment she felt icy liquid splash on top of her head and dribble down her face. The drenching was followed by a shower of greasy chicken bones and cold French fries. They landed in her hair and fell down inside her blouse. Then the lid of the Dumpster slammed down above her, leaving her in murky darkness.

Before Nina could even anticipate his next move, she heard the roar of an engine and the squeal of tires. Through the peephole, she watched in stunned disbelief as the hearse peeled out of the parking lot. Her gaze fixed on the illuminated Missouri license plate until she could no longer read the word on it that identified her nemesis: BONEMAN.

She dropped the Spam can, her fingers shaking. The Bonecrusher hadn't annihilated her, he'd just dumped his garbage on top of her. Maybe it was a warning. Maybe he'd read Karla's story and discovered she'd be one of his judges at the Reviewers' Choice competition. Maybe that's why he'd kept up his campaign of terror.

It was working.

She rose up, her knees wobbly, still unable to believe she'd come out of this confrontation relatively unscathed. Then she hit her head on the Dumpster lid.

It stuck there.

Wincing, she reached up to feel a thick, sticky wad of chewing gum adhering her hair to the lid. "Wonderful," she muttered. "Like I don't already have enough problems."

At least she was alive. She had gum in her hair and a chicken wing in her bra, but she was alive. Now she just had to figure out how to stay that way.

TWO DAYS and seven showers later, Nina had a plan. It wasn't the best plan, but then, she wasn't a rocket scientist like her brother. Or a brain surgeon like her mother. Still, Molly McKenna, who lived two doors down in her apartment building, liked it and had even agreed to tag along.

"So where are all the naked men?" Molly asked, as they stepped through the front door of the Ninth Street Gym.

"We're not here to see naked men," Nina replied, trying her best to look inconspicuous in a room full of grunting, muscle-bound males. The air was warm and heavy with the sour odor of perspiration. She grabbed Molly's elbow and steered her toward an unoccupied treadmill.

The Ninth Street Gym was an old warehouse that had been converted into a gym with a makeshift boxing ring in the center of the room. The decor was Early Macho and catered to street fighters and blue-collar bodybuilders. Most of them were now staring at Nina and Molly, the only women in the place—unless you counted the silicon-enhanced sex kittens on the posters lining the gray concrete-block walls.

Molly scowled at her. "You told me there would be naked men."

"That's because it was the only way I could convince you to come with me."

Molly was twenty-four and momentarily unattached. A dessert chef with wide hazel eyes and short, spiky auburn hair, she collected boyfriends like other women collected recipes. A connoisseur of the opposite sex, Molly provided the expert opinion Nina so desperately needed. Molly specialized in tall, tan and temporary.

Nina lowered her voice to a whisper. "Now here's the plan...."

"Look," Molly gasped, pointing toward the sauna, "he's almost naked." They watched in silent awe as a strapping young man walked by, a skimpy white towel hanging low on his hips.

Nina tried not to stare, but it had been a long time

since she'd seen an almost-naked man. Longer than she wanted to admit. "He's not bad."

Molly rolled her eyes. "Not bad? You're going to be picky again, aren't you?"

"I'm not picky. I just like a man to have certain...qualifications."

Molly fanned herself with her hand as another towel-clad hunk crossed their path. "I'll take his qualifications anytime. Day or night."

Nina's mouth went dry as she followed Molly's gaze. She had to admit the towel left little to the imagination. And she had a great imagination.

Molly placed a hand on a stair-step machine to steady herself. "I feel a little woozy."

"It's all the testosterone in the air," Nina said, feeling a little light-headed herself. "They should put up a warning sign."

"You mean like the one on the front door that says No Women Allowed?"

"We're not here to exercise," Nina replied, momentarily distracted by the bulging quadriceps of the hunk at the weight machine.

"Then why are we here?"

"I already told you. I need a man."

"Then you're in luck," Molly quipped. "There's one standing right behind you."

Nina turned to face a huge wall of hairless chest. She backed up a step and saw that the rest of him was hairless too, except for the brown handlebar mustache under his hawk-like nose. Her gaze dropped to his snug red Spandex biking shorts, then quickly flew back up again.

"I'm gonna have to ask you babes to leave." His voice sounded rough, like gravel on asphalt, and his brown eyes looked small and mean.

He was perfect. Nina swallowed, her throat dry. She really wanted this one. "I'm not a babe, I'm Nina Walker and I write a food review column for the *St. Louis Post-Dispatch*. It's called 'Nina's Nibbles.' How would you like me to review the dining facilities of the Ninth Street Gym in my next column?"

"All we got is a vending machine and jar of beef jerky."

"I love beef jerky." She took a step closer to him and heard Molly utter a warning squeak behind her.

Nina smiled up at him. "I don't believe I caught your name." She knew it had to be something hard, like the rest of him. Rocky or Brick or Flint. She'd known a Flint once. He'd decapitated her favorite Barbie doll and slashed the tires on her bicycle.

"Tiff." He spit the word between his clenched teeth.

Nina took a step back. "Excuse me?"

"My name is Tiff Atherton and I'm the manager here."

Tiff? Well, a girl can't have everything. If she couldn't have a Flint, she'd definitely settle for Tiff. She held out her hand. "Nice to meet you, Tiff."

"Our meeting is over," he said, ignoring her outstretched hand. "If you're not out the door by the time I count to three, I'll throw you out myself."

His ominous tone sent a thrilling tingle down her spine. This man just oozed intimidation.

"Let's get out of here," Molly hissed, her fingers gripping Nina's forearm.

Nina stood her ground. She couldn't pass up this golden opportunity. Not when she had the man of her dreams standing right in front or her. "If you'll just give me a chance to explain—"

With one smooth movement, Tiff hefted her over his brawny shoulder, giving her a close-up view of his chiseled butt.

"Put me down!"

She heard a high-pitched squeal and craned her head far enough to see Molly succumb to the same fate. Another burly bodybuilder had obviously decided to join in the fun and now had Molly draped over his shoulder. Only she wasn't struggling with her captor. She was probably giving him her phone number.

Maybe Nina had used the wrong strategy. Maybe she should have flirted with Tiff. Shared a romantic moment over a piece of beef jerky. Worn a bikini. Anything to convince him to help her.

"Tiff, wait a minute," Nina shouted as she bounced on his shoulder. "I have a proposition for you."

"I'm married."

"It's not that kind of proposition."

He hesitated at the front door. "Does it involve paying me money?"

"No, but…"

"Wrong answer," he clipped, then dumped her out the front door. She landed with a hard thud on the grassy embankment. Molly dropped down beside her a split-second later.

"Wait!" Nina lunged for Tiff's thick ankle. She couldn't let him get away.

Tiff frowned down at her, shaking his leg in an attempt to loosen her grip.

She held on tight. "Just listen. Come with me to Chicago for the weekend. You can even bring Mrs. Tiff. I'm sure we'd have a lot of fun together."

"I'm not into that kinky stuff."

"No kinky stuff," she promised, wrapping both arms around his ankle. "Just a relaxing weekend at the Ambassador Towers. All expenses paid."

He stilled for a moment. "What's the catch?"

She peered up at him. "The catch is that I'd need you to act as my bodyguard. I'm one of the judges in the Reviewers' Choice culinary competition, only one of the chefs wants to use me to sharpen his meat cleaver."

Tiff snorted, wrenching his leg out of her grasp. "You don't need a bodyguard, lady. You need a good psychiatrist." Then Tiff and his accomplice strode back inside the gym, their pumped-up bodies disappearing behind the heavy condensation on the windows.

"Now what?" Molly asked, rising to her feet and rubbing her backside.

"I'm out of ideas." Nina picked a blade of grass out of her hair. "Tiff would have been perfect."

"You should have lied about the money."

"You know I can't lie," Nina muttered. "Don't you think I've tried?"

Molly sighed. "I've seen you try. It's pretty pathetic."

Nina had never been able to lie. A tragic shortcoming when you grew up in a family of overachievers. She'd never been able to cover up her own failures with a good lie because her cheeks flamed bright red and her tongue twisted in her mouth and she broke out in a cold sweat. At least her nose didn't grow. But she'd still been pegged with the nickname Pinocchio as a child.

Which made it all the more amazing that her curse had actually turned out to be a blessing in disguise. Her penchant for truthfulness had made her the most popular restaurant reviewer in St. Louis. Readers lauded her review columns as witty, entertaining and, best of all, honest. Most of her readers anyway.

Molly stood up. "So much for that stupid plan."

"It wasn't stupid," Nina said, rising to her feet. "I just approached it the wrong way. I should have brought a leash and a collar."

"I thought you wanted a bodyguard, not a guard dog."

"I want protection. Unfortunately, both bodyguards and guard dogs cost money. So I needed to come up with a creative solution to my problem."

Molly sighed. "We can try hitting the other gyms tomorrow night. Surely you can convince one muscle man in this town to whisk you away for a romantic weekend.''

Nina turned toward her. "This weekend trip is business, *strictly* business. And I already have plans tomorrow night. I have to review some coffeehouse on Third Street.''

Molly's eyes widened. "You mean Café Romeo?''

Nina shrugged. "I don't remember the name. All I know is I can't stand the taste of coffee or cappuccino or even latté, so how can I possibly give the place an objective review?''

Molly clapped her hands together. "That's the answer! You can find a man at Café Romeo.''

"Do they have a bouncer at the door who will meet all my requirements?''

"Even better.'' Molly grinned. "They have a matchmaker.''

"A what?''

"A matchmaker. Some old dame reads your coffee grounds, then fixes you up with the perfect man. I can't believe you haven't heard about this place.''

Nina shrugged. "I review so many restaurants it's hard to keep track of them all. My editor did mention that he liked the biscotti there.''

"Who cares about biscotti when you can have great buns? And I'm talking male buns. Better than the ones we just glimpsed underneath those towels. All you have to do is fill out the application with the requirements for your perfect man.''

Nina's mind began to race. This was it. The answer to all her problems. Could it really be this easy?

"Right now my perfect man is about six foot five, two hundred and fifty pounds, and bench-presses cement trucks. And most important, he'll be temporary. I only need him for the weekend."

"What if he wants more than that?"

"I'll worry about the minor details later." Nina brushed away the dirt and grass clinging to her black denim jeans. "Let's go fill out an application."

"Wait a minute," Molly said, shaking her head. "It won't work. Madame Sophia needs to read your coffee grounds to find your perfect match and you don't like coffee."

"I'll drink Brazilian bog water if that's what it takes. Besides, I'm not looking for love. All I want is one bodyguard-to-go from Café Romeo."

NINA SOON DISCOVERED that her take-out order wasn't going to be that easy. She sat at one end of the long coffee bar in Café Romeo and stared dismally at the still half-full cup of Jamaican almond blend in front of her. She'd wanted her coffee served in one of those tiny espresso cups, but Madame Sophia had been quite adamant.

She swept a surreptitious glance over her shoulder. Madame Sophia was conversing with a lone customer at a corner table. Molly was flirting with the hunky cashier near the door. With a quick flip of her wrist, Nina dumped her remaining coffee in the potted fern sitting on the end of the coffee bar. Then she hastily placed the empty cup back on the saucer, the sound of china clinking together unusually loud in the almost-empty coffeehouse.

"Done already?" Madame Sophia's melodic voice made her jump.

Nina forced a smile. "It's all gone." A wave of heat washed up her cheeks at the evasion, but it *was* the truth.

Madame Sophia climbed onto the padded bar-stool next to her and reached for Nina's cup and saucer. "Let's see if we can find your perfect man in here."

"I was hoping for someone a little bigger," Nina quipped.

Madame Sophia didn't respond or even smile as she gazed thoughtfully at the soggy ground. She tipped the cup one way, then another. "Hmm. Interesting."

Nina leaned over for a closer look. "Really?"

Madame Sophia acted as if she didn't hear her. A long, pregnant silence stretched out between them. Nina watched the older woman work, wondering how many people fell for her act. No doubt Madame Sophia worked her matchmaking magic by paying more attention to the detailed application Nina had filled out than to the dregs in the bottom of a coffee cup.

"The reading is a little muddled," Madame Sophia proclaimed at last. "But I think I see..." her voice trailed off, then a satisfied smile curved her mouth. "Yes, I'm almost sure of it."

"A man?" Nina ventured.

"Definitely."

She twisted her fingers together in her lap. "Is he big? Mean? Scary?"

Madame Sophia bestowed an ethereal smile on her. "He's your perfect match."

Nina smiled back, but she didn't believe her. She couldn't afford to believe her. Not after she'd let so many other men in her life derail her from her chosen career track. It was almost as if she lost all common sense whenever love came into her life.

At eighteen, she'd met Erik, and willingly given up her scholarship to Brown to attend the local community college so she could be close to him. He'd decided to join the Navy after the first week of classes and had ended up in Turkey.

Then she'd fallen hard and fast for Brent, shortly before finals week in her senior year. Nina had been wild about the guy. An electric guitarist in a popular local band, he'd dumped her after three weeks for a seventeen-year-old groupie. Unfortunately, he hadn't dumped her soon enough. She'd spent every minute of her spare time with him instead of studying. After flunking three out of five of her final exams, she'd had to make up the classes in summer school so she could graduate.

She lost her internship with KMOV Channel Four News after Manuel convinced her to "see the world" with him. Their romance lasted as far as Pensacola, where he found a new traveling companion.

The list went on and on. No matter how handsome, how charming, how sexy, men had screwed up her life for years. That's why she'd declared a moratorium on men six months ago, when she'd landed this job as a food critic for the *St. Louis Dispatch-Post*. She'd lost too many opportunities to take any more chances with romance. It never worked out for her anyway.

Maybe once she achieved the level of success she'd always craved, she'd reconsider. But for now, the moratorium was in full effect.

"How soon can I meet him?" Nina asked, hoping he'd consider a free weekend in Chicago adequate compensation for services rendered. Especially since all he had to do was stand next to her and growl.

"How about tomorrow night? Right here, at Café Romeo."

"Perfect." It all seemed so simple. Maybe it was a sign. Maybe this time her dreams would finally come true.

2

"This is a nightmare," Jake Callahan muttered, as the photographer's assistant misted his bare chest with water from a spray bottle. He sat posed on a stool at the coffee bar of Café Romeo wearing nothing more than a pair of skintight black leather pants. Thankfully the coffeehouse hadn't opened yet, so the only witnesses to this spectacle were the female photographer and her assistant, his Aunt Sophie and his brother Trace, who stood off to one side with a smirk on his face.

"Just wait, Trace," he growled, "it's your turn next."

"At least I get to keep my shirt on," Trace said with a grin. He wore his work clothes, a sleeveless blue T-shirt and a pair of faded blue denim jeans, his brown leather toolbelt slung low on his hips. The photo shoot was Aunt Sophie's latest publicity project for Café Romeo.

The photographer motioned to her assistant. "Now give him the red rose. We want this shot just to ooze romance."

Aunt Sophie thoughtfully tapped her chin with one

finger. "I think he should hold the rose between his teeth."

"Yummy," the photographer exclaimed. "My heart's beating faster already. Put the rose in his mouth, Mindy."

Jake folded his arms across his chest. "I'm not putting a flower in my mouth. That's where I draw the line."

Trace's grin widened. "Isn't that what you said about the leather pants?"

"I mean it this time." Jake turned to his aunt. "If you want this advertising campaign to bring more business into Café Romeo, you need to use real models."

"You told me I couldn't afford real models," Aunt Sophie countered. "Besides, no model could compare to my nephews." She turned to Mindy. "Aren't they gorgeous?"

"Yeah, gorgeous," Mindy muttered, as she attempted to wedge the thorny stem of the rose between Jake's clenched teeth. He finally took it from her hand and flung it over his shoulder.

"So how exactly did Noah weasel out of this?" Trace asked.

"He's in Atlanta investigating a case for that big insurance company of his," Aunt Sophie replied. "Otherwise, I know he'd be here. I have every confidence this new advertising campaign will pull Café Romeo out of its little slump."

Jake just hoped it would be enough. He'd been over the cash flow for Café Romeo a dozen times, and it didn't look good. Unless sales improved dramatically, his aunt would be out of business in a few months. He couldn't let it happen. Jake Callahan didn't like to lose.

Not only had he invested a considerable chunk of his own money in this place, but Aunt Sophie had put her heart and soul into the coffeehouse. After all she'd sacrificed to help raise Jake and his two younger brothers, she deserved some success in her life.

So if Jake could help her by posing half-naked on a bar stool, then he'd damn well do it. It wasn't as if he didn't have time. His work as a business manager for Café Romeo and a chain of fitness centers made it possible for him to set his own hours. He actually had too much time on his hands. Time to wonder what was missing in his life.

Jake mentally shook himself. He hated whiners. If he was unhappy with his life, it was up to him to change it. Now he just had to figure out how.

"That's all, Jake," the photographer said, lowering her camera. "We've got some great shots here. I can't wait to see the posters."

Jake turned slowly to his aunt. "Posters? You never said anything about posters."

She waved a hand in the air, the silver bracelets jangling on her wrist. "I had a vision."

Jake and Trace both groaned.

Aunt Sophie got that familiar, faraway look in her eyes. "I can see it now. The Men of Café Romeo at bus stops, train stations and maternity wards. Everywhere women gather.'' Then she blinked and looked at her nephews. "Isn't that perfect?''

Perfect wasn't exactly the word on Jake's tongue, but he refrained from saying it in mixed company. He also didn't want to imagine life-sized posters of himself in skintight leather pants plastered all over St. Louis.

"We should have known,'' Trace muttered under his breath as he brushed by Jake to take his place in front of the camera.

Jake nodded. Trace was right. They should have known. Nothing was ever simple with Aunt Sophie. He'd never forget the time she'd volunteered as a room mother at his elementary school. Instead of providing the customary cookies and juice, she'd organized a sit-in to protest the conditions in the school cafeteria.

Then there was the time she'd invited her carnival friends over to entertain Jake when he had the chicken pox. He still didn't know how she'd managed to fit that baby elephant through the front door.

He didn't want to even think about the succession of blind dates she'd arranged to make his life miserable. The worst had been the weekend ski trip with the twin sister of the Bearded Lady. His date's five o'clock shadow had definitely put a damper on the romance.

A reluctant smile tugged at Jake's lips as he remembered some of Aunt Sophie's other ill-fated matchmaking attempts. She might be a little flaky, but she loved all three of her nephews unconditionally.

His smile didn't last long.

"There's one more thing I think you should know," Aunt Sophie said, hooking her arm through his and pulling him away from the photo shoot.

"What?"

When she smiled up at him, his stomach twisted into a tight knot. "You have a date tonight."

"A date?"

Sophie nodded. "At Café Romeo. Seven o'clock. She's a lovely young woman. Her name is Nina and she can't wait to meet you."

"Then she'll be disappointed." He set his jaw. "I'm not letting you set me up on another blind date."

"I wouldn't exactly call it a blind date. You know I have a gift for matching up perfect couples." She leaned toward him. "Jake, I've read her coffee grounds and I believe this woman could be your soul-mate."

He closed his eyes and silently counted to ten. His jaw clenched and he could feel his right eyelid twitch. But he wouldn't lose his temper. He'd learned the hard way that losing control could lead to disaster.

At last he began to calm, aware of Aunt Sophie's long, bony fingers still curled around his arm and the voice of the photographer behind him, instructing Trace to hold a screwdriver between his teeth.

"Jake?"

He opened his eyes and spoke in a calm, even voice. "Aunt Sophie, I've told you a dozen times I don't need or want a matchmaker in my life."

She sniffed. "Would you rather see me go to jail?"

"What are you talking about?"

"Truth in advertising. How can I claim you and Trace are the Men of Café Romeo when you've never been matched up with one of my customers?"

"I don't think they'll lock you up just because I refuse to go out for an evening of dinner and dancing."

"Maybe not," Aunt Sophie conceded, "but what about Café Romeo's reputation? The word of mouth from one disgruntled customer could ruin the entire business."

He shrugged as he turned to watch Trace flex his biceps for the camera. "So fix her up with someone else."

"Impossible. No other man fits her requirements."

He turned back around. "Requirements?"

Sophie nodded. "She made it very clear that her date had to meet certain…specifications."

"Such as?"

"He has to be at least six feet, two inches tall, weigh between two hundred and two hundred and fifty pounds, and have a size seventeen neck."

Jake motioned toward his brother. "Trace fits that description as well as I do. Why not send him?"

"Because that would be a disaster," Aunt Sophie muttered under her breath. Then she squared her shoulders. "Besides, you're the one who won the Golden Gloves title ten years ago."

Jake stilled. "So?"

"So one of her specifications is that her date be skilled in karate or judo or..."

"Boxing," he breathed, his throat tight.

"That's right. She told me she was looking for her very own Terminator."

He narrowed his eyes. "What kind of nut is this woman? And just what exactly does she have in mind for our date? A tag team match?"

Aunt Sophie smiled. "So you're going?"

"Of course I'm not going. Although I'll admit I'm curious about a woman whose idea of the perfect date is Arnold Schwarzenegger. And they say men are shallow."

"She's very pretty," Aunt Sophie remarked. "Intelligent, too. I met her last night when she filled out the application for her ideal man."

"Is speech one of her requirements for an ideal man, or does he just need to grunt?"

Aunt Sophie smiled. "Why don't you show up at Café Romeo tonight and find out."

"Forget it."

Aunt Sophie stepped closer to him. "If you just agree to meet her for this one date," she took a deep breath, "I promise never to try to match up you with a woman again."

He stared at her in disbelief. His aunt had been meddling in his love life for as long as he could remember. She'd been after his coffee grounds for years, certain she could see the future Mrs. Jake Callahan in them. "Are you serious?"

"Completely. One date, Jake. That's all I ask in return."

One date. One wasted evening in return for romantic freedom for the rest of his life. No more surprise blind dates. No more hiding his coffee grounds. He'd be free to live his life exactly as he wanted. Alone.

His mouth curved into a slow smile. "You've got a deal."

She clapped her hands together. "Wonderful! Now all we need to do is dress you for the part."

"Do I have to wear an Arnold Schwarzenegger mask?"

"Of course not. You're much more handsome than Schwarzenegger. But your wardrobe is a little... bland." She reached behind the coffee bar and pulled out a shopping bag. "I brought you a few things to loosen up your image."

He frowned. "What kind of things?"

"A black mesh muscle shirt to go with the leather pants, a gold chain, a pair of leopard-print bikini underwear...."

He frowned down at the scrap of silk underwear. "Aunt Sophie, I'm a business manager, not a gigolo."

"I know, dear, but don't apologize." She shoved the shopping bag into his hands. "When Nina sees you in these clothes, she won't be able to resist you."

The last thing he wanted was for this woman to find him irresistible. His aunt would be much more likely to stick to her side of the bargain if this Nina never wanted to see him again.

So why not make it happen?

Jake bit back a smile as an idea formed in his mind. If his plan worked, his date would take one look at him and say *hasta la vista,* Baby.

IT WASN'T love at first sight.

Nina sat alone in a corner booth of Café Romeo, shivering under the blast of the air conditioner vent directly above her. Usually she reserved judgment about a place until she'd at least tasted the food, but Café Romeo had already left a bad taste in her mouth.

First, she couldn't find a parking place and had ended up walking three blocks in the rain—without an umbrella. Then the heel on one of her brand-new leather pumps had broken when she'd slipped on the step leading to the front entrance of Café Romeo. At least she hadn't fallen down—until she'd lost her balance on the slick, ceramic floor in the ladies' room, landing near the pedestal sink and bruising her tailbone.

She'd managed to slowly limp to her table without further damage, but the review for Café Romeo she was composing in her head wasn't a rave. In fact, she doubted if it would meet the minimum word count once the copy editor deleted all the expletives. She leaned back against the padded seat cushion, wincing at the pressure on her sore tailbone.

When the pain eased, she let her gaze wander around the coffeehouse. The polished hardwood floors and the high ceilings gave the place an old-world charm. She noticed a small water spot staining one wall and a crack in one of the decorative stained glass windows. Overall, Café Romeo looked a little rundown, but the rich aroma of fresh-ground coffee and the private, high-backed booths made it quite cozy.

At long last a waiter approached her, his dark, shoulder-length hair pulled back into a neat ponytail and his mouth pressed into a thin line. He set a pair of menus and a cup of steaming coffee in front of her, then turned to go.

"Excuse me," Nina called after him.

He glanced at her over his shoulder. "Yes?"

She pointed to the coffee cup in front of her. "What's this?"

With an audible sigh, he returned to the table. "Jamaican almond blend. It's the house specialty." He cleared his throat. "I'm Ramon, and due to circumstances beyond my control, I'm forced to be your waiter this evening."

Lovely. Now on top of everything else, she had a flaky waiter to deal with. "Well, Ramon, I didn't order this coffee."

"It's on the house."

"I'd rather have a cup of hot tea."

He sniffed. "I'm afraid that's impossible."

"You don't serve tea here?"

He rolled his eyes. "Of course we do. But *you* have to drink the coffee."

She gritted her teeth.

"I don't like coffee."

"Too bad. Madame Sophia wants another reading

of your coffee grounds, just to double check. The last one was a little murky.''

"Double-check what?''

He shrugged. "Don't ask me, I just work here. Now if you don't want anything else...."

She pushed the coffee cup away. "I want a cup of hot tea. And if you won't get it for me, then I want to talk to the manager.''

His lower lip trembled. "Please don't make this difficult for me. I'm not even supposed to be working this evening. I'm supposed to be...'' Ramon slumped into the chair across from her, laid his head on the table and began sobbing.

Nina flushed under the stares of the other customers as his sobs grew louder. She'd never made a waiter cry before and didn't know quite what to do. When his sobs didn't subside, she reached out and patted him awkwardly on his thin shoulder. "Don't cry, Ramon. It's nothing personal. I just don't like coffee.''

Ramon lifted his head. "Then what in the world are you doing in a coffeehouse? No, don't tell me,'' he said with a disdainful sniff. "You're here to find love.''

"That's the last thing I want.''

He sat up and tore a paper napkin out of the dispenser. "Well, good for you, because it doesn't exist. Do you know where I should be right now?''

A mental institution? Nina cleared her throat. "No, where?''

"Visiting my fiancée at the Women's Eastern Correctional Center in Vandalia.''

"Your fiancée is in prison?"

"Actually, she's my ex-fiancée," Ramon said, his eyes misting again as he choked on another sob. "It's all over between us."

Nina handed him another napkin. "Maybe you're better off without her."

Ramon blew his nose. "That's what my mom says."

His mother must be turning cartwheels. Nina didn't even want to imagine what her parents' reaction would be if she brought an ex-con home to the family. They still hadn't recovered from the shock of her dating a college drop-out two years ago. "Has your mom ever met her?"

Ramon nodded. "She introduced us. Mom's her cellmate."

Nina's mouth fell open, but no words came out. Ramon's face crunched up and she knew it was only a matter of moments before he began weeping again. She pushed the coffee toward him. "Here, you drink it."

"It will screw up the reading," he said, but picked up the cup anyway. "But what does it really matter? Love is just a myth. A fairy tale. There are no happily ever afters in the real world."

Now she was not only sore, cold and damp, but thoroughly depressed. Café Romeo was in the running for her Worst Restaurant of the Year review. And she hadn't even ordered any food yet.

"My fiancée broke up with me for a jock," Ramon said, still brooding about his broken heart. "He's the prison basketball coach and quite a stud, according to Mom.'' He narrowed his eyes. ''I hate jocks.''

Poor Ramon could never be suspected of being a jock. He was tall and rail-thin, with long lashes fringing his big brown eyes. He reminded her of a stray puppy. ''Not all women are attracted to jocks.''

Ramon snorted. ''You must be, or you wouldn't have ended up with Jake Callahan as your dream date.''

''He's a jock?'' she asked, surprised by the tiny flutter in her stomach. She had no reason to be nervous. This date was strictly business.

''A boxer,'' he replied, his lips pursed in disapproval. ''An ex-boxer, actually. He won the Golden Gloves title when he was eighteen, then went on the boxing circuit. They used to call him The Jackhammer.''

The Jackhammer. A thrilling tingle leapt up her spine. She could see him now. Big. Mean. Relentless. Just the kind of man she needed. For the weekend, anyway. ''I can't wait to meet him.''

''You're in for a real treat.''

The sneer in his voice unsettled her. ''You don't like him?''

''Like him?'' Ramon echoed. ''Like him? I loathe the man.'' He feigned spitting on the floor. ''Don't tell me I didn't warn you.''

What did that mean? Nina's nervousness gave way to panic. Maybe she was making a big mistake. She was about to ask a total stranger to go away with her for the weekend. "Maybe he won't show up. He should have been here ten minutes ago."

"He'll show up. The jocks always end up with the p-p-retty ones." Ramon's voice broke on a sob and he reached for another napkin. His elbow bumped her coffee cup, tipping it over. The now-tepid brew streamed across the table and spilled onto Nina's lap.

"Oh, no!" She jumped up as the warm liquid soaked into her ivory silk skirt and ran down her legs.

"See what kind of day I've had?" Ramon watched her dab at her skirt with a fistful of napkins. He shook his head at her efforts. "Believe me, that Jamaican almond stain will never come out."

"I believe you," she said, trying not to cry herself at the sight of her ruined skirt.

Ramon squinted up at her. "You know, you look sort of familiar to me. Have you ever been in prison?"

"No," Nina said, giving up on the stain. She sat back down in her chair, gasping as pain from her sore tailbone shot up her spine.

"What's wrong?"

"I fell in the ladies' room and bruised my, uh... tailbone. I'm still a little sore."

"Bummer," Ramon replied sympathetically. Then he tilted his head to one side. "I know I've seen you somewhere. Are you sure we haven't met before?"

"Positive." She knew he probably recognized her from her picture at the top of the "Nina's Nibbles" column, but she never liked to draw attention to herself when conducting a review. Rather a moot point, since her table had provided non-stop entertainment for the few customers in the place.

Ramon stood up with a long sigh. "No offense, but I don't have time to sit here and chat all evening. Will there be anything else?"

"I'd kill for a cup of hot tea."

He gave her a wobbly smile. "My ex-fiancée used to say things like that. Maybe that's why she hasn't made parole yet." He pulled a pencil out of his shirt pocket and jotted down her order. "One cup of hot tea coming up."

"Ramon," she called before he turned away. "Why don't you like Jake Callahan?"

"Because he's an overbearing control freak who happens to be Madame Sophia's nephew as well as her business manager. He thinks I'm too emotional for this job. *Me.* Can you believe it? Like I can't handle a little stress." His lower lip quivered. "If Madame Sophia wasn't here to protect me, Jake would probably beat me up, then put me through the coffee grinder." He leaned toward her and lowered his voice to a whisper. "So if you ever see Ramon D'Onofrio on the menu, call the police."

She nodded, knowing she'd never have to worry about it because she was never stepping foot inside this place again. After Ramon left, she closed her eyes and focused on her plan. She wanted The Jackhammer to like her. But not too much. Just enough to escort her to Chicago for the weekend and play bodyguard for free.

A deep baritone interrupted her reverie. "Are you Nina?"

She kept her eyes closed for a moment, letting the sound of his voice swirl around inside of her. It was low and dark and dangerous, and her pulse kicked up a notch at the sound of it. Then she opened her eyes and slowly looked up at him.

She noticed the pocket protector first. It was neon yellow against his chartreuse-green shirt and crammed with pencils. The shirt was buttoned clear up to the collar and strained against his neck. A small Garfield cartoon bandage was strapped across his square chin.

The crick in her neck told her he fit her height requirement, but that awful shirt and a baggy pair of high-water khaki pants hid the rest of his body. She tried not to grimace at his hair, parted in the middle and slicked down at the sides with some kind of styling gel. The only attractive feature on the man was a pair of midnight-blue eyes, almost hidden behind the black horn-rimmed glasses sliding down his nose. But they couldn't hide the truth.

The Jackhammer was a complete nerd.

3
_____

JAKE WATCHED his date's eyes widen at the sight of him. He had to admit she had nice eyes. A deep, mossy green that reminded him of crushed velvet. Nice hair, too. Her tangle of damp blond curls framed a heart-shaped face, and he couldn't help but notice the lush fullness of her pink lips when her mouth fell open.

"Yes, I'm Nina Walker," she said at last. "Are you...Jake Callahan?"

"At your thervithe," he replied with a pronounced lisp. Then he slid into the booth across the table from her, reminding himself that her eyes and her hair and her mouth didn't matter, because he never planned to see her again. The way she filled out that silk suit didn't matter either. If he showed one spark of interest in this woman, his aunt would start stocking up on organic rice to throw at the wedding. He wasn't about to fall into one of Sophie's matchmaking traps.

No matter how enticing the bait.

Her gaze fell to the table and she muttered something under her breath that sounded like, "This just isn't my day."

He ignored the pinprick of guilt he felt at her

words. He didn't like to disappoint any woman, but it was better for her to discover he wasn't her perfect match right away. A clean break always healed the fastest. Besides, the sooner he proved how incompatible they were, the faster he could end this date before those green eyes made him have second thoughts.

"Thorry I'm late," he said, sticking to his strategy. "I wath watching *Gilligan'th Island* and couldn't tear mythelf away."

"Really?" Those velvety green eyes sparked with interest. "Which one?"

He froze. "What?"

"Which episode?" she clarified. "My favorite is the one where Gilligan finds the radioactive vegetable seeds and all the castaways develop superhuman powers. Mary Ann ate the carrots and could see really far, and the Skipper ate the spinach and was incredibly strong. Or is it the one where the Skipper thinks he's allergic to Gilligan?"

"Uh…yeah. That one." He hadn't seen an episode of *Gilligan's Island* in over a decade, and he certainly couldn't remember any details. He cleared his throat and decided to try a different tactic. "A Three Thtoogeth marathon ith playing at the Rivoli tonight. Can you believe Moe never won an Othcar?"

"Can you believe I've never seen the Three Stooges?" she said with a smile that made his breathing hitch. "It sounds like fun."

She couldn't be serious. He'd never met a woman who wanted to watch the Three Stooges voluntarily. Most considered it a sadistic form of video torture.

Then her smile faded. "Unfortunately, I can't go anywhere looking like this." She stood up and frowned down at her shapely figure.

All Jake saw were long, long legs that led up to a short skirt that hugged her rounded hips. The low-cut bodice of the silk jacket revealed a generous amount of equally silky skin. She was right. She didn't belong in a movie theater. Not one man in the joint would have his eyes on the movie screen.

Her fingers splayed over the waistband of her skirt. "I doubt I'll ever get this off on my own. I'm afraid it will take a professional."

He swallowed as he looked up at her. He'd never had any problems removing a woman's skirt before, although he'd hardly call himself a professional. Before he had time to consider the consequences, he heard himself say, "I'll be happy to help."

"You know a good drycleaner?"

He hesitated. "Drycleaner?"

"To get this stain off." She brushed her hand over the light-brown stain in the center of her ivory skirt.

He hadn't even noticed the stain before now. Probably because he'd been too busy noticing *her*. That way lay madness. Or at least a second date.

But before he had time to reconsider his game plan, Ramon approached the table and pointed at Nina. "I know who you are now." He set a cup of steaming tea in front of her. "You're Nina Nibbles."

"Try Nina Walker," Jake interjected, irritated at the interruption.

Ramon scowled at him. "I meant she writes that

great restaurant review column called 'Nina's Nibbles' in the newspaper.''

The words hit him like a sucker punch to the gut. ''Nina's Nibbles''? This woman wrote the most influential restaurant review column in the city? He'd been calling the newspaper for months requesting a review in her column for Café Romeo. Now she was here. And he was doing his best to make her never want to come back.

''Oh, hell,'' Jake muttered under his breath.

Ramon turned to Nina. ''Hey, I'll bet you're here doing a review of Café Romeo.''

''Well, yes, but...''

Ramon drowned her next words with a loud groan. ''Just my luck to spill a cup of Jamaican almond blend on you tonight. I haven't spilled any java on a customer for at least a week.'' He sighed. ''So how's your tailbone?''

''Tailbone?'' Jake echoed, looking from the waiter to Nina. A soft pink blush suffused her cheeks.

''She took a dive in the ladies' room,'' Ramon informed him. ''Probably cracked the bone.''

''I'm usually not so clumsy,'' Nina explained. ''But I broke the heel of my shoe on the step outside the front door....''

''That step is a death trap,'' Ramon interjected. ''I'm surprised we haven't been sued yet.''

Jake didn't know whether to kick Ramon or himself. He'd blown it. Big time. But maybe he could repair some of the damage before it was too late. He stood up so fast his leg bumped against the table, sloshing hot tea out of her cup and onto her jacket sleeve.

"Very smooth, Callahan," Ramon muttered out of the side of his mouth. He grabbed a handful of napkins out of the dispenser. "Here, Miss Nibbles, let me clean up the mess for you. Have you ever heard of tea-dyeing? I've got a big pot of Earl Grey steeping back in the kitchen. We could dunk your suit in it a few times and it will look good as new."

Jake didn't wait around to hear her response. He practically ran to the small office at the rear of the coffeehouse, tugging so hard at his shirt collar that buttons flew. Once inside, he closed the door behind him and quickly peeled down to his light-blue boxer shorts.

He found the black leather pants, mesh shirt, and leopard-print thong exactly where he'd left them this afternoon, in the shopping bag on top of the filing cabinet. With a grimace, he added the gold chain to the ensemble.

After hastily changing into the new clothes, he tossed the vintage glasses aside, then reached for a comb. He didn't have time to wash the gel out of his hair, so he slicked it straight back off his forehead. He might not look exactly like Schwarzenegger, but he could probably scare old ladies in this outfit.

"If this is what Nina wants," he muttered, moving toward the door, "this is what Nina gets."

He opened the door and the woman standing on the other side of it screamed. Then she clasped one hand to her chest. "Jake! I almost didn't recognize you. Thank goodness I found you."

"Aunt Sophie," he said, grabbing her arm and steering her inside the office. "What's wrong?"

"Everything. Have you seen your date yet?"

"Yes. She's a knockout. She's also the one person capable of saving Café Romeo from bankruptcy. Now, if you'll excuse me, I have to get back to her."

"No!" Aunt Sophie grabbed his arm. "She's all wrong for you, Jake. I hate to admit it, but I made a horrendous mistake." She took a deep breath. "Nina Walker is not your perfect match."

"That's fine with me, Aunt Sophie. I don't want to marry the woman. I just want to wine and dine her until she falls in love with Café Romeo."

Aunt Sophie leaned toward him. "Jake, listen to me. Ramon just brought me that woman's coffee grounds, and I did a second reading. She's not a stable person. She could even be one of those crazy stalkers. I don't think you should have anything to do with her."

He swallowed a sigh of exasperation. "I can take care of myself, Aunt Sophie."

"Except we both know you won't," she retorted, a spark of annoyance in her blue eyes. "What if she's dangerous?"

"The only danger from Nina Walker is a rotten review. Which is just what we'll get if I don't get back out there and turn on the charm." He headed for the door, hoping Ramon hadn't done any more damage to Café Romeo's reputation in the short time he'd been gone.

"Jake, wait!" Sophie called after him.

But Jake couldn't delay any longer. He had a lot of work ahead of him. It might even take all night. And he'd be more than willing to make the sacrifice—for the sake of Café Romeo.

Only, when he rounded the corner that led to his table, he found out he was too late.

Nina was gone.

THE RAIN had dissipated to a steady drizzle by the time Nina made her escape from Café Romeo. She hurried toward her car, slipping and sliding on the wet, greasy sidewalk. Thunder rumbled and a flash of lightning illuminated the night sky.

The entire evening had been a disaster. But Ramon's suggestion that she stand naked in the kitchen while he dyed her suit a lovely shade of Earl Grey had been the last straw. Especially when he'd tried to unzip her skirt as she was leaving. At least he hadn't followed her out the door.

She did feel bad about abandoning her date. Poor, nerdy Jake. He might actually have some potential with a good makeover and some speech therapy.

Three blocks and two blisters later, she reached her car, fumbling inside her purse for her keys. She found them at the same second an iron hand clamped down on her shoulder.

The Bonecrusher.

With a terrified squeak, she rounded on him, her

purse flying and landing with a thud against the man's temple. He dropped like a rock.

Adrenaline pumping, Nina whirled back to her car. Her fingers shook as she located the correct key and inserted it into the lock. A low moan from the ground behind her made her hesitate.

With her purse at the ready, she turned and really looked, for the first time, at her attacker. He was sprawled flat on the asphalt, one leg slightly bent at the knee. Water shimmered off his painted-on black pants. His black shirt molded to a muscular chest and broad shoulders. Another flash of lightning illuminated the Garfield bandage on his chin.

"Jake?" She fell to her knees for a closer look. It really was Jake Callahan. A new and improved Jake Callahan. Except for that ugly, blue knot already forming on his temple. She cradled his head in her lap. "Jake, speak to me."

His eyelids fluttered open, then he stared up at her. "What the hell do you have in your purse? An anvil?"

"A brick." She brushed the damp strands of his hair off his forehead. "I have it in there for protection."

"Have you ever thought about just buying a gun?"

"Guns scare me."

He snorted. "They used to scare me too, until I got broadsided with a brick. Next time I think I'd rather take my chances with a bullet."

"Wait a minute," Nina said, realizing for the first

time that his appearance wasn't the only thing different about this man. "What happened to your lisp?"

His Adam's apple bobbed in his throat. "Uh…you must have cured it when you decked me. It's a miracle."

"It's a scam." She jumped up, her quick movement dropping his head back onto the asphalt.

"Hey," he said, rubbing the back of his head as he sat up. "That hurt."

"Good." She folded her arms across her chest. "Now are you ready to tell me what's really going on here?"

"Well…you just attacked me with a brick and I'm trying not to take it personally." He slowly rose to his feet, wobbling a little as he took a step closer to her. "Especially since I'm hoping we can get to know each other better."

She backed up against her car door. "That's not what I meant. One minute you're a mild-mannered guy, and the next minute you're…" Her voice trailed off as she stared at him. His new clothes didn't hide anything. Jake's muscular physique would make a superhero look like a wimp. She swallowed. "What happened to the other guy?"

He wrinkled his brow. "Ramon?"

"No. The other Jake Callahan. The one with the glasses and the pocket protector."

One corner of his mouth tipped up. "Would you believe me if I told you I had a split personality?"

"No."

"An evil twin?"

"Try again."

He glanced up at the swollen sky. "Maybe we should go somewhere dry to discuss this. Perhaps over a warm brandy."

She wasn't going to let him get off that easily. "I want to discuss it now. It's not like we can get any wetter."

He sighed. "All right, I'll tell you the truth."

Finally. She tilted up her chin. "Don't worry, I can take it."

"I didn't want to go out on a date with you."

For all her bravado, his words still stung. "Oh."

"It's nothing personal," he said quickly. "I'm just tired of my aunt trying to interfere in my love life. So when she told me your description of the perfect man...."

"You decided to be just the opposite." Nina couldn't hide the sharp tone of her voice. But she was more angry with herself than with Jake. How could she ever have fallen for his nerd act? Looking at him now, with his wet clothes molded to his magnificent body, he looked like nothing less than a hardened, take-no-prisoners warrior. She'd never felt so stupid.

Or so safe.

"Please let me make it up to you," he pleaded. "I didn't know you'd be so..." his voice trailed off as his eyes skimmed over her.

Too late she realized her wet silk suit was just as revealing. Thankful he couldn't see her blush in the darkness, Nina ever so casually held her purse up in front of her chest. "You didn't know I'd be so... what?"

His gaze slid up to her face. "So...surprising. I also had no idea you wrote 'Nina's Nibbles'. If I had, I never would have tried to fool you. Or let Ramon be your waiter. And I sincerely hope you won't hold it against Café Romeo." He moved another step closer to her. "I'll do anything to make it up to you."

Her pulse quickened. "Anything?"

He took a deep breath. "You name it, Nina. I'll do it."

She smiled. "You've got a deal."

ONE WEEK LATER, Jake opened his front door, suitcase in hand, and found Trace standing on the front stoop. "What are you doing here?"

"I'm here to stop you from making the biggest mistake of your life."

Jake glanced at his watch. "I have a plane to catch."

Trace walked past him into the living room. "Just give me five minutes."

With a sigh of irritation, Jake set down his suitcase and closed the door. "Okay. You've got five minutes."

Despite his impatience, he'd always made it a point to make time for his brothers. Even at the height of his boxing days, when his training had consumed every spare moment, Trace and Noah had known they could count on him. They'd kept him hopping, too.

As a teenager, Trace's numerous scrapes with the law had led to more than one trip to the police station.

Noah never got into trouble with the law, but there had been times Jake wished someone would arrest his little brother for breaking so many hearts. He couldn't count the number of Noah's old girlfriends who had cried on his shoulder. If arthritis ever set in, he was sending the medical bills to his playboy brother.

Trace seated himself on the black leather sofa, looking nothing like the sullen hood he used to be. He wore his hair shorter now and had traded his torn jeans, ratty T-shirts and biker jacket for khaki shorts and a white polo shirt. He also drove a brand new Blazer instead of a used motorcycle, thanks to his success as a contractor. The black sheep of the family had done well for himself. But that didn't mean he could boss around his big brother.

"Got any beer?"

"You don't have time for a beer." Jake leaned against the credenza and folded his arms across his chest. "You're leaving soon, remember?"

"Not if I can talk you out of going away with this Nina woman."

"You can't. It's all set, and I'm not backing out now."

Trace pointed at Jake's head. "What the hell is that?"

"What?"

"That bruise on your forehead. What did you do, walk into a wall?"

"Actually, it was a brick. Nina carries one in her

purse. And believe me," Jake said, absently rubbing the swollen knot on his temple, "she knows how to use it."

Trace sat up on the sofa. "Let me get this straight. This woman nails you with a brick and you still want to marry her?"

Jake laughed. "Marry her? Where did you get that crazy idea?"

"From Aunt Sophie. I've never seen her so upset. She told me if you marry this woman, you'll be miserable for the rest of your life."

"Well, you can set Aunt Sophie's mind at rest. I don't plan to marry Nina or anyone. Ever."

Trace looked skeptical, but this subject wasn't up for debate. Marriage wasn't an option for Jake Callahan. He loved women, but he couldn't risk falling in love. Not when love made people do silly, stupid things. Made them lose control of their emotions. He couldn't afford to ever let that happen to him again.

Trace glanced at the packed suitcase by the door. "So you're not eloping?"

"Of course not. I'm just going to Chicago for the weekend."

"So this is just a romantic weekend fling?"

"Not exactly."

Trace arched a brow. "Care to elaborate?"

"I'm mixing business with pleasure. Nina is none other than Nina Walker, the food critic for the *St. Louis Post-Dispatch*. She was doing a review for Café Romeo the night we met."

"How did it go?"

"Let me put it this way. Ramon was her waiter."

"Damn," Trace muttered. "How did that happen?"

"It happened because Aunt Sophie refuses to fire the guy. I don't have anything personal against the man, but he's a walking disaster area."

"I take it Miss Walker was less than impressed?"

"That's putting it mildly. Especially after I showed up."

Trace looked surprised. "You've never had any problem impressing the ladies before."

"Except this time, I went out of my way to make a bad impression. Look, I don't want to go into all the gory details. Let's just say the only way I could make it up to her was to agree to go to Chicago with her for the weekend. In return, she'll give Café Romeo a rave review."

"She said that?"

Jake shrugged. "Not in so many words. But it was implied."

Trace shook his head. "How many times do I have to tell you that women need everything spelled out in black and white? You can't just assume their minds work the same way as ours."

"You mean rationally?"

"That's exactly what I mean."

"You don't know Nina. She seems like a very rational person."

"Did you decide this before or after she hit you with a brick?"

"All right, so she's not perfect. At least she didn't

drive off and leave me lying unconscious in the parking lot.''

Trace's eyes widened. "You were unconscious?"

"Only for a few minutes."

His brother set his jaw. "I'd never go within a hundred feet of a woman who knocked me unconscious. And I have to wonder why she wants to spend a weekend with a man she just met."

Jake shrugged. "She was a little vague on the details. And I was still a little woozy from the brick, so I didn't press her. Maybe she's just lonely."

"Or desperate. Or some kind of psychopath. You know anything is possible when Aunt Sophie's involved."

"I know. But I'm willing to take that risk." How could he do any less after everything Sophie had done for him and his brothers? She'd left the carnival and moved in a week after their mother went AWOL. Along with her exotic momentos and outlandish stories, she'd brought life and love back to his shell-shocked family.

Sophie had made the Callahans whole again.

But in the process she'd given up her career and the possibility of a family of her own. Now it was his turn to give something back to her.

"I'm sure Nina is harmless," Jake said, brushing away his brother's concern. "Besides, I don't care what her reasons are if it helps bring business to Café Romeo."

"That's a big if. Take it from me, Jake. You need to spell out to a woman exactly what you expect from her. And what she can expect from you. That way there are no misunderstandings."

Jake walked to the door. "Since when did you become an expert on women?"

"I never said I was an expert." A slow smile creased Trace's face. "Although I've dedicated myself to an extensive study of the subject. By the time I'm through, I'll find a woman who will make the perfect wife."

Jake suppressed a shudder as he picked up his suitcase and opened the door. "I think that's an oxymoron."

Trace ambled after him. "You just need to take charge of the situation. Make it clear to Nina from the start that you won't put up with any silly female nonsense." Trace turned in the doorway. "Oh, and you might want to convince her to take the brick out of her purse."

"Thanks for the advice," Jake said dryly.

"Anytime, big brother." Trace slapped him on the shoulder. "Anytime."

NINA SAT in the center of her living room on top of her overstuffed suitcase. She had grabbed onto the thin metal zipper pull and was straining to zip it shut when she heard a knock on her front door. "It's open!"

Molly strolled into the apartment, carrying a small red gift bag, adorned with a profusion of curly gold ribbon. "Wait! You're not done packing. I brought you a bon voyage gift."

Nina looked up from her suitcase struggle. "If I try to cram one more thing in here it's going to explode."

"But this is a necessity," Molly countered, handing her the gift bag.

Nina looked inside, then pulled out a jumbo box of condoms.

"It's the rainbow variety pack," Molly informed her as she flopped down on the sofa. Pepper, Nina's gray tabby, jumped up next to Molly and curled against her hip.

Nina was still staring at the box. "You shouldn't have."

"Don't mention it."

"No, I mean you *really* shouldn't have." She dropped the box back into the bag. "I won't need them."

Molly grinned. "I know it's been a while, but they're not for you, they're for Jake."

"He won't need them, either."

"Does Jake know that?"

"Not exactly." Nina turned her attention back to the suitcase.

Molly scooted forward on the sofa cushion. "But you did tell him about The Bonecrusher."

"Not exactly."

"Okay…so what did you tell him?"

With one last forceful tug, Nina pulled the zipper home, then rose up off the floor. "I just asked him if he'd like to go to Chicago with me for the weekend."

"And that's it? You didn't mention the Reviewers'

Choice competition, or the fact that one of the chefs wants to purée you?''

"It didn't seem like a good time. It was raining, and Jake wasn't completely lucid.''

"Are you even planning to tell him?''

Nina pulled her suitcase upright, then wrapped both hands around the handle and hauled it toward the door. "Definitely. When the time is right.''

"And when will that be?''

"At about thirty thousand feet.''

Molly laughed. "I just hope he doesn't toss you out of the plane. I can't believe any man would agree to a platonic weekend with you—no strings attached.''

Nina shrugged. "I may not have actually told him we'd have a strictly platonic relationship, but it was implied. We got off to a rocky start at Café Romeo, and I think he really just wants to make it up to me.'' Slowly she looked around the apartment for anything she might have missed. "Now, are you sure it's not any trouble to watch Pepper for the weekend?''

"Are you kidding?'' Molly nuzzled Pepper's furry face close to hers and made smooching noises. Pepper closed his eyes, patiently enduring the attention. "I love cats. In fact, I'm thinking of getting one of my own.''

"Okay, his food is in the pantry, and the litter box...''

"...is in the laundry room,'' Molly finished for her. "You already told me this. Now go. Pepper will be fine.''

Nina took a deep breath. "All right." She opened the door and dragged her suitcase behind her out into the hall. Then she whirled around. "Tell me I'm not making a big mistake."

"You are not making a big mistake. Just have fun. You get to spend a weekend at a great hotel with a gorgeous guy."

Nina's throat tightened as panic gripped her. "But I don't know anything about him. Except that he's an ex-boxer. What if he's a male chauvinist? Or a playboy? Or some kind of kinky psychopath?"

A worried frown creased Molly's brow. "I thought you liked him."

"I do," Nina admitted, suddenly realizing the reason for her sudden case of cold feet. She'd liked Jake when she'd first met him. She'd liked him even better when he'd shed his nerd costume. As a matter of fact, she hadn't found a man as appealing as Jake Callahan in a very long time. That was the problem.

"And he must like you a little, or he wouldn't have agreed to spend the weekend with you." Molly winked. "Maybe even more than a little."

"I don't want him to like me, I just want him to protect me."

Molly rolled her eyes. "Is this about that stupid moratorium? I can't believe you've stuck to it this long."

"It's not stupid. Look at the great things that have happened to me since I've given up men. I got a good job on a big-city newspaper. My review column is a hit. And I've been invited to judge one of the most prestigious competitions in the industry. Who knows where this could lead?''

''It sounds to me like it could lead to a lot of lonely nights.''

Nina shook her head. ''The moratorium is not going to last forever, just until I get my career firmly on track. I'm twenty-seven years old and I've wasted too much time already. This weekend could be my big break. I can't let Jake Callahan or any other man make me lose my focus.''

Molly looked doubtful. ''But what if he's irresistible?''

Nina squared her shoulders. ''I'll only have to resist him for seventy-two hours. How hard can that be?''

4

NINA REGRETTED her words as soon as she saw him. Jake Callahan looked even better than she remembered. He stood near the entrance to the airport terminal, wearing stone-washed blue denim jeans and a red polo shirt. He smiled when he saw her walking toward him and her heart skipped a beat.

"This is business," Nina muttered to herself. "Strictly business."

"It's almost time to board." Jake took the heavy suitcase out of her hand. "Man, what do you have in here? More bricks?"

"Just a few necessities," she said, pulling their tickets out of her purse. The sponsor of the Reviewers' Choice contest had sent her two complimentary airplane tickets. Normally, Nina avoided flying like food poisoning, but she wasn't in a financial position to turn down free transportation to Chicago.

By the time they had checked their luggage and boarded the airplane, Nina's panic had returned in full force. Part of it was due to her fear of flying. The other part was due to the man seated next to her. He not only looked good, he smelled good. She took a deep, calming breath, inhaling the spicy scent of his cologne. Seventy-two hours suddenly seemed like an eternity.

"Nervous?" Jake glanced down at her hands clenched around the arms of her seat.

"A little. I don't really like to fly."

"I love it," he said, as the jet engines roared to life.

Nina squeezed her eyes shut as the airplane picked up speed. Her body tensed as the plane's momentum pushed her back against the cushioned seat. Every airplane disaster story she'd ever heard raced through her mind.

"There is a far greater risk of dying in a car accident than in an airplane crash," Jake said next to her. He sounded calm. Rational. Perfectly relaxed.

It irritated the hell out of her.

"In fact," he continued, "when an airplane crashes, more people die from smoke inhalation than from the impact. That's why it's always a good idea to know where the emergency exits are, so you can make a quick escape."

"This is not helping," she said through her teeth.

"Relax, Nina. Air travel is perfectly safe. Think of all the hundreds of flights every day. What's amazing to me is that there aren't more mid-air collisions. Especially since the job of an air traffic controller was recently rated as the most stressful."

"Mid-air collisions?" Nina squeaked, her eyes open now and glued to the small square window searching for oncoming planes.

"That hardly ever happens," Jake assured her, unfastening his seat belt. "Most airplane disasters are caused by equipment failures." He looked around the crowded cabin. "I wonder how old this plane is?"

For the first time she noticed the frayed tweed fabric on the arm of her seat and the scratches on the window casing. The plane looked old to her. Very old. "What kind of equipment failures?"

He shrugged. "Could be anything. Engine problems or trouble with the landing gear. I once heard a story about a duck flying south for the winter that ran into an airplane window and broke it. Three passengers were sucked out before they got everything back under control."

Nina's heart pounded hard in her chest. "That's it. I want to get off."

"Hey, I'm just joking." He reached over and began rubbing her tense shoulders. "You're perfectly safe."

"At least until we run into a flock of migrating ducks."

He laughed. "Birds don't fly this high. We're at thirty thousand feet."

Thirty thousand feet. That was her cue to give him his job description for the weekend. But since she wasn't convinced they'd even survive the flight, what was the point?

Jake's hand moved to the back of her neck, kneading the tight muscles. Almost against her will, her body began to relax.

"That's better," he murmured. "You just need to

take your mind off flying. Think about something else.''

Easier said than done. Still, he might be right. She licked her dry lips. ''So how many people have you beaten up?''

His hand stilled on her neck. ''What?''

''You're a boxer, right?'' She tilted her head forward to give him better access to her taut neck muscles.

After a long moment he began massaging her neck once more. ''Ex-boxer. My record was twenty-three and one.''

''Wow, that's great.'' She was starting to feel better already. ''Did you knock any of them out?''

''Eleven were TKOs.''

''What's that?''

''Technical knock-outs. That's when the referee calls the fight.''

''Oh.'' She couldn't help the stab of disappointment at his words. Still, a TKO was better than a loss. Which made her ask her next question. ''What about you?''

''What about me?''

''Did you ever get knocked out, or technically knocked out?''

He hesitated for a moment. ''I lost my last fight.'' Then his hand moved along her jawline, his rough fingers caressing the curve of her cheek. ''You really have beautiful skin.''

Warning bells went off in Nina's head. She pulled away from his touch. ''About this weekend...''

"I know a great restaurant just off Michigan Avenue," he said, folding his hands in his lap. "Do you like Taiwanese food?"

"Um...yes...I mean no." She knew she sounded ditzy, but his compliment had caught her completely off guard. "I mean we won't have time to eat."

Jake arched one dark brow. "Really? Even to keep our strength up?"

Her cheeks warmed. "I think you're deliberately misunderstanding me."

One corner of his mouth curved up in a smile. "I sincerely hope not."

She took a deep breath. "Maybe I should explain. The Ambassador Towers is the site of the Reviewers' Choice competition this weekend and I'm one of the judges."

"So we'll be eating in."

"I'll be eating all weekend long. You can eat wherever you want, or order something from room service."

"You mean this is strictly a working vacation? No time for play?"

"None," she said firmly, then unbuckled her seatbelt and turned to face him. "Jake, I'm afraid I asked you to go to Chicago with me under false pretenses."

His smile faded. "You lied to me?"

She shook her head. "No...I just didn't fully explain what I expect of you."

"Go on."

She swallowed, finding this harder than she'd imagined. "I need a bodyguard."

He didn't say anything. She stared into the midnight depths of his blue eyes, waiting for some kind of reaction. "I need a bodyguard," she repeated.

"And?" he prompted.

"And you're it."

He hesitated for a long moment. "Tell me you're joking."

"I'm completely serious," she assured him. "And I think you'll be perfect."

"Trace was right," he muttered.

"Who's Trace?"

"My brother. He knows all about women. I should have listened to him." He raked one hand through his hair. "Sorry, but I'm going to have to pass."

"What does that mean?"

"It means you'll have to find some other guy to trick into becoming your bodyguard. As soon as we land, I'm turning around and heading back to St. Louis."

"But you can't do that!"

He set his jaw. "Just watch me."

Before she could find a way to convince him, the stewardess wheeled her serving cart up to them.

"Good afternoon," she chimed, flashing a come-hither smile at Jake. "Thank you for flying with us."

Jake smiled back at her. "Anytime."

Nina watched him flirt with the stewardess while she mentally kicked herself for her poor timing. She should have waited until they'd reached the hotel. Unless she came up with some reason to convince him to stay, Jake was going to abandon her at O'Hare International Airport.

After handing them each a bag of peanuts and a soft drink, the stewardess pushed her cart to the row in front of them, the bottles clinking as the airplane bucked.

"What was that?" Nina gasped, grabbing Jake's arm. "A duck?"

"Just a little turbulence," he assured her, before taking a sip of his soft drink. "Now why don't you tell me why you need a bodyguard."

Hope momentarily dispelled her fear. "Does this mean you've reconsidered?"

"No. I just thought talking about it might take your mind off the flight."

The airplane lurched again and the pilot's calm, monotone voice carried over the intercom. "This is your captain speaking. We are experiencing a little turbulence. There is absolutely no danger, but just as a precaution, we ask that you please fasten your seat belts."

"We're going to crash, aren't we?" Nina said, her heart racing in her chest. "That's why he told us to fasten our seat belts."

"No," Jake replied calmly as he snapped his seat belt together. Then he reached over and fastened hers. "If we were going to crash, he'd tell us to assume the crash position."

"Shouldn't we be in Chicago by now?" She looked out the window at the misty clouds below them.

"Soon. It will take just long enough for you to tell me why you need a bodyguard."

She turned to him. "I thought you weren't interested in the position."

"I'm not, but I am interested in the story. Are you a rich heiress?"

She rolled her eyes. "If I was an heiress, we wouldn't be flying coach. I need a bodyguard because one of the chefs I reviewed in my column is a little…sensitive. He's been stalking me for the last three weeks."

"Stalking you?" He frowned. "Why?"

"Well, number one, I criticized his cooking. And number two—he's one of the contestants in the competition this weekend."

"So let me get this straight. You want me to protect you from a chef? One of those flaky guys who collects recipes and wears an apron?"

"This isn't funny," she scolded. "I think the man is unbalanced."

"Maybe his puffy white hat is too big." Jake settled back in his seat. "I think I can handle a chef."

Her pulse kicked up a notch. "Does this mean you're reconsidering?"

He mulled it over for a moment, then nodded. "I'll do it. But I'll expect compensation."

Her hopes fell. "I can't pay you. My car was rear-ended last month and the repairs sucked my bank account dry."

Jake's gaze locked on her face. "I don't want your money, Nina."

Heat pooled low in her stomach, then flowed up to her cheeks. She'd never bartered with her body before. But then, she'd never had a man like Jake Callahan interested in her body before. Curiosity and lust made her momentarily consider his proposition.

"What exactly do you want from me?" she asked, her voice low and husky.

"A review."

She blinked back her surprise. "A review? You mean like a...performance review?"

"I want the works. I guarantee you will have a wonderful time."

The man certainly wasn't modest. But what exactly was he asking for—a publicity quote on his sexual prowess? She could picture it now: "The Jackhammer lives up to his name."

"So do we have a deal?"

She swallowed. "I'm sorry, Jake, I'm not that kind of girl."

"What do you mean?"

"I mean the kind who will kiss and tell. I realize that in this instance you actually *want* me to tell, but I've never reviewed a lover before. I mean...I wouldn't even know where to start."

He stared at her for the space of several heartbeats. "I was talking about a review for my aunt's coffeehouse, not for me."

"Oh." Her flush deepened and she wondered if the high altitude was affecting her brain.

"Although, I have to admit the idea intrigues me." His eyes burned a slow trail down her body. "I've never had a woman review me before. Although, I've certainly never had any complaints.''

"Getting back to Café Romeo," she prompted, half hoping a duck really would hit her window and suck her right out of this situation.

"Right." He leaned toward her and lowered his voice. "I'll make you a deal, Nina. In exchange for acting as your bodyguard for the weekend, you'll agree to give Café Romeo a second chance. A rave in your column could make Café Romeo the hottest coffeehouse in St. Louis.''

She could tell him that giving Café Romeo a rave review was a long shot. But he hadn't specifically told her he expected a rave, just that he wanted another review. It might be a little unusual, but there was no legal or ethical reason she couldn't give the coffeehouse a second chance. After all, her experiences at Café Romeo the other evening had been a little unusual.

"So what do you say?''

She nodded, relieved he'd finally come around. "You've got a deal.''

His gaze drifted to her mouth. "Good. It sounds like this weekend could be mutually satisfying for both of us.''

She licked her lips. "What exactly does that mean?''

"I think we both know what it means. You're a beautiful woman, Nina. We could have a wonderful time together this weekend.''

She took a deep breath, determined to make her position perfectly clear. "No."

"No?"

"It's nothing personal," she assured him. "I've given up men. Temporarily, anyway."

He gave her a slow smile. "Maybe I can convince you to change your mind."

She shook her head, feeling much better now that everything was out in the open. "You'd be wasting your time, Jake. I'd better warn you that I've got tremendous willpower when I set my mind to something. There is nothing you could say or do to sway me."

"Hey, I just heard something."

"Engine failure?" she asked, her fingers flexing on the armrest.

"No. It sounded more like a gauntlet." He grinned. "You just threw it down right in front of me. I'd better warn you that I can never resist a challenge. I'm a competitor at heart, Nina. And I'll do everything in my power to sway you...among other things."

"Take your best shot, Callahan." The plane hit another pocket of turbulence and lurched violently. Nina squeezed her eyes shut, awaiting disaster.

"I'll do that," he replied. Then he kissed her.

Her eyes flew open when his mouth touched hers. His hand cradled her cheek, his thumb lightly brushing the hair at her temple. At first, she was too stunned to pull back. Then she didn't want to pull back. She leaned into him, her hand on his broad shoulder as he deepened the kiss. He traced the seam of her lips with his tongue, groaning low in his throat when her lips parted.

Nina knew this was idiotic. Impulsive. Insane. She also knew she had to put a stop to it so Jake couldn't claim victory before the battle had even begun. She drew back from him. "Nice try."

Jake's gaze slowly lifted from her mouth to her eyes. "Hey, I'm just doing my job."

Her body felt warm and tingly all over. "Your job doesn't include kissing me."

"The turbulence scared you." He leaned back in his seat and closed his eyes. A satisfied smile curved his mouth. "I thought a little distraction might be in order."

It had worked. She'd forgotten about the turbulence. She'd forgotten she was even on an airplane. Jake's kiss had almost convinced her she could fly without one. From now on she needed to keep both feet on the ground. And Jake Callahan needed to keep that sexy mouth to himself.

Nina faced forward in her seat and tightened her seat belt, purposely ignoring him as the plane began its descent.

It was going to be a bumpy weekend.

5

NINA TRIED not to stare at the king-size bed in the middle of her hotel room, which was hard since Jake was lying right in the middle of it. His proprietary manner annoyed her, especially since he had a king-size bed of his very own in the adjoining room.

He lay propped against the pillows, his arms folded behind his neck. "So when do I get to meet this homicidal hash-slinger?"

"Tonight at the cocktail reception. All the judges and contestants are expected to be there." She turned to her suitcase, busying herself with unpacking her clothes and placing them neatly in the drawers of the mahogany wardrobe. Her anxiety hadn't eased when she'd stepped off the airplane. If anything it had gotten worse. She had so much at stake this weekend. So much to lose.

Possibly even her life—although she hadn't seen any sign of The Bonecrusher since they'd arrived at the Ambassador Towers. Maybe he'd backed out of the contest at the last minute. Or missed his flight. Or choked on a chicken bone.

One could hope. Or one could imagine he was secreted in his hotel room planning his next move against her. Not that her bodyguard seemed overly concerned. Jake had spent the last half hour studying the room-service menu. And now he was intently studying the floor.

"You dropped something," he announced.

She glanced down to see her new black lace Wonderbra in a heap at her feet, the price tag still attached. She snatched it up and stuffed it in the drawer, a blush burning her cheeks. "Thanks."

He smiled. "My pleasure. But just for the record, you don't need to wear that to impress me. I happen to like you just the way you are."

She closed her eyes at the seductive purr in his voice. He was doing it again. Teasing her. Enticing her. Most single women would give up chocolate to have a six-foot-two-inch hunk of male temptation stretched out on their bed. But not Nina. This was a test. If she could just resist Jake Callahan for the next seventy-two hours, her career dreams would come true. And she wanted that to happen. Wanted it more than she'd ever wanted anything in her life.

She opened her eyes, steadier now and more determined than ever. "Believe me, Jake, the last thing I want to do is impress you."

"Then who *are* you trying to impress?"

She closed the lid of her empty suitcase and set it on the luggage rack. "If you must know, his name is W. Murphy Hayes."

"What does the W stand for?"

She shrugged. "I don't know. Everybody calls him Murphy. His friends, anyway."

"Are you one of them?"

She shook her head. "Please. I've never even been in the same city with him before. Until now."

"I've never even heard of him until now."

"He's the publisher of *The Epicurean,* the Cadillac of culinary magazines. It's based in New York and has world-wide circulation. The magazine just happens to have an opening for a restaurant reviewer. It's been rumored that the three judges selected by Mr. Hayes for the Reviewers' Choice competition are the top contenders for the job."

"And wearing a padded bra is one of the job requirements?"

A blush heated her cheeks. "Of course not. I just want to put my best foot forward."

"I don't think it goes on your foot."

Her blush deepened. "Look, if you must know, Hayes has a reputation for liking well-endowed women. Yes, it's sexist, and I'd rather be hired on my writing abilities, but I *really* want this job."

He sat up on the bed. "Why?"

She couldn't believe she had to spell it out for him. "Because I won't have an opportunity like this again. *The Epicurean* is the pinnacle. I'll be at the top of my profession. I'll have clout, prestige, not to mention a great salary. I'd be crazy not to want this job."

She opened the wardrobe and pulled out her silky pink robe. "Now, as my bodyguard, I'll expect you to escort me to the reception. It's my hope that just having you around will be enough to deter The Bonecrusher. Especially if I happen to drop a few hints that you're a boxer called The Jackhammer.''

"Ex-boxer."

"Whatever. As long as you look mean and intimidating."

"Should I wear my boxing gloves to the party, or will a coat and tie do?"

She refused to be baited. "A coat and tie will be fine." She folded the robe over her arm. "Now if you'll excuse me, I need to get ready."

He got to his feet with a reluctant sigh. "How am I supposed to protect you from the next room?"

"I think I'll be safe in the bathtub."

"Think again. Over forty percent of domestic injuries happen in the bathroom."

As if she needed something else to worry about. "You're making this up."

"No, it's true. My little brother's in the insurance business. Guess some of it's rubbed off." He paused by the connecting door. "Are you sure you don't want me to wash your back?" He grinned. "I've got great hands—so I'm told."

She didn't doubt it for a moment. "Thanks, but I can manage just fine on my own."

He headed into his room. "Give me a holler if you change your mind."

Nina closed the connecting door with a sigh of relief. She'd survived Round 1 with The Jackhammer.

JAKE HAD met his match. In the romantic arena, anyway. He had to give Nina credit. She'd successfully dodged each of his romantic overtures and double entendres. He peeled off his shirt and dropped onto the floor to begin his daily exercises. Their verbal sparring had invigorated him, so he did twice the number of stomach crunches and one-handed push-ups that he'd incorporated into a modified exercise routine. It wasn't as grueling as the training he'd endured on the boxing circuit, but it still kept him in top physical condition.

But his ability to bench-press three hundred pounds wouldn't help him woo Nina. She might be smart and stubborn, but passion lurked beneath that boxy gray business suit. He'd seen it in her eyes. Tasted it in her kiss.

A thought struck him as he reached for the fluffy white towel he'd draped over a chair. What if he did succeed? And what if Nina wanted more than a weekend together? Could this silly game between them possibly jeopardize Café Romeo's review? He toweled the sweat off his face and chest, wondering if the stakes were too high.

He'd played a high-stakes game before—and lost. Jake stared at the towel in his hand, remembering another night a lifetime ago. A noisy auditorium, reeking of cigarette smoke and beer. Sweat. Blood. A soul-searing hunger.

Jake had been pumped for the biggest fight of his life, the fight that could catapult him from the ranks of amateurs into the professional boxing circuit. In those days, he'd lived to box. Embraced the intense training and dedication it took to excel at the sport.

Best of all, once he stepped into that ring, he could let loose all the emotions he had stored up inside of him. Only that night his emotions had controlled him.

That night he'd crossed the line from boxer to killer.

Jake blinked at the towel clamped tightly in his hand, his knuckles as white as the nappy fabric. He took a deep breath, his body filmed in cold, clammy sweat. He wiped down again and tried to wipe those old memories out of his mind. He'd never let it happen again. Never let his emotions take over.

He slung the towel around his neck, ready for a hot shower to ease the tension out of his body. But a muffled shout froze him in his tracks.

"Help!"

Nina. He raced for the connecting door, relieved to find it unlocked. But his relief quickly turned to worry when he found her room empty on the other side.

"Jake!"

The bathroom. His heart pounded in his chest as he tried the bathroom door. Locked. She was trapped in the bathroom with that crazy chef. Because Jake hadn't been doing his job. A job he never would have accepted if he'd thought she was in any real danger. He simply hadn't believed a man who wore an apron for a living could be a threat to anyone.

Now Nina was going to suffer for his stupidity.

He backed up a few steps, then rammed his shoulder against the door. Wood splintered, but the door didn't give. He could hear Nina's voice, but couldn't make out the words over the sound of the running bath water. Was she cursing her bodyguard? Or begging for her life? He rammed his shoulder into the door again, and this time it swung open on impact. His momentum sent him sailing into the small bathroom, his feet hitting the slippery, wet floor. They flew out from under him, and he landed on the ceramic tiles with a teeth-rattling thud.

Tepid water soaked through his jeans and boxer shorts. He looked up to see Nina furiously bailing water with a plastic ice bucket—first dipping it into the overflowing bathtub, then dumping it in the marble sink. She was safe. She was alone. She was also naked underneath her skimpy silk robe.

Jake's heart still beat triple time. "What the hell is going on here?"

Lavender-scented steam filled the air. She dipped the plastic ice bucket into the tub. "The knob broke on the tap and I can't turn off the water."

"Did you pull the plug?" he asked, as water lapped over the edge of the tub.

"Of course I pulled the plug," she replied, still bailing. "As you can see, it didn't help much."

Jake carefully rose to his feet, then reached for the broken knob lying on top of the toilet tank. With a few deft twists and a lot of luck, he finally got the water stopped.

"Well, now I feel really stupid," she said, her face flushed and moist with exertion. Damp blond curls clung to her temples. "How did you fix it?"

"I don't have the faintest idea. Just don't touch that knob or you could have another flood on your hands.

You'd better call maintenance before you decide to take another bath.'' He straightened up, wiping his wet hands on his wet jeans. ''Oh, and one more thing.''

''What?''

''Don't ever scare me like that again.'' He took a step closer to her. ''Do you have any idea what I thought when I heard you scream like that?'' He didn't wait for her to answer. He grabbed her by both arms, his fear still palpable. ''I thought that chef was in here with his cleaver. I thought...'' His voice trailed off as he gazed down into her face.

''You thought...what?'' she asked softly.

''Nothing,'' he bit out.

''Then what are you thinking now?''

''I'm not.'' Then he did something really stupid. He kissed her. Before she could even react, his mouth caught her lips and his arms wrapped around her waist and pulled her close. He kissed her hard and deep, with hot, aching need that pulsed from his mouth into her own. The heat from her sweet, supple body penetrated his damp clothes. His fingers splayed over her cheeks, her skin as soft as the silk of her robe. A ripple of desire shot through him as she pressed against his hard length.

Alarmed by the intensity of his reaction, Jake broke the kiss. ''You're all wet.''

''That's an understatement,'' she muttered. Then she cleared her throat. ''I'm sorry I scared you. I guess I panicked when the water started hitting the floor.''

He backed up a step so he could think straight. "Why did you let me break down the door? Why didn't you just open it?"

"I had to put on my robe first," she retorted, tugging the sash more tightly around her waist. "I told you to wait."

"I didn't hear you."

She set her jaw. "You might want to get your ears checked. Because I've also told you I'm not interested in romance. Yet you've already kissed me today. Twice."

"It won't happen again." He meant it, too. He still didn't understand what had come over him. He'd kissed her. Twice. The first kiss had been planned— a smooth maneuver to calm her nerves and satisfy his curiosity.

But this second kiss had come as a complete surprise—to both of them. Jake rubbed one hand over his jaw, wondering what had come over him. He *never* acted on impulse. Never let his emotions drive him anymore. But something had driven him to pull Nina into his arms.

That kiss had been a wake-up call. More like a wake-up punch, actually, right in his solar plexus. He couldn't let himself lose control of this situation. Of any situation.

For a moment he let himself consider what might have happened if Nina's life really had been threatened. He'd acted on pure impulse when he'd heard her scream. He knew he would have fought to save her. Hell, he'd fight to defend the life of anyone in danger. *But at what cost to himself?* Once he crossed that line again, could he ever go back?

"Jake? Are you all right?"

He sucked in a breath as her voice returned him to reality. Nina was safe. Safe. Beautiful. Sexy. His desire for her had sharpened into a physical ache. But he needed to go slower. Let this heat between them just simmer for a while until he got his emotions back firmly under control.

"I'm fine," he lied.

She arched a brow. "So did you really mean it?"

"Mean what?" he asked, still trying to get his bearings.

"That you won't kiss me again."

"Of course."

She folded her arms across her chest. "Why should I believe you?"

"Because I'm a man of my word," he said firmly. "You're right, Nina. I've taken advantage of you. The next time we kiss, you'll be the one who initiates it."

A spark flashed in her green eyes. "There won't be a next time."

He smiled, relieved to be back in familiar territory. He loved women, even if he could never allow himself to fall in love. He also loved the intricate tango that men and women had engaged in for centuries. Only he'd better make certain she knew that their dance would eventually come to an end.

"I can live with that." He trailed one finger over the soft curve of her cheek. "I won't like it, but I can live with it. I think we could have a fun weekend together. But that's all I want, Nina. A weekend. No long-term relationship. No commitment. I should have made that clear from the beginning.''

She turned away from him and busied herself by dropping fluffy towels onto the floor to absorb the puddles of water. ''At least you're honest about it. I'll admit that's refreshing.''

His mouth went dry as he watched the way her silk robe outlined her slender figure. ''Now that we've established the ground rules, shall we let the games begin?''

She glanced at him over her shoulder. ''You're impossible. Besides, I don't have time for games. I have a reception to attend. Can you be ready in twenty minutes?''

He winked at her as he moved toward the door. ''I'm always ready.''

No wonder they called him The Jackhammer.

Nina's knees still shook a little as she and Jake entered the large reception hall. The aftermath of his kiss still vibrated through her, making her entire body thrum. What was wrong with her? She'd been attracted to men before. None of them had ever been quite like Jake Callahan, but she'd had her share of heart-pounding moments.

Her heart pounded just looking at him. He easily overshadowed every other man in the room in his tailored gray suit and crimson tie. No doubt he'd surpass every other man here without the suit, too. He'd only been half-dressed when he'd come to her rescue in the bathroom, giving her a close-up view of that taut, washboard stomach. Those thick biceps. The surprising breadth of his shoulders.

She remembered the way his jeans had been slung low on his lean hips, the way the dark hair on his chest gradually tapered until it disappeared beneath his waistband. The way his blue eyes had darkened just before he kissed her.

"Nina?"

She blinked, Jake's deep voice breaking into her reverie. "What?"

He smiled. "You look nervous."

Nervous? Panic-stricken was more like it. Because instead of concentrating on her career, she was standing next to the buffet table fantasizing about Jake. Even after he'd told her he was a one-weekend man. Even after she'd promised herself not to let another man distract her from her goals.

Nina squared her shoulders, determined to regain her equilibrium. "I'm fine."

"Good. I'm starving. Can we eat before we mingle?"

"Go ahead," she replied, avidly scanning the crowd for a sign of The Bonecrusher. At six feet, seven inches, he should be hard to miss, although it was difficult to picture him among this sedate crowd. Men and woman mingled around the opulent reception hall as a string quartet in the corner played a selection of tranquil chamber music.

"Well, if you insist...."

But before he could walk away, Nina grabbed his forearm. "I don't believe it. He's here!"

Jake's muscles tensed beneath her fingertips. He looked up at the silver-haired man approaching them. "That's your stalker? He looks more like a mortician than a chef."

"Keep your voice down," she admonished, then leaned closer to him. "That's W. Murphy Hayes. The publisher of *The Epicurean.*"

He frowned as his gaze flicked to the fully padded front of her shimmery azure cocktail dress, then back up again. "I see you're fully prepared to meet him."

"Go stuff something in your mouth, Jake," she said under her breath, as Hayes closed the distance between them.

"And miss meeting the famous W? Not on your life."

Before she could argue with him, Hayes held out his hand. "Miss Walker, I presume?"

"Yes," she said, extending her hand. "Please call me Nina."

"And you must call me Murphy." He lifted her hand to his mouth and brushed a dry kiss across her knuckles.

"It's a pleasure to meet you, Murphy," she said, a little breathless with anticipation. This man held more than her hand. He held her future.

"The pleasure is indeed mine." His gaze drifted down below her neck and stuck there. "I must tell you how much I enjoy your...columns."

"Dim sum?" Jake offered, holding a small plate filled with Chinese dumplings under Murphy's nose.

The publisher stepped back a pace, the hors d'oeuvre plate effectively blocking his view of Nina's new and improved cleavage. "Uh…no, thank you. I'm having a late dinner with a friend."

Nina flashed a warning glare at Jake, then smiled at Hayes. "I just want to thank you again, Murphy, for inviting me to be one of the judges at this year's Reviewers' Choice competition. It's quite an honor."

"I only request the best." He nodded in acknowledgment to an elderly couple on her left. "So many people, so little time. I hope we can meet later and discuss your talents in more detail."

"Any time," she said, as Murphy drifted off to greet the other guests. A tiny thrill shot through her. He'd singled her out. Kissed her hand. Asked her to meet with him again. To interview her, perhaps? She watched as he approached another judge, a lithesome blond woman, noting with satisfaction that he didn't kiss her hand.

Then Jake stepped into her line of vision. "Dim sum?"

She laughed, too buoyant to be irritated by his earlier interference. "Is that all you can say?"

"No." He smiled as he took a step closer to her. "I could say you're looking beautiful tonight. But that would be an understatement."

"Thank you, Jake. I think Murphy liked me."

His smile faded. "That would also be an understatement. Do you really want to work for a guy who slobbers all over your hand?''

''He's very continental,'' she said, moving away from the buffet table as a line began to form. ''Now, let's go mingle.''

But they'd only taken a few steps when she ran into one of the last people she wanted to see.

''Well, if it isn't The Nibbler!'' Karla Ruskin held a full glass of beer in one hand and an even fuller hors d'oeuvre plate in the other. She looked up at Jake and her finely tweezed eyebrows rose half an inch. ''And who's your scrumptious sidekick?''

''This is Jake Callahan,'' Nina said flatly. ''Jake, this is Karla Ruskin. She works for the Dispatch.''

''Callahan,'' Karla murmured, rolling the name around on her tongue. ''Jake Callahan. Of course!'' Her eyes widened in recognition. ''Jake 'The Jackhammer' Callahan.''

''I'm a business manager now.''

''Really? Are you here for the bout?''

He smiled. ''Bout?''

''Between The Nibbler and The Bonecrusher.''

''Karla!'' Nina admonished under her breath. For all the good it did her. Karla didn't let anyone or anything stop her pursuit of a story.

Jake's brow furrowed. ''Who's The Bonecrusher?''

Karla staggered back in mock amazement. ''Who's The Bonecrusher? Are you kidding me? He's only the best…the most awesome…the king of the ring.''

''He's a professional wrestler,'' Nina informed him. ''Or at least, he used to be.''

Jake turned to Nina. "And you're...The Nibbler?"

"That's right," Karla affirmed. "Because she chewed up The Bonecrusher and spit him out in her column. He retaliated with a turkey-bone simulation, and the fun's just continued from there."

Jake wasn't smiling anymore. "You mean...."

She nodded, hurrying to tell him before Karla could make matters worse. "He's the one, Jake. The Bonecrusher, also known as Chef Bo Bonham. And I use the term *chef* very loosely."

"Ooh, look!" Karla squealed, pointing toward the wide double doors. "There he is now!"

6

JAKE STARED, unable to believe his eyes. The chef filling the doorway wasn't the temperamental twit he'd imagined. He was a colossus. He was...The Bonecrusher. And it was Jake's job to stand between Nina and this human wrecking machine.

"Here he comes," Karla said, barely able to contain her excitement. "Oh, why didn't I bring my camera?"

"Why didn't I bring my tranquilizer gun," Jake muttered under his breath. Only he doubted that that would be enough to stop the man striding toward them. He looked as if a Mack truck couldn't stop him.

At least Jake's will was in order. He'd left everything to Aunt Sophie. With the income from his various investments, she should have enough money to keep Café Romeo in the black for the next few years.

Nina edged closer to him and he sensed her fear. What kind of bully picked on a woman? He clenched his fists as a spark of anger ignited inside him. Taking slow, deep breaths, he fought for control.

"We meet again, Miss Walker." The Bonecrusher's deep baritone carried across the room. Several heads turned to stare at the tempest now brewing in the center of the room.

Nina lifted her chin. "Chef Bonham."

Jake tensed as The Bonecrusher took another step closer to her. One more step and he'd have to do something. He reached for her hand. "Let's go, Nina."

"No, wait," The Bonecrusher boomed. "I've got something to say to Miss Walker."

"This really isn't the time or the place," Nina said, holding tightly onto Jake's hand.

Karla stepped into the fray.

"No, say it! This party could use a little excitement. It's been a real bore up until now."

The Bonecrusher glared at her. "Who are you?"

Karla's eyes widened. "I'm a reporter for the *St. Louis Post-Dispatch.* I've been a fan of yours for years, Mr. Bonecrusher. I've written several articles heralding your outstanding career. They haven't all been published yet...."

"Whatever." He turned away from her and cleared his throat. "Miss Walker, I've decided to let bygones be bygones."

Nina blinked. "*You've* decided? You're the one who dropped chicken bones on my head!"

"Chicken bones?" Jake echoed, wondering why Nina hadn't bothered to fill him in earlier. She'd obviously left out a lot of important details.

"They're a trick of the trade. I keep a large supply in my hearse."

Maybe Jake did need his hearing checked. "Did you say *hearse?*"

"Oh, it's so cool," Karla gushed. "It's all black with red velvet curtains in the windows. The license plate says BONEMAN."

"Whatever." The Bonecrusher turned back to Nina. "My manager is the one who wanted me to carry on a vendetta against you—for purely promotional reasons. My transition from professional wrestler to professional chef hasn't been easy for him." He hitched a thumb over his shoulder. "That's him, sulking behind the potted palm. Name's Benny Otis. He's the one who really hates you."

"Well, that makes me feel so much better," Nina said dryly.

Jake's gaze narrowed on Otis. Through the palm fronds he could discern a wiry man with stooped shoulders, a sullen face and a thin, barely visible mustache. He recognized a groupie when he saw one. A loser who liked to bask on the edge of his hero's limelight.

Nina's fingers flexed in his hand. "You mean this whole thing was just a publicity stunt? The chicken bones? The threats?"

The Bonecrusher shrugged. "I'll admit I was a little upset when I read your review. But I got over it. I just hope you don't hold it against me in the judging."

Her shoulders relaxed a fraction. "Of course not. I plan to give every contestant the score they deserve."

The Bonecrusher grinned, and for the first time

Jake noticed that two of his front teeth had been filed into sharp points. "I'm not sure I like the sound of that. But just keep an open mind, Miss Walker. You may be in for a surprise."

"That sounds ominous," Karla said, after The Bonecrusher stalked off, clearing a wide path through the crowd. "What do you suppose it means, Nina? Poison in the pesto? Crushed bone fragments in the cannelloni?"

"He apologized, Karla. It's over." Nina breathed a sigh of relief. "And no one is happier about it than I am."

Karla's eyes widened in surprise. "You actually believed him? The Bonecrusher is famous for his devious tactics. He'll lull you into a false sense of security, and then *bam*—he's got you pinned to the mat with his trademark death-hold. Take my word for it," she said, as she trailed after her hero. "It isn't over yet."

Those were the last words Jake wanted to hear. He'd managed to keep Nina safe. This time. But what if Karla was right? What if Nina needed him to do more than hold her hand?

"I don't see Murphy anywhere," Nina said, scanning the crowd, her mind obviously now on more important matters. "Do you suppose that spectacle scared him off? I want to stand out in his mind, but not as The Nibbler."

In Jake's mind, she already stood out in this crowd. Her blue cocktail dress shimmered under the lights of the chandelier and molded perfectly to her body. The deep vee of her bodice had him directing more than one "hands off" glare to the other men in the room. She combined elegance and sex appeal in a way that he'd never seen before. And he wasn't sure he wanted to see it again. It was too distracting. Too unsettling.

Just like everything else about her.

"Don't worry. I saw W leave before *Chef Bonham* arrived." He folded his arms across his chest. "Now do you want to tell me why you kept his identity a secret?"

"Because I kept hoping he'd just go away. I'm sorry, Jake. I probably should have told you the whole story from the beginning."

"*Probably?* Damn straight you should have told me. I was expecting some little twerp in an apron."

"It doesn't matter now," she said, placing one hand on his forearm. "It's finally over."

His resentment swiftly faded. "Not according to Karla."

She rolled her eyes. "Karla needs to get a life. She also needs to accept the fact that the battle between The Nibbler and The Bonecrusher ended in a draw."

"Are you sure?"

"Positive."

Her confident tone convinced him. Jake pushed the Bonecrusher to the back of his mind and concentrated on Nina. "What about us?"

She looked up at him. "Us?"

He smiled as he slipped his arm around her waist and drew her close. "Are you ready to take on The Jackhammer?"

She laughed. "You're impossible. Don't you ever give up?"

He shrugged. "I can't help myself. You're irresistible."

"Flattery will get you nowhere."

"Then what *do* you want?"

"Something even better than sex," she quipped, stepping smoothly out of his arms. "The lobster canapés."

He grinned in spite of himself. *Score one for Nina.* She was not only beautiful, she was witty and articulate. Score one for Aunt Sophie as well. Nina Walker might not be his perfect match, but she was perfect in just about every other way. She was also determined to keep him at arm's length.

Unless she changed her mind sometime during the long, lonely night. A man could hope. Or he could follow Nina's example and head for the buffet table.

He just hoped there were enough lobster canapés to satisfy him.

NINA TOSSED and turned in her bed that night, unable to fall asleep. Her drapes were wide open, giving her a beautiful view of the Chicago skyline. Somehow she doubted she'd ever sleep again. Not when her dreams were finally about to come true.

W. Murphy Hayes had left her a message at the front desk, asking her to meet him for an early breakfast. She hugged her pillow to herself as she stared up at the ceiling. *Finally.* Finally, she had a chance to make it into the Walker family newsletter. After a lifetime of false starts and unrealized expectations, success was in her reach. All she had to do was reach out and grab it.

If she could just keep from grabbing Jake Callahan first.

She pressed the pillow to her nose and breathed deeply, inhaling the scent of his spicy aftershave that still lingered there. He was impossible. Irreverent. Irresistible. At least she could admit it to herself, even if she knew better than to admit it to him. And despite his amorous arsenal, her defenses hadn't weakened. Not much, anyway.

She sighed, rolling onto her stomach and bunching the pillow beneath her chin. W. Murphy Hayes should be the only man on her mind now. He'd hinted that the job was hers if she wanted it. The black lace bra had really done the trick.

She frowned at the thought, telling herself the man responsible for such a successful magazine couldn't possibly base his business decisions on bust size. Still, did she dare *not* wear the black lace Wonderbra to breakfast tomorrow?

Before she could analyze the ramifications of an overnight breast reduction, a sharp knock sounded on her hotel-room door. She sat up, her hands clutching the sheets.

The Bonecrusher.

Maybe. Or maybe not. He'd told her his reign of terror was over. It was probably housekeeping. She'd called them earlier requesting towels to replace the soaked ones still strewn across her bathroom floor.

She got out of bed and walked to the door, double-checking the dead bolt to make certain it was locked before she peered through the peephole.

It wasn't The Bonecrusher.

But it didn't make Nina feel much better to see Karla standing outside the door. She swore under her breath as she flipped the dead bolt and opened the door. It was after midnight. Didn't obnoxious reporters ever sleep?

Karla looked just as unhappy to see Nina. Her jaw dropped as she shifted the wine bottle and two glasses she held in her hands. "What are you doing here?"

"This is my room," Nina replied. "And I could ask you the same question."

Karla tried to peer over Nina's shoulder. "I was told this was Jake Callahan's room."

Nina folded her arms across her chest. She'd have to have a long talk with the hotel manager tomorrow if the staff was giving out that kind of information. But there wasn't any reason she couldn't have a little fun with it now. "What makes you think this *isn't* his room?"

Karla blanched. "Are you and Jake…together?"

Before she could reply, she heard Jake's deep voice behind her. "Nina, are you all right?"

She turned around to see him walking toward her— and almost started drooling. He wore cotton drawstring pajama pants and nothing else. A fine layer of dark hair spanned his broad, chiseled chest. His biceps were so big she doubted she could get both hands around them.

"I thought I heard someone..." his voice trailed off as his gaze fell on Karla. "Oh, hello."

"Hi, Jake," Karla replied, looking a little dazzled by his appearance herself. "I thought we might share a nightcap and trade some good boxing stories." She frowned at Nina. "But I didn't realize you had a roommate."

Share a nightcap? Nina couldn't believe the woman was that transparent. As if Jake would fall for such a tired line.

He moved up to stand beside her, one hand braced on the open door. "Nina and I aren't roommates. I'm in the next room. Come on over."

JAKE LED KARLA past a wide-eyed Nina, through the connecting door and into his room. Then he shut the door firmly behind him. That door had been driving him to distraction all night. Thankfully, he now had another distraction—Karla and her bottle of merlot. He wasn't exactly thrilled about sharing a drink with her, but he'd do anything to take his mind off Nina. Especially since she was wearing that damn pink robe again; her blond curls tousled as if she'd just gotten out of bed. He just wished it had been his bed.

Get a grip, Callahan. So much for the distraction. He looked up to see Karla watching him and forced a smile. Maybe inviting her into his room had been a mistake. He grabbed the shirt he'd draped across a chair and shrugged it on. Despite her easy smile and cute pixie face, Jake just couldn't work up any enthusiasm for flirting with her. Much. less anything else.

"So, to what do I owe the pleasure of this visit?" he asked as he poured them each half a glass of wine.

She took a sip, studying him over the rim of her glass. Then she set it on the table in front of her and folded her hands together. "I just couldn't sleep until I found out how it feels to almost kill a man."

Jake choked on his wine. When he recovered, he set his glass down. "No comment."

"That's what you said five years ago." Karla leaned forward in her chair. "After practically killing off two promising boxing careers with one punch, you can't just walk away without a word. My readers want to know the inside scoop, even after all these years. It was a big story back then, you know."

He knew that only too well. He'd lived it. "No comment."

"Off the record," she persisted. "How did it feel when they started performing CPR on your opponent? Did you hear his wife screaming in the front row? Did all the booing bother you?"

"No comment," he said tersely.

But Karla didn't give up easily. She had a buoyant enthusiasm that irritated him almost as much as her incessant questions. "I heard no manager would take you after that night. Rumor or truth? Is boxing still in your blood? Do you dream about being back in the ring?" Her eyes widened. "That's why you're here with The Nibbler, isn't it? You want to take on The Bonecrusher to resurrect your career!"

He grabbed his wineglass and drained it in one gulp. "You should be writing fiction, Karla. It seems to be your forte."

She arched a brow. "Romantic fiction, perhaps? Are you and The Nibbler practicing your moves on each other? Is this a tag team affair of the heart?"

He yawned. "Excuse me. Fairy tales make me sleepy. Perhaps we should call it a night."

"Just answer one question, then I'll leave without another peep."

"Forget it," he said firmly.

"I just want to know how can you stand by and let The Nibbler defame another athlete." Her face twisted, making her look older, harder. "She absolutely skewered The Bonecrusher in her column."

"You don't like her, do you?" Jake leaned his elbows on the table. "Aren't reporters supposed to be objective?"

"We're human," she retorted. "And so are professional wrestlers. They have feelings just like everyone else."

"He's not a wrestler anymore, he's a chef who moonlights as a stalker. Did you know he's been threatening Nina?"

"Oh, please. Now who can't take a little criticism?" Then Karla grinned, reminding him of a perky pixie once more. "But I suppose you're right. I suppose as a big wrestling fan I am a little biased."

"A little?"

She laughed. "All right. A lot. I promise to work

on it, if you'll promise to think about giving me an exclusive.''

He pushed his chair back and stood up. "Not in this lifetime."

She took his cue and rose to her feet. "I like you, Callahan. You're stubborn and sexy—my favorite combination." She moved toward him. "If you don't want to do an exclusive, how about a little pillow talk instead?"

THE SILENCE was deafening.

Nina didn't normally eavesdrop on people, but tonight her curiosity overcame her ethics—and her good sense. She stood with her ear pressed to the connecting door. Either the Ambassador Towers had great sound-proofing or Jake and Karla were doing something other than talking.

She straightened, irritated at herself for caring. This was not suitable behavior for a mature, successful career woman. She should just go to bed and get a good night's sleep. Her gaze fell on the telephone as a more appetizing idea popped into her head. She could order something from room service. Her stomach rumbled, casting the deciding vote. She picked up the telephone, dialed room service and ordered a slice of strawberry cheesecake.

In her twenty-seven years she'd learned that cheesecake could soothe a lot of life's aches and pains. She reserved chocolate cheesecake for true emotional emergencies—like family reunions and phone calls from her perpetually disappointed parents.

Tonight, she thought she could get by with strawberry cheesecake. And perhaps a side order of onion rings if sleep still eluded her.

While she waited for her cheesecake to be delivered, Nina picked up her latest copy of *The Epicurean* off the nightstand. She flipped through the glossy pages, impressed as always by the high quality of the photographs and the innovative articles. The featured restaurant-of-the-month was a tiny bistro located just outside Paris, France. The owner, a stout Frenchman, had a reason to be smiling. Now that he had *The Epicurean*'s seal of approval, his bistro's success was guaranteed.

She'd give her sweet tooth to work for a magazine as classy and influential as *The Epicurean*. But until such a sacrifice proved necessary, she'd indulge in the sinfully sweet strawberry cheesecake now knocking at her hotel room door.

When she opened the door, she was surprised to find no one on the other side, just the white plastic room service tray on the floor. "At least I don't have to tip," she muttered. Picking up the tray, she carried it into the room, kicking the door shut behind her. She set it on the table next to the window and sat down, her mouth watering.

Only she didn't see a comforting slice of cheesecake when she lifted the silver cover off the plate.

A pile of crushed, splintered bone fragments lay on the dish, a small piece of white paper folded neatly on top of them. She picked it up, her fingers shaking. The message was short and simple.

Say goodnight, Nina.

She crumpled the note in her hand and slammed the cover back on top of the plate. Then she grabbed the tray and put it right back where she had found it on the hallway carpet.

The nerve of that pumped-up cretin! She was sick and tired of The Bonecrusher's games. Fed up with his threats. And really ticked off that he'd taken her strawberry cheesecake. Incensed, she moved toward the connecting door, ready to send her bodyguard after him.

Nina didn't stop to think until her hand touched the knob. What if her bodyguard was already occupied? What if he had his hands full...with Karla? That thought didn't improve her mood. With an irritated sigh, she leaned against the door, pressing her ear firmly to the veneer surface. If she heard any panting or moaning, she'd have to come up with a different plan.

She'd also have to throw up.

At that instant the door opened, and Nina tumbled head-first into Jake's room. She landed flat on her back on the plush carpet, staring up into the surprised faces of Jake and Karla.

"I told you she was trouble," Karla chimed, then stood on the tips of her toes to kiss Jake's cheek. "Goodnight, Jake. I had a wonderful time." She stepped over Nina's prostrate body and walked through the connecting door, obviously taking the scenic route through Nina's room on her way out.

Jake grinned down at her. "Were you actually listening at the door?"

Nina rose up on her elbows. "Of course not. I was...." Her voice trailed off as she struggled to come up with a reasonable explanation. "All right, I was listening at the door. But only because I didn't want to interrupt anything." She got to her feet. "I didn't, did I?"

"What do you want?" he asked, ignoring her question.

She wanted to know what he and Karla had been doing for the last twenty minutes. Instead, she tipped up her chin and said, "I want an apology."

"An apology? For what?"

"Dereliction of duty. While you were...cavorting with Karla, I got another message from The Bonecrusher."

His grin faded. "What kind of message?"

"I'll show you." She turned around and headed for her room, Jake right on her heels. Retrieving the tray from the hallway once again, she pointed to the covered dish in the center of the tray.

"You're afraid of a midnight snack?" Jake asked wryly.

"See for yourself," she said, setting the tray on the table, then lifting the lid with a flourish. A pristine slice of vanilla cheesecake slathered with strawberry sauce sat on a delicate china plate. Nina's mouth dropped open as she stared at it.

Jake bent down for a closer look.

"So that's his evil plan. He going to kill you with high cholesterol."

She looked over at him, sputtering for a moment before she finally found her voice. "This wasn't here before."

"Don't worry," he said, seating himself at the table and picking up the fork. "I'll take care of this for you." He took a huge bite, then closed his eyes in appreciation. "Hmm. Now this is what I call a dessert to die for."

She swatted him on the shoulder. "Would you be serious! Something very weird is going on here. I swear there was a pile of bones on that plate before."

Jake skewered a plump strawberry. "Bones?"

"Yes, bones. It looked like crushed chicken bones. That seems to be his specialty."

"No wonder you gave him a bad review."

She slid into the chair next to him, deciding now was the time to fill him in on all the gory details. "As much as I hate to say it, Karla was right. The Bone-crusher is playing games with me. He's no one to take lightly, either. He sent twelve of his opponents to the hospital. Once he even ate an entire roast turkey, bones and all, for a publicity stunt."

Jake scooped up the last forkful of cheesecake and chewed thoughtfully. "Well, there aren't any bones in here."

She frowned down at the empty plate. Missing out on her cheesecake didn't improve her mood. "You don't believe me?"

"Actually I do. But we don't know for certain The

Bonecrusher is to blame. It could be his promoter. Or even one of his kooky fans.''

"Or Karla."

He shook his head. "Karla might have a motive, but she also has an alibi. She was with me, remember?"

Only too well. Nina couldn't contain her curiosity any longer. "So what exactly were you two doing there?"

He stared at her for a long moment. "What do you think we were doing?"

She shrugged. "A bottle of wine, a hotel room, two attractive single people, naturally I assumed...."

"The worst," he interjected before she had a chance to finish her sentence. He actually had the gall to look offended. "For your information, I don't go to bed with just anyone. I'm a one-woman man. One woman at a time, anyway. And you're the only woman I want right now."

Right now. The operative words. Despite their mutual attraction, his romantic intentions were strictly temporary. So why couldn't she put him out of her mind? Why, even now, did her body tingle at his nearness? *Forbidden fruit.* That must be the answer. She wanted him so badly because she knew she couldn't have him. If she succumbed to Jake's considerable charms, history was doomed to repeat itself. And Nina would be doomed to remain a failure. The Walker family embarrassment.

She took a deep breath, suddenly feeling very tired. "Right now, I just want to get some sleep."

"And I want you in my bed."

She stood up. "You just don't give up, do you? I admire tenacity, but this is ridiculous."

He rose to his feet. "Nina…"

"No," she held up one hand, "let me finish. I'm not sleeping with you. I'll admit I'm attracted to you. I'll admit we have fun together. I'll even admit that I think we'd be *great* together in bed. But there's more to life than great sex."

"There is?"

She nodded, trying desperately to come up with something. "Of course. You should explore celibacy, Jake. You might find the experience very enriching."

"At the moment I just find it frustrating." He took a step toward her and lowered his voice to a husky whisper. "Nina?"

She swallowed hard, her lips tingling in anticipation of his kiss. She wanted to stay strong, but she wasn't made of iron. "Yes, Jake?"

"I have no intention of sleeping with you tonight."

Her gaze lifted from his mouth to his eyes. "But you said you wanted me in your bed."

"I do. And I plan to sleep in your bed. We're switching rooms. That way if this joker decides he wants to play with more than chicken bones, he'll find me in here instead of you."

"Oh."

He tipped up her chin with his finger. "I already told you that I'm not going to kiss you, or try to seduce you, or push you into doing something you don't want to do."

"Oh...good."

"I also don't take advantage of a woman when she's scared and vulnerable." He traced his finger lightly up the curve of her cheek and tucked an errant curl behind her ear. "Sweet dreams, Nina. You're perfectly safe with me."

Somehow, that didn't make her feel any better.

7

JAKE WOKE UP the next morning in Nina's bed. *Alone* in Nina's bed. He sighed as he stared up at the ceiling. This weekend wasn't going exactly as he'd planned. His frustration turned to panic when he didn't find Nina in his bed either.

Twenty minutes later he was shaved, dressed and fuming as he walked into the hotel restaurant. How could he possibly protect her from The Bonecrusher or anyone else when she took off without telling him? At least he'd found her note taped to the bathroom mirror before he'd torn the hotel apart. He set his jaw, wondering why he'd ever agreed to this crazy weekend. Maybe Trace was right. Maybe Nina *was* trouble.

So why did he dream about her last night? Why couldn't he quash the fantasies induced by that impulsive kiss? He scanned the crowded restaurant, finally spotting her at a corner table.

She looked up at Jake and smiled as he approached her table. "Good morning."

"Is it?"

"Well, it would have been better if Murphy had actually shown up for our breakfast meeting. But he left a message with the mâitre d'—with a very gracious apology and a promise to make it up to me.'' She could barely contain her excitement. ''He wants me to meet him in his suite tonight at eight o'clock to discuss the job opening at *The Epicurean.* Who knows where this could lead?''

''I know exactly where it could lead,'' Jake replied. ''And I can't believe you fell for one of the oldest lines around.''

Her brow crinkled. ''What are you talking about?''

''The come-up-to-my-suite-and-look-at-my-etchings line.''

''He didn't say a word about etchings.''

Jake snorted. ''Close enough. But won't good old W be surprised when I show up with you tonight?''

She carefully dabbed her lips with her linen napkin. ''You won't be with me.''

Jake folded his arms across his chest. ''I'm your bodyguard, remember? You shouldn't have even come down to breakfast without me. I certainly can't allow you to wander the hotel hallways alone at night.''

She considered that for a moment. ''All right. But you'll have to wait outside the door.''

''How can I protect you if I'm not in the same room with you?''

She laughed. ''Murphy isn't dangerous.''

''If you really believe that, then I'm definitely not letting you go there alone.''

She studied him as a waitress paused by their table

to fill his coffee cup. "Are you always this cranky in the morning?"

He picked up his cup, blowing gently on the steaming brew. "I don't like waking up alone."

"So you've said."

He scowled. "That's not what I mean. You should have told me about your breakfast meeting instead of leaving it in a note."

"You're probably right."

"Of course I'm right. I'm always right."

She smiled. "You're also modest."

He shook his head, both bewildered and bemused at her ability to counter his every verbal spar. "Look, Nina, you have to trust me. I want to keep my end of the bargain. I can't do that if you disappear again."

She wrapped her hands around her teacup. "I just wish we knew how those chicken bones got there last night. And who pulled the switch? Is it The Bonecrusher again or do I have a new enemy?"

"I plan to talk to the hotel manager this morning. Someone on his staff is obviously giving out your room number." He looked at her over his coffee cup, noting with dismay that she'd worn her black lace Wonderbra to breakfast. "You haven't given it out to anyone, have you?"

"Just Murphy."

The easy way she said his name made something hot and indefinable rush through his veins. He blew on his coffee until the unfamiliar feeling passed. "Why would W. Murphy Hayes possibly need to know your hotel-room number?"

She shrugged. "In case he wants to call me or stop by for a chat or a job interview."

"So now we can add another suspect to our list."

"It's *not* Murphy," she insisted. "Karla probably bribed the desk clerk. She's pretty relentless when she's after information."

"Tell me about it," he muttered before taking another sip of his coffee. "So it's possible the culprit discovered your room number the same way."

"Or else he and Karla are in cahoots." She frowned at him. "What are you smiling about?"

His smile widened. "I've never actually heard anyone use the word *cahoots* in a sentence before. It's kind of cute."

"Jake, I'm serious!"

"I know. That's what makes it cute."

She didn't bother to hide her sigh of exasperation. "Look, we have a long day ahead of us. You'd better order some breakfast."

He hailed the waitress and placed an order for three eggs sunny-side up, a rasher of bacon, a side order of hash browns and a large stack of pancakes. Then he frowned at the small glass of orange juice and the dry toast in front of Nina.

"Is that all you're having?" he asked, after the waitress walked off.

She put a hand to her stomach. "To tell you the truth, I'm a little nervous. I've never judged a culinary competition before."

Jake leaned back in his chair. "So what exactly do you have to do?"

"Well, today each of the chefs will compete in one of three preliminary categories—appetizer, vegetable, or dessert. I'm judging the dessert category."

"Lucky you. No wonder you didn't order much breakfast. Maybe, as your bodyguard, I should taste them ahead of you, just to make sure they're safe?"

She shivered slightly. "I wouldn't put anything past The Bonecrusher."

Jake didn't like the shadows he saw in her eyes, so he tried to steer the subject back on course. "So how do you choose a winner?"

"Each category is scored on a point system. The ten chefs with the highest points at the end of the day will qualify to compete in the original entrée category tomorrow morning. Then the winner will be announced at the awards brunch."

"Sounds simple enough."

"It won't be," she declared, picking up a piece of toast. "I'm still amazed at the talent they have assembled here. These chefs are the best of the best."

He watched Nina nibble at her toast. "Including Chef Bonham?"

"Not in my opinion."

"Then how did he ever garner an invitation?"

The waitress approached with Jake's order and Nina waited until she left to continue the conversation. "Good question. A fluke, maybe? Or just incredibly good luck?"

"Or maybe more than luck. Isn't *The Epicurean* sponsoring this competition?"

"Yes, they've sponsored it for years."

"So maybe Benny Otis convinced good old W that The Bonecrusher would generate publicity for the contest." Jake sprinkled salt and pepper on his eggs, then dug into his breakfast.

"Maybe."

After a few moments of silence, Jake glanced up to find Nina watching him. "What?"

She smiled. "Nothing. I've just never seen anyone eat with so much enthusiasm before."

"I'm hungry. And these multigrain pancakes are great." He held up a forkful, dripping with warm, golden maple syrup. "Here, try a bite."

She hesitated a moment, then leaned forward. Jake slid the fork into her mouth and watched her eyes close as she leaned back and chewed. His gaze dropped to her mouth and he saw a tiny drop of maple syrup clinging to her lower lip. He sat there, mesmerized by that tiny droplet. Then her tongue darted out and the drop disappeared.

"That was ecstasy," she murmured.

He scooped up another forkful of pancakes and held it out to her. "Want some more?" He could watch her eat pancakes all day.

"I'm tempted," she said, then glanced at her watch. "But the dessert class starts in ten minutes, so I'd better not fill up. Oh, and I have to make arrangements to have my black dress pressed before my meeting with Murphy tonight."

"I still think Hayes has an ulterior motive." He didn't like the idea of Nina alone with Hayes in a hotel suite. He didn't like it at all.

And that bothered him.

"I have a better idea," Jake said. "Why don't you call up Hayes and tell him you'll meet him in the lounge? Think of it as neutral territory."

Now it was Nina's turn to frown. "Absolutely not. If W. Murphy Hayes wants to meet with me in his suite, that's where we'll meet. If he wanted to meet me on the roof of the hotel, I'd be up there clinging to the chimney stack."

"That's ridiculous," he snapped, despite the look he saw in her eyes. The same steely determination that he'd seen in only a handful of his boxing opponents. The ones who refused to go down. The ones who lived and breathed the sport of boxing. At that moment he had no doubt that she'd attain all her dreams.

She squared her shoulders. "Ridiculous, but true. This could be it, Jake. The chance I've been waiting for all my life. And I'll do anything to make it happen. Anything."

NINA TOOK another step closer to her dream when she entered the middle section of the partitioned auditorium. An array of tantalizing aromas assailed her nostrils. Colorful banners stretched over the long rows of cooking stations, each one proudly displaying the name of a company sponsor. She saw advertisements for top-quality ovens, copper cookware, organic fruits and vegetables and every type of cooking accessory imaginable.

Her pulse quickened at the frenetic activity and she

noticed the furtive glances at the judge's badge she wore on the lapel of her blazer. Thanks to her Wonderbra, it was hard to miss.

She slowly scanned the endless rows of cooking stations. Each one included a stove, a stainless-steel countertop, a small display table and a chef. Only one chef was missing—The Bonecrusher.

She'd been assigned the dessert category, Chef Bonham's purported specialty, although she'd been less than impressed with his Full-Nelson Flambé.

Jake stood next to her. "Chef Bonham must have decided to try his luck with another category. Looks like you're safe."

"From The Bonecrusher, yes. From cavities, no." A sugary-sweet aroma filled the air and a melodic chime sounded to indicate that the judging was about to begin. It was loud enough to be heard on either side of the partitions, where her fellow judges were in charge of the vegetable and appetizer categories.

"Don't worry, I'll be with you every step of the way. I even saved a little room for dessert."

She shook her head. "Sorry, Jake, but you have to stay behind the roped-off section with the rest of the spectators. You can watch, but you can't taste."

"I think you just want all that dessert for yourself."

She grabbed her clipboard off a nearby table. "Hey, it's a fattening job, but somebody's got to do it."

Ten thousand calories later, she turned in her clipboard and slumped down into a chair next to Jake. "I never want to look at another meringue again."

He grinned. "Does that mean no midnight cheese-cake tonight?"

She groaned. "Don't mention the word *cheesecake*. In fact, don't mention food at all." In addition to a stomachache, all that refined sugar had given her a slight buzz.

"That bad, was it?"

"No, that good. I've never tasted so many sinfully rich, exotic desserts. The problem is I more than tasted them. I devoured them." She ran her tongue over her teeth. "I think I can actually feel my teeth disintegrating from all that sugar."

"Look on the bright side—Workers' Comp will probably pay for your dentures."

Her laugh turned to a moan as her stomach cramped. "I think I'd better go lie down for a while." She stood up, swaying slightly.

Jake was at her side in an instant. "I know what you need."

"An intravenous line of antacid?"

"Some fresh air."

Too miserable to protest, she let him pull her from the room. The next thing she knew, they were stand-ing outside the hotel, the warm afternoon breeze ruf-fling her hair. She leaned against the sun-warmed brick of the building and closed her eyes.

"Feel better?" Jake asked, standing beside her.

She breathed deeply, then opened her eyes. "Much better, actually."

"Good." His smile made her heart skip a beat. "Then how about a little excursion?"

"Is there a diet center in the neighborhood?"

"No, but we're only a few blocks from the Navy Pier. Ever been there?"

She shook her head, now feeling a little giddy. Must be a reaction to all that sugar.

"Then, let's go," he said, grabbing her hand once more and heading east on North Water Street.

The exercise and fresh air did wonders for her digestive system. They turned south on North McClurg, then walked at a leisurely pace until they reached East Grand Street, holding hands all the way. If Nina didn't know better she could almost call this a date. Jake was courteous, cordial and downright charming.

For a brief moment, she wondered if she should risk going out with him like this, but then she got her first glimpse of Navy Pier and forgot all about it. "Wow. This is really something."

"A tourist's paradise," Jake said, then turned to her. "So are you ready for a Ferris-wheel ride? It's only fifteen stories high."

She looked up at the towering Ferris wheel. "I think I'll pass. If you think I'm bad on airplanes, you should see me on a Ferris wheel."

He took a step closer to her. "I'll be there to protect you."

"But will you be there to hold the barf bag?"

He grimaced. "Okay, we'll skip the Ferris wheel. How does your stomach feel about a carousel ride?"

"Now, *that* I can handle," she chimed, feeling better than she had all weekend. The stress of The Bone-crusher's threats had taken their toll. Add to that her anxiety over meeting W. Murphy Hayes, and it was no wonder that she needed some time to play.

And play they did. She and Jake rode the carousel three times, then they spent the next several hours browsing through the unique kiosks lining the pier. Taking a leisurely break on a park bench, Nina watched the colorful array of sailboats floating on Lake Michigan while Jake was off on some mysterious mission. When he returned, he treated her to a frozen lemonade and a fresh-baked pretzel, still warm from the oven.

"Now for an expert opinion," he said, tearing off a bite-sized chunk of the pretzel, dipping it in mustard sauce, then placing it in Nina's mouth.

She chewed thoughtfully, furrowing her brow as if in deep concentration. "Soft, but not doughy. Salty, but not bitter. The mustard sauce is piquant, but..."

"But what?"

"But I prefer cheese sauce with my pretzel," she said with a grin.

He gave a snort of disgust. "And you call yourself a connoisseur."

"That's why they pay me the measly bucks. Speaking of measly, why do we only have one pretzel?"

"Because I wanted to save my money to buy you something really special. C'mon." He grabbed her elbow and pulled her down the pier toward a small kiosk displaying gold and silver jewelry. He turned toward the pudgy teenage boy working the cash register. "Is it ready?"

The boy nodded and handed him a small box wrapped in sky-blue tissue paper and topped with a shiny gold bow.

"Here," Jake said, after they'd threaded their way through the crowd to an empty park bench. "This is for you."

Nina took the package from him, too stunned to speak for a moment. "Jake, you didn't have to buy me anything." They'd stopped at that kiosk earlier and looked over the selection, but she didn't remember calling his attention to any particular piece of jewelry.

"I saw it," he said softly, "and thought of you."

She carefully unwrapped the package, then opened the small cardboard box. Inside, nestled on a strip of white cotton batting, was a thin gold bracelet. She picked it up, light reflecting off the tiny gold stars dangling from it. "Oh, Jake. It's lovely."

"It will probably turn your wrist green."

She looked up at him. "My favorite color."

He gazed into her eyes. "Mine, too."

Nina's breath caught in her throat at Jake's expression. She couldn't remember the last time a man had looked at her that way. Maybe no one ever had.

"This bracelet has a special meaning behind it," he said at last. "I've been knocked around the boxing ring plenty of times." His mouth curved up in a wry smile. "But you're the only person who has ever made me see stars."

"I did?" Her voice sounded high and breathless to her ears.

"That's right. I saw plenty of stars after you clobbered me with that brick."

She blinked once, then laughed out loud. So much for romance. "Help me put it on." She scooted closer to him on the bench and held out her arm.

He bent over her wrist and circled the bracelet around it. "There," he said, hooking the clasp, then straightening. "It looks even better on you."

He looked even better up close. She could see the hint of dark whiskers on his jawline. The way his thick lashes curled slightly at the tip. The small scar below his left eye. Too late she realized she was staring. And he was staring right back at her. They were in the middle of bustling Navy Pier, surrounded by tourists, hucksters and strolling musicians, yet they were only aware of each other.

Nina leaned closer, aware of Jake's sudden stillness and the anticipation in his eyes. She lingered for a moment with her mouth only a hairbreadth from his own. But he didn't move, didn't try to take control of this moment away from her. Desire swirled deep inside her as she brushed her lips against his mouth. Once. Twice. A tantalizing, light touch that drew a low moan from his throat.

When she couldn't stand it any longer, she circled her arms around his neck and pulled him close, deepening the kiss. His tongue met her own as they delved. Explored. Tasted. Their last kiss had been hot and spicy. A delectable appetizer that had left her wanting more. This kiss was like a perfect soufflé. Tender. Succulent. Uniquely satisfying.

Nina finally broke the kiss, vaguely aware of the crowd of people around them. The hunger in Jake's blue eyes made her blood race. He definitely knew how to make a woman feel desirable. With just a look. A touch. A kiss.

"Now what?" Nina asked, her voice almost a whisper.

"Now…" Jake's voice trailed off as his gaze dropped back to her mouth. He inched closer.

Nina licked her lips in anticipation.

"Now it's time for the big surprise."

She could hardly wait. But instead of heading back to the hotel room, Jake led her in the opposite direction. Nina followed along, her heart pounding and her cheeks flushed. Her mind whirled in a way she couldn't blame on a sugar overdose.

Something was happening. Something that she hadn't wanted to happen but now seemed powerless to stop. Her step faltered when she realized how easily she'd let down all her defenses.

He tugged at her hand. "We've got to hurry or we're going to be too late."

"For what?"

"For the surprise." He grinned. "I made reservations for a dinner cruise on the *Spirit of Chicago*. It's one of the best floating restaurants in town."

Nina stood her ground. It was happening again. She'd let this wonderful time with Jake make her forget all her priorities. Let the laughter and the bracelet and that kiss seduce her into wanting something she couldn't afford to have. Not when she had her future all mapped out.

An affair with Jake Callahan would be more than a detour—it would be a dead end. It would mean rearranging all her priorities. Putting her career on the back burner.

It would mean failing. Again.

"Jake, I can't..." she began.

But he wasn't listening. "We can talk on the boat," he said, pulling her along once again. "If we don't hurry it will sail without us."

She trailed after him, almost running to keep up with his long strides. The setting sun cast long shadows over the dock. It would be dark soon. That thought caused a frisson of panic to shoot through her. She didn't even know why until she glanced at her watch.

Nina dug in her heels. "What time do you have?"

"We can make it," Jake replied. "But we have to hurry."

Something smelled fishy, and it wasn't the lake. Then it hit her. She wrenched her hand from his grasp. "You did this on purpose!"

Jake turned to her, looking more stern than romantic. "Nina, I said we'll talk on the boat. Now let's go."

"I'm not going anywhere with you." She whirled around and headed in the opposite direction. Colorful lights glowed on the amusement rides but Nina barely noticed them or the people dodging out of her path.

Jake was soon right beside her. "What about dinner?"

"I already have plans, as you well know," she retorted, lengthening her stride. "With the publisher of *The Epicurean*. This was all a scheme to make me miss my meeting, wasn't it? The carousel ride, the dinner cruise, the bracelet."

"Not the bracelet," he bit out. "That wasn't part of it."

"Ha! So you admit it." She was walking so fast now that her breath came in short, shallow gasps. Cold fury submerged all those other, more confusing emotions. She welcomed it—feeding it with self-recriminations.

"All right, I admit it. I was just doing my job."

Nina hoisted her purse strap higher up on her shoulder, really wishing she hadn't removed the brick. "Let me set you straight once and for all. Your job isn't to kiss me. It isn't to sabotage my career. All I want you to do is protect me."

"Well, if there's one man you need protection from it's W. Lecher Hayes. If you ask me, he's a bigger threat to you than The Bonecrusher!"

"In the first place," she said between clenched teeth, "I didn't ask you. And in the second place, you have no right to interfere in my life. I was perfectly happy until you came barging into it."

"You asked for me, remember?" he snapped, losing some of that cool calmness that irritated her so much.

"That was the biggest mistake I ever made," she

retorted, turning on to the street that led to the Ambassador Towers. "And believe me, that's saying a lot."

Jake turned, walking backwards so he could face her. "All right. Maybe I shouldn't have tried to trick you."

"Maybe?"

"But I really did want to go on the dinner cruise with you."

She looked up at the skyscrapers. "This from a man who dressed up like a nerd and talked with a lisp just because he didn't want to date me." Then her gaze fell on Jake. "Do you lie to all the women you meet, or am I just one of the lucky ones?"

"I'm not lying," he said, stumbling over a crack in the sidewalk. "And I think you're overreacting."

She whirled around to face him as he hit the ground. "Overreacting? You don't know how much this meeting means to me. You don't know anything about me!"

He sat on the cement, his elbows resting on his bent knees, oblivious to the people passing him on either side. "I know you're a talented writer. I know your column is extremely popular in St. Louis. What more do you want?"

"I want to make it big. I've wanted that my entire life. You don't know what it's like to grow up in a family like mine."

"So tell me."

She took a deep breath, still winded from her sprint. "My mother is one of the top neurosurgeons in the country. My brother works as an astrophysicist at NASA. My sister Ellen just made tenure at Brown University. She's an expert in Renaissance history. Just like my Dad. He's just published his fourth book on the subject.''

''So?''

''So? Don't you see? I'm nothing.''

He frowned. ''Tell me you don't really believe that.''

''All I know is that I've wanted to be someone special my entire life. I may not save lives, or explore space or know anything about life during the Renaissance, but I can write a damn good restaurant review column.''

''I know. I've seen it.''

''After all these years I've finally found something I can do. Not only do, but do well. But I want to be the best. In my business, that means working for the best.''

''The Epicurean?''

She nodded. ''That's the brass ring. If I landed a job there, I'd make the front page of the Walker Family Newsletter.''

He scowled. ''The what?''

''The Walker Family Newsletter,'' she repeated with a sigh of irritation. ''I know it sounds stupid, but it's actually a very professionally done newsletter. My parents send it out to family and friends once a year to catalog all the Walker family achievements. It's usually no less than five pages.''

''Don't tell me you've never been in it.'' His scowl

deepened and she could see the disapproval in his eyes.

"No, but it's not what you think. It's not a punishment. I just haven't done anything to deserve it yet. My parents love me. And they'd be so proud if I actually made something of myself."

"So you're doing it for them?"

She squared her shoulders, realizing she'd wasted too much time already. "No, Jake. I'm doing it for me." Then she turned on her heel and headed for the front entrance of the Ambassador Towers. She still couldn't believe she'd fallen for his act. He'd almost romanced her out of the career opportunity of a lifetime. And for what? A moonlight cruise? A kiss under the stars? Neither one would boost her up the career ladder. Thankfully, she'd come to her senses just in time.

Only she didn't feel thankful. She felt sick at heart. Hurt. Disappointed. And most of all, disillusioned. Had Jake been playing out another masquerade today, just as he had the first time they met?

The hotel loomed in front of her. Thanks to Jake's scheming she wouldn't even have time to change or freshen her makeup before her meeting with Hayes.

"Nina, please wait," he called after her.

She ignored him, striding into the hotel and straight toward the elevators. She stepped inside an open car and stabbed the number-eleven button with her index finger.

"Nina," Jake said, only a few paces behind her.

"Stay away from me." She held up one hand to

keep him from following her inside. "I don't need you, Jake. And I don't want you anymore," she said, as the elevator door closed between them.

She just wished she really meant it.

8

I DON'T WANT YOU ANYMORE.

Nina's words pounded in Jake's head as he jogged up the hotel stairwell, taking the steps two at a time. He'd hoped the exercise would burn off his pent-up frustration. But he'd run up four flights so far and anger still roiled inside him. The only problem was he didn't know whether he was angry at Hayes, Nina or himself.

He'd blown it. What a stupid, asinine ploy. Why had he ever thought a woman as sharp as Nina would fall for it? She was right—he was a jerk. This rendezvous with Hayes might be suspect, but it was her decision to make. She was a grown woman, and he knew from personal experience that she could take care of herself.

His heart hammered in his chest and his lungs screamed for air as he raced up the stairs. He wouldn't let his emotions overtake him. Not again. Never again.

Jake finally reached the seventh floor and leaned against the door that led into the hallway, panting hard. He was turning into a wimp. He used to run stairs like this every day when he was in training, then go three rounds in the ring. Now he felt like passing out. Or throwing up. Or both.

He closed his eyes, focusing on taking slow, deep breaths. Gradually, his heartbeat slowed and his sweat-drenched body began to feel normal again.

He opened his eyes, staring up at the holes in the acoustic ceiling. *It wasn't worth it.* He might be attracted to Nina—maybe even more than attracted— but if that meant losing control, then he needed to back off. He'd lost control five years ago and barely avoided disaster. He definitely didn't want to repeat the experience.

Jake opened the door and strode out into the hallway toward his room, his calf muscles already protesting that seven-flight sprint. He'd be sore for a few days. Maybe that was good—a physical reminder to keep his distance from Nina.

He unlocked the door to his hotel room, then walked inside, kicking off his athletic shoes and stripping off his socks. Trying hard not to think of Nina alone with Hayes. Or of how she'd claimed she'd do anything for her career.

She'd even worn that stupid Wonderbra.

The telephone rang just as he turned on the shower. He left the hot water on, letting steam fill the bathroom, finally picking up the phone on the third ring. "Hello?"

Silence on the other end of the line. "Hello," he said, his voice louder and more strident now.

Then he heard a woman's shrill whisper. "Jake, help me. I'm in 1101...."

His blood turned to ice as the line went dead. *Nina.* He dropped the phone and bolted toward the door. Hayes must have her cornered. He'd known the creep couldn't be trusted. Hayes probably had his own private interview couch for potential female staff members of *The Epicurean*. That thought made him move even faster.

Too impatient to wait for the elevator, Jake hit the stairwell again, pure adrenaline fueling him now. He raced up to the eleventh floor, then sprinted down the hallway until he reached the door to Suite 1101. It was only then he noticed he wasn't wearing shoes. Or socks.

He raised one fist and pounded on the door. "Open up!"

He waited, unnerved by the eerie silence on the other side of the door. Then he pounded again. "C'mon, Hayes, I know you're in there."

The door suddenly swung open and Jake stepped back in surprise. It wasn't W. Murphy Hayes standing in the doorway.

It was Benny Otis.

The scrawny promoter scowled at him. "What the hell do you want?"

Jake's hands curled into fists as hot fury bubbled inside him. He took a deep breath and fought for control. "Nina."

"Jake?" Nina's voice sounded from somewhere inside the suite.

He took a step over the threshold, but Otis placed

a restraining hand on his chest. "Not so fast, Callahan."

Jake looked down at Otis's hand, then back up again. Adrenaline pumped through his veins, reminiscent of the buzz he used to get before a big fight. He used to feed on it, letting his emotions build until he hovered on the razor's edge of control.

A tenuous balance. That had been part of the thrill. It was what had made him such a powerful, explosive fighter. He could mow down this peon with one punch.

But could he stop?

Otis read the indecision on his face and sneered. "Looks like I heard right. The Jackhammer is afraid to fight."

Jake pushed past him into the suite. He rounded a corner and saw Nina seated in a chair, her green eyes huge and terrified. Another wave of anger washed over him. He took a deep breath, willing himself not to give in to it.

"Jake," she whispered.

He rushed to her side and pulled her to her feet. "Are you hurt?"

She shook. "No, I'm fine now that you're here. Otis is crazy. He's the one who sent those messages, not Murphy. But I didn't realize it until it was too late. Then he wouldn't let me leave."

"That's because the party just got started." Otis had followed Jake and now stood watching both of them, his hands in his pants pockets. "Your boyfriend is welcome to stay."

Nina turned to Jake. "He wants me to taste the entrée The Bonecrusher plans to enter in the contest tomorrow."

"That's right." Otis nodded toward the chafing dish on the table. "Call it a sneak preview."

"I just call it sneaky," Nina said, her hand on Jake's arm. "I also refuse to give The Bonecrusher a score he doesn't deserve."

A chilling smile curved Otis's thin mouth. "Maybe I can find a way to make the idea more appetizing."

She lifted her chin. "Just try it and you'll be very sorry. Jake isn't my boyfriend, he's my bodyguard. He also happens to be a very good boxer."

Otis chuckled. "I know all about Jake Callahan."

"Then you'd better let me go—or pay the consequences."

He waved her threat away as if it were a pesky fly. "Miss Walker, I think it's time we come to an understanding."

"I understand that you're trying to intimidate me. Did Bonham put you up to it?"

A muscle knotted his jaw. "People look at me and think I'm just The Bonecrusher's flunkie. But I'm a damn good promoter. I may not have as much brawn as The Bonecrusher, but I've got a damn sight more brains. And I do what needs to be done."

Jake pulled Nina closer. "Including kidnapping?"

His eyes widened in surprise. "I believe Ms. Walker came here of her own free will. Isn't that correct?"

Nina glanced at Jake. "Yes, but that doesn't give you the right to lock me in here!"

Otis shrugged. "You're free to go."

She looked surprised. "I am?"

"As soon as you taste The Bonecrusher's latest creation."

She glanced disdainfully at the chafing dish. "I get it now. You're going to poison me."

Otis's eyes narrowed. "Don't tempt me, Miss Walker."

Jake had heard enough. "Get out of here, Nina."

"She's staying," Otis said, moving toward her.

Jake stepped in front of her and Otis's fist shot out and caught him in the stomach. His breath left his chest in a whoosh as he bent over from the unexpected blow. Too late he saw the gleam of brass knuckles on Otis's right hand.

"Go," Jake shouted, as he gagged from the brutal impact.

Nina backed up a step, a look of horror on her face as Otis struck him again, this time with an uppercut to the jaw. Every instinct in Jake urged him to strike back. To pummel Otis with his fists. *To kill him.* He closed his eyes, fighting both nausea and dizziness.

Otis hit him again. And again. By some miracle, Jake stayed on his feet. He heard Nina's shocked gasps with each blow. The room whirled, but he kept all his concentration on Nina, making certain he stood between her and Otis. The promoter laughed as he struck out at will, the brass knuckles now smeared with blood.

"Stop! Please stop!" Nina's voice sounded far away.

But Otis didn't stop. Blow after blow struck Jake in the face and ribs. With each one he backed up a step, keeping Nina behind him as they moved toward the door. He desperately wished she'd run while she had the chance. He turned to tell her to do just that, suffering for it with a rabbit punch to the kidneys. Then he saw the look of horror on her face and heard her muffled warning. Too late he turned back around to see that Otis now had a new weapon.

The promoter grinned as he swung the lamp in his hands. Jake felt the cold brass base smash into his chin.

Then he didn't feel anything at all.

"LEAVE HIM ALONE!" she cried as Jake hit the floor. She watched in horrified disbelief as he sprawled motionless on the carpet.

Otis laughed. He took two quick steps, then catapulted his wiry body into the air. She winced as he landed right on top of Jake.

"Isn't that a great move? It's a Bonecrusher classic."

"Stop it!" She ran for the telephone, remembering too late that Otis had torn the cord out of the wall when she'd called Jake. She turned back in time to see Jake rise unsteadily to his knees.

"C'mon, sissy boy," Otis taunted, his skinny arms outstretched as he slowly circled him. "Show me your stuff."

She expected Jake to come at him with both fists

flying. Instead he got unsteadily to his feet and just stood there. A perfect target.

He looked at her, his right eye almost swollen shut. "Leave, Nina. Now."

Otis took advantage of Jake's inattention with a vicious undercut, the brass knuckles drawing more blood.

Jake's head snapped back, but he remained on his feet. "Nina...go!"

She wasn't going anywhere. Not until she put a stop to this madness. She frantically looked around for something, anything, to stop the beating. She ran to the wet bar, picked up the ice bucket and flung the contents at Otis. Finely chipped ice rained down on him.

He shook himself like a dog, then grinned at her. "Thanks, I needed that."

She turned to Jake, who leaned semi-conscious against the sofa. "Do something!" she cried. "Fight. Defend yourself! Run!"

Jake pulled himself up, his hands curled into tight fists. A muscle knotted his jaw and she could see the tension emanating from him.

"Jake, please do something!"

"Get...out...of...here."

The next moment Otis went in for the kill. He hurled himself at Jake, knocking him off the sofa. Then he fell on top of him, pinning Jake's shoulders to the floor. His forearm pressed viciously into Jake's throat.

"One," Otis cried, like the referee at a prize fight, "two…"

Nina gasped as Jake twisted his body far enough for one shoulder to lift off the carpet. "Stay down, you idiot!"

But Jake had used his momentum to flip onto his stomach, and was now paying for it. Otis stood up and ground the heel of his cowboy boot into Jake's spine.

Nina whirled on the promoter, fear and desperation clawing at her. "Leave him alone. I'll give you what you want. Just leave him alone!"

He lifted his boot off Jake's back while he considered her offer. "A perfect score at tomorrow's entrée competition?"

She nodded, her throat tight. What else could she do? Just stand by and watch the little man beat Jake to death before her eyes?

Otis smiled. "That's more like it, Miss Walker."

Jake groaned as he slowly rolled onto his back. Nina knelt down beside him, sliding her arm under his shoulders and carefully lifting him to a sitting position. He looked awful. The puffy skin surrounding his right eye had turned purple and blood streamed from one nostril.

She lifted Jake to his feet, staggering a little under his body weight. His head lolled on his shoulders and she was afraid he was about to lose consciousness. She moved toward the door, half-dragging Jake along with her.

"Just understand one thing," Otis called after her.

"Nobody double-crosses Benny Otis. So either you give The Bonecrusher a perfect score tomorrow or…" His words hung in the air, the threat in them unmistakable.

"Or what?" Nina asked when they reached the doorway.

"Or your *bodyguard* better get ready for Round 2. And next time, I won't go so easy on him."

JAKE HURT EVERYWHERE. He ached in places he didn't even know had nerve endings. His ribs hurt. His head hurt. Even his hair hurt.

"I think we should take you to a hospital," Nina said, after propping another pillow behind his head. He lay on the king-size bed in his hotel room, watching his bruises swell. He'd never actually been body-slammed before. It wasn't an experience he wanted to repeat.

Nina leaned over him and began unbuttoning his shirt, her silky blond hair brushing against his collarbone.

"What do you think you're doing?" he asked, too stiff and sore to try and stop her.

"Checking the damage. If it's as bad as I suspect, we're calling an ambulance. Then we're calling the police."

"No," he bit out. "No ambulance. No police."

"But…"

"No," he interjected, then closed his eyes with a sigh. "I'm fine."

"Then why did I practically have to carry you to

the room?'' she asked, as she reached the last button. He could feel the cool air caress his skin as she pulled his shirt apart.

"Oh, Jake."

He opened his eyes and glanced down at his chest. It was already starting to turn an unflattering shade of black and blue. An angry red mark streaked just above his navel. "It's nothing," he said, trying not to groan as she gently pressed her fingers against his ribs. "I bruise easily."

"I don't think anything is broken."

Just his pride. But that would heal, in say, ten to twenty years. Jake Callahan had just been thoroughly trounced. By a ninety-eight-pound weakling. In front of a woman. *In front of Nina.*

"Do you hurt anywhere else?"

"I told you, I'm fine," he bit out, more sharply than he intended. He closed his eyes, wishing Otis had hit him hard enough to erase his memory. Talk about the ultimate humiliation.

But, unfortunately, his memory was all too clear. He did have a throbbing headache, though. And past experience told him a slight concussion was a possibility.

He closed his eyes as Nina rose off the bed and turned away. Good. She was leaving. Now he could relive every humiliating moment in solitude. But his respite didn't last long.

"What exactly happened back there?" she asked, coming back into the room with a wet washcloth in her hand. She placed it gently over the most ugly bruise on his chest.

He sucked in his breath at the icy chill of the washcloth. "I think that's pretty obvious."

"Not to me." She moved the washcloth over his chest, the brief touch of her fingers causing goosebumps to rise over his skin. He waited, certain he knew exactly what her next question would be. Why hadn't he fought Otis? Or at least defended himself with a few well-aimed punches?

Time to change the subject. "First, tell me...what happened with Murphy?"

Nina's gaze flicked away from him. "He never wanted to meet with me. Otis left both messages just to set me up. And I fell for it. Murphy isn't interested in me. I haven't even seen him since the reception last night."

"So call him," Jake said, trying not to wince at her ministrations. "Only forget the Wonderbra and don't kiss up to him. You're good, Nina. Damn... good. Tell him you want the job and then...give him the reasons why you deserve it."

She looked at him. "You make it sound so easy."

"Aunt Sophie always told us to go after...our dreams."

She hesitated, then glanced over at the telephone. "Your message light is blinking. Do you want me to put it on the speaker phone?"

"Sure," he replied, grateful for the extra amenities of the hotel. He didn't think he could move now if his life depended on it. Which it just might if Otis decided to come back and finish the job.

Nina pressed a series of buttons on the keypad and the next moment a familiar, exasperated voice filled the room.

"Jake, are you completely insane? Our aunt matches you up with some fruitcake and now you're whisking her away for a romantic weekend? Please tell me it isn't true. How could you encourage Aunt Sophie like this? Now she'll never leave any of us in peace.

"And if I hear that you're even considering the M word, I'm kidnapping you and taking you to Mexico until I can knock some sense into that thick skull of yours. Oh, and that reminds me—Trace said you're acting as this woman's bodyguard. What the hell is that about? Why would you ever become involved with a woman who needs a bodyguard? I thought you took a vow never to fight again. So what is this—a suicide mission? Call me."

The line had barely gone dead before Nina started her interrogation. "Who was that?"

"My brother," Jake said, silently cursing Noah for his lousy timing. "Or I guess I should say, one of my brothers. The youngest one, Noah. He also has the biggest mouth."

"I noticed." She planted her hands on her hips. "So who told him I was a fruitcake?"

"Not me," Jake assured her. "It was probably Trace."

"And Trace is…?"

"My other brother."

"Nice family. What have I done to get them so riled up?"

"It's nothing you've done," he replied, shifting on the bed to find a more comfortable position. Or, at least, a less painful one. "I'm starved. Shall we order up some room service?"

"Nice try." She stretched across him to fluff his pillow. "But you're not getting out of it that easily."

Jake suppressed a sigh. His little brother was going to pay for putting him in this position. "I don't suppose you'd consider just letting this drop?"

"Not until I find out why I've hired a bodyguard who won't fight to save me. Or himself."

"IT'S A LONG STORY," he said, closing his eyes once more. "Ancient history."

Nina refused to let him put her off any longer. "I minored in history in college," she said, getting more comfortable on the mattress. "And we have all night."

She wanted to know if her bodyguard was more of a hazard than a help. But more than that, she wanted to know more about Jake Callahan. Despite their rocky relationship, she couldn't deny the magnetic pull he had on her.

And she didn't like it. She didn't like it one bit.

Not when a romance between them had no future. Not when his kisses took all her carefully laid career plans and turned them upside down. Not when he made going after her dreams sound so simple. She'd

blamed all the men in her past for screwing up her life. Maybe the only person she really needed to blame was herself.

But before she could question her choices for the past decade, she needed to discover the real Jake Callahan. She'd told herself he wasn't different than other men. Rationalized her intense attraction to him as just a blip on her hormonal radar screen. A temporary balm for the loneliness that sometimes enveloped her. But none of that was true.

And now, more than anything, she needed the truth.

"It happened five years ago," he began, after she'd almost given up hope of getting the story. "Five years, three months and eleven days to be exact."

"You killed a man," she ventured.

"No."

"Maimed him?"

He scowled at her. "Do you want to tell this story, or should I?"

She lay on her stomach on the bed, her chin propped in her palm. "Go ahead."

"Thanks. Now where was I?"

"Once upon a time five years, three months and eleven days ago...."

"Right." He stared up at the ceiling, his mind obviously drifting to another place. "I had a big fight scheduled. Not just any fight—the fight that could catapult me into the professional boxing circuit. If I won."

She bit her tongue to keep from asking him if he did. Jake obviously wanted to tell this story in his own way and in his own time. Somehow she sensed that he'd never told it before.

"I trained hard for that fight. It was against the reigning amateur heavyweight champ, and I knew he was no slouch. In fact, he had more KOs on his boxing record than I did."

"Weren't you afraid?" Nina asked, before she could help herself.

"No, I was never afraid to get into the ring. I was always impatient. I love the art of boxing. It takes skill, stamina and strategy." He hesitated. "Best of all, I loved letting loose all the emotions I had stored up inside me."

She nodded, remembering times when she would have relished an opportunity to land a few punches on her smug siblings. "I think I can relate."

"Well, I may have gotten all the moves down and learned the craft, but I was mentally undisciplined."

"And that's important?"

"The most important part of the sport. Any sport, really. It takes more than talent to win—it takes mental toughness."

"Sounds like the job description for a restaurant reviewer."

His split lip curved into a half smile. "I suppose it's true for any competitive profession."

"Somehow I can't believe you aren't mentally tough."

"I am," he replied. "Now. But back then, I was too emotional. I let my feelings control me in the ring."

"So what happened?"

He looked at her, shadows darkening his blue eyes. "It was a great fight. My opponent was tough. Very tough. If I beat him, I'd be on my way to the top."

He leaned carefully back against the pillows. "Only he wouldn't go down. I knocked him to the mat twice, but he kept getting back up. By the tenth round the crowd was on its feet, the noise deafening. I was determined to come out the winner. But by the fifteenth round, I was sweating it. I knew the fight was close, and I knew the champ's past record would carry a lot of weight with the three judges. If I wanted a guaranteed win, I had to knock him out. I knew I would do anything to win. *Anything.*"

She swallowed, remembering how recently she'd said those same words herself.

"I cornered him in the ring, landing a series of hard punches to the face." He hesitated a long moment. "I told myself I'd kill him if necessary. I wanted to kill him."

She couldn't say anything, her throat tight. Somehow she knew this story didn't have a happy ending.

"I landed a right hook under his chin and he dropped to the mat like a rock. Flat out. No movement. No expression. Nothing. I wasn't even sure he was breathing."

She looked down at her hands, surprised to see them clutching the bedcover. She flexed her fingers, then looked back at Jake.

"The referee started the eight count," he continued, his voice low and mesmerizing, "and the crowd was on its feet, cheering wildly. Only the champ still wasn't moving. I could see his trainers in the corner, frantically hailing a doctor. I realized at that moment I'd crossed the line from boxer to killer.''

"You didn't really mean it," Nina said, unable to remain silent any longer. "It was the heat of the moment.''

Jake shook his head. "At that moment, I meant it. And it scared the hell out of me.''

She was almost afraid to ask the next question. "What happened to him? Was he…all right?''

"He was better than all right. In fact, he won the fight.''

She stared at him in disbelief. "What? You mean…he got back up?''

"Nope. He was out cold.''

"Then how could he possibly win?''

"When the referee reached the count of six, I threw in the towel.''

"What does that mean?''

"In boxing, when you throw your towel into the ring, it's considered a forfeit. So the champ was declared the winner.''

She struggled with the concept of throwing your dreams away in an instant. Once the referee had reached eight, Jake would have been declared the winner. He could have gone on the professional circuit. He could have become a big-time boxer.

"The crowd booed me out of the arena. My manager was furious and quit on the spot. But I'd already decided to walk away from boxing. I didn't like the man I'd almost become in that ring.''

Nina knew then. The awful truth hit her with the wallop of a knockout punch. She was surprised she didn't fall off the bed.

She was falling in love with him.

How could she help but love a man who put character above his dreams? Who showed more courage by losing than by winning? How could she help but fall in love with a real-life hero like Jake Callahan?

Right now her love for him was a tiny glimmer, but she knew in her bones it was growing, warming her from the inside out. That soon it would become a deep, abiding love. The kind that lasted. The kind that had always eluded her.

He sighed, totally unaware of her unwelcome revelation. ''After that day I vowed to never fight again. I can't trust myself to stay in control.''

She disagreed. He showed more control, more self-possession, than anyone she'd ever met. But she could understand his reticence, even if she thought it was unnecessary. In fact, it was more than unnecessary. Under the present circumstances, it was downright dangerous.

Jake folded his arms behind his head, wincing slightly at the movement. ''So now what do you have to say?''

Nina swallowed, wanting to say so much. Wanting to touch him. To hold him in her arms. To tenderly kiss each cut and bruise; his badges of honor. She wanted to tell him how much she regretted dragging him into this mess in the first place. And how much she admired him.

Instead, she whispered just two words. "You're fired."

9

JAKE WONDERED if his concussion had made him delusional. Or hard of hearing. "What did you say?"

She stood up, her cheeks flushed. "The deal is off. You're no longer my bodyguard. Your brother was right, this is a suicide mission."

He struggled to sit up in bed, trying to ignore the stabbing pain in his midsection. "You can't fire me. We made a deal."

She took a step back from the bed, almost as if she were afraid he'd come after her. "The deal's off."

If Jake could have moved, he just might have gone after her. She looked so damn beautiful. And he felt so much better now that the story that had haunted him for the past five years was finally out in the open. His bruises and scrapes still hurt like hell, but a weight had been lifted from his soul.

Thanks to Nina. Despite her reaction and her illogical thinking, he wanted to hold her again. Kiss her again. This time in the privacy of the hotel room instead of the middle of bustling Navy Pier.

He shook his head, attempting to clear it of the fantasy rapidly rising in his brain. It must be the concussion. He couldn't think clearly when she was this close to him. Which had been his problem since the first time he'd met her.

Only she wasn't thinking clearly either. "I mean it, Jake. I want you to stay away from me."

"You're crazy, Nina. What happened tonight should prove more than ever that you need a bodyguard. What if Otis comes after you again?"

"He won't. Because I agreed to give him what he wants."

Jake stared at her. "A perfect score for The Bonecrusher. You didn't really mean it, did you?"

She took a deep breath. "I'll do whatever I have to do."

He shook his head. "You can't let Otis strong-arm you into cheating. It isn't right. And it isn't fair."

"I don't plan to cheat. I plan to disqualify myself as a judge."

He stared at her in disbelief. "You can't do that."

"I have to!"

"But Murphy will be furious. You won't stand a chance of getting that job at *The Epicurean* if you renege on your judging duties."

"I don't have any other choice," she cried. "I won't give The Bonecrusher a score he doesn't deserve. And I refuse to put you in danger again. Otis could have seriously hurt you tonight."

Otis *had* seriously hurt him, but Jake wasn't about to admit that out loud. Any more than he would allow Nina to give up the dream job she'd wanted for so long.

"Look, Nina, we had a deal. I agreed to act as your

bodyguard for the weekend and you agreed to give Café Romeo a rave review.''

Her mouth dropped open. ''I never agreed to a rave!''

''Yes, you did,'' he countered, his voice rising at the same rate as his temper. ''On the airplane, after you dropped your bomb about making me your body-guard.''

''You should have turned me down.''

''I did. Only you wouldn't take no for an answer. So I finagled a deal for Café Romeo instead. One rave review for one bodyguard.''

She shook her head. ''You misunderstood me. I agreed to give Café Romeo a second chance. I plan to review it again when we get back to St. Louis. But Café Romeo will have to succeed on its own merits.''

''Fine. And I'm still willing to go through with my part of the deal, too.'' He couldn't help noticing the way Nina kept staring at his chest. He knew those bruises looked hideous, but the last thing he wanted was for her to see a constant reminder of his failure. ''I won't let anyone hurt you, Nina. I promise.''

''I know,'' she said softly. ''That's why I have to withdraw from judging the contest.''

He hurt too much to argue with her any more. But he didn't intend to let her throw away the biggest career opportunity of her life. Not when it meant so much to her.

Not when she meant so much to him.

He couldn't fight both his physical pain and his feelings for her. They flooded through him, impervious to the brick wall he'd erected in his heart all those years ago. Cleansing him. Healing him. Confiding in her had been the catharsis he needed.

Too bad it was at the expense of her dreams.

Now he just had to find some way to make it up to her.

THE NEXT MORNING, Nina made it as far as the elevator before Jake caught up with her. "You should be in bed."

He followed her inside the empty elevator car. "I'm fine."

She had to admit he did look better. His right eye was still black, blue and bloodshot, but the swelling had gone down. Small cuts and bruises still covered his face, and his bottom lip puffed out a little. But all the damage to his torso was now covered with a navy blue polo shirt tucked into a pair of snug blue denim jeans. As the elevator lurched into motion, he bent down to tie the laces of his white Nikes, then straightened again, moving with considerably more ease than he had last night.

"How's your head this morning?" she asked, remembering how she'd dosed him with ibuprofen every four hours. At three-thirty in the morning, she'd stumbled into her own bed, too exhausted to even change into her nightgown.

"It hurts like hell."

"How's your memory?"

He glanced at her as the elevator doors slid open

and they both stepped out into the main lobby. "My memory is fine. Why?"

She turned to face him, aware of the bustle of people outside the auditorium. "Because I fired you last night, remember?"

"And I told you I never welsh on a deal."

"I'll still review Café Romeo, if that's what you're worried about."

"No, actually, I'm worried about you. Otis is still around. And so is The Bonecrusher. Frankly, I don't trust either one of those two cretins. And I'm certainly not going to lounge about in my hotel room and let you wander around alone."

"The only place I'm going is the airport, right after I find Murphy and tell him I can't judge the final round."

"You don't have to do that, Nina."

She reached out to touch his forearm. "Jake, we've already been through this. I won't throw the contest and I won't let you put yourself in danger because of me. I've got enough to worry about without worrying about you, too."

He set his jaw. "So just pretend I'm not here."

As if that were even remotely possible. She was so aware of him her entire body tingled. His nearness assailed all of her senses. She could smell the spicy scent of his aftershave, feel the finely honed muscles of his forearm, see the stubborn glint in his blue eyes, hear the determination of his voice. And worst of all, she could remember the taste of his mouth on her own. Firm. Hot. Demanding.

She swallowed hard as his gaze met hers. Did he remember as well? Did he want to repeat the experience as much as she did?

The elevator dinged beside them, announcing a new arrival. Saved by the bell, literally. She'd almost thrown herself at him. It's hard to convince a guy you don't want him around if you're plastered to his torso. And she definitely didn't want him around her. Not with Otis in the vicinity.

Jake took a step closer to her. "Nina, listen...."

"Hey," Karla Ruskin stepped off the elevator and walked up to Jake and Nina. "Have you two heard the latest news?" Then she took a good look at Jake and gasped. "What happened to you?"

"I ran into someone. Or I guess I should say, he ran into me."

"Looks like he bulldozed you." She reached out and poked the swollen lump on his jaw. "I bet that hurts."

Jake sucked in a breath. "You're right, it does."

"You had some news?" Nina intervened, before Karla did any more damage.

"I'll say." Karla leaned toward them and whispered, "The Bonecrusher is disqualified. Can you believe it?"

Nina blinked. "Disqualified?"

"That's right. Seems his promoter, Benny Otis, tried to influence one of the judges. Murphy found out about it and now The Bonecrusher is history." She moved toward the auditorium. "I've got to be

there when they break the news to The Bonecrusher.
I bet he'll tear the place apart. What a story!''

Nina watched Karla disappear into the auditorium,
then she turned slowly to Jake. "You talked to Murphy."

He nodded. "On the telephone this morning.
Seems one of the other judges had been complaining
about Otis harassing her, too, but she didn't have any
proof to back it up. So I agreed to meet him at his
suite and show him proof."

Nina reached up and tenderly cradled his bruised
cheek. "This kind of proof?"

He gave her a wry smile.

"Pretty convincing, wouldn't you say?"

"Oh, Jake. What if Otis still comes after you? He'll
be furious when he hears the news."

"Don't worry about me. I'll be fine." He nodded
toward the auditorium. "The final round is about
ready to begin. Are you ready to show W. Murphy
Hayes your stuff?"

She smiled. "Callahan, I'm always ready."

CHEF BO BONHAM, aka The Bonecrusher, didn't take
the news well.

Nina heard his bellow of rage as she and Jake
walked into the auditorium. All the chefs were at their
stations, and everyone in the place was staring at Station Four, where The Bonecrusher was in the process
of pulverizing his promoter.

Then he looked up and saw Nina.

He dropped Otis, who crumpled onto the floor with

a pitiful wail. The Bonecrusher tore off his apron and flung it at the trembling contest official. "I'm outta here."

"Just ignore him," Jake advised under his breath. "He won't do anything to you in front of all these people."

"I think you're forgetting that he's used to annihilating people in front of an audience," Nina whispered. "Look at what he did to Otis. He likes performing in front of a crowd."

The Bonecrusher strode toward the door, then turned on Nina. "This is all your fault!"

Jake pulled her behind him, putting himself between her and her nemesis. It was a typical macho move, but she loved him for it anyway.

The Bonecrusher glared at her over Jake's shoulder. "You screwed me once, lady. I don't let anyone screw me twice."

Jake took a step toward him. "Only a coward threatens a woman."

Bonham sneered at him. "Speaking of cowards, I'm surprised you had the guts to show up today. Otis told me he mopped the floor with you. If you're smart, you'll stay out of my way."

Jake faced him toe-to-toe, his voice low and even. "If you're smart, you'll leave right now."

The Bonecrusher smiled, a truly chilling sight.

"I'd rather hurt somebody."

The hairs prickled on the back of Nina's neck. "Run, Jake. Run!"

But he ignored her. "Take cover," he ordered, as

he feinted to the left, barely avoiding an elbow shot to the nose by Bonham. It enraged the larger man, and he sailed through the air, straight at Jake. At the last possible moment, Jake bobbed out of the way and The Bonecrusher landed on the floor with a pained grunt.

Nina could see W. Murphy Hayes looking on in horror and Karla scribbling furiously in her notepad. One of the photographers started snapping pictures of The Bonecrusher lying in a heap on the floor. Big mistake. The next moment, Bonham reached up, plucked the camera from the photographer's grasp, and hurled it against the wall.

The crowd backed away from him. He slowly turned to face Jake, his face twisted with anger. "Now you're going to be sorry, sissy boy."

"Go for it," Jake said, squaring his shoulders.

But instead of going for Jake's throat, The Bonecrusher whirled and dove straight toward Nina. He clipped her on the jaw with his elbow before she could dodge out of the way. She went down hard on the floor, the jolt snapping her teeth together. A sharp pain, reminiscent of her last visit to Café Romeo, shot straight through her tailbone.

A woman behind her screamed as The Bonecrusher spun to come at Nina again. She tried to scoot out of his way, but the agonizing pain slowed her progress. She closed her eyes, waiting for the impact.

It never came.

Instead she heard the distinct crunch of bone. She

opened her eyes, fearing the worst. But Jake wasn't crumpled on the floor.

He was fighting back.

She stared at him, almost unable to believe the transformation. He stood with his broad shoulders back, his powerful body poised to strike. Then he raised his fists in the classic boxer stance, his cool, determined gaze fixed on his opponent.

The Bonecrusher wiped the blood off his lip. Then a slow smile revealed his pointed teeth. He slowly circled Jake. "Ready or not, here I come."

Nina tensed as The Bonecrusher rushed Jake. Her breathing hitched as she saw Jake's fist fly out, catching Bonham on the chin. His massive head snapped back. Once. Twice. Three times. Then he fell to his knees, his eyes glazed.

Jake stood over him, his fists still clenched. Bonham suddenly swept one leg out, catching Jake off guard behind the knees. He staggered for a moment, then delivered a hard blow to Bonham's gut. The Bonecrusher doubled over, making his jaw a perfect target for a solid uppercut.

It knocked him out cold.

Jake stood there, just staring at him. After a moment, his taut shoulders relaxed and he stared down at the red, swollen knuckles on his hands.

Nina got up and limped over to him, gently touching his forearm. "Are you all right?"

"I'm fine," he said, sounding a little surprised. Then he turned to her, lightly trailing his fingers over her tender jaw. "He hurt you."

"Just a little," she assured him. "Now we'll have matching bruises."

He reached out and pulled her into his arms, holding her so tightly she couldn't breathe. "If anything ever happened to you..." he murmured against her hair.

"I'm fine," she whispered, wrapping her arms around him. They held onto each other for a long time, barely aware of the crowd of people surrounding them or the security guards arriving to haul The Bonecrusher away.

At long last, Jake pulled back far enough to look into her face. "Nina, I...."

She licked her dry lips, unnerved by the raw emotions she saw in his eyes. Her own emotions threatened to overwhelm her. A mixture of relief and fear flowed through her. But her fear had nothing to do with her physical safety. She'd never felt as safe as she did in Jake's arms. In fact, she never wanted to leave them. And that scared her more than anything.

"Yes, Jake?" Her voice sounded low and husky to her ears and her knees went weak. She knew intuitively that this was one of those moments that could change her life forever.

He gazed into her eyes. "I...could wring your neck."

JAKE WANTED to kick himself as soon as the words fell out of his mouth. He felt Nina stiffen in his arms and knew he'd just made a big mistake. His gut clenched at the memory of that three-hundred-pound brute barreling toward her. If only she'd taken cover as he'd asked her to do. But it wasn't really Nina's fault. Jake was solely to blame for not doing a better job of protecting her.

"What did you say?" Nina asked, stepping out of his arms.

Jake had to force himself not to grab her and haul her against him once more. Just like some caveman who had fought for his woman and won. He rubbed one hand over his face, wondering what was wrong with him.

"Forget it," he said gruffly. She had enough to worry about without trying to figure out how to let him down easy. They both knew that her first priority was her career.

"I don't understand."

"Neither do I," Jake muttered. "Sometimes a minor concussion can make you blurt out the strangest things."

She studied his face for a long moment. "Oh."

Only Nina didn't look reassured by his words. In fact, she looked a little sick. Her face had gone pale and she swayed slightly on her feet. Of course, that could be a reaction to the run-in with Bonham. The jerk had hit her pretty hard.

"Why don't you sit down," he suggested, leading her to the nearest chair. "Can I get you something? How about a glass of water or a cup of hot tea?"

"Whiskey would be good," she said, wrapping her arms around her middle. "A double. Straight up."

Jake wasn't sure where he could find whiskey at

ten o'clock on a Sunday morning, but he damn well wasn't going to disappoint her. If she wanted whiskey, he'd find a bottle of the best aged Scotch whiskey around. He might even join her in a shot or two.

One last drink before they said goodbye.

NINA WAITED until Jake was out of sight, then frantically searched the lobby for a pay telephone. She gave the operator her credit card number, then placed the call.

After the fifth ring, Molly finally picked up. "Hello?"

"Help me," Nina cried. "I'm in big trouble and I don't know what to do."

"Whoa, slow down. Nina, is that you?"

"Yes, it's me." She sagged against the wall, her knees still shaky.

"Where are you?" Molly asked.

"I'm still in Chicago."

"Is it The Bonecrusher? Is he still after you?"

"No," Nina replied, twisting the telephone cord between her fingers. "It's Jake Callahan."

"Jake's after you?" Molly said, sounding surprised.

"No! I mean, yes. I mean, I'm not sure."

"Okay, take a deep breath. Then tell me exactly what's going on."

Nina inhaled, then exhaled slowly. It made her feel a little better. "All right. The thing is…I think I'm falling for Jake."

"After only one weekend together?"

Nina frowned into the telephone receiver. "That's long enough to fall in love."

"Maybe for rabbits. You're probably just in lust with him. I knew you should have taken the condoms. Especially after I got a good look at him."

"What do you mean? You've never met Jake."

"Not in the flesh. But I went to a Cardinals game and saw a poster of him in the ladies' room at Busch Stadium." Molly smacked her lips. "That man is yummy."

A poster? Now Nina was more confused than ever. She closed her eyes and groaned. "What am I going to do?"

"Jump him. You want to, don't you?"

"Yes. No. I don't know."

"You've never been this indecisive before."

"I know! And it's driving me crazy. I knew exactly what I wanted before I met Jake."

"So what's the problem?"

"The problem is…I don't know what I want anymore." She rubbed her left temple, trying to ease the sudden ache.

"Nina," Molly said, now the voice of reason. "One weekend together does not a commitment make. It's not like he's asked you to marry him."

Nina didn't say anything, suddenly realizing how ridiculous she must sound. Then she heard the screech of a cat. Her cat, if she wasn't mistaken. "Is that Pepper?"

"Uh…yeah. But he's okay." Another screech

sounded, louder this time. "Oops, gotta go. Pepper's in the aquarium again."

"Molly, wait..." Nina began, then heard a loud click followed by a dial tone.

Great. Now on top of everything else, she had to worry about her cat. Nina bit her lip as she hung up the telephone receiver. Pepper was all she'd have left if she walked away from the man of her dreams.

Then she turned around and found herself face-to-face with the *other* man of her dreams.

"Hello, Nina," W. Murphy Hayes said, his face creased in a wide smile. "I was hoping I'd catch you before the judging begins. I'd like to apologize."

"Apologize?" she echoed, hoping she didn't look as dumbstruck as she sounded.

"For all the trouble Chef Bonham and Mr. Otis caused you. I hope it didn't entirely ruin your weekend." Then he snorted. "Chef Bonham. Now that's an oxymoron if I've ever heard one."

"You don't like his cooking?" Nina asked, surprised by his tone.

"Like it? The man should be legally barred from coming within fifty paces of a kitchen. He's a menace to the palate."

"But I thought you invited him...?"

"Otis convinced me it would be good publicity for the competition. Unfortunately this isn't exactly the kind of publicity I wanted." He shook his head in dismay as the police and ambulance personnel arrived in the auditorium. Then he turned back to Nina. "But

I'm not here to talk about my problems. I want to talk business—if you have the time.''

Nina's heart skipped a beat. The publisher of *The Epicurean* wanted to talk business. With her. She told herself not to get her hopes up. "I think I can spare a few minutes."

"Good. When I met with Mr. Callahan this morning, he told me I might be able to lure you away from St. Louis—if the price was right." He flashed her another smile, then motioned to a pair of wicker chairs in the corner. "Why don't we get comfortable?"

Nina settled into her chair, taking slow deep breaths so she wouldn't hyperventilate. She tried the old trick of imagining W. Murphy Hayes in his underwear, but for some reason she couldn't do it. The next moment, her mind flashed a full-color picture of Jake in his underwear, and she could picture him all too well.

Handsome hunk didn't begin to do him justice. He was delectable. She'd love to get her hands on him. To show him just how much she really loved him. To touch him everywhere. To kiss…

"Nina," Murphy said, breaking into her reverie.

She started. "Yes?"

"Are you all right? You look a little dazed."

Dazed was putting it mildly. Less than an hour ago, she'd been ready to give up her dream of a job at *The Epicurean* to protect Jake. Now her dream was about to come true. Nina mentally shook herself and forced herself to focus on what Murphy was saying.

"I'm very impressed with your work, Nina. I've followed your columns for several months now and, frankly, I think you're wasting your talents at the *Dispatch*. You need a larger arena to stretch your creative wings."

"Do you have any particular arena in mind?"

He chuckled. "As a matter of fact, I do. I'd like to offer you a position as a regular columnist on our staff. The salary is negotiable, of course. But I will throw in a bonus if your first column makes the September issue."

"That soon?"

He chuckled. "Can you think of any good reason to wait?"

Jake. He lived in St. Louis. She was headed to New York. But then, he'd known that would be the case when he'd told Murphy she wanted the job. So, obviously, there was nothing to hold her back. "You're right, Murphy. Why wait?"

"Good. Your column has got just the kind of witty, refreshing style *The Epicurean* needs."

Nina sat, still stunned that her dream had just fallen in her lap, and wondering why she didn't feel happier about it. Maybe she was just numb from the shock.

"Well," Murphy boomed, "what do you say? Does *The Epicurean* have a new columnist?"

She smiled. "First, let me tell you what I want."

10

JAKE'S STEP FALTERED as he rounded the corner and saw Murphy and Nina shaking hands.

"Welcome to *The Epicurean*, Nina. I know you'll be a fine addition to our staff." Then he looked up and saw Jake. "This lady knows how to drive a hard bargain, Callahan. You should have warned me."

Nina laughed. "Jake taught me everything I know."

He didn't feel like laughing, but he did manage a smile. "Congratulations, Nina."

"Thank you." She moved toward him and kissed him on the cheek, careful to avoid his bruises. "I owe it all to you."

Hayes turned to her. "Say, why don't you fly back with me and visit New York City for a couple of weeks? You can take a tour of the office, get a real feel for the place. It will also give me an opportunity to introduce you to the rest of the staff."

Nina looked at Jake. "What do you think?"

He personally hated the idea. Who would calm her down when she started worrying about kamikaze ducks? "It's completely up to you."

She nodded. "Right. Well...why not?"

"Good. I'll go make another plane reservation—first class all the way. And we can have dinner at the Chalet this evening," Hayes said, rubbing his hands together. "It's a new French restaurant that just opened in Manhattan. The chef is a native of Provence."

She smiled. "The best wine in the world comes from Provence."

"So do the best chefs. Just wait until you taste his pastry. I guarantee you'll fall in love." Murphy winked at her, then headed back into the auditorium.

Jake suddenly realized he didn't want her to fall in love with anyone. Not until he could examine his own feelings, still rusty from disuse. He knew he liked Nina. Really liked her. And he definitely desired her. But could he really be in love with her after only one weekend? Could he risk telling her before he knew for certain?

The answer to that question was as easy as it was painful. No. He had to let her go. He wouldn't let anything or anyone, especially himself, stand in the way of her dream.

A chime sounded and Nina took a deep breath. "That's my cue. It's time for the judging to resume."

"Good luck," Jake said, swallowing the lump in his throat.

Her brow furrowed. "Aren't you coming in with me?"

He shook his head. "I should probably go pack. And the police still want a statement from me. The plane leaves at one...." His voice trailed off as he ran out of excuses. He couldn't stay with her and keep from touching her.

"Oh...right," she said, looking slightly confused. "Well, I guess I'd better go."

"Nina," he called as she turned away. He wanted one last look at those incredible green eyes.

She turned back to him. "Yes, Jake?"

"I hope all your dreams come true."

She smiled, and his heart kicked up a notch. "I intend to see that they do."

Two WEEKS LATER, Jake could still see her smile when he closed his eyes.

"You made the right decision," Trace said, the muscles in his neck, arms and chest straining as he lifted the barbell above his head.

"You think so?" Jake opened his eyes, then wiped the sweat off his forehead with a towel. It had been two long weeks since he'd left Chicago and now his life was back to normal. Or so he kept telling himself.

He and Trace regularly met every Thursday evening at the Ninth Street Gym to work out. Tiff Atherton, the owner, was one of Jake's old sparring partners and one scary guy. But not as scary as his wife. Which was the reason Tiff enforced the No Women Allowed rule so vigilantly.

"I know so," Trace said, slowly lowering the barbell until it was level with his knees, then letting it drop. The sound of the heavy weights hitting the cement floor echoed across the gym. "Nina Walker was all wrong for you."

Jake moved to a treadmill and began jogging. "In what way?"

"In every conceivable way." Trace slung a towel around his neck and climbed on an adjacent treadmill. "She's pretty, right?"

"Beautiful."

"Mistake number one. Haven't you ever heard that song that says if you want to be happy, you should never make a pretty woman your wife?"

"Please tell me you're joking."

"Hey, I think it has some validity." Trace heightened the incline on his treadmill, then he walked it with a slow, steady pace. "And it's not like being pretty is all that's wrong with her."

"What else?"

"She's untrustworthy. You said she promised to give Café Romeo a rave review and all I've seen in the paper is reprints of her old columns."

"She'll do it," Jake said, knowing implicitly that he could trust her to keep her word. "But she didn't exactly promise a rave."

"Well, soon it won't matter what she writes, because Café Romeo won't last much longer. The coffeehouse competition is fierce in this town."

Jake didn't need his brother to tell him the financial facts of life. He'd already squeezed every last drop out of Café Romeo's cash flow. A favorable review still could help, though. Nina might even be back from New York by now. The thought of seeing her again made his heart race in a way no treadmill ever could. "Maybe I should call her."

"Absolutely not." Trace wiped his face with his towel. "As far as I'm concerned, she can stay in New York. Café Romeo doesn't need her and neither do you. We'll figure some other way to save Aunt Sophie's business."

"What have you got against Nina?" Jake turned up the speed on his treadmill. "You've never even met her."

"I'm the one who picked you up at the airport two weeks ago, remember? I almost didn't recognize you. And the way you went on and on about the woman. It was disgusting. Nina might not have caused all those bruises, but she's definitely to blame for the strange way you've been acting lately."

"You're exaggerating." Jake wished Trace would forget about that ride home from the airport. He'd tried to forget about that entire weekend. Now here he was, thinking about seeing her again. How many times did he have to get knocked down before he gave up the fight? Nina wanted a high-profile career in New York, not him.

Jake's legs pumped faster, as if trying to physically purge Nina Walker from his system. It wouldn't work. Nothing worked. He'd even considered accepting Karla Ruskin's recent invitation to dinner. But no woman could compare to Nina. "Do me a favor."

Trace looked over at him. "What?"

"No matter what Aunt Sophie says or does, don't let her fix you up with a woman."

Trace snorted. "Don't worry about me. I'm not about to fall into one of her bachelor traps. I just wish you'd quit mooning over this woman."

Jake scowled at him. "I am not mooning over her."

Trace laughed. "You took the picture from her column, had it blown up into a big eight-by-ten photo, framed it and hung it on your bedroom wall."

Jake hopped off the treadmill. "What the hell were you doing in my bedroom?"

"Snooping. Isn't that what little brothers do best?"

It was time for Jake to show him what big brothers do best. "How about going a couple of rounds with me in the ring?"

Trace grinned at him. "Lead the way."

Two weeks after she arrived in New York City, Nina got called into her new boss's office.

"Don't you like it here?" W. Murphy Hayes leaned back in his big leather office chair, peering at Nina over his bifocals.

"I love New York," Nina said, gazing out the big plate glass window at the Manhattan skyline. The offices of *The Epicurean* were on the sixteenth floor of a posh high rise. "It's big, diverse and exciting. But...." Her voice trailed off as she turned from the window and took a seat on the antique horsehair divan.

"But you still insist on working out of St. Louis?"

She smiled at him. "That *is* what we agreed to in Chicago."

"I know," he said with a resigned sigh. "But I had big hopes that you would love New York enough to want to stay."

She fingered the tiny gold stars dangling from her bracelet. "I do love New York. I just happen to love Jake Callahan more."

He grinned. "Is that why you've been mooning around here for the last two weeks?"

Nina gaped at him in surprise. "Mooning?"

His smile widened. "Yesterday at lunch you poured ketchup on your spinach salad."

Her cheeks warmed. "I might have been a little distracted."

"At least now I know the reason." He chuckled as he shuffled some folders on the top of his desk. "You had me worried, Nina. I was afraid you were having second thoughts about the job."

"Absolutely not. It's even better than I'd imagined." Murphy was a better boss than she'd imagined, too. He might admire the "columns" of his female employees, but he was definitely a "hands-off" employer.

And he'd done his best to entertain her during her two-week stay in New York. The longest two weeks of her life. Time and distance hadn't diminished her feelings for Jake. If anything, they'd grown stronger. She'd used the solitude of her New York City hotel suite to reflect on what she really wanted for her future.

Then she'd called her mother, finally tracking her down at the Mayo Clinic. Her excuse for calling had been to tell the family all about her new job at *The Epicurean*. Instead, she'd ended up telling her mother all about Jake. To Nina's surprise, Dr. Lauren Walker had advised Nina to follow her heart.

Lauren had also hinted that she'd love some grandchildren. Nina smiled, realizing grandchildren were the one thing her successful siblings hadn't produced. Her throat tightened when she thought of holding Jake's baby in her arms. Of course, she had a few little details to work out first. Like convincing him to marry her. But she could do that more effectively in St. Louis than New York.

Murphy leaned forward, picking up a slender gold pen and sliding it back and forth between his fingers. "The board of directors approved your work plan. Since you'll be travelling all over the country doing restaurant reviews, it really doesn't matter if you're based in St. Louis or New York. You can fax in your column and just fly in for the quarterly staff meetings."

"That sounds perfect."

He chuckled. "Then you'll also be pleased to know that they approved your contract. You're a tough negotiator, Nina. I like that in a woman."

"Thank you." She only hoped her negotiations with Jake would go this smoothly. She'd have to find just the right words to convince him.

Fortunately, words were her specialty.

ONE WEEK LATER, Jake walked into Café Romeo—
and immediately walked back out to double-check
the blue neon sign above the door. Either this place
wasn't Café Romeo, or he'd just walked into the
"Twilight Zone."

The place was packed. Every booth and table was
filled and the coffee bar was lined three deep with
young men and women. Laughter filled the air, min-
gling with the melodic clink of coffee cups and silverware.

Jake stared around him in amazement, then he
spotted Ramon sprinting toward the coffee bar with
an order pad clutched in his hand. Jake reached out
and grabbed him by the shoulder. "What's going on
here?" he yelled above the noise.

Ramon clapped his hand to his chest, his eyes
wild. "I'm having heart palpitations. I can't deal
with all this stress. I'm this close," he inched his
thumb and forefinger together, "to having a nervous
breakdown."

"Where's Aunt Sophie?"

Ramon shrugged. "She's probably been crushed
beneath the mob. And now they're going to turn on
me because we're out of chocolate biscotti." He
stuck out his lower lip. "And hasn't anyone ever
heard of a twenty-percent tip before? My last table
left me a dime. A dime! As if I didn't have any
feelings. Why not just kick me until I'm dead?"

"You're getting hysterical again," Jake said,

handing Ramon his handkerchief. "Try not to take everything so personally."

"Ha! Easy for you to say." Ramon sniffed. "You're not the one who just got a Dear John letter from his ex-fiancée."

Jake frowned. "The jailbird fiancée? I thought she broke up with you weeks ago?"

"She did. But she obviously got her addresses mixed up, because this letter was addressed to some guy named John. I think she's been two-timing me." Ramon glared up at him. "What does this John have that I don't have?"

Jake could venture a guess, but Ramon seemed upset enough already. And to Jake's amazement, he actually found himself feeling sorry for the guy. For the first time he realized they had something in common.

Losing the women they loved.

Only Jake intended to find his woman. And to keep her this time. He clapped Ramon on the shoulder. "Be a man, Ramon. You can do it."

Ramon tipped up his chin, then took a deep, shuddering breath. "I'll try." Then he headed off to the next table.

Jake edged through the crowd, searching once again for his aunt. He finally found her inside her office, surrounded by teetering towers of coffee cups waiting to be read.

"Aunt Sophie, what's going on here?"

She looked up from studying the blue coffee mug

on her desk, her mouth dropping open in surprise. "Jake! You came!"

"I came to say goodbye," he clarified. "I can only stay a minute."

"You can't leave," Sophie exclaimed, her eyes widening in horror. "Not now."

"I should have left days ago," Jake said. "I just hope it's not too late."

Just then Trace barreled through the door. "Aunt Sophie, I..." His voice trailed off as he stared in disbelief at Jake. "What the hell are you doing here?"

"Saying a quick goodbye. My plane takes off in an hour."

"Good plan." Trace said, raking his fingers through his short, brown hair. "We can sneak out the back door. I've got my car running, so we can make a quick getaway. How long do you think you'll need to stay in hiding?"

"He's not going anywhere," Aunt Sophie cried, then sidled around her desk and flung herself across the open doorway. "Not unless it's over my dead body. You walk out this door, Jacob Andrew Callahan, and my death will be on your head."

He looked between the two of them, thoroughly confused now. "Will someone please tell me what's going on here? Why are you two acting so nuts? And why is this place so packed?"

Trace scowled as he folded his arms across his chest. "Everyone came to see the show."

"What show?" Jake asked. "Is Ramon doing his Jerry Lewis impression again?"

"You don't know?" Aunt Sophie asked, moving toward him.

"Know *what?*"

Aunt Sophie picked up the folded newspaper lying on the corner of her desk. "About this."

Jake gazed down at the "Nina's Nibbles" column. He'd been reading it faithfully for the last three weeks, even though they'd been reprints of her older columns. But he'd saved today's column to read on the airplane, when he'd have time to relish each word of Nina's inimitable style.

"I don't believe it," he said, quickly scanning the column. Then he read it again, his heart hammering in his chest.

Nina's Nibbles

I can now say unequivocally that Café Romeo is my favorite coffeehouse in St. Louis. No, make that North America. All right, the world. Not because of their renowned chocolate biscotti. Not because of their espresso or eclectic array of flavored coffees. Not because of the quirky staff, who do their best to make your visit to Café Romeo one you'll never forget. But simply because Café Romeo is the place to go if you want to find romance.

It happened to me.

I went to Café Romeo looking for latté and

found love instead. It was written in the coffee grounds, according to matchmaking proprietor Madame Sophia. That's how I met Jake Callahan and lost my heart.

Only he doesn't know it yet.

So, for the first time ever, I'm going to use this column to convey a personal message: Jake, I love you. If you're still seeing stars, please meet me at Café Romeo this evening at seven o'clock. I'll be the one eating cheesecake.

I have a special message for my readers too: If you're thirsting for romance, place an order for love-to-go at Café Romeo.

Jake slowly lowered the newspaper. "She's here? Today? Now?"

"Yes," Trace replied, his brow furrowed. "Isn't that the reason you're on the run?"

Jake slowly shook his head. "I was going to New York City to track her down. I'm wild about her." He grinned. "And it sounds like she's wild about me, too."

Aunt Sophie clapped her hands together. "I knew it! I knew it would work! You can't escape fate."

Jake laughed. "I thought you said she was all wrong for me. What changed your mind?"

"Not a what, a who," Sophie explained. "Ramon saw how upset I was after reading those coffee grounds and finally admitted that he drank Nina's coffee that night. So Nina *is* your perfect match. Just stay away from Ramon."

"As far as possible," Jake promised. Then he gave a whoop of delight as he picked up his aunt and twirled her around in a circle. "She loves me, Aunt Sophie. Nina loves me!"

"I know." Sophie's eyes shimmered with tears as Jake set her back down on the floor. She wrapped her frail arms around his neck and hugged him tight. Then she gave him a shove toward the door. "Now stop making me dizzy and go find that girl."

Trace stepped forward and grabbed his brother by the shoulders, giving him a hard shake. "Jake, snap out of it! I think that woman really did some damage when she hit you with that brick. You've been acting odd for weeks. Go see a neurologist before you do anything rash."

"He's already found the best medicine," Aunt Sophie chimed, pulling Trace away from him. "Love."

Love. It all seemed so simple now. Jake had realized it this morning, lying in his bed alone and wishing with all his heart and soul that Nina was lying beside him. He'd wasted precious time already, letting his doubts and fears keep them apart.

He wasn't about to waste one minute more.

He was out the door in a flash, ignoring Trace's protests. Immediately he was caught up in the mob of people. He stood up on his toes, catching a glimpse of Nina's face bobbing in the crowd several yards away. "Nina!"

"Jake?" Her voice carried over the room, and his heart skipped a beat at the sound of it.

But he couldn't get to her fast enough. So he

climbed on top of the nearest table, the occupants hastily drawing their coffee cups out of range of his size-twelve shoes. He could see her easily now, caught in the crowd near the front door. "Nina!"

She looked up, her green eyes glowing when she saw him. "Jake!"

He took a deep breath and shouted at the top of his lungs. "Will you marry me?"

Silence instantly descended on the coffeehouse. It was so quiet now, you could hear the steam hissing out of the cappuccino machine.

Jake saw Nina's eyes fill with tears. She'd never looked so beautiful to him as at that moment. "Yes, I'll marry you!"

The crowd burst into raucous shouting and applause as two hefty young men lifted Nina onto their shoulders and carried her toward Jake.

She climbed onto the table and stepped straight into his arms. He planned to keep her there forever. "I love you, Nina."

Her arms wrapped around him, holding him tight. "I can't believe this is real. I love you, Jake. I think I've loved you from the moment we met."

He grinned. "Are you *thure* about that, *Mith* Walker?"

She laughed. "All right, maybe not the very first moment." Then her expression grew serious. "But I'm sure now. I've never been more sure of anything in my entire life."

"Nina," he whispered, drawing her close. "You

are my life. How did I ever think I could live without you?''

''Must have been that concussion.''

''Thank God I've finally come to my senses. We'll move to New York City and live happily ever after. I know how important your dreams are to you, Nina. I'll do whatever I can to help them come true.''

She put one finger to his lips. ''Jake, my biggest dream already came true. I've got you.'' Then she grinned. ''And we'll be staying in St. Louis.''

His brows drew together. ''But what about your job with *The Epicurean*?''

''I can write my column anywhere. I've already negotiated all the terms with Murphy.'' Then she leaned closer to him. ''Now I have a question.''

''Yes?''

''Are you ever going to kiss me?''

He grinned. ''In front of all these witnesses?''

She arched one blond brow. ''It will be good practice for the wedding.''

He cupped her cheek with one hand. ''Well, you know what they say—practice makes perfect.''

Then he tasted perfection, trailing his lips along her brow, then down the creamy smoothness of her cheek, until he finally teased his way to her lips. He brushed them gently with his own, savoring their sweetness.

Nina wrapped her arms around his neck and pressed close against him. The sweetness soon turned to sizzle as their kiss deepened into something hot and erotic and full of passionate promise.

At long last, they both came up for air, completely oblivious to the roaring crowd surrounding them. Jake licked his lips as he looked into her eyes, now darkened with passion. "I hope you negotiated time for a honeymoon in that contract," he said hoarsely. "A long honeymoon."

Her cheeks turned a delightful shade of pink. "Actually, I did. A working honeymoon. What do you think about a month-long tour of some of the great cities of Europe—London, Paris, Vienna, Rome? With dinner at the finest restaurants—all expenses paid."

He grinned. "I think I could fly there without the plane."

She laughed and shook her head. "No flying. We're taking a slow boat to Europe. And we'll have the cruise liner's honeymoon suite all to ourselves."

He leaned down to nuzzle her neck. "I like the way your mind works."

"You mean you're not marrying me for my body?"

"That too."

"I love you," she whispered in his ear, her warm breath sending a delicious tingle through him. He realized then that he'd fallen head-over-heels into the bachelor trap.

And he couldn't be happier about it.

TRACE CALLAHAN heard the loud cheering of the crowd and sank down in the office chair, burying his head in his hands. His big brother was doomed.

"Don't take it so hard," Aunt Sophie said, tenderly ruffling his hair. "It was inevitable."

Trace looked up at her. "What do you mean?"

Aunt Sophie sighed. "I probably shouldn't be telling you this, but I happened to get my hands on Jake's coffee grounds. I knew from the beginning that Nina was the right woman for him. Well... almost from the beginning."

The hairs on the back of his neck prickled. "How did you get his coffee grounds?"

She waved his question away. "The how isn't important. I'm just glad it came about so quickly. Now maybe you and Noah won't be so skittish when it's your turn."

"Our turn?" Trace rose slowly to his feet. "Don't tell me you've read our coffee grounds as well?"

"That's right." A smile wreathed her lined face. "Soon you and Noah will be as happy as your big brother."

Trace's face drained of color. "You mean...?"

Sophie patted his arm, trying to soothe his distress. "You're next, Trace. Then Noah. It will be much easier on you if you don't try to resist fate."

Trace whirled toward the desk and grabbed the phone. Then he punched out a number.

"What are you doing?"

"Calling Noah to tell him to stay in Atlanta. That way he'll be safe."

"Safe? From love?"

"From disaster. Sorry, Aunt Sophie, but Jake and Nina are a fluke. I don't even want to think what you've got in store for Noah and me."

She grabbed his arm. "You're not going to leave town, are you?"

He leaned over and kissed her cheek. "Of course not. I'm made of stronger stuff than my brothers. I can resist whatever kooky woman you throw at me."

She held back her laughter until he walked out the door. "Oh, my darling Trace. You'll never even know what hit you."

* * * * *

Don't miss Trace Callahan's story,
BACHELOR BY DESIGN, Duets #27,
on sale next month.

CARRIE
ALEXANDER

Custom-Built
Cowboy

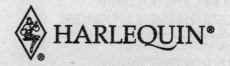

TORONTO • NEW YORK • LONDON
AMSTERDAM • PARIS • SYDNEY • HAMBURG
STOCKHOLM • ATHENS • TOKYO • MILAN • MADRID
PRAGUE • WARSAW • BUDAPEST • AUCKLAND

Dear Reader,

A confession. I bought my first Harlequin romance because of the gorgeous stud on the cover. He was a magnificent creature—sleek, sculpted muscles, deep chest, flowing mane...ah, yes, what a horse!

I was thirteen and horse crazy. If there was an actual man on the cover, I don't recall. So it's only fitting that all these years later, I should write a boy-meets-girl-meets-horse story for Harlequin Duets. This time, though, my emphasis is on the *other* gorgeous stud....

Grace, Molly and Laramie started The Cowgirl Club as horse-crazy ten-year-olds. Fifteen years later, they're living in Manhattan and still dreaming of cowboys, never imagining that one—the Custom-Built Cowboy—has arrived in the city to sell Grace his horse. And we're off to a galloping good time.

If you enjoy the ride, please look for Molly's story, *The Counterfeit Cowboy,* in July, and then coming up in October read how Laramie ropes her man in *Keepsake Cowboy.* And if, like me, you're still waiting to grow out of your horse-crazy phase, drop me a line at P.O. Box 611, Marquette, MI 49855.

Best wishes,

Carrie Alexander

Books by Carrie Alexander

HARLEQUIN LOVE & LAUGHTER
8—THE MADCAP HEIRESS
28—THE AMOROUS HEIRESS

HARLEQUIN TEMPTATION
689—BLACK VELVET
704—A TOUCH OF BLACK VELVET
720—BLACK VELVET VALENTINES

Prologue

"MOLLY, GRACE, LARAMIE," the camp counselor read from her clipboard. She pointed to one of the ponies tied to the paddock fence, a mean-looking piebald with a scrub brush for a tail. "You three are assigned to Rattlesnake for the month."

Ten-year-old Grace Farrow stepped out of the group of campers and rolled her eyes at the dusty pony, who rolled his yellowed eyes right back at her. She stuck out her tongue. Rattlesnake peeled bristly lips back from his big yellowed teeth and gave a horsy yawn. "C'mon, Molly," Grace said, coaxing her shy cabinmate over to the pony. "Rattlesnake doesn't bite. Or if he does, at least he's not poisonous."

Molly Broome hung back. "We should wait for our other partner." Ponies weren't as large as horses, but Molly was a little bit afraid of them anyhow. She wished she was like Grace, who was funny and confident and already knew how to ride. She even wore her own helmet, jodhpurs and paddock boots. All Molly had was the embarrassing cowboy hat her Grandpa Joe had given her for a camp going away present.

Grace's eyes were as green and curious as a cat's. "Do you know Laramie?"

"She's that tall girl with the black braids and the funny black hat. She doesn't say much."

"Oh, yeah, the charity girl." Although the campers weren't supposed to know who was at Skowhegan on scholarship, of course they did. Grace put her hands on her hips, skinny arms akimbo, and decided she was glad their riding partner was different. Laramie was different-interesting, not different-weird. "She's kinda cool."

At that, Molly and Grace turned to watch Laramie Jones walk slowly across the sandy paddock. She wore a baggy T-shirt, faded jeans and black cowboy hat that was so beat-up it looked like rattlesnake had already tromped on it. She stopped before them, skimmed the lackluster pony with her solemn gaze and said, "Hi."

A friendly smile spread across Grace's small, freckled face. "Hi! I'm Grace from New York, and that's Molly from Connecticut. You're from Wyoming, I bet, 'cause of your name."

"Sort of." Laramie stabbed the toe of her sneaker in the dirt. "But I'm really from everywhere, I guess." She glanced at Molly. "What are you wearing?"

Molly's plump cheeks turned pink. She pushed the red cowboy hat with white stitching off her head so it dangled down her back, its elastic string catching at her throat. "My grandpa got it," she mumbled. "I know it's a stupid baby hat, but he made me promise to wear it."

"Is yours real?" Grace asked.

"My dad was a cowboy." Laramie made the claim

proudly, even though she wasn't positive that it was true. "He gave his hat to me when I was born. In Wyoming." Her stomach squeezed in on itself, but she took a deep breath and vowed, "Someday I'm gonna go back there."

"I'll go, too." Grace's eyes sparkled at the idea of taking off into the unknown. "Cowboys and Indians and mustangs—oh my!"

Molly giggled. She wasn't sure she actually wanted to visit the site of so many of Grandpa Joe's favorite Western movies, but she said, "Me, too," anyway.

The girls eyed each other with interest, starting to feel like friends.

"Hey, you cowgirls over there," called the counselor from across the paddock. "Quit the yak-yak club and keep an eye on your pony."

"That's us," Grace said while she untied Rattlesnake. He'd stuck his head through the planks of the fence and was snatching at mouthfuls of grass and spiny purple thistle. "We're the Cowgirl Club!"

Laramie helped Grace tug at Rattlesnake's head. "Yeah," she said, smiling in a way that made her seem pretty despite her ragtag gawkiness. "The Cowgirl Club. I like the way that sounds."

Molly darted past Rattlesnake's twitchy hindquarters and grabbed the rope with the others. "The Cowgirl Club," she chimed in, and together the three of them pulled up the stubborn pony's head.

1

LARAMIE JONES TOSSED her black Stetson up in the air, unconcerned about disturbing the other patrons of the posh riding club lounge. She let out a whoop. "The Cowgirl Club is now in session!"

"Yee-haw," Grace Farrow called in jubilant agreement, catching the spinning hat between her palms. She put it on and slid into their group's usual remote corner booth. Saturday afternoon with her "ropin' and ridin'" girlfriends—still tongue-in-cheekily referred to as the Cowgirl Club even after all these years—was the highlight of her week.

"Oh my, yes, and yippee-ki-yi-yae, too," Grace's sister-in-law, Caroline Farrow, responded in the driest, most tiresome version of her upper-crust accent. She draped herself across the padded leather seat, passive-aggressively anticowgirl in her English riding habit: black velvet helmet, pristine cream jodhpurs and tailored navy jacket.

"We're missing Jill." Molly Broome dusted a few lingering horse hairs off the seat of her jeans and slid in beside Laramie.

"Jill hasn't shown up at the stable for weeks now," Laramie said, "not since she started hanging with that group of radical vegans." Laramie was tall and angular, with a long dark braid that swung between her shoulder blades when she shook her head. "As far as I'm concerned, Jill's out." She flipped her thumb.

"Of the Cowgirl Club?" Molly said, alarmed. "For good?"

Caroline arched an interested brow. "Do tell."

Grace shot straight up in the leather booth, Laramie's cowboy hat cocked on the back of her head. "What? And I suppose you're going to kick me out, too, now that I'm engaged." She wasn't prepared for her acceptance of Michael Lynden's proposal to cost her *that* much!

As leader—some might say instigator—of their urban cowgirl club, Laramie Jones paused to consider Grace's questionable status. While the rest of them saw their get-togethers as a chance to horseback ride, eat barbecue and drool like teenagers over hunky cowboys, Grace knew that since they'd met at Camp Skowhegan fifteen years ago Laramie had come to count the Cowgirl Club as an extension of her dubious birthright. According to Laramie's post-hippie-dippy mother, her daughter had been conceived in, and named after, Laramie, Wyoming, home of her cowboy father. Laramie took the name seriously.

"Naw," she said at last, "I think we'll keep you." Leaning across the table, she tapped the crown of her precious cowboy hat, settling it into place on Grace's head. "On probation."

"Jeez, thanks a lot."

Laramie shook a scolding finger. "It's the price you pay for getting hitched to a noncowboy. In fact, a forfeit may be in order."

"Ah, yes, a forfeit," Caroline said, roused from her lassitude.

"Wait a minute," Molly protested. You could always count on Molly. "I thought we were here to celebrate Grace's engagement."

"Of course." Laramie draped an arm across the

back of the booth. "But this is the Cowgirl Club—
we're wild women of the imaginary West. Grace has
got to prove that Michael is cowboy enough to marry
one of us."

Grace's laugh rang a little hollow. "C'mon, Laramie. It's not like we ever honestly expected to lasso
ourselves some cowpokes. I mean, seriously, here we
are in the middle of Manhattan. We do most of our
riding in Central Park. The place is not exactly teeming with prospects!"

"It's the principle of the matter," Laramie replied
firmly. "We all agreed that cowboys represent the
perfect man, right?" She looked from Grace to Molly,
her glance skipping across Caroline, who was with
them on sufferance rather than out of empathy. "As
members of the Cowgirl Club, we are pledged to live
out our ideals, which, in case you forget, are straight
talk, hard work, open skies and—"

"Tight jeans!" they sang out as a trio, gleeful as
ever over their cowgirl mantra.

Caroline's eyes rolled. "Here we go again."

"Not to forget cowboy hats," Laramie said, grabbing hers from Grace and hanging it off the corner of
the booth for safekeeping. She stuck out the toe of
one of her custom-made snakeskin boots. "And cowboy boots."

"And weatherworn tanned faces with sky-blue
eyes that can see for a mile," Molly said dreamily.
"Big, strong, gentle hands…"

"I'm partial to chaps, myself," Grace stated.
"With lots of long fringe and those cute little silver
conchas."

"Buy Michael a Stetson and a pair of chaps as a
wedding present," Laramie suggested with a teasing
smile.

Molly giggled. Her warm brown eyes danced with daring as she leaned closer to whisper, "Make him wear them on your honeymoon...*and nothing else!*"

"That'll be the day." Beneath the houndstooth twill of her well-used hacking jacket, Grace's shoulders rose and fell with a sigh of pent-up longing. Michael was a good, solid, suitable man, but she had to admit that their love life wasn't very adventurous. "I don't see it happening, cowgirls."

"Buttless chaps," scoffed Caroline. She tipped off the riding helmet and smoothed her pale blond chignon. Her lips were puckered with disapproval. "Definitely not Michael's style."

Grace frowned at her sister-in-law, whom she'd privately nicknamed The Lemon-Sucker. At times she'd wondered why her older brother, Victor, had chosen to marry such a sour, unforgiving woman. Recent subtle—but firm—family pressure for Grace to make her own favorable marriage now that she was twenty-five had given her insight into his choice. She could only pray that Michael Lynden would not turn out to be as big a sourpuss as the impeccably well-bred Caroline.

From top to bottom, the Farrows were a family of achievers. The elder generations expected nothing but the best from Victor and Grace. Academic honors and degrees were supposed to come first, then a quick start on a prestigious career, a good marriage that begat at least two outstanding children, more honors and grander achievements—both for the good of the world and for the accumulation of worldly goods—followed by comfortably enriched middle years and the final glory of an iconic old age.

Victor and Caroline were well on their way to ful-

filling the Farrow destiny. Grace, however, was…
reluctant. Well-intentioned, but reluctant.

Up to now, the Cowgirl Club had been the outlet
that relieved the pressure. She hadn't considered just
how completely marriage to Michael might stop her
up.

"I guess I'm never going to get my cowboy fantasy," she admitted in a low voice. "That's the one
thing I regret about my engagement."

"The *one* thing?" Laramie said. She was too keen
to fool, and had grown from a silent, solemn girl to
a confident, outspoken, yet still somewhat reserved
woman.

Grace chose to ignore the implication, at least out-
wardly. "Let's face it. Michael's just not the type to
participate in fantasies. Of any sort."

"He is very, um, serious," Molly said carefully.
She was sweet and generous to a fault, unwilling to
hurt anyone's—least of all a friend's—feelings.

"And that's exactly what Grace needs." The tilt of
Caroline's head was supercilious. No allowance there.
"He'll settle her down."

As per the Farrow party line, Grace acknowledged
with a silent nod.

"Yeah." Laramie snorted. "Settle you down in
New York City. Saddle you with a ten-room Upper
East Side apartment and so many stifling expectations
that you'll never again know what it's like to be
free."

"What a terrible fate," Caroline said, her sarcasm
audible.

Laramie's jaw set stubbornly. "Well, it's not following the Cowgirl Club code."

Grace weighed the alternatives and for the fiftieth
time decided that she would not regret marrying Mi-

chael. He might be uptight, but he was no lemon-sucker. Most of her friends counted him as a rare find—a well-off, well-mannered, relatively neurosis-free New York bachelor willing to commit. True, he was lacking a certain height, but then so was she. He couldn't be blamed for coming up short as far as her unrealistic cowboy dreams went. For her to do so would be illogical.

Michael was also a very patient man, agreeing to a long engagement without argument. Of course, he'd assumed that the delay was simply to give the Far-rows enough time to book the approved church for the ceremony and plan a big, splashy wedding party at the Plaza.

Which was everyone's assumption, Grace admitted to herself as her fingers bit into the cushy seat of the nail-studded booth. When she closed her eyes and shifted restively it was easy to imagine that the creak-ing leather was a Western saddle, which immediately sent her into a reverie about stinging cold air, steam-ing horseflesh and battered leather chaps that clung to the legs of a tall, silent man whose eyes were so deep they said everything she needed to hear....

Oh, but there she went, galloping off to her fantasy world again! Now that she was engaged, she'd sworn to herself that she'd put a halt to her wayward desires. Or at least rein them in.

Grace forced the cherished cowboy fantasy out of her mind, even though she didn't particularly care to return to thoughts of her reluctant engagement, either. To be brutally frank, the prospect of spending the next fifty years as a married New Yorker made her feel all tight and twisty and itchy inside.

Certainly not a proper reaction for a bride-to-be.

Barely resisting the urge to scratch her prickling

scalp, Grace sank her fingers into her thick, curly hair and cradled her head in her hands, her expression hangdog. What had she done? Why had she agreed to marry Michael? And—to paraphrase the lyrics of the latest Cowgirl Club theme song—where the heck had all the cowboys gone when a girl really needed one?

A waiter in a hunter-green apron arrived at the table and asked for their drink orders. Grace closed her eyes and let out a soft groan of despair, all that—as a Farrow—she could allow herself. Some celebration!

"I think Grace needs a swig of firewater out of a dented canteen," Molly said with sympathy. "Isn't that what cowboys drink?"

Laramie slapped the table. "Set her up with a shot of whiskey, barkeep!"

"Ignore these fools," Caroline said in her most imperious manner. "We'll have a bottle of your best champagne." When the bemused waiter had departed, she cocked her chin at the trio of wannabe cowgirls. "We *will* celebrate Grace's engagement. Because I, for one, think that Michael Lynden is all the man she could ask for. Perhaps their engagement means that she's finally going to give up this cowgirl nonsense and grow up."

"Give up…?" Molly was baffled. "Grow up…?"

"Heresy," snapped Laramie. "I'm appalled." She crossed her arms and looked a question at Grace.

Grace's resolution wavered. On one hand, she had the Farrow expectations to live up to. On the other was her hankering for cowboys and all things Western. She put her elbows on the table and knitted her fingers together at her nape, stalling even though she already knew that while the Cowgirl Club was a wonderful diversion, its policies weren't very practical for a city woman to enforce.

In the Farrows' cosmopolitan world, simple values, clean living and cowboys in tight jeans were nothing but quaint anachronisms.

Grace decided. Again. "Bring on the forfeit," she said with as much conviction as she could muster. "I'm marrying Michael."

"If that's the way you want it," Laramie said after a long pause.

Molly's round face was crimped with concern. "Oh, Grace, are you sure?"

"I…" *I think so.* Grace dropped her hands to the table and stared at her brand new engagement ring. The diamond winked back at her when her fists clenched. "Yes. *Yes.* Yes, I am."

"Well," Laramie said, with a certain finality, "that cuts it. Michael's not a cowboy, but I suppose he's not all that bad, either. Your forfeit won't have to be too severe." She glanced around the quiet, dim lounge, an après-horseback haven of Persian rugs, leather club chairs and tumblers of mellow Scotch for the ritzy equestrian set. "Okay. How about this?" She hooked her old black Stetson off the back of the booth. "As her forfeit, Grace must do a boot-scootin' boogie with the first man who arrives at our table wearing a cowboy hat."

Grace laughed in disbelief, but as far as Cowgirl Club shenanigans went, performing a little dance with what would probably end up being the waiter was a relatively mild forfeit. In the past, she'd been known to mount the back of the booth like a saddle bronc…which was probably why the maître d' always made sure the semiprivate corner booth was available to them.

Laramie was twirling the cowboy hat on her finger. "You've got your eye on the waiter," Grace said, rightfully suspicious of her friend's intentions. "I've noticed him before. I think his name is Spenser. Doesn't sound very cowboyish."

Laramie's shrug was noncommittal, but her dark eyes glinted with mischief. Molly was busy trying to get a second look at Spenser.

Grace finally agreed to the forfeit. "Okay. Sounds harmless enough...."

Caroline's lips were pursing again. "Really, Grace," she said mincingly. "Think of your engagement. You absolutely must begin cultivating a more ladylike demeanor. I'm sure Michael expects it of you."

Even though Laramie and Molly made faces at the prospect—after all they hadn't formed the Cow*ladies* Club—Grace had to silently agree with The Lemon-Sucker. So far, Michael had tolerated her occasionally wayward tendencies, as had her exasperated parents. But their patience was running short. And therein lay one of Grace's thornier, itchier problems.

Like any well-brought-up urbanite of the Farrows' sort, she'd been drilled on proper etiquette in her early years. Outmoded as most of it was, she knew how to waltz, how to address a foreign dignitary, when to wear diamonds and when to wear pearls, the best way to exit a car in high heels and a low neckline. She'd refined the art of meaningless social chitchat. She could maintain her smile even when corporate executives called her Michael's little lady.

She knew *how* to behave. She just couldn't seem to sustain proper decorum for very long.

Her true belief was that life was too precious and potentially too exciting to be spent worrying about the rules of polite society. Although she went along with the Farrow regimen up to a point, always at the back of her mind was the dream of escaping to another world, one where she'd be free to spend every day in a T-shirt and jeans instead of power suits and heels, one where she and her horse could gallop the open countryside instead of circling a schooling ring. A life in the country, not the city. A life her fiancé and the rest of the Farrows would see as a dreadful waste. Only the members of the Cowgirl Club understood.

Grace squirmed. Michael's idea of a country house was an overpriced cottage on Martha's Vineyard. And even before she'd met him, her family's dire disapproval had kept her from escaping the city on her own. Besides, knowing her inclination toward mishaps, she'd have likely been bitten by a rattlesnake or trampled by a herd of cattle her first day out, and then all the Farrows would have gathered to shake their heads over the fatal foolishness of trying to escape the Farrow destiny.

"What is it with you three and cowboys?" Caroline sniped. She gave a distasteful shudder, Farrow to the bone, even if only by marriage. "As I see it, they're dirty, smelly creatures with bad teeth and sun-damaged skin."

Laramie nudged Molly. "It's a leather thing, right? Some women simply don't get it."

"It's a commitment-to-simple-values thing," Molly insisted, entirely sincere. "Straight talk, hard work—"

Caroline waved one of her pale, delicate hands. "Spare me the mantra. Straight talk is all one can expect from cowboys because they're dumb as mules.

Hard work equals low pay. Open skies? Wake up and smell the subway, ladies—we live in *New York*.''

"That's what I was saying," Grace pointed out.

"Then, for heaven's sake, Grace, give it up. Cowboys are nothing but—but hicks in hats." Caroline shuddered again with a true sophisticate's distaste for the vast, untamed country west of the Eastern Seaboard. There had to be something wrong with people who refused to be chic, Ralph Lauren's cowboy phase notwithstanding.

Laramie glowered. "Did I hear you correctly? Hicks in hats?"

Molly's cheeks curved with a gentle smile that forgave Caroline's lack of vision. "I'm afraid you're right, Laramie. Some women just don't get it."

Grace wondered in which category she belonged, now that she was marrying Michael. And she *was* marrying Michael. She was ninety-five percent sure.

Prissily Caroline tugged on the cuffs of her tailored riding jacket. "Be that as it may, I will never understand how Grace can be thinking about cowboys when she has Michael Lynden."

Laramie leaned in and stage-whispered to Grace, "Remember, we're dealing here with a woman whose fantasy life is so limited she can't comprehend the appeal of leather chaps." She leaned back. "I bet your husband counts himself one lucky guy, Caroline."

"And what, may I ask, leads you to think a cowboy knows how to please a woman?" the snooty blonde replied. "Have you ever seen a Western movie with a really good love scene?" Her puckered lips spread into a smug grin as the three members of the Cowgirl Club turned to each other in dismay, momentarily flummoxed.

Their waiter brought the bottle of champagne to the table, gingerly uncorked it and poured, wary of the usually raucous group's complete silence.

Caroline was the first to lift her glass. "Best wishes, Grace. I am so pleased that at twenty-five you've finally outgrown your teenage fascination with cowboys. Welcome to the real world."

Molly and Laramie exchanged a look, then raised their glasses. "Best wishes," they said, carefully polite, and, "Congratulations. I'm sure you'll be very happy together."

Although Grace felt let down, she tried not to show it as she sipped the champagne. Farrows put on a brave face and did what they had to do. Hence her engagement.

"Thanks, everyone," she said, solemn as her father, the judge. "Rest assured that I intend to carry on the Cowgirl Club tradition even after marriage." Suddenly she brightened. "Say, maybe I can lure Michael to a dude ranch for our honeymoon!" Her friends, knowing Michael, appeared skeptical. "Then again, maybe not..."

"This does put a crimp in our plans for Laramie," Molly said, adding, for Caroline's benefit, "Laramie, Wyoming, not our own Laramie Jones."

"Not necessarily," Grace said quickly. "Remember, the wedding's scheduled for next June. We can still spend the spring in Laramie." But she couldn't help sounding doubtful. Even though they'd been discussing their dream vacation for months now, it had always seemed more like a fantasy than reality. At least for Grace. She knew that Laramie-the-cowgirl was bound and determined to make her way west one way or another.

"To spring in Wyoming," Molly exclaimed, raising her glass in a toast.

"Spring in Wyoming," Grace echoed faintly.

"The final fling of the Cowgirl Club," Laramie said, clicking glasses.

Caroline reached for the bottle. "Praise be."

"I KNOW, I KNOW," Grace said twenty minutes later. They were well into their second bottle of champagne. "Michael's a wunnerful guy, blah, blah, blah. It's not like I'm talking 'bout hopping a plane to Texas and going on a cowboy roundup." She hiccuped. "But please, *pleaze* let me have my little fantasy, anyhow. It's the only thing I—" She stopped abruptly. Her dream cowboy was the only thing she had left? Was she really *that* negative about her engagement?

Her friends put down their champagne flutes and looked at her with interest. The Lemon-Sucker's face puckered with its usual disapproval.

Grace cleared her throat. "It's the only thing...Michael can never...be...to me," she finished. The attempt was as lame as a broken-down Central Park carriage horse. "'Cause he's not the cowboy type. You know, rugged and manly and—"

Caroline's salon-maintained brows arched so high Grace thought they might merge with her chignon. "In the cowboy way," she hastened to add. "And that's okay. Really it is. I don' expect—"

Molly saved her. "Of course not. It's only a fantasy. I have them, too." She chuckled. "But I still don't expect the stockbroker-of-the-month to wear spurs to bed."

"I should hope not," Caroline said. "Think of the wear and tear on the Anichini sheets." It took more than two bottles of champagne to loosen up The Lemon-Sucker.

With an effort, Grace focused both eyes on the rock decorating her left hand. It was a gorgeous, expensive, six-carat diamond solitaire from Tiffany's. She'd felt very adult, responsible and Farrowlike when Michael had placed it on her finger. And now all she could think about was how itchy it was wearing it; her skin was practically crawling. Was she allergic to diamonds and gold…or just marriage to Michael?

She slid the ring up to her knuckle so she could scratch beneath it. "All the same," she said, picking up the conversation with a small *hic,* "I wouldn'ta minded riding off into the sunset with a Marlboro Man jus' once, somewhere along the way. Now izz too late."

Laramie's eyes were distant. "Cowboys don't happen to contemporary career woman," she murmured. "At least not in Manhattan. That's why we have to go West."

"Westward the Women," Molly said in agreement. She was their Western movie expert.

Grace dipped her ring finger into the glass of champagne to soothe its itchiness. "I gave it a shot. Spring break, freshman year, me 'n Molly took a bus tour of Nevada ghost towns. Remember, Mol? We thought we'd turn up some cowboys, even ghost cowboys, but all we met were other tourists."

"There was that cute guy who played a cattle rustler in the Wild West show.…"

Grace shook her head. "He was from Reno. He didn't ride a bronco, he drove one. He modeled underwear for Sears part-time."

"He wore chaps."

"And liked to admire them in a full-length mirror.'' Grace giggled when her engagement ring slid off her finger and into the champagne with a fizzy little plop. Sort of like a very expensive Alka-Seltzer. She stamped the stem of the fragile glass on the table and declared, ''I want a real cowboy!''

''Awww, poor Gracie...'' Molly said, reaching across the table to pat her friend's arm. ''We all do.''

''Guess I'll never get one. Was a silly dream anyhow.'' Grace lifted the glass to her lips, wondering if her engagement would have to be called off if she swallowed her ring. Naw. Her mother would hire Manhattan's leading thoracic surgeon to do an emergency ring-ectomy if it meant getting her daughter to the church on time.

Caroline had had enough. ''Look, just because Michael doesn't wear chaps, buttless or otherwise—''

''All chaps are buttless,'' Laramie interrupted.

''Plus which, they'd look awfully silly over one of Michael's three-piece suits,'' Molly quipped.

''Honestly.'' Caroline snatched Grace's glass away from her. ''You've drunk too much champagne if you can't see that Michael Lynden is immensely more desirable than a hick in a hat.''

''Maybe you should marry him, then,'' Laramie said.

Caroline's features froze.

If only, Grace thought, not really noticing that her sister-in-law had turned to iced lemonade. Grace was thinking that there had to be a way to cure her itch, because as often as she had told herself that fantasies should be kept as fantasies and not lived out, she wasn't quite convinced. Before the wedding, she needed to know, incontrovertibly, that she'd gotten her cowboy craving out of her system. It wouldn't be fair to Michael otherwise. He deserved a fully devoted wife.

And she deserved a shot at a cowboy.

"Speaking of hicks in hats," Molly said, sounding odd. "Don't look now, but isn't that a—"

Grace looked. Immediately. "A cowboy," she said, her voice sounding even odder than Molly's, as if she'd fallen down a well. *Help, Lassie, help,* she thought giddily, staring across the lounge, unable to believe her eyes. Even when she blinked several times, opening her lids wider with every blink, the cowboy didn't disappear. *Incredible.* She'd been sure that he was a champagne-fueled figment of her imagination!

The discreet amber glow of the mica lighting fixtures was too dim for her to make out much more than the shape of the stranger's cowboy hat and the impressive width of his square shoulders. Hardly daring to breathe, she rose halfway out of the booth without realizing it, every inch of her tingling with anticipation as she strained to see more.

"A *cowboy,*" Laramie said, as startled as Molly. Grace didn't notice.

"You've got to be kidding." Caroline rolled her eyes, refusing to look. "There are no cowboys in Manhattan."

"It is a cowboy," Grace said breathlessly. She gulped air, trying to reoxygenate her spinning brain. "A real one." She knew it instinctively.

"Real?" Laramie's eyes narrowed as the man entered the riding club lounge. "Well, real or not, he's very good-looking."

Molly's smile had turned goofy; her head bobbed up and down. "Oh, yeah. Very definitely absolutely good-looking."

Caroline whipped around, a rictus of suspicion on her face.

"Aw, you guys..." Grace had finally realized that a Cowgirl Club stunt was afoot. *Or aboot,* she said to herself, goofy from the champagne. "You all planned this—"

"Howdy-do, cowboy," Laramie said under her breath. Small stars twinkled in her dark shining eyes. "Hold on to your hats, cowgals. He's a-comin' this way."

Of course he was. Grace sat. Collapsed. Like a bale tossed out of a haymow. "This is a joke, isn't it?" Even from across the darkened room, she'd discerned that the cowboy was tall, well-built and sort of...worn and weathered. By all appearances, authentic. But how could she trust her instincts? She'd never actually met a real-life cowboy. "You guys set me up."

"Not me," Molly and Laramie said together, but in Grace's opinion they looked like court jesters, nodding and grinning, sitting side-by-side in the booth.

She consumed the last of her champagne in one large swallow. Not even the sharp click of the diamond against her teeth was enough to jolt her back to her senses. With a crooked pinkie, she casually scooped the ring out of the glass, her eyes drawn back to the approaching stranger.

"Wow. My very own cowboy..." She marveled at the lengths to which her friends had gone to celebrate her engagement. "Gee, thanks, guys."

"Really, Grace, we didn't—"

"Gracie, I swear I had nothing to do with—"

"Yes, and cowboys regularly roam the streets of Manhattan," Caroline sneered. "This is *someone's* idea of a bad joke." She aimed her scowl at Laramie.

"A custom-built cowboy," whispered Grace. Could he be real?

She shook her head, trying to configure the logic of it. Too much of a coincidence, she decided. He wasn't real. But he *was* hers.

A moment later the cowboy's formidable figure loomed over the table. Slowly she turned her face up to his...and was mesmerized.

The man was magnificent—everything a fantasy cowboy should be. Beneath the brim of a silver-gray hat, his eyes were a deep, piercing green, staring out at her from a sun-browned face that was as chiseled and remote as the peaks of the Rockies. Dark stubble had encroached all across the rough terrain of his jaw and the hollows beneath his jutting cheekbones, setting off a slightly crooked nose and firm mouth to road-weary, saddle-tramp perfection.

Grace stared, thunderstruck, longing for him to be real. A shocking, sensuous, deliciously deep heat had begun to flow through her like a river.

The man is an imposter—a party favor, she tried to tell herself, but it didn't matter. He was that good. And she was...so ready. So very ready.

His cowboy hat was battered, stained by rain and mud, faded by the sun. His shirt was a mossy-green brushed flannel with metal snaps, the sleeves pushed up to display tanned forearms and the biggest, strongest, roughest hands she'd ever seen in her life. Her gaze caught on them and held. They were capable hands. Oh, yes. Hands capable of...

Capable of anything, Grace thought. And *everything*. Her molten response surged dangerously high. She was in danger of being swept away. Somewhere at the back of her mind was the sobering knowledge that she *wanted* to be swept away.

Her wondering gaze dropped to the cowboy's belt buckle, a silver oval braided with gold. With hyper-sensitive vision she picked out the tiny golden letters that read Silver Springs Rodeo, Best All-Around Cowboy.

He was the best all-around cowboy, all right—and she wanted him all around her! The giddy, swirling heat of *that* mental picture consumed her, melting away lingering inhibitions concerning proper behavior and familial responsibility. She rose toward the cowboy as if pulled by a string.

But wait. She had to remember that this was a joke, no matter how authentic he looked. Except that when she stole a quick glance at Laramie and Molly, they were both staring up at the cowboy in awe. Impressed by their own creation?

"Grace Farrow?" he said, his voice low and husky, carrying just the right subtle hint of a Western drawl. Too much "aw shucks, ma'am" would have been a dead cornpone giveaway.

Still, his saying her name put Grace on firmer footing, regardless of how much she wanted to be swept up in the fantasy. A genuine cowboy in Manhattan was just barely possible, but there was no way on earth that he'd know her name.

It was a setup. It *had* to be a setup. Unfortunately, even that likelihood didn't entirely cool her desire.

"I'm Grace," she chirped when the cowboy's gaze turned expectantly toward Caroline. She scrambled out of the booth, crushing her sister-in-law's toes beneath a boot heel in her hurry to claim the cowboy. He might be only a fake cowboy custom built to fit her fantasy but, by gosh, she meant to take advantage of the gift!

She extended her hand. "Grace Farrow. Pleased to meetcha!"

The cowboy seemed taken aback, but he accepted the gesture, enveloping her hand in his. The flow of heat blossomed into high color across her cheeks; she blushed inordinately at his frank evaluation of her face and, more fleetingly, her figure.

He glanced up from her riding clothes, his expression revealing little. Nonetheless she'd gotten the feeling that he was not particularly impressed. "Miss Farrow." He squeezed and released her hand. "I'm Shane—"

"Oh, that's perfect," she blurted. "Shane! Just like the movie!"

"I…guess so." The cowboy seemed rather hesitant, considering that he was only playacting. Maybe he was just for show.

Or for dancing, she thought, remembering the forfeit decreed by Laramie. Grace was to dance with the first cowboy who came to their table, and lo and behold, here he was.

Of course! The man was an exotic dancer, just like the one who'd been hired as the cheesy entertainment at Nina Getty's bachelorette party. The dancer had crashed their gathering dressed as a policeman and had then proceeded to bump and grind and tear away his uniform until all he was wearing was a bulging leather thong.

Perhaps the cowboy needed some encouragement to strip down to his bulging, fringed-suede thong. Not that such a thing—the thong; she couldn't speak for his bulges—would be particularly authentic…

Recklessness nudged Graced forward. "Go ahead," she found herself purring as she eased up tight against the cowboy, "show me your stuff."

Even before he stiffened at her request, she'd discovered that his body was awfully hard—long and lanky, roped with muscle. The scent of leather, hay and horse that clung to him was *extremely* authentic. She breathed deeply, decided the guy must be a method stripper, and let herself go with the flow. "Ooh, Shane, I do hope you've got your thingie in a thong." Standing on tiptoes, she giggled in his ear. "*Thong* you very much."

The cowboy recoiled. "Pardon?"

"Dance with me." Holding on to his wide shoulders, she bumped her hip into his. "I believe we all are s'posed to do the boot-scootin' boogie, so whaddya say, handsome, wanna dance?" Her hips swished back and forth suggestively.

Caroline gasped. "Grace!"

Laughing, bobbing her head so that the loosened corkscrew strands of her hair sprang up all around her face, she stepped back to regard the confused cowboy. Oh, yeah. He was perfect, right down to a pair of gorgeous long legs encased in faded blue jeans and scuffed cowboy boots.

"C'mon," she said, shimmying her torso in encouragement. She snapped her fingers, unmindful of the ring sliding around her pinkie. "You're an exotic dancer, aren'tcha? A strip-o-gram?"

She reached out and popped a few of the snaps at the collar of his shirt, letting the tip of one finger curl into the crisp mat of his brown chest hair. His skin against her knuckle was as hot as her own. "Mmm. This is a real *good* fantasy," she breathed, hooking the fingers of her left hand behind his silver belt buckle up to the second knuckle and using it to tug him against herself.

"Um, Grace," Molly said, the tremor in her voice

so genuine that it was impossible to ignore. "In all honesty, Grace, I don't think he's a stripper."

Grace looked at Laramie.

"Don't look at me," she said, hands up.

Suddenly a different kind of heat was flooding Grace, one she was terribly familiar with. But couldn't quite accept. "Okay, then, he's a…a hired gun," she said desperately, eyes glued to the cowboy's shirtfront. Her laugh had turned brittle and high-pitched, her cheeks to fire. "So to speak."

She aimed a frantic glance over her shoulder. "Please tell me you've hired him as a Cowgirl Club stunt…?"

Laramie shook her head. Molly mouthed *Sorry.*

The warm river that had been pounding through Grace's veins turned to Arctic sludge. Her fingers were frozen around the stranger's belt buckle. She couldn't seem to unclench them.

"Well, he looks like a refugee from the Village People to me," Caroline pronounced. She rose from the booth, dismissing the stranger with a twitch of her pursed lips. "Didn't fool me for a second."

Grace swallowed and looked up into the cowboy's face. His expression was as silent and unyielding as a block of granite. She'd hoped for at least a smidgen of good-humored understanding. Instead his lips formed a straight, solemn line and his jaw was clamped tight. She waited, but he didn't say anything. Not even any*thong.*

Please speak, she silently pleaded.

"Ma'am?" he said.

Grace whimpered when his callused hand covered hers and began to pry her numb fingers off his rodeo buckle. For one crazy moment she relished the touch...until she realized that her engagement ring was dangling from the tip of her pinkie.

And her pinkie was still inside his waistband.

"Uh," she said hesitantly. He was trying to push her hand away. "Don't do that. Er, please let me—"

"Maybe when we know each other better," he said.

Now he gives me humor. "Stop," she warned, twisting her hand this way and that. "Don't—"

He thrust her hand off his belt buckle.

Grace looked down at her fingers. No ring.

No ring!

She looked at the cowboy's fly.

Ring.

Or at least a very suspicious bump.

He followed the direction of her stare. "What the hell?"

"Guess what?" she squeaked. "I think my ring fell off inside your...down your...next to your..." She tried to think of a polite way to put it. "Down your, uh, jeans, by your, uh, zipper."

Grace forced herself to concentrate on the location of the diamond even though Molly and Laramie were laughing and Caroline was muttering dire threats about humiliating the family name. "And guess what else?" she said, gesturing at the cowboy's fly, on the verge of her own hysterical laughter. "It's not just any old ring—it's an engagement ring!"

Meaning to be helpful, she reached for his zipper. He brushed her hands away. "Let me do it." He cocked his hip and fished two fingers down the front of his jeans. The bump slid a little lower, just out of reach.

Grace bit her lip. The Cowgirl Club *would* have to specify tight jeans! "Maybe if you unzip?"

The cowboy regarded her dubiously. "I'd rather not." He stamped his boot and the ring moved again, into a region whose contours she didn't dare study too closely unless they were displayed in a thong.

"Could you...?" She knelt and tugged his jeans away from his boot, trying to open a pathway for the ring. He straightened his leg and shook it as vigorously as a wet dog.

"I think I see it," she said, excited enough to momentarily forget her humiliation. She put her hand on his thigh and felt through the denim. "Yup, here it is." Her fingertips pressed into firm muscle. "Your jeans are too tight, though. I'll have to work it down."

At Shane's thick silence she glanced up and was startled to find him blushing. "I meant the ring, of course," she explained needlessly.

He tugged at the brim of his cowboy hat, pulling it lower over his face. "I'd rather do it on my own, ma'am." His eyes avoided hers. "If you don't mind?"

"Sure." She stood, stifling a nervous giggle as he put his hand on his thigh and directed the ring along the length of it. One last shake and it dropped past his shin and onto the toe of his boot. They both stared at the diamond for a few embarrassed seconds before Shane retrieved it and handed it to Grace.

She plucked it from his open palm. "Thanks." Her smile wobbled. "And sorry. About, well—" she gestured at his jeans, at his... "—everything."

Shane nodded warily.

She found herself gibbering. "Omigawd. This is almost like the time I learned from my brother that the Santa at Macy's was an imposter. I went up to him and peeled off his beard and kicked him in the shins and tipped over his elf, but of course I was only eight years old, so no one pressed charges.'' She darted a glance at the cowboy, hoping he'd laugh. ''Seeing as how I'd just had my heart broken by the cruel truth and therefore wasn't responsible for my actions...'' Could the same excuse still apply?

Shane took another step back. He hooked his thumbs in his pockets and stared at her as if she were a prime candidate for Bellevue.

Her face crumpled. ''I really am sorry. Extremely sorry.''

He still didn't say anything.

Grace's defenses surged. Why weren't Molly and Laramie jumping in to support her, cowgirls one and all? ''But you just can't do that, you know. You can't walk up to someone in a cowboy costume in New York City and expect them to take you seriously—''

''It's not a costume, Miz Farrow.'' Shane lifted the Stetson, ran a hand through a healthy crop of short brown hair and resettled the hat, pulling the brim down low over his forehead the same way she'd seen a zillion movie cowboys do.

''Oh.'' It wasn't a costume? Desire pattered against her nerve endings like warm raindrops, gathering, swelling, ready to gush through the smallest crack in her defenses. She tried to hold back her hopes, but the chance that this man might be genuine was more than she could withstand. ''You know my name,'' she blurted, feeling the seductive warmth rising inside her.

''That's right. You gave it to me.''

''I d-did?''

''I'm Shane McHenry. From Goldstream Ranch in Treetop, Wyoming. You're buying my horse, ma'am.''

2

SHANE WAS TRYING not to stare at her, but not staring was getting tougher with each passing second. Every word out of her sassy mouth, every toss of her head and spring in her step made him want to stare until his eyes were full.

Grace Farrow was not what he'd expected. Not at all.

Hellfire.

The woman who'd departed from the group as they'd left the upper level lounge area—the sour blonde in the stark English riding gear—had fit his stereotype to a T. When he'd first walked over to their booth he'd been hoping that she was Grace Farrow, because then he could have continued to dislike her without question. Selling Lion to a spoiled city woman with more money than brains was already a sore point. Fixating on an image of a snobbish Grace Farrow was the only thing that had relieved his regret during the long drive to New York City.

But *this* Grace, she was…well, she was something else.

"Ma'am?" he said as she did a little hop and skip along the raked concrete aisle of the stable.

She flashed a wide grin at him over her shoulder. The force of it—added to the brilliance of her green eyes—rocked him back on his boot heels. "Please don't call me ma'am," she said, crinkling her cute little nose. It was speckled like a cinnamon bun. "I'm not a ma'am—yet!"

"Then, uh...Miss?"

She spun around to face him. "Grace!"

"Pardon?"

"Call me Grace!" She spoke in constant exclamations.

"Grace," he said. Cautiously, because the name didn't suit her. The girl was a pocket firecracker, too small and lively to be inhibited by elegance or grace.

"This is it, Grace." He put his hand on the door of the stall where he'd been directed to leave the horse, astonished at how much he enjoyed saying her name. What did *that* mean?

"Then why didn't you say so?" She tossed her head and rose up on her toes to see into the box stall. Her breath caught. "Oh...he's magnificent."

Shane didn't see the need to reply. Even though Lion was still wearing the heavy blanket and leg wraps that had protected him during the journey, anyone with a lick of horse sense could see that he was a rare specimen. Even a flibbertigibbet like Grace Farrow.

She wound her fingers through the decorative iron grillwork that topped the long row of box stalls. At her soft chirrup, Lion swung around and came to investigate his visitor, his wide nostrils flared to pick up her scent.

Shane inhaled, detecting a hint of sweet vanilla among the standard ripe, horsy smells of the warm stable. The girl even smelled like a cinnamon bun.

Grace made a cooing sound and straightened her fingers, letting the horse whiff at her palm. "No treats this time, big fella," she said, and scraped her fingertips across the bristle of whiskers on his muzzle.

Lion snorted and flung up his head, his eyes showing white as he rolled them, making a display of his outrage at her presumption.

Grace's eyes lit up like sparklers when she laughed. "Oh, yes, he's magnificent!"

"He is," Shane agreed, feeling cross. For no good reason, he was put out that she hadn't even flinched at Lion's fire-breathing-stallion act. The ill-informed city woman he'd been expecting would have quailed.

Lion was pawing at the thick bed of straw, lashing his long bronze tail. "What a drama queen," Grace said with another glittering laugh. She peered through the grillwork like a little girl in a candy store, one booted calf hooked around the other.

Her companions joined her. The exotic one with the long black braid dangling from her cowboy hat said, "Drama *king,* Grace. Get a load of the equipment."

The curvy, quiet one brushed aside her glossy sable bangs and smiled up at Shane. "He's a very handsome stallion, Mr. McHenry."

"Shane."

She stuck out her hand. "Molly Broome."

The other woman was watching him with measuring eyes and an occasional flicker of a smile. "Laramie Jones," she said, also offering him her hand.

"Shane McHenry," he replied, aware that the woman was testing his grip. Hers was not bad. But not especially challenging to a man accustomed to restraining a twisting ton of sweaty steer on a regular basis. "Interesting name—Laramie." He released her hand. "Are you from Wyoming?"

"Not exactly."

"Oops, sorry." Still occupied with examining the horse, Grace gave a distracted wave. "I should have introduced you guys. This is Molly, and that's Laramie. Put us all together and we make up the Cowgirl Club.''

Shane blinked. ''The Cowgirl Club.'' He supposed that explained their preoccupation with cowboy ''costumes.'' ''Have you got officers and bylaws and all that?''

''It's not as silly as it sounds,'' Grace said. ''Mainly, we just like to ride together. I stable my horse here. Molly and Laramie rent theirs by the hour.'' She bent to pick up a flake of hay.

Who could account for the whims of city women? Shane glanced innocently at Grace's riding boots and then not so innocently at the way her tight brown jodhpurs clung to the tantalizing curve of her rear end, and suddenly every thought in his head piled up like bumper cars at a carnival. Pure physical attraction thickened his veins. He took off his hat and held it near his belt buckle while he swiped at his forehead with a blue bandanna kerchief, disturbed that ten minutes after the fact he was still feeling the intimate pressure of Grace's fingertips on his thigh.

He slid the folded kerchief into his back pocket and cleared his throat. ''Where does the cowgirl part come in?''

Grace turned from offering Lion a handful of hay and pointed at Laramie. He'd all but forgotten about her and Molly, standing in the aisle, inspecting him as though cowboys were bugs and they were entomologists.

Laramie touched the brim of her battered black Stetson. ''In another life, I was born to be a cowgirl.''

''And in this one?''

''I'm a travel agent,'' she answered. ''There must

have been a mix-up when they were passing out the work assignments. I swear I belong on a ranch.''

She was at least five-ten in her boots, with square shoulders and a slim, fit figure. She looked capable enough. More than his own sister, who'd been brought up on the ranch, same as he, but had been pronounced too delicate for barn chores. ''And you?'' he asked pretty Molly Broome, figuring it was better for his faculties if he didn't concentrate on Grace.

Self-consciously Molly slid her palms along the generous flare of her hips. ''In another life, I was probably the chuckwagon cook. In this one, I do corporate party planning.'' She shrugged. ''It's not the same.''

He turned to Grace. She had rested her crossed arms on the stall door to admire Lion as he munched the alfalfa hay, her distracting hindquarters thrust back at Shane. He tried not to look. Barring that, he tried not to crush the brim of his hat in his fists. ''What about you?'' he said, sounding strangled. ''Grace?''

She swung around reluctantly. ''I can't imagine being anything but a Farrow—in any life. It's probably one of those Hindu-mystic-karma things. In each reincarnation I evolve into a better and better version of a Farrow. Obviously, at present I'm stuck on a lower plane of enlightenment.''

Shane was confused. Was word of the Farrow name supposed to have reached as far as Treetop, Wyoming? Were they rich like the Rockefellers or famous like the Barrymores?

''But I used to have a fantasy that maybe I was adopted and my real parents were Roy Rogers and Dale Evans,'' she continued blithely. ''Which ought to be enough to qualify me for the Cowgirl Club.''

"I'm afraid we're giving you the wrong impression, Shane." Laramie shot Grace a quelling look. "We're not kooks."

"We're Western buffs," Molly said helpfully.

Grace tipped her head to one side as she looked him up and down. Her eyes were bold, her cheeks and lips flushed with expectation. "Have you got a pair of chaps?"

"Uh, yeah, sure."

"*Rrr.*" She rolled her tongue in a throaty Cat-woman purr that made him wonder what maneuvers it might attempt in a more intimate situation. "Do they have fringe?"

"No."

"Cute little silver conchas?"

He frowned at her. "'Fraid not."

Laramie put her hands on her hips. "He's a real working cowboy, Grace. Not a dress-up, Rose Parade one."

"Forget Redford in *The Electric Cowboy,*" Molly said. "Think *The Horse Whisperer.* Think John Wayne."

The three women were inching closer, their eyes bright and their expressions avid. Shane backed off a few steps, having gained a new understanding of how an animal in a zoo must feel when the gates opened and the crush descended. "I need to take care of the horse," he said to stave them off, when it was obvious that what he really needed was to get out of New York as soon as possible. He'd never imagined that city women would be so...enthusiastic.

He stepped past them and reached for the latch of the stall door. Grace popped up beside him. "Oh, yes, super, let's take the horse out. I want to get a better look." The heavy door creaked as she shoved it open.

When she made a move to dart into the stall, Shane clamped his hand on her shoulder. She let out a squeak and stopped in her tracks. He hesitated, lightening his grip, but not removing it. Small as she was, he knew he hadn't hurt her.

She turned up her face, her eyes wide and glistening, tilted at the corners like a Persian cat's. But with her rusty red-brown hair, triangular face and wide mouthful of gleaming white teeth, she reminded him even more of a fox—quick, sharp, lithe. All the same, he had to fight back an urge to hold her in his arms and pet her till she purred.

"Stay back," he said gruffly, forcing her away.

She gave him an impudent salute. "Yes, sir." Smirking at Molly and Laramie, she added, "John Wayne, sir."

"*Rio Bravo?*" suggested Molly.

Grace's grin split her face. "More like *Red River*. And I'm the cattle he's herding."

Shane ignored the exchange, except to think, with a hollow, sinking feeling that made him remember he hadn't eaten since breakfast, that damn, she was one of *those*. A romanticized-movie-cowboy lover. But he'd already known that, from her previous reactions. Not including the weird, out of left field thing about the thong. He didn't even want to know what that had been about.

Even so, he smiled to himself as he snapped a lead rope onto Lion's halter. Better the Duke than Dirk Diggler.

Not that it mattered. He was going to harden his heart, complete this transaction, check into a cheap hotel for a few hours of shut-eye and then be on his way back to Wyoming at sunrise. With any luck, by the time he hit Pennsylvania the enthusiastic peculiarities of city women would be a distant memory. Someday he'd recall Grace Farrow only long enough to tell the boys at the Thunderhead Saloon about his strange adventure in New York City.

"What's his name again?" Grace asked as Shane led the horse into the aisle. Laramie and Molly had retreated to a respectable distance, but eager Grace was crowding closer and closer.

"Vermilion." Shane put his hand out to keep her at bay.

She darted around him when he turned to pull off the blanket, but was caught up short by the sight of Lion's glossy chestnut coat. "Ahhh." She took in the horse from ears to tail, turning his name over in her mouth in a way that Shane appreciated. "Vermilion. Vermilion...for his color. Gilded red and bronze."

Shane's mother had named the horse. He'd wondered if it sounded pretentious, but Grace Farrow's approval made him think that it wasn't so bad, after all. "Very appropriate," she said with a sigh. "Perfection, in fact."

His last selfish hope that she might back out of the deal faded. Of course an amateur would be enchanted by the stallion's flashy appearance, never mind his suitability. "Lion is his stable name."

Despite Shane's surliness, Grace's smile took another chip out of the steep mountain between them. "Lion," she repeated, her hands clasped beneath her chin. "Hmm...yes, I like it."

"He can be a man eater," Shane warned. He went to replace the blanket over Lion's back and the horse danced out from beneath it, shoes clattering on the concrete. The stallion whinnied, setting off a round of nervous replies among his potential stablemates.

"He needs exercise." Grace pointed along the row

of stalls. "There's an indoor arena down at the other end. If it's empty, you can let him loose to kick up his heels."

Shane nodded and took a firm hold of the halter. Lion on a stampede, snorting, kicking and bucking his brains out, was a formidable sight. Maybe Grace would be daunted, although nothing she'd said or done so far had given him reason to believe she was the dauntable type.

"This I gotta see," Laramie said as Shane led the prancing horse into the arena.

Intensely aware of Grace's eyes following his every movement, Shane slid a soothing hand beneath Lion's mane. Though obedient, the stallion radiated so much pent-up energy it was clear he was ready to go off like a bottle rocket.

Shane extended the end of the lead to Grace. "Think you can hold him while I take off the leg wraps?"

She stepped forward. "Certainly!"

He watched her out of the corner of his eye while he bent to the task. Lion stood perfectly still, his nostrils working like a bellows as he pressed his muzzle to Grace's sternum. One flick of the animal's powerful head and she'd be out cold from a serious clunk under the chin, but all Lion did was lip at the collar of her shirt like a docile pony.

Grace giggled and cooed at him. The horse's fine-tuned ears flipped back and forth, gauging the situation. His muscles bunched and quivered; he pawed the ground.

Shane backed off as a ripple ran through Lion's shining neck and shoulder. "You'd better—" he started to warn Grace, but she'd neatly unsnapped the lead rope and stepped away a split second before the stallion made a tremendous leap forward. His muscular hindquarters came up, horseshoes flashing beneath the fluorescent lights as he let fly with a mighty kick. A fine spray of sand pelted Shane and Grace.

"Spectacular," she gurgled, spitting dirt.

Lion charged across the arena like a runaway train, turning at the last moment to avoid crashing into the wall. He bucked his way back toward his audience and Grace shrank into Shane's arms, letting out one small gasp as the horse galloped past them, red coat glistening like fire.

Shane's fingers spread across Grace's shoulders. For a moment he wanted to ease his arms downward, reach all the way around her waist so he could tug her up against himself the way she'd tugged him by his belt buckle back at the lounge. He knew she'd nestle against him, a perfect fit. Already he could feel her rampant curls grazing his chin, the press of her warm, firm bottom against his thighs....

Instead of succumbing to the impulse, he turned Grace toward the doorway, where Molly and Laramie were waiting. And watching. Then he released her. "You're safer here."

She turned back, tilting her head to peer beneath the brim of his hat. "You know very well that Lion won't run me over. He's playing." The horse thundered past them.

"All the same..." Shane touched his brim. "Stay put, will you, Miss Farrow?"

"Grace!" she reminded him as he turned and walked into the center of the arena. When he didn't glance back, she collapsed against the wall and exhaled, fanning her warm face. "Whew."

"My goodness," Molly said in a low voice. "Apparently he's the real thing." She sighed lustily.

"But, oh, Grace, what are you going to do with him?"

Grace hugged herself. "I'm buying the horse, not the cowboy."

"Maybe you can arrange a two-for-one deal," Laramie suggested. She and Grace laughed and slapped hands.

Molly grabbed Grace's wrist in midair and tapped a fingernail against the flashy diamond ring. "*This* is what I mean. What are you going to do about this?"

Laramie snickered. "Besides drop it down that cowboy's jeans."

Grace sobered. She didn't want to have to admit that because of her engagement, what she should do was nothing, nothing at all. That didn't seem fair—to her, anyway—when Shane McHenry was so perfectly suited to fulfill her fantasy.

Strange, she thought, how good fortune could so quickly turn sour when its time expired. If she'd had any idea that her search for a new horse would place a cowboy on her doorstep, she'd have put off accepting Michael's proposal for a few more days. Maybe weeks. Maybe even...forever.

But she did still intend to marry him. She was eighty percent sure.

"You can't be serious about buying the horse, either." Molly pressed herself to the wall as Lion made another rampaging turn around the arena. "He's practically wild."

"I've already agreed to," Grace answered. "You know I've had horse agents scouting for months now because I wanted a more challenging ride than Dulcie."

Even Laramie was uncertain. "You can back out of the deal."

"Why should I?" Grace gestured. "He's absolutely magnificent!"

Lion had slowed to a swift trot. He crisscrossed the arena, head high, ears pricked, listening intently to Shane's low, coaxing voice. His flashing hooves carved divots out of the thick dirt floor.

"He's rather untamed," Molly said.

Grace nodded approvingly. "That's how I like 'em."

Laramie looked askance. "Are we speaking of the horse or the cowboy?"

"Well…" Grace watched Lion circle the arena. "I can't say that I was expecting quite so fiery a horse." She looked at Shane, who stood with his back to them so she could freely admire the breadth of his shoulders and the very interesting way that cowboys broke in their jeans. There was something about authentically faded denim molded to real cowboy muscle that beat the synthetic results of Madison Avenue boutiques and health clubs hands down. "Or that the horse would be delivered by a genuine Wyoming cowboy," she marveled. "Imagine."

"And you thought he was a stripper," Molly said. "Good Lord, Grace!"

She briefly closed her eyes. "How was I to know? What with Laramie's forfeit, I thought you guys had set the whole thing up. Who'd expect a cowboy to show up out of the blue like that, at just the right moment?" With an inward cringe, she thought of how she'd urged Shane to strip for her. "Which I, of course, turned into the wrong moment."

"But you *were* expecting a horse," Laramie pointed out.

"Sure. Only not until this weekend. And I had no

reason to think that there'd be a cowboy included in the package.''

Especially not a custom-built cowboy, she added silently, watching as Shane slowly approached Lion, one hand extended. He was easy in his ways. The mere existence of an engagement ring wasn't enough to halt her deep craving to know his touch. It was a million-to-one chance that a deprived Manhattan cowgirl would get such a shot, she calculated as another moist flush of heat oozed over her skin, dampening her palms and armpits and everything in between. Shouldn't she be allowed to take advantage of beating the odds?

Shane was walking Lion in their direction. ''I have to get ready to leave. Want to give it a whirl?''

Grace blinked. ''What—?''

Gently he took the snap end of the lead rope from her clenched hand and attached it to the metal ring on Lion's halter. ''The horse needs a cool down. Can you manage?''

Every time he turned his eyes on her and spoke, her brain got scrambled like a skillet full of eggs. She opened her mouth, anyway. ''Walk a horse in a circle? Why, yes, I do think I can manage that, yes, indeed!''

''Good.'' Without another word, he left the arena.

Grace stayed where she was, the inner heat drizzling downward until it had pooled in her boots. Her socks were going to need wringing out. ''Did he leave?'' she finally whispered to the other women.

''Duh.'' Laramie knocked her knuckles against Grace's head. ''You in there, Grace? Because you're acting like a thirteen-year-old squealing over her first sighting of the Backstreet Boys. I know we're the

Cowgirl Club, but let's try to keep a little composure or we'll scare him off.''

Grace took a deep breath. Why didn't Michael make her head spin and her pores sweat? Life would be a lot easier if he did. ''I can't seem to...help myself,'' she said haltingly. ''He's so real...it's a shock.''

''Come on.'' Molly touched Grace's arm. ''Let's walk. It'll calm us all down.''

They'd circled the arena twice, Lion traveling sedately beside them, before Grace got her wits back, sort of. ''Molly, tell me. Am I crazy or is that cowboy really good-looking? I mean, he seems like a nice guy, too, if a tad grumpy, but isn't he really good-looking? And really *real*.'' She blew out another ratchety breath. Lion snorted companionably.

Molly gave a humming sigh. ''Oh, he's a stud, all right.''

''I can't believe my luck. I really can't.'' Grace worked her engagement ring around so the diamond bit into her palm when she made a fist. ''Engaged for a week, and *then* I meet the cowboy I've dreamed of all my life!'' She punched the air.

''It is rather ironic.''

They made another circuit. Grace's silence must have begun to worry Molly, because she said, ''Michael—remember Michael. You wouldn't...''

''I wouldn't! I made a promise.'' Grace frowned. *And I'm seventy-five percent sure that I can keep it.*

They kept walking.

''Bo-ring,'' Laramie sang out when they came around again.

Grace's head snapped back. ''You're right. This is boring. Since when did I let myself get boring?'' Afraid that Laramie would answer ''Since Michael

Lynden," she hurriedly thrust the lead into Molly's hands and went around to Lion's left side. With her leg bent at the knee, she waggled her riding boot at Laramie. "Give me a leg up, will you?"

Molly glanced nervously at Lion even though he was completely relaxed, his head hung low. "Grace…"

"I just want to get the feel of him. We won't go faster than a walk." She put her hands on Lion's withers and waggled her boot again.

"As long as you're sure you know what you're doing." Laramie made a stirrup of her hands and hoisted Grace onto the horse's back.

"What could happen?" She settled herself carefully, suddenly aware of just how tall Lion was. He had at least a hand and a half on Dulcinea, her long-time riding horse. Six inches had never seemed so much like six feet. "Uh, maybe you should stay at his head, Mol. Just in case." The horse shifted beneath her, a thousand or so pounds of sinew and muscle sliding over hard bone.

Molly was gathering up the lead rope when the door to the arena opened and another horse and rider appeared. Lion snorted with interest and bounded forward, jerking the rope from Molly's hand. Grace grabbed her mount's mane, his choppy trot making her "Whoa-oa-oa" sound as if it had been mangled by an eggbeater.

When the unsuspecting rider turned to see Lion bearing down on her, she wrenched a high-pitched shriek from the bottom of her lungs and sent it echoing off the ceiling of the cavernous arena. Her equally frightened horse swung around and gave a mighty kick at the charging stallion.

Lion shied to avoid the wallop. Grace lurched sideways as well, barely keeping her seat. Lion reared up on his hind legs, loosening her grip further. Heart in mouth, she realized she was slipping toward the nervous horse's lethal churning hooves.

3

I CAN DO THIS! Even though she'd slithered sickeningly off balance, Grace managed to cling to Lion's neck as his front hooves came down, hitting the dirt with such a jolt her vertebrae rattled like Crackerjack.

But she had no control. The stallion galloped for the far end of the arena, taking her along for the ride. As they careened around the corner, she slewed dangerously to one side despite her death grip. Terrified by the looming blur that was the dirt churning beneath Lion's hooves, she let out a weak scream. *Nosiree,* she realized, somewhat drunkenly, *I* can't *do this!*

Lion whizzed past Laramie and Molly and the alarmed horse and rider. Past Shane, arriving in the doorway. One glimpse of his expression cleared Grace's head. He was angry. If she didn't gain control of his stallion he'd send her straight back to Pony Club.

"Whoa, boy," she crooned. Lion's ears flicked. His speed came down a notch, from breakneck to merely sprain-neck, but it gave Grace the chance to think. She'd sat many a gallop. All she had to do was ease her weight off Lion's neck, settle back and signal her mastery over the horse through her seat and legs. He was trained, discounting runaway gallops.

"Slow down, Lion, please...." Unclenching her panicky muscles was a battle. Her fingers were tangled in the horse's mane and wouldn't let go, no way, no how. *"Whoa!"*

Suddenly the other horse appeared beside them, running hard. Grace only had time to glance over into Shane's face and say a little thank-you prayer before he'd leaned sideways in the saddle and scooped her off Lion in one smooth motion. For a fraction of a second she clutched at nothing, her legs dangling in midair, and then she was pulled toward Shane in a sidesaddle position, held so close and tight that she felt a deep inner sense of satisfaction slide firmly into place. She thought of consummation, of two halves becoming whole, but that was crazy, wasn't it?

Nonetheless, safely enfolded in Shane's arms, she let out a sigh of relief and laid her head against his chest. The rapid thud of his heartbeat matched her own. She was trembling from shock; he was all that kept her from sliding out of the saddle like a blob of warm butter.

"Grace, are you okay?" he asked softly as the borrowed horse slowed to a walk. Lion had pulled up in the center of the arena in a cloud of dirt, snorting and dancing and flicking his tail.

"I'm okay." She looked up briefly before closing her eyes again, her arms wound around his waist. *Just don't ask me to let go.*

Surprisingly, he didn't. Even though they'd stopped, even though Molly and Laramie were running toward the horses, making noisy exclamations. "Thanks for rescuing me," she said, slowly lifting her gaze to his face. He had every reason to be angry at her, but—also surprisingly—it seemed that he no longer was.

He touched her cheek with the side of his thumb,

a gentle brushing that shot slivers of sensation beneath her skin. "Never do that again."

She tried for a smile. "Not if I can help it."

Considering the circumstances, a strange sense of peace and comfort had settled between them. *Warm and cozy,* Grace thought, her lashes fluttering because suddenly she was stricken with shyness, unsure where to look. They were so close. *Two halves...*

Shane cupped her chin, tilting her face toward his. "Promise me." His deep voice cut through her confusion. "Never do that again."

His eyes burned hot as coals in the shadow cast by the brim of his cowboy hat, but feminine intuition told her that it still wasn't anger that fueled them. It was desire. Her lips parted, beckoning a kiss, through no conscious fault of her own. She was reacting on pure instinct.

And Shane's face moved infinitesimally toward hers....

"Grace! Are you okay?" Molly's worried voice shredded their intimate cocoon. "I'm sorry, I couldn't hold on when—" She skidded to a stop, her eyes going from Grace's face to Shane's. "Ohh..."

Shane shifted in the saddle, dropping his hand to Grace's waist. Impersonally.

She unwound her arms and tried awkwardly to sit so she was supported by the pommel of the saddle rather than her rescuer. "It wasn't your fault, Mol."

"No," Shane said, "it was Grace's."

She looked at him sharply. "It was Lion's."

"You were supposed to walk him, not ride him."

"For good reason." She stuck her nose up in the air, although considering the circumstances it was difficult to be properly outraged. "He's far too wild to ride."

Shane's jaw tightened. "With the proper rider, he's—"

"I'm a good rider!"

"Sure. On a meek stable horse, inside a fence…" The saddle creaked as he shifted back against the cantle, scowling beneath his brim. "I warned you— Lion's got a charge in him. He's not the horse for you. He eats beginners for breakfast."

Grace steamed with insult, but it was difficult to argue when she was still sitting in Shane's lap no matter how they tried to move in opposite directions. They were practically nose-to-nose. And even though normally she'd have fought for her honor as an equestrian, by all evidence her passion for cowboys was taking precedence. Darn it, but she was still turned on! She wanted to kiss him! By the gleam in his eye, she suspected that Shane felt the same way.

He stared her down, not moving, not so much as a twitch. Only the slight flare of his nostrils and the intense heat radiating between them gave him away. *Good self-control,* she told him silently, looking straight into his eyes, *but I can feel the pounding of your heart. It's outracing even mine.*

She grabbed two handfuls of his shirt and laid a loud, smacking kiss full on his lips. As kisses went, it was a high five. Scarcely better than nothing. "Thanks for being my hero, cowboy," she said, and launched herself off the horse with a certain flair that wasn't quite what she'd hoped for because as soon as she hit the ground her knees almost buckled.

She took one step, as wobbly as a newborn filly, and then Molly was there to support her, murmuring encouragement. "Great dismount, cowgirl."

Grace glanced at Shane. He hadn't been stricken by her kiss or impressed by her je ne sais quoi; he was calmly collecting Lion from Laramie and returning the other horse to its owner. The two equines nudged noses in a friendly manner, ten minutes too late, as far as Grace was concerned.

"That was almost like the movies," she said to Molly, her laugh as shaky as her knees. "You know the scene. The screaming virgin schoolmarm or the feisty rancher's daughter on a runaway horse frightened by a rattlesnake and the cowboy hero who arrives in the nick of time to swoop her from danger…"

Molly squeezed Grace's arm. "Yes, I know the scene. Sorry to interrupt the clinch."

"It probably wouldn't have gone as far as a kiss." *But for a second there…* "I don't think Shane was as concerned for my safety as he might have been."

Molly smiled. "Well, by then he knew that you were okay. But I got a glimpse of his face when he walked into the arena and saw you on the back of a rearing stallion. He was panicked."

"He was thinking about Lion."

"Then why did he call your name?"

Grace stopped, surprised at the revelation. "He did?" Slowly she shook her head. "I didn't hear it."

"You were otherwise occupied."

"I know, I know," she wailed. "Why do these things always happen to me?"

Molly wasn't as sympathetic as usual. "You know why."

"Because I don't think. I never remember to think. I'm a slave to my impulses."

"You can say that again," Laramie said, joining them. "Whatever possessed you to try to ride a horse like Lion bareback?" She flicked her braid over her shoulder. "And I emphasize *try*."

"You gave me a leg up," Grace protested, but her

heart wasn't in it. She rushed to the stable row, suddenly intent on expressing her apologies to Shane and his horse. She *had* been at fault.

The sight of them pulled her up short. "How is he?" she asked, even though Lion was cross-tied in the aisle, looking as gentle as a family pet as he relaxed under the vigorous massage of a curry brush. Nonetheless, she approached cautiously.

Shane swiped his wrist across his forehead. "He's fine. No thanks to you."

Grace bit back her apology. "Does he always bolt like that?"

Shane shrugged and repositioned his Stetson. "Funny thing. I forgot to train him to canter in circles like a circus horse."

They reached for the dandy brush at the same time. Grace was so startled by his hand settling over hers that she blurted, "Oh, Shane, I am sorry. I didn't mean any harm."

He withdrew. "Yeah, too bad that things didn't work out."

"So you're going to take Lion back to Wyoming." To occupy herself while she tried to figure out how she felt about that, she smoothed away the horse's bronze mane and started brushing his neck. "What about the hard sell? Don't you even want to give it a shot? Maybe I can be persuaded."

Shane was tight-lipped. "I wasn't looking to sell Lion in the first place. Your man approached *me*."

"Oh. Right." The confusion in his eyes—the irritation, attraction, relief, possibly regret—baffled her.

He turned away. "The guy made me an offer—"

"You couldn't refuse." Her palm coasted along Lion's satiny hide; the horse was in prime condition, but not as cosseted as the usual show horse. An intriguing prospect, she decided. "I suppose I ought to write you out a check for expenses, then."

"Much appreciated, ma'am."

This didn't feel right. None of it. For a change, Grace kept quiet and ran through her options while she continued to brush Lion's chestnut flank. As a stallion, he was too much horse for her. But he was magnificent. Just because they'd had a bad first ride didn't mean a partnership was entirely hopeless. Especially when she considered how her first times were always awkward: first day of school (she'd pasted her eyelids shut during arts and crafts); first kiss (she and Billy Forbes had locked braces); first pony (Rattlesnake had lived up to his name); first horse show (her new pony, Pippin, had stopped in the middle of their round to chomp on the brush jump); first real boyfriend (how could she have chosen a wrestler?); even her first *time* (wrestlers were not known for their sensitivity).

First cowboy, she thought suddenly.

One and only cowboy.

"Listen," she said, forgetting to think it through all the way to the end, "I find that I haven't quite made up my mind about Lion. And you can't leave until tomorrow, anyway. So why don't we get him settled for the night and we'll all sleep on it? I can put you up—I've got loads of extra bedrooms at my place. And in the morning we can talk. About Lion." She hesitated. "Not that we couldn't talk about other things, of course! We can talk…" Shane was flagrantly silent. "That is, I can talk…well, um, you know what I mean…?"

As the silence lengthened, Grace fixed her gaze on Lion's wide, dark, red-lashed eye. One of his metal horseshoes scraped the floor. Her body temperature rose until she knew her face must look like a stewed tomato. Apparently the je ne sais quoi that worked so well on stockbrokers-of-the-month had been left in the dirt by her custom-built cowboy.

Finally Shane made a sound—a noncommittal grunt. She decided to take it as an agreement. "Okay, then! Here's what we do—"

He interrupted. "I can find my own room."

"Well, ye-e-es, I suppose you can." She peered over Lion's withers. "If you'd rather spend a couple of hundred bucks instead of accepting my generous invitation when I have four empty bedrooms going to waste. My new apartment is so huge we won't have to see each other, let alone talk. Just remember to drop a trail of crumbs so you can find your way out."

"A couple of hundred, huh?"

She smiled, victorious. "For any hotel room that's even remotely acceptable."

"I could check into the Plaza and bill you."

Her eyes narrowed. How did he know about the Plaza? Cowboys didn't stay at the Plaza. "I don't think you're that kind of person."

"Nope."

"Do you mean nope, I certainly am not that kind of person, or nope, I wouldn't accept your offer of a room even if I have to stay at a dump in the Bowery with a manager named One-Eyed Guido and no heat, water, clean sheets or lock to keep the hookers and their clients out?"

Shane fought back his laugh. "Since you put it that way…"

GRACE WAS ARGUING about traffic patterns and alternate routes with their cab driver, using some sort of New York shorthand Shane couldn't begin to understand. He looked out the window to the left toward the trees of Central Park. In Wyoming, most of the leaves had already fallen, but in New York the trees were still clinging to their fading colors: red, orange, salmon and a rusty amber that was nearly the same shade as Grace's hair.

When he turned, New York City sprang back into existence. It was his first time here, and he hadn't thought that he'd like it. But there was something about the air—granted, it was thick, dirty, polluted air—that, with its aura of energy and limitless possibility, was engaging to the senses. Even to him, a man who'd never thought of wanting anything but the ranch.

They were caught in a snarl of traffic on the west side of the park, working their way crosstown to the Upper East Side, according to Grace. She'd made him leave his pickup and stock trailer at the stable, a privilege that had involved such a lengthy negotiation that Molly Broome and Laramie Jones had finally given up on dinner plans and grabbed a cab heading downtown, also according to Grace, who had explained all this to Shane as if the distances involved were on a par with crossing the continent in a covered wagon.

He craned his neck to study the skyline. As far as he was concerned, the provincialism of New Yorkers had seriously mangled their perception. Take Central Park. Eight hundred acres, Grace had proudly claimed. He supposed that made for a nice piece of land on an island the size of Manhattan, but from the viewpoint of a rancher...well, he couldn't say he was all that impressed.

Grace glanced out the window to see what he was looking at. "That's the Museum of Natural History," she said, and launched into a travelogue about all the

Big Apple sights he must not miss. The driver muttered something unintelligible and leaned on the horn until the florist's van idling directly in front of them moved over enough for their cab to inch its way forward, scraping another streak of paint off its dented door. In Shane's opinion, the driver wrangled the steering wheel like a champ.

"And there's the Dakota Apartments," Grace said after traffic had started moving. "Where they filmed *Rosemary's Baby*. Grand, isn't it, in a gruesome sort of way?"

He stared at the Gothic monstrosity. "I wouldn't want to live there, myself."

She gave a short, wry laugh that he didn't understand, so he looked out the window again. The city was jam-packed with people—all of them serious, single-minded, pushing and rushing, hell-bent for leather. All of them anonymous. Back home, the Rockies and the vast, wild, lonely ranges dwarfed the town of Treetop and the surrounding humble ranches, but Shane figured that folks still felt significant. You had to be pretty darn sure of yourself if you were going to battle deep snow, frigid cold and the wind that came screeching off the mountains like a thousand banshees.

The taxicab was moving faster. "Papaya King," Grace said after a while, pointing to a neon-lit diner. "Great hot dogs. I apologize about the stripper thing. The papaya juice is delicious."

Shane fingered the hat he'd placed on his knee. In the tight confines of the cab, Grace loomed larger in his senses than the skyscrapers that blocked out the sky. She was only smiling and chattering and occasionally laughing, not even in any particularly seductive way, and still he was astonished by how much he wanted her.

How the heck had that happened?

"Do you do that often?" he asked.

"Eat at Papaya King?" Her fascinating lips curved with amusement.

He gave her a good long look. "Mistake men for strippers. Lose diamond rings inside their jeans."

She raked a hand through her hair, pulling a few more curly strands out of the clip that was doing a poor job of restraining them. He wanted to see her with her hair all wild and loose around her face, blowing in the wind. She, for one, wouldn't complain about the harsh weather and reach for a scarf; she would shake her head and laugh with her arms wide-open, embracing the sky.

"Not precisely," she said, sounding as if she were admitting to a flaw. "But close enough."

"I don't get you."

"Let's just say I'm not always on my best behavior."

He mulled this over. "You were expecting a stripper?"

She tossed back her head, her eyes bright with laughter. "Not really, but I wasn't expecting a cowboy, either!"

"Do you always connect the two?"

"In Manhattan, one is more likely to meet a stripper who's a cowboy rather than a cowboy who's really a cowboy. D'you see?"

He shook his head. "This is a very strange place."

She said "Yes!" with such glee that he had to laugh.

Eventually they reached Fifth Avenue, a street he'd heard enough of to know that it wasn't the kind of place he'd ever imagined spending a night. Central Park's eight hundred acres were right there, only partly screened by a wide avenue of screeching traffic and scurrying pedestrians. He saw a skinny-as-a-rail Latino boy walking six dogs and talking on a cell phone, all at once. A man entered the park wearing lots of leather and hair shorn like a cockatiel. A woman in sweatpants and sneakers dodged traffic with a three-wheeled baby carriage.

"This is where I live, Colfax Towers," Grace said as they exited the cab. "Everyone calls it the Castle."

Holding his hat and the old duffel bag he'd packed with a change of clothes and a few basic toiletries, Shane halted on the sidewalk to look up at the immense stone bulwark of Grace's apartment building. She hadn't exaggerated. It was a castle.

"Holy shi—uh, holy cow." Embarrassed, he glanced at Grace. She seemed amused by his slip of the tongue. He reminded himself that she wasn't the sort of uptight society dame who'd be insulted by a touch of salty language.

This building, though...

"You actually live here?" He understood now why she'd laughed about his earlier comment about the other apartment building. Two circular towers made from massive, rough-hewn blocks of granite soared into the platinum sky. Beneath a black-and-white-striped awning, a man in a castle guard uniform was holding a heavy ironclad oak door open for them.

"I know what you're thinking." Grace took his arm. "And it is as stodgy as it looks. But what New Yorker in her right mind would turn down an apartment in the Castle? It's an East Side landmark, on a par with the Dakota."

"Which one—North or South?" he asked, only

half kidding as he paused at the door, waiting for her to enter first.

She patted him on the chest as she went by. "Smarty-pants!"

His pleasure at her easy affection took him by surprise. It was a few seconds before he remembered to follow her inside.

He found himself in an entrance hall so huge he was sure it would echo if a person dared to break the oppressive silence by raising his voice. The vaulted ceiling was forty feet tall if it was an inch, but all that empty space didn't make him feel any less confined by the dense stone walls and stuffy atmosphere. He wasn't claustrophobic—just accustomed to an endless Wyoming sky. Grace's place was well named, though; the metal clang and heavy wooden thud of the door closing made him think of being locked in a dungeon.

Another of the palace guard was holding the elevator. Grace hurried Shane away from the worn tapestries, electrified torches and a fire that crackled behind a hand-forged Gothic screen.

"Good evening, Eddie," she said as they entered the paneled elevator car. "This is my cowboy, Shane McHenry."

"Evening, Miss Farrow." The palace guard pulled the spiked gate shut and looked suspiciously at Shane and his duffel. "Sir."

My cowboy. Shane wondered at that. Did she still think he was playing dress-up? He set his hat on the back of his head like a cowpoke and said easily, "Yup, my sidekick will be along any minute now."

Grace's eyes danced; her mouth widened into the smile that had already grown familiar. She thought he'd made a good joke, but not on her. Foolish woman. He was better off far, far away from her and her million-dollar castle apartment and her billion-dollar smile.

And yet he continued to study the smile, upgrading it to priceless, which should have shocked him. Being a rancher, he'd learned to be ruthlessly practical. Almost everything had a price…even Lion. Up to now, only his honor and the ranch itself had been deemed nonnegotiable.

"How's Zanzibar?" Eddie asked.

"Shaggy," Grace said, to Shane's confusion. "Dusty."

Eddie *tsk-tsk*ed as the elevator shuddered to a stop. He opened the gate. "Here you are, Miss Farrow." His baleful glare tracked Shane as he left the elevator and followed Grace into a sixth-floor foyer that was a miniature version of the grand entrance hall, minus the fireplace and a few of the furnishings. Four doors opened off it, preparing him as much as possible for the size of apartment 6B.

Grace flung open the door. "Home sweet home!"

Shane took off his hat. They were in another stone foyer, this one lined with Gothic arches that opened onto several large, dark, overfurnished rooms. He got glimpses of stained glass, brass and lots of heavy, carved wood as Grace swept him along a wide passageway, saying cheerfully, "Let's not stand on ceremony." She opened a door, then another across the flagstone hall. "You can pick your own bedroom. They're equally horrid."

"I'm sure they're—"

"Don't try to snow me! They're dreadful. But I moved in only days ago, so I haven't had time to do anything about it." She looked up at him and fell into a sudden silence. Her eyes traced a path along his jawline, so palpably that he itched with the corresponding prickles. She exhaled. "Yes. You'll want to get cleaned up. The hot water's balky, but I'm sure you can rough it. Shall we meet in the kitchen in ten minutes? I don't know about you, but I'm famished!" She stripped off her jacket, stuffed it into her riding helmet and with one last sensational smile disappeared through a door at the end of the hallway.

Shane took the first room without looking. It was a Victorian-style chamber of horrors—dark-green wallpaper crawling with a pattern of vines, flowers and forest creatures; a half-dozen needlepoint rugs scattered over a hard carpeted floor; massive walnut furnishings that were black with age. The four-poster bed was mounded with florid cherub pillows, built so high that the mattress came up to his waist. He tossed his hat and duffel on it. Someone of Grace's size would need a stepladder to climb aboard.

He stood there for a minute, imagining her sneaking his door open after midnight, peeking inside, alert, wide-eyed, taking a running start and leaping into the bed with her nightgown flying up to reveal her naked legs. Did her thighs have freckles or were they as pale and smooth as cream? Did she smile even when she made love, her lips glossy, open, welcoming?

He looked in the rippled mirror tilted at a tipsy angle above a doily-sprinkled dresser and didn't recognize himself. The sudden feelings for Grace were as strange and abnormal to him as pulling a two-headed calf. He'd been alone for too long. Not completely alone—there was his mother and sister to consider—but alone…in that way. Without a woman.

He'd been solely in charge of the ranch for fourteen years, since he was seventeen and his father had died in a freak spring lightning storm. There had been flir-

tations, a handful of fleeting affairs, even a few mar-
riage-minded local gals who'd expressed a certain
willingness, but he'd already been weighed down
with his responsibilities to the ranch. He couldn't see
adding a wife to the stew. And as the years went by
it became harder and harder to even imagine what it
might be like to have a woman who was a partner
and friend as well as a lover.

For sure he didn't know how to treat a woman like
Grace Farrow. If she'd been stuck-up and standoffish
as she was supposed to be or even delicate and refined
like his sister, he'd have had some idea of what to
do. But she was not. She was Grace—bright and
friendly and eager as a puppy dog, but still alien—
citified, he supposed—in many of her ways. She
smiled at him, though; she touched him; she sent out
signals that made him picture her tumbling around
with him in that big four-poster bed.

He rubbed his thigh. Then again, look at the way
she'd dropped her ring down his jeans and treated
Lion like an amusement park ride. Look at her apartment, her lifestyle. He wasn't interested in taking on
a woman who might well be a spoiled heiress with a
cowboy fetish.

His safest option was to do as he'd planned. Sell
Lion—much as he hated to. Say goodbye. Hit the
road. Put a few thousand miles between him and the
crowded electric circus that was New York City.

Try to forget that Grace Farrow's smile had stirred
his lonely heart.

4

GRACE HEARD THE CLAP of Shane's boot heels on the stone-flagged floor and decided with an anticipatory rush of warmth that maybe there was no reason to put down more of her Navajo carpets, after all. Having a cowboy in the house gave her a different perspective on a lot of things.

Clack, clack, clack. He paused by the entrance to the dining room, a baronial hall of family portraits with a massive sideboard and a table for twelve. Clack. Clack. Scrape. He'd tried the door to the butler's pantry.

She touched the tip of her tongue to her upper lip. "In here, Shane."

He walked through the pantry, one eyebrow quirked in a way she found undeniably attractive. "Think I was lost?"

"It's been known to happen. One Thanksgiving Cousin Thaddeus went looking for the powder room and never came back. We found him snoring in the maid's quarters, but then he'd been imbibing the cranberry wine all during cocktail hour, so..." She held up a yellow squash and a red bell pepper and shook them like maracas. "Are you a meat and potatoes man?"

"Reckon so."

"Well, see, I have eggs. I have veggies. I have a

loaf of French bread that's going stale. Can you make do with a ratatouille omelette?''

"Sure. Whatever." He rolled up the sleeves of a fresh shirt—this one ecru with piping that matched the dark indigo of jeans so new they still had a crease. They looked sharp, but she missed the soft, faded ones that clung to his legs so distractingly.

"May I help?" he asked.

"Thanks, but no—you're a guest. Please take a seat." She pointed her chopping knife at a stool. "You can watch while I do my Julia Child show. Usually my audience is only imaginary, unless we count the cockroaches."

He sat abruptly, hooked his boot heels on the bottom rung and said, "Cockroaches?" with utter distaste.

"There's one—crawling up your leg!"

He jumped off the stool and beat at his jeans with the flat of his hands before glancing up and catching her eye. His grin was sheepish as he returned to his seat. "We don't have cockroaches in Wyoming."

"So I gathered." She chortled. "I just couldn't resist."

"Shame on you," he scolded, "taking advantage of the rube from the country."

She looked up from the vegetables she'd begun chopping, checking out his expression to be certain that he was only kidding, even though she was already wagering that he was a lot savvier than one might assume.

Shane winked at her. Her breath caught short; her face heated up like a steam grate. And no wonder. A wink from a leering construction worker on the street was one thing. Or a wink from a boozy advertiser during a three-martini lunch. Even a wink from the cute bicycle messenger who frequented the station. But a lazy, sexy wink from a cowboy with a sneaky grin and a five o'clock shadow was enough to make her forget that she was a city woman who'd thought she'd seen it all.

"Careful," Shane said, and she looked down in time to watch the blade miss her fingertips by a hair-breadth. *Get a grip,* she thought. *He's only a cowboy.*

Her one and only custom-built cowboy, gorgeous as all get out.

"So," he said while she went to the pantry for onions and garlic and to the sub-zero refrigerator to rummage for a somewhat withered eggplant, "you have family living in the city?"

"More or less." She took a deep sniff of the onion to clear her head. "At the moment we're sort of scattered. A month ago my dad retired from the bench, so he and Mom decided it was the perfect time to go to Africa on a photo safari like they'd always wanted to. And then my grandmother upped and eloped to Palm Springs with her boyfriend, Aristotle. This place was hers...." She gave Shane a sassy grin and said as an aside, "Castles ain't my style," then continued, "But seeing as I was finally on the verge of getting en—"

She stopped short, remembering that her ring finger was bare. Most likely she'd left the ring on the marble ledge in the shower stall, where she'd washed after changing out of her riding clothes. No big deal...except that suddenly she didn't want to emphasize the point that she was "taken." Even though getting cagey about it when Shane had already had an extremely personal encounter with her diamond was not exactly logical.

Luckily, logic was not her strong suit.

"That is, since Victor and Caroline had already bought a new place on Central Park West, which let me tell you was some pretty quick thinking on Caroline's part, um, so then naturally Grandmother Farrow's apartment came to me," she said in a rush, her voice rising several octaves in her effort to avoid mentioning her engagement. *Sorry, Michael, but tonight I might just forget that you're my fiancé.*

Shane locked his fingers around his knee. "It's a lot of apartment for a little gal like you."

She nodded, savoring the soft-as-suede look in his eyes. He was flirting, she decided, in a laid-back cowboy way. "A week ago I was living in a nice clean contemporary loft in the Village. Now I'm stuck rattling around this place like a marble in a maze. My grandmother might decide to come back, so I can't touch her junk." She waved the knife, sending several chunks of diced onions skipping over the kitchen island. "Brocade ottomans! Victorian fainting couches! Antimacassars! Can you imagine? I don't even want to know what antimacassars *are*, let alone own them, but Gran expects me to live with her antiques out of a sense of family tradition. Try telling that to my big toe when I stub it on an English satinwood chiffonnier in the middle of the night for, like, the tenth time."

Grace stopped to take a breath. "Just call me yakkety-yak," she said apologetically, but even as she did she was struck with a notion. Shane hadn't gotten the same glazed, smiley, see-how-tolerant-I-can-be? look that Michael did whenever she lost herself in what he'd begun to condescendingly refer to as her "babble."

Instead, Shane appeared to be fascinated. How refreshing.

But disconcerting, too.

She gave herself a good mental shake. "And now…" She executed a fancy flourish with her knife. "The cook will attempt a ratatouille. First, we need a skillet." After much clashing and clattering, she found one of the appropriate size. "If my assistant would be so kind…" She heated a tablespoon of olive oil and motioned for Shane to dump in the eggplant. He quickly complied.

She sautéed happily, flipping bits and pieces into the air with carefree abandon, warbling in her fluty chef voice throughout the off-the-cuff cooking demonstration. Michael had once laughed at her Julia show, but recently—if you'd call the past five or six months recent—he'd taken to going wherever the TV was to watch *SportsCenter* or check stock quotes while she cooked. She hadn't realized until now that it even bothered her.

Shane, of course, was a captive audience. He sat at the island, drinking a cup of black coffee, shaking his head at her more fanciful extemporizations, sometimes grinning and sometimes breaking out in a fullfledged laugh when he couldn't help it. He had a way of turning his head away when he smiled, as if he was unaccustomed to sharing his softer side, and something in his bashfulness touched her, charmed her, made her stomach clench and her heart go pittypat. She stopped thinking of him as a cowboy and started thinking of him as a man.

Dangerous, that. Better he should stay a fantasy figure.

Except that she'd never been good at denying herself what she wanted. It was her nemesis, the followyour-impulses thing again. Up to now, most of her follies had been merely personally embarrassing. When the crucial moment of choice came, she'd generally surrendered to the crunch. If she were to seduce a cowboy, however, even for a one-night fling, her engagement would definitely be over and all the weighty Farrow expectations would come crashing down on her head.

Shane propped his chin on his hand. Through her lashes, she watched his callused fingertips skim over the shadow of his beard. *Yum.* Wasn't there a country-and-western song with a lyric about hard-working hands needing someone soft to hold? She wouldn't mind being the someone, especially since it was so incredibly easy to imagine his hands stroking her skin—her cheeks, her breasts, the yearning, trembling curve of her belly. *Maybe he's worth it,* she mused.

Maybe I am.

Now there was a thought. Such a stupendous thought that she was too chicken to follow up on it, especially when it would be much safer to lapse into comedy. "Then you put the egg in the skillet and the lime in the coconut—oh, dear-r-r me, wr-r-rong r-r-recipe!" she sang, rolling her *R*'s with abandon. "Something tells me Julia's been at the cooking sher-r-r-ry again!"

Shane's head tilted thoughtfully. His eyes were heating up again, but all he said was, "Or the piña coladas."

Grace giggled. She sang what she could remember of "The Piña Colada Song" while she spooned filling onto the second omelette, doing a hip roll when she got to the "mor-or-or-orning" part. She didn't look too closely at Shane; her feelings about him were already strong enough, thank you, sir, very much, sir. She didn't need to see how handsome and rugged, and therefore exotic, he was—a cowboy sitting so calmly in a kitchen in an apartment in the Castle on Fifth Avenue in New York City!

After charring the French bread under the broiler— okay, so she'd sneaked a few peeks at Shane and gotten distracted—she quickly set out her own bright Mexican woven placemats, her grandmother's silverware and cut-crystal glasses and a bottle of red wine.

"I hope this will do." She arranged their place settings on either side of the tiled island. "I prefer eating in the kitchen, but if you'd rather…?"

Shane shook his head and deadpanned, "I've seen the dining room."

Ah. He was simpatico. By rights, the tightly wound knot that had lodged itself in her chest should have relaxed at that, but it didn't. It got a little tighter. *Because* he was simpatico. And thus threatening to her already seesawing Farrow status quo.

She uncorked the wine and said, "Tell me about Lion."

Shane halted a forkful of omelette halfway to his mouth. "Did you still want the hard sell?"

"No. I want the inside scoop, the real story." She filled their glasses. "There's got to be one. Being that I've never heard of a cowboy using a horse like Lion for ranch work."

"He's not the usual quarter horse, no." Shane put the bite of omelette into his mouth and immediately forked up another. She passed the bread basket and he took two pieces, unfazed by the blackened edges. "Lion's a natural jumper."

"What's his lineage?"

"His sire's a Thoroughbred owned by a friend of mine. His dam, Gildersleeve, is a mare bred from a Hanoverian warmblood that was once my father's hunter—"

"Fox hunting?" Grace was surprised. "Really? In Wyoming?"

Shane shook his head. "My father wasn't a rancher originally. He was born in Virginia to what my mother calls a 'good' family. He went to all the right schools, played polo and lacrosse, did some fox hunting. Some years later he ended up in Wyoming with a wife and a child and a ranch he'd bought on a whim. For the adventure, he said. I was three or four."

"I see," Grace said, although she didn't, not entirely. Shane's breeding was apparently as convoluted and intriguing as Lion's. And as successful.

"It was my father who bred a few jumpers over the years. Out of sentiment, I guess. Homesickness." Shane looked up from his plate. "Lion was Gildersleeve's last foal. It was obvious he wasn't a cow horse, and since I prefer a Western saddle, I sent him to a proper trainer." He paused to polish off the rest of his omelette. "This past summer, while I was working the ranch, the trainer took Lion around to a few small jumping competitions on the coast, which is where your horse trader spotted him, from what I hear." He paused again, staring at his empty plate with a hopeful expression. "I should warn you that I've been riding him Western at the ranch. Maybe I've messed up his training…?"

Grace rose from her stool and went over to the cooktop to make another omelette. "Oh, but that's what's exciting! Lion's unconventional breeding and training have kept him fresh. My sources say that his untapped potential is huge, and now that I've sort of seen him in action, I agree. I only hope that he's not beyond my capabilities." A few minutes later, she brought the skillet over to the island and slid the steaming omelette onto Shane's plate, gratified that he had a healthy appetite. He hadn't touched the wine, so she refilled his coffee cup.

He nodded his thanks. "At least you're finally being sensible about it."

She wasn't sure that she wanted to be sensible, of all things. Certainly not this evening. "Oh, I didn't say I was going to go that far!" she trilled, but her conscience wouldn't allow her to verbalize all the glorious ways they could be insensible together. "Regarding Lion, that is. See, I'm not quite the chump you might think. I rode Dulcie in the Maclay finals at Madison Square Garden when I was seventeen."

Shane barely paused in his consumption of the second omelette. "And now?"

"Well, yes, I'm a doddering twenty-five, and, no, I'm not an elite rider with a score of trophies and an invitation to the Olympics. But Dulcie and I hold our own—"

"In Central Park."

"Central Park's nothing to sneer at." She speared a chunk of zucchini with her fork and brandished it threateningly. If he didn't grant her equestrian skills some respect she'd give him a good poke in the ribs. "I'll have you know that Dulcie and I are very adept at dodging winos and cantering circles around the muggers."

Shane shook his head. "Then why do you need Lion?"

"For the challenge." She became more serious, wondering over the question herself. "I've been restless. I needed, oh, something...." Apparently an engagement and a new place to live weren't enough, at least when they were neither the man nor the location she'd set her stubbornly nonconformist heart on.

Shane swabbed his plate with the remaining crust

of bread and shoveled it into his mouth. He drained his coffee cup, looking levelly at Grace over the rim. She couldn't look away; didn't, in fact, want to. His eyes had turned a serious, murky-swamp green, his brows drawn in a flat brown line above them. With the cowboy hat removed, she could see that the skin near his hairline was a shade paler than the rest of his face, and was probably smoother, too—if she touched it. She wanted to. She wanted to complete the embrace they'd shared earlier, wanted to hold him close and press her lips to his forehead, her nose buried in his hair. She already knew that he didn't smell of expensive designer cologne like her fiancé; Shane carried the scent of the wild outdoors.

He set down the cup. "Lion is not a debutante's plaything."

No, he's not, Grace silently agreed. *But perhaps you are!*

THE GREAT HAIRY BEAST loomed from the shadows, frozen in a perpetual snarl, its sharp curved horns gone yellow, its eyes a flat, lifeless black.

"It's a wildebeest," Grace said distastefully. "My great-granddaddy Barclay Farrow was a big-game hunter."

After Shane had loaded the dishwasher and Grace had hand washed the few pieces of glass and silver, she'd offered to give him a tour of her inherited apartment. He'd been curious enough to accept. If all the extra rooms filled with boatloads of antique whatnots hadn't already done so, the mounted heads that lined the paneled walls of the study would have surely driven home the point that people like the Farrows would forever remain a mystery to him.

Plenty of well-heeled hunters came to Wyoming to

shoot elk and bighorn sheep. Shane had even done a little hunting himself, for meat, not sport. He couldn't understand the mentality that drove a city dweller to hang the head of a stuffed zebra on his wall.

"I've tried naming them, but that doesn't help." Grace whipped a dust sheet off a wing chair and tossed it like a shroud over the zebra. "That one especially bothers me. I'd yank them all down if I could, but I just know that Gran will come back from Palm Springs in a few months and expect the apartment to look exactly the same. The only room I dare to redecorate is the one I've chosen for myself."

"Then why move in in the first place?"

"I told you." She plopped into the uncovered chair. "No one turns down an apartment in the Castle."

"You could have been the first."

She slumped lower on her spine, her expression darkening. "It was my Farrow duty."

One thing Shane understood was the pressure of facing up to family responsibilities, although in his case he'd wanted Goldstream as his own from the moment he'd roped his first calf. Even before then. His mother still occasionally commented on the bother of washing corral muck out of rompers.

"I imagine the Farrows can afford such things as locks and keys, housekeepers and maintenance men," he commented. Not that it was any of his business.

Grace shrugged. "Haven't you ever had to do something you didn't want to do?"

"Sure." He sat heavily across from her, nearly knocked off his feet by the rush of feelings that gripped him at her innocent question. His emotions made no sense. He had no use for Lion. The horse was the final proof of the absurdity of his father's folly with ranching. And yet...

"Shane?"

When he looked at Grace the truth came out in two stark words: *"Sell Lion."* Letting go of the stallion was like letting go of his dad all over again.

"Oh, Shane." Grace slid forward to the edge of her seat so their knees nearly touched, her hands dangling between them. Her eyes searched his. "Why have you come all the way to New York if you don't really want to sell Lion," she said softly, not even making a question of it because it was likely she already knew the answer. But not the cause, he thought. She didn't know that he would do anything to bring joy to his sister and maybe finally a reprieve to his mother. Even this.

"Money," he said. "Plain and simple as that."

Grace's chin went up. "Money?"

That she questioned.

"I understand that ranching is not always profitable," she ventured when he didn't speak, her brow puckering in the mystified way of a girl who'd probably never had to balance a checkbook.

His answer was forceful. "The ranch is fine." He'd worked like a stevedore for all these years to be able to say so. "The ranch is holding its own just fine."

"That's good, then." Her eyes glittered with curiosity.

He looked past the grate into the smoke-blackened hole of the stone fireplace and found himself confessing, "It's Eleanor, my sister. She's a pianist. Exceptionally talented, they tell me. She has a chance to attend a music school in San Francisco. I intend to see that she gets there. But it's...expensive."

Grace's fingers settled lightly over his. "You must

care for your sister very much if you're willing to give up Lion to help her." She clasped his hands and squeezed.

"He's only a horse. I'll get over it."

Although Shane tried to stay tough, Grace's expression was so sweet and kind, he began to ache with a need that was as emotional as it was physical, that seemed to grow stronger and therefore more confounding every moment they were together. Her smile was generous; her voice and eyes and hands were as warm and welcoming as the first rays of sunshine on a chill morning in the mountains. He wanted to bask in her glow, in her free and easy manner. It was not sympathy she offered him, but balm just the same.

Yet the very nature of it nagged at him. He wasn't accustomed to being less than the rock at the center of his own small universe. How best to respond to a female who was giving instead of needy was a mystery to him.

He knew enough to kiss her, though—it hadn't been *that* long. All he had to do was tighten his hands around hers and use them to draw her closer, closer...until the scent of her clouded his head and her lashes brushed the cinnamon speckles dusted across her cheeks. Her breath mingled with his as she parted her lips the tiniest bit in invitation. She was all-woman, open and accepting, curved and warm, with a mouth that promised the ultimate sweetness if only he could risk sampling it....

"I'm engaged," she said out of nowhere.

The bottom dropped out of Shane's stomach. "You're engaged. Uh, yeah, I already knew that." But for a brief time, he'd let himself forget.

Her eyes were huge, the inky pupils blotting out

the brilliant emerald irises. "Shucks. I am definitely engaged."

"I heard you." He let go of her hands, shocked that his disappointment had such an infinite depth.

Her lower lip quivered. "Well, yes, I just thought that we should both be reminded."

Deliberately he settled back, his legs stretched before him, one crossed over the other so that he would look easy and relaxed—if she didn't notice that he was gripping the hard wooden knobs at the ends of the chair's arms as if bracing himself for the bronc ride of his life. Raging needs were so dammed up inside him he could barely choke out the question that needed to be asked: "Who's the lucky guy?"

Grace dropped her face into her hands and said, with what sounded to Shane like a frustrated moan, "His name's Michael Lynden. We've been engaged for about a week." Her face lifted, pale and drawn in the dusky light. "Excellent timing, hmm?"

Shane wasn't following. He studied her, trying to place her words and reactions in a form that was recognizable. Back home, a gal who'd just gotten engaged tended to squeal, giggle and wave her ring under her girlfriends' noses, but maybe they did things differently in the city.

"Congratulations?" he said.

Grace let out a stifled laugh, her lips compressed. "Thank you. I guess."

He cocked an eyebrow.

"Oh, I'm terrible, I know! I don't understand what's wrong with me." She smiled bravely. "Michael's a great guy, just great. We've been seeing each other for a year now, so it was time to get engaged. Everyone said so. And really, he'll be a wonderful husband and a caring father and good provider, all that practical, meaningful stuff that's far more important than pounding pulses and sweaty palms, if you know what I mean...." She trailed off, looking less brave than uncertain.

"I like a good pounding pulse, myself," Shane said. "Lets me know I'm alive."

"Of course." Restlessly she ran her hands over her hair. A number of barrettes and bobby pins had been stuck in it at all angles; odd-shaped clumps and corkscrewed wisps poked out here, there and everywhere, giving her the comic look of a half-plucked porcupine. "Of course, of course," she repeated, mainly to herself, "but it's nothing you can take to the bank."

"Is that what's important to you?"

"A solid, stable, suitable marriage, yes, of course," she said, fidgeting with her hair, loosening another ginger-colored strand with each agitated yes and of course. "It's what my family wants for me, yes, absolutely, and so do I."

Even though Shane knew he should just shut up and call it a night, he asked, "Then why do you seem so unconvinced?"

Grace's shoulders straightened; her nervous fingers fell to her lap and knitted together like one of his mother's misshapen mittens. She didn't speak for what was the longest minute Shane had ever known, but when finally she did he wished she hadn't.

"Why, that's your fault, cowboy," she said with a teasing drawl, looking straight at him so her desire was plain to see, staining her cheeks a luscious pink.

He couldn't pretend he hadn't followed *that* one, not when he'd twice come within a heartbeat of kissing the daylights out of her. "Excellent timing," he mimicked, shooting a lopsided grin her way in hopes that she'd laugh the whole thing off as a temporary short circuit of their electrical systems.

"Depends." She considered. "Are you referring to the fact that you showed up a week too late, or..." Her eyes honed in on his mouth. Unmistakably. "Or on the welcome you received when you did arrive?" Her gaze slowly lowered until it was tracing the length of his outstretched legs. Significantly.

Not that, he thought, remembering the diamond down his jeans. "Stopping a split second before we kissed," he said. "That's what I meant."

She drew a deep breath. "Right. We wouldn't have wanted something scandalous to occur beneath my great-granddaddy's trophy heads. Think how shocked they'd have been."

"To say nothing of your great-granddaddy."

"He's dust. The heads outlived him."

"So to speak."

"Do keep speaking, Shane. A pause could lead to all sorts of unspeakable acts."

He opened his mouth. Nothing came out except what seemed very much like a pause.

Grace's pouting lips were very, very kissable. Her gaze continued to linger meaningfully.

"Sorry, ma'am." He jumped to his feet faster than an unseated rodeo rider. "I don't do requests."

She rose; so did her voice. "Did I ask?"

Correspondingly, his voice came out as rough as sandpaper. "You asked. Without saying a word."

He flinched when she reached out, but all she did was lightly touch the rodeo buckle he'd won when he'd been nineteen and recklessly immortal. Just the same, he could have sworn she'd reached right inside him, grabbed hold of his heart and gave it a healthy squeeze—it was beating that fast.

"It's a shame," she murmured, tapping a fingernail against the silver buckle. "I always wondered what being the best all-around cowboy entailed."

He stepped away, one of the toughest things he'd ever done. "Nothing illegal," he vowed, then changed that to, "Nothing immoral."

She closed her eyes. "Yes," she said through gritted teeth. "Of course."

"Don't think that I'm not interested, Grace."

Her eyelids cracked.

"I just don't believe in poaching."

"Poaching?"

"On another man's territory."

She faked a laugh. "What is this, the seventeenth century? I'm no one's property, Shane."

"Is that so? Then it must've been me, 'cause I got the distinct feeling that you're not living by your own rules." He touched two fingers to an imaginary Stetson. "Miss Farrow."

Although Grace's eyes widened and her mouth opened as if she wanted to respond, she was speechless. After congratulating himself on *that* accomplishment—no small feat—Shane grabbed the opportunity to saunter out of the room with his dad-blamed morals intact. He was wagering that he could search out the Victorian hellhole on his own, but he'd bet dollars to doughnuts that he wasn't going to get a wink of sleep once there.

5

SOMEHOW, SHE'D TALKED him into a horseback ride.

Not that he could complain. The October day was a dazzler, bursting with sunshine and color, the air so brisk and sharp it cut through the traffic fumes like a knife. They rode along a Central Park bridle path, Grace all gussied up in her English riding costume on her beloved mare, Dulcinea, and Shane, with his hat, denim jacket and Western saddle—well-used, all three—astride Lion. In his opinion, they made a mighty odd pair.

Grace was talking about Lion, sounding as though she might buy him, after all. Shane felt two ways about that. For one, the generous sales price would mean that Ellie would have her chance in San Francisco, and that their mother would finally have a way off the ranch. Then again...

Lion would be gone for good.

As would Grace.

She'd be out of his life either way, Shane reminded himself. Agreeing to a test ride through the park was only a delaying tactic—on both their parts. Grace had been a chatterbox at breakfast, talking a mile a minute to convince him that a horseback ride was in order before he departed. If only she knew it, all she'd had to do was smile and he would have agreed to jump Lion over the Empire State Building. Maybe he was lucky she had no real comprehension of his susceptibility to her charms. Knowing Grace, she'd think leaping tall buildings might be a fun stunt to try.

Knowing Grace? Shane sincerely wished he did. Or could.

"Let's canter!" she said, beaming at him over her shoulder as her bay mare stepped into a rocking-horse lope. It was a very tame gait. Very ladylike. But not very Grace.

Lion snorted and barged after Dulcie, pulling like a plow horse, fighting for his head. Accustomed to long runs across the Goldstream rangeland, the stallion was raring to go. The new surroundings and brisk, sunny weather had his blood up. As did the scent of the strange mare.

Recognizing the feeling, Shane surrendered to the basic male urge for action. He adjusted his hat, let out a short, exuberant whoop and gave Lion a half inch of rein. The stallion shot past Grace's mount like a bullet, his stride lengthening until it ate up the track in voracious leaps and bounds. Grace shouted and leaned low over her mare's withers, urging Dulcie faster, faster. They were game.

The trees gave way to an open space, small by Shane's standards, but spacious enough for a gallop. Even under check, Lion easily outdistanced Dulcie. The field flew by in a golden-brown blink and they entered the quiet wood again. The horses' hoofbeats thudded on thick leafy loam. Squirrels chattered in the trees. The city's roar was reduced to a distant hum.

As the bridle path was unfamiliar, caution should have prevailed. But for once Shane was not concerned with practicality. He sat tight and let his horse canter the twisting path through bushy evergreens, copper-colored maples and the bare limbs of ancient elms.

A disarming happiness accompanied his expanding world. He was suffused with vigor, potency—possibility! Eight hundred acres wasn't nearly enough space to contain him.

Grace shouted something about a road and suddenly Lion reached it, his metal shoes clattering as they entered the dank, black space beneath an arched bridge. With a swish of his tail and a swirl of crackling leaves, the horse bounded toward the daylight on the other side. The bridle path skirted a marsh bristling with cattails, and Shane slowed Lion to a trot, letting Dulcie catch up as the trees became sparse and the pedestrians profuse.

Grace's face was glowing. "You're hell on wheels," she said, laughing through her breathlessness, her eyes bejeweled by the sunshine. "The both of you!"

Shane gathered up the reins, Lion dancing beneath him. "I lost my head."

"But not your hat!" She tapped the hard shell of her black velvet riding helmet, which was buckled beneath her chin. "How'd you manage that?"

He laughed and answered in *Grace!* fashion. "Big brains!"

"Thick skull!"

"Good riding."

With a touch of her boot heel she brought Dulcie up beside Lion, who nickered in welcome and nudged the mare with his nose. "I'll grant you that. You must be one of the rare ranchers who uses horses instead of a helicopter to round up your cattle."

"Goldstream's a small outfit, for sure."

She hunched her shoulders. "What's it like, then?"

Of one accord, their horses had slowed to a walk. Through the scattered trees, Shane watched Canada geese skim across a lake, their wings beating frantically at the water as they lifted off the surface and into a blue vista bordered only by the silver-gray rickrack of Manhattan's skyscrapers. It was like one of those riddle questions, he thought. How tired must a goose be to touch down in the city? How motivated must a cowboy be to bring his best horse to Manhattan?

He shook his head, disgusted with himself. He was making more of this than need be.

"Goldstream Ranch is nothing special except to me," he told Grace, his voice roughened by the effort of containing his profound love of the ranch. "Not enough acreage to compete with the big boys, too rough and remote to appeal to the gentleman farmer."

Her gaze was focused far ahead, as if she were seeing all the way to Wyoming. "Still, I'll bet it's lovely...."

"Yes and no, according to your outlook." He thought of his mother—Lucilla LeGros McHenry, a woman of no great means but many grand illusions. Grander than the ranch, at any rate, or so she'd been saying since she'd first set foot upon it.

Grace was not deterred. "My guess is that it's beautiful."

She seemed exalted by the idea of it. Even though Shane was encouraged by her enthusiasm, he thought it wise to take her down a notch. Her expectations had been colored by Hollywood. "You've seen too many cowboy movies," he said gravely.

Her eyes swiveled in his direction. "And what of it?"

"Real life—"

"Bah humbug! Life is what you make of it!" She jounced in her postage-stamp-size English saddle for emphasis. Dulcie flung her head up and down, curb chain jingling. Lion joined in, arching his neck and tossing his mane. "You see? The horses agree."

"You have no idea what you're talking about."

Suddenly the light went out in Grace's eyes. "You're right. Look what I've made of *my* life."

Shane was startled. "I didn't mean—that is, I wasn't trying to…" He stopped, confused. "You have it all, don't you?"

"Like you said, that depends on your outlook." She settled in her saddle with a sigh. "I have a castle in Manhattan, you have a ranch in Wyoming. Which of us is better off?"

His short laugh was disbelieving.

"I'm not speaking of bank accounts or stock portfolios," she said.

"Sometimes it's hard not to," he replied, then regretted it when he felt a twinge of wounded pride. She was right, though. He was rich in the ways that ultimately mattered the most to him.

Then why did thoughts of the very ranch that used to fill his cup to the brim quickly turn to the loneliness of his quiet life and empty bed? Funny how the bed had begun to seem a lot larger and emptier since he'd met Grace.

Her chin was up, her heels down, her gaze discreetly directed at the tips of Dulcie's ears. "You know, I'm not exactly the daddy's little debutante that you seem to think I am. It's true I have some of the trappings, thanks to a generous trust fund and Gran's apartment. But I work, too, and not at some job that's only a filler till marriage. All Farrows are expected to have careers…some of them admittedly more important than others." Her lashes flickered. "My father was a judge and my mother worked in network news before they both recently retired. My older brother, Victor, is a doctor. Even Caroline works—at least until she gets pregnant. Which according to the Farrow schedule should be any day now.''

No farmers, ranchers or blue collar workers for the Farrows, Shane thought, but all he said was, ''Very impressive.''

''Isn't it?'' Grace sat very still in the saddle, her shoulders squared and her spine rigid as a fence post. Only her chin had come down a notch. ''I'm the family foul-up,'' she confessed in a low voice. ''My dad 'encouraged' me into a year of law school, but I just couldn't hack all that talk of torts and procedures and billable hours.'' Her sharp little chin shot up in the air. ''I didn't want my hours to be billable! I wanted them to have better value than that.''

''So do they?''

She shrugged sheepishly. ''Depends if you think children are Farrow-worthy.''

''Children?'' *Farrow-worthy?*

''I have a staff position with *The Johnny Jump-up Show*. I'm a production assistant, prop master and script supervisor, all rolled up into one.'' She halted Dulcie on a slope beneath the spreading branches of a large elm that had dropped most of its leaves. ''Let's take a break.''

He waited until they'd dismounted and sat down on a small rug she produced from the saddlebags before asking what the heck *The Johnny Jump-up Show* was. It sounded like Grace, though, he thought, admiring the way her freckled face turned like a wildflower toward the warmth of the sun when she took off her helmet and ran her fingers through her tied-back hair.

She talked with her eyes closed, her lashes tipped

red-gold by the sunshine. "I work at a small cable station. We produce thirty minutes—twenty-two minus commercials—of the adventures of Johnny Jump-up and his hand puppets, Ko-Ko and Mr. Niblets. I got the job two years ago through my mom's connections." Her hands fidgeted. "She thought I was interviewing for a position with the news team, but the station's personnel director took a long look at me and my resumé and hired me for *Johnny Jump-up* instead." One eyelid cracked. "Think that means anything?"

Shane nodded. "Yeah, I think that means a lot."

"In the greater scheme of things?"

"I'll leave that judgment up to Him." He pointed at the sky.

Suddenly Grace leaned over and kissed him on the cheek. Her hand squeezed his thigh. "You're a good guy, Shane. All that a cowboy should be."

He reached for her, but she was gone, kneeling over the saddlebags, jabbering about how outings at Camp Skowhegan had taught her to never venture into the wilderness without provisions. Shane looked at his empty hands. When had he lost his reflexes? This was the second time Grace had kissed him and the second time he'd been too slow to expand on the opportunity. She was as quick as a jackrabbit. Too bad he'd left his lasso at the ranch.

She tossed him a can of pop and, wouldn't you know it, his reflexes worked just fine. "The Cowgirl Club's gonna penalize me again," she said with a bemused curve of a smile. "I should have brought canteens."

The pop was still cold; he swigged deeply. "About this Cowgirl Club…"

"Didn't we explain it?" she asked, scowling as she

threaded her fingers together around the soft drink can. Even her frown was cute.

"It sounds…" *Absurd* was what he wanted to say.

"Like something three ten-year-olds would make up when they're at a camp far from home, getting a little homesick and maybe needing the comfort and camaraderie of new friends?"

He was brought up short. "Uh, yeah. That's what I reckoned."

Setting the can aside, Grace rolled onto her stomach and started gathering leaves that had fallen from the elm. "Molly was shy and Laramie was guarded and I was…" Her hands plunged into the heap of dry leaves. "I needed to be somebody. Even if it was only the vice president of a club with three members."

"But why the *Cowgirl* Club when you live in New York City?"

She rolled onto her side and made one of her funny faces at him. "You think only boys like to play cowboy? Not all of us are lucky enough to live in Wyoming, y'know."

"Have you ever set foot on a ranch?"

"Well…Molly and I once spent part of spring break at a dude ra—"

He interrupted. "I meant a working ranch."

"Dude ranches don't qualify, huh, cowboy?"

"It's a whole 'nother species."

"Snob."

"Hey, from what I gather, dude ranching is lucrative. It's just not my preference."

A shout of laughter propelled her back onto her stomach. "Ooh, man, the way you looked when you said *dude ranching*—as if it stunk like a skunk in a funk!" She threw a handful of leaves at him, but since her face was lit up again, gladdening his heart, he didn't care if she buried him in the stuff. She stuck out her tongue. "Shane McHenry, you are a snob!"

"A snob?" he repeated, brushing himself off. "Why, ma'am, that's a new one on me."

"A ranching snob…a country slicker…a he-man-of-the-Wild-Wild-West-and-don't-you-forget-it-little-lady!" she gushed, bobbing her head, stirring the leaves and swinging her heels in the air.

Shane used the brim of his hat to hide his amusement. Her joy was infectious; nothing wrong with that, though it made him feel…unlike himself. He was accustomed to hard living and little luxury, even emotionally.

He glanced around at the unfamiliar surroundings. If his sense of direction hadn't been addled by the confusion of the teeming city, they had made a loop around the reservoir and a good section of the park and were pointed back toward the stable. Lion was tied to a tree, at ease but alert, his ears and eyes swiveling to take in the activity on the paths at the bottom of the slope.

"An honest-to-goodness cowboy," Grace murmured, recapturing Shane's attention. Her chin was in her hands as she looked up at him, marveling again as if he were an endangered species. He supposed that he was, particularly in New York City, but somehow her awe didn't sit right. He didn't want to be a superhuman icon, especially to her.

"All right, you've made your point," he said. "And just so you know, I have nothing in particular against dude ranches. I simply wouldn't want to run one myself." Or, heaven forbid, see Goldstream turned into one—even if the comfortable lifestyle would have better suited the female side of his family.

Grace sat up. "There are lots and lots of people

who can't live on ranches but still want a taste of the authentic Western experience...."

Then don't send them to a dude ranch, he thought.

She caught his eye. "Yes, I know, what most of them actually want is a romanticized, sanitized version of the real thing. But what's wrong with that? Tourism keeps many a failing ranch afloat."

"In one form or another."

"Watch out. You're getting that skunky look again...." Grinning, she pinched her nostrils.

"Point made and *taken,*" he emphasized, redirecting his gaze down the leaf-strewn slope. Runners, power-walkers and bicyclists clogged the road. Loiterers lolled on benches, basking in the sun. A noisy game of touch football was being played on a flat expanse of grass off in the distance.

Grace nudged him with her elbow. "Not so bad, is it, country boy? No muggers or gang-bangers in sight."

"Not much like *NYPD Blue,*" he admitted.

"I could make a point out of that, but I'm far too big a person to stomp all over your faulty logic, Mr. You've-Watched-Too-Many-Movies." She dragged the saddlebags across the rug. "I won't even comment about all the tourists who take a bite out of the Big Apple like it was one big dude-ranch-slash-amusement-park. Want one?"

He confronted the apple she held in front of his face. "Your middle name's not Eve, is it?"

"No," she said, making a smoochy shape with her lips to coax him into a bite, "but be forewarned. I'm seething with sinful desires just the same."

"A regular big city temptress?"

Her eyes glittered. "Oh, I certainly hope so! I've always coveted the power to corrupt."

"I'd prefer not to be your victim." He snatched the apple off her outstretched palm and tossed it toward the horses. Lion gave a nervous little hop, then caught the fruity scent and nosed through the leaves in search of the apple. His strong teeth crunched it up in two bites.

"Not very nice."

Shane looked at Grace.

She didn't smile. "Lion didn't even share it with Dulcie."

"Listen, Grace. You—you're engaged."

"Yes. As I recall, we settled that question last night."

"Did we?"

"Sure." She held up her left hand. "I even wore my ring so there'd be no question." They both looked at her ring finger.

Make that her ring*less* finger.

Grace's eyes darted toward his fly, for no good reason that Shane could see. He definitely would've remembered if her nimble fingers had approached such a sensitive region a second time. "Oh, no, my ring!" she said, a beat too late and a shade too dramatically, leading him to wonder if her engagement was all it was cracked up to be. Her distress lacked...commitment.

Grace had spun around and was flinging handfuls of crisp autumn leaves this way and that. "It must have slipped off my finger."

"Again? Maybe your fiancé ought to get the thing sized." He would if she was his woman. Maybe even make the ring a half size too small, to ensure a snug fit.

"It fits." She had cleared away most of the leaves she'd been playing with and was running her hands

over the patchy grass and dirt. "It fits perfectly fine."
Bits of leaf and twig were sprinkled in her hair and
up and down the sleeves of her houndstooth jacket.
Shane leaned closer to pluck a crumpled gum wrapper
out of her collar, in time to hear her mutter under her
breath, "But it itches."

"The ring itches?"

She glanced over her shoulder. "Well, no. My finger does. I might be allergic." Turning aside to peel
up the corner of the rug, she added, again under her
breath, "Allergic to being a Farrow."

She hopped up, forestalling Shane's comment.
"We've got to find that ring!" she declared, trying
to tug the rug out from beneath him. "It's six carats
of expensive. Michael cashed in some of his stocks
to buy the gaudy thing."

*True love, upwardly mobile urban professional ver-
sion.* Shane got to his feet and brushed off his jeans,
wondering why Grace seemed worried only about the
ring's monetary value. She didn't come off as superficial otherwise, so her lack of sentiment might mean
that she didn't particularly value her fiancé, either.

"And Michael cherishes his Intel stock like a
baby," she continued, upending the pop cans as she
shook out the rug. Brown flecks of crumbled leaves
showered down like confetti, but there was no sign
of the ring. "He's gonna kill me."

"You could have lost it anywhere." Shane didn't
feel very sympathetic. He glanced back the way
they'd come, through woods and fields and ditches.
"Eight hundred acres, you said?"

"Eight hundred forty-three!" she wailed. "But
wait—I had it when we sat down. It was starting to
itch again, so I slid it around my finger a few times
and then, let's see, I took out the soda, which was

cold, so I rubbed my finger against the can and then—"

"At some point, you threw a handful of leaves at me."

She eyed his open collar. "You don't suppose..." Her gaze dropped to his belt buckle.

"No!"

She sidled over to him, the corners of her mouth twitching with suppressed laughter. "You're sure...?" She motioned along the length of his legs, clearly offering to feel for six-carat lumps.

He wanted her hands on him so badly that he definitely couldn't let her get her hands on him. "I'm sure!" he barked, his face hot. "I would have felt it!" Cripes, Grace's exclamations were catching.

"One would think." She gave his jeans a lingering inspection, then abruptly dropped to her knees. "Here's what we do. There's only about five square feet to cover. I'll start here on my hands and knees and you begin on that side and we'll meet in the middle. If we're careful, we can't possibly overlook the diamond." She started sifting through the leaves on her elbows and knees, nose hovering near the grass, bottom thrust up in the air.

He allowed himself a short survey of her rounded contours before looking deliberately up at the sky. He swallowed, trying to convince himself that he didn't feel what he was feeling. And that he didn't mind groveling in the dirt to rescue another man's engagement ring as a favor to a woman he wasn't feeling anything for.

"Yuk." Grace buried a snail beneath a handful of crusty leaves. She probed the grass, dislodging a pebble. "I could use some help here. Cowboys are supposed to be chivalrous."

He took a few careful steps and knelt across from her. "What gave you that idea?"

She shot him a quick smile. "Movies. Books. Legend."

He stirred the scattered leaves. "I don't recall any Westerns where the hero had to get down on his hands and knees to search for another man's engagement ring."

"We can gloss over that part of our plot."

"Not if I'm chivalrous." They were close enough now that he caught a whiff of her vanilla perfume. Enough to make it impossible to deny what he was feeling. Bad omen. He'd never before been turned on by a cinnamon bun.

He cleared his throat. "Remember what happened to Sir Lancelot."

Grace kept her head down. All he could see was the froth of her kinky ponytail and the crooked white line of her part. "Now you're talking knights in shining armor. A different genre altogether." She paused thoughtfully. "Sort of."

Shane rolled aside one of the leaking pop cans to reveal the diamond ring, plastered in muck. For an instant he thought of passing by as if he hadn't seen it, maybe even grinding it into the soft earth with a careless kneecap, but of course he couldn't. "Found it," he said, plucking the ring out of a clump of leaf debris. "Here you go. It's kinda sticky."

Grace sat back on her heels. "Wonderful." No exclamation point. She took the ring gingerly. "You saved my life."

Or condemned it? Shane wondered, knowing he shouldn't be thinking along those lines. No use setting his sights on her when he was leaving as soon as possible. Maybe today, but tomorrow for sure. Unless he wanted to avoid the weekend tourist traffic. Monday, then. He'd definitely leave by Monday.

"Yuk," Grace said, wiping the smudged diamond in the grass.

Shane looked away. "The horses are getting restless. We should return to the stable."

"Right." Frowning, she held the ring up between two fingertips. "I hate to ask, but I don't have a pocket that buttons, so d'you think you could, like, keep the ring for me? It's too disgusting to wear, but I don't want to risk losing it again." She peered hopefully into his eyes, her brow furrowed, her lips sweetly puckered.

"I guess…"

"Thanks." Her smile widened as she reached for him. He unbuttoned the pocket of his denim jacket. Instead she went straight for the breast pocket of his blue flannel shirt, her fingers light and nimble and yet completely provocative, just the way he remembered from her previous "strip search." A steel band wound around his ribs as she slid the ring into his pocket and snapped it shut, her head bowed near his so that when he inhaled, her scent was inside him, vanilla and sunshine and exotic, pampered female flesh. The steel band tightened as he drank her in, and still he couldn't stop because she was another man's fiancée and this was all he could ever have of her, only this, the fierce, poignant ache of wanting Grace as his.

She snapped the flap shut. And patted the pocket, three taps, right over his heart. "Safe and sound."

His chest felt so tight he couldn't speak. He nodded instead.

Grace stood and lifted off his hat. Her lips touched his forehead. "You are my knight in faded denim."

Engaged, engaged, she's engaged, Shane told himself over and over again until at last she'd stepped out of arm's reach.

RESTLESSNESS MOVED through Grace like ripples in water. She'd always been the fidgety sort, never one to sit still, quiet and ladylike, though heaven knew she'd been forced to on more occasions than she cared to count. Luckily this wasn't one of them, because she was likely to jump right out of her skin if she had to keep docile while waiting for the Lancelot of Honorable Intentions to make a move on her!

Her custom-built cowboy didn't know from opportunities. And she'd been throwing them at him hand over fist.

Probably it was a good thing that one of them had the iron to stick to his guns. She thought of her diamond ring and how she'd been dearly tempted to toss it to the squirrels and call herself nuts rather than face the chore of putting it back on her darned itchy finger.

Instead she'd wimped out all around, and by all rights should have now been stricken with guilt. That she wasn't meant it was *she* who was the skunk—phewie! A two-timing skunk, even though technically she and Shane hadn't done anything wrong. Which was more to his credit than hers, so no doubt she qualified as a two-timing skunk-in-the-making. Unless straying eyes and infidelity of the heart counted against her. Which they did, she admitted when her gaze turned longingly to Shane's strong profile as he replaced his hat. Oh, he most certainly did. Big-time.

He turned to appraise her, his expression so intent, his eyes so hungry that it was clear his chivalry had not been born of disinterest. She leaned against Dulcie's warm flank as her untethered heart took a long slow glide into the pit of her stomach. For all her frivolity, she was not unaware. Beneath her flip exterior, she *knew*.

What was happening between her and Shane was serious. And immensely significant.

Grace reacted as always—on impulse. "Here's an idea," she announced, squaring her shoulders to deflect his sure objection. "I shall ride Lion back to the stable!"

Shane did object, but she pooh-poohed his every concern. He said a tryout within a fenced arena would be safer. Affronted, she pointed out that she'd been riding since the age of eight and jumping since she was eleven. He hesitated, so she simply stood there and smiled up at him expectantly, batting her lashes, knowing she looked cute as a button in her fitted jacket and tight white breeches.

He gave in. Awfully fast. Maybe he suspected that her next move would be toward him.

Determined to seem capable, she brushed aside his offer of a leg up. Putting her foot into the clunky leather stirrup of the Western saddle, she grabbed the tooled pommel and with a bounce propelled herself up, *up,* up, onto Lion's back. The horse's ears pricked with interest at her light weight. While Shane adjusted her stirrups, she took up the reins to let the stallion get the feel of her hands on his mouth.

"All set." Shane took her heel in his hand and placed her booted foot into the shortened stirrup. There was a carefulness—a caring—about the act that made her breath catch. "Be smart now," he warned, getting all solemn and me-big-mannish. "Remember what I said—Lion's not a plaything."

She turned the horse in a neat circle, showing off

a little. "There, you see, Mr. Worrywart?" She patted Lion's neck. "We'll do just fine together."

"But you're not used to a Western saddle."

"Whaddya mean? This thing is as big and comfy as an easy chair. I couldn't fall out of it if I tried."

Shane's grin held a grudging admiration. "I think you could do anything you set your mind to."

"Exactly!" She pressed her heels to the horse's sides. Lion stepped into a smart, tail-swishing walk. "It's you who's going to have problems with a strange saddle. But don't worry, Dulcie will stop when you fall off." She laughed gaily as Shane hurried over to mount the patient bay mare.

He urged Dulcie into a trot to catch up, the loose irons dangling against his shins. "Let's show him," Grace whispered to Lion, easing her hands higher up on the stallion's neck. Their pace grew brisker.

The earlier exercise had mellowed Lion out. Despite her awkwardness in the Western saddle, he responded to her aids like a trained-to-perfection show horse, doing extended trots and flying lead changes without turning a hair. He even popped over a log and leapt a small ditch, putting Grace at her confident best. She rose in the stirrups as they galloped, loving the thrill, every muscle charged with adrenaline. *This is living!* she shouted inside, turning to shoot a smile at Shane. Speed, action, freedom, a custom-built cowboy at her side—what more could an urban cowgirl ask for? How had she survived so long without it? For that matter, now that she knew what she was missing, how could she succumb to Farrowdom ever after?

It was a sobering question. By the time they'd slowed to a cooling walk as they left the park and crossed busy city streets to reach the stable, Grace had decided that her first step would be purchasing Lion. Keeping the horse might be the best way to keep the cowboy. She didn't quite dare think beyond that.

She regarded Shane cautiously; he'd hung back on Dulcie, giving her room to ride even as he kept a close eye on her. "So, cowboy, what did you think?"

The horses' shoes clip-clopped on the concrete. "You were adequate," Shane said after a long pause.

Her nose wrinkled. "Adequate!"

"Not bad," he conceded with a tug of his hat brim. "For a city girl."

She tipped up her chin. "I'll take that as a compliment—laconic cowboy style."

They passed beneath the stable's brick archway. Shane brought Dulcie alongside Lion. "I meant it as a compliment." He looked her up and down until she could no longer pretend that the flush of her skin had come from the damp heat of exertion rising off their horses. Fanning herself, Grace sneaked a peek at him from the corner of her eye. He winked when he caught her; she broke out into goose bumps. Was that even possible? she wondered, astonished by her uncontrollable reactions to this man. She had to laugh. Possible or not, one thing was clear—Shane McHenry had her running hot and cold and every degree in between!

They halted. She swung her leg over Lion's hindquarters and dropped to the ground, then reached up to loosen the saddle. The girth was a wide ribbon of leather wrapped through a metal ring, and she struggled to free it, finally diving under the skirted stirrup so she could use both hands.

Suddenly Shane was there, flipping back the stirrup, laying one of his big hands over both of hers.

Her pulse skipped. "I've got it," she insisted, digging her fingertips beneath the knotted leather strap.

"You don't have to prove yourself to me."

She hesitated, her eyes downcast, surrendering to their simmering attraction for just one moment. Then she tossed her head defiantly. "Hell, yes, I most certainly do!" Worming her forefinger under the strap, she tugged until it loosened. "There, you see? I've got it. No problem."

Shane squeezed her hand. "Right. No problem." He looked concerned nonetheless. She hadn't meant to engage his sympathy, but since she had it anyway...

"Uh, say," she ventured, "is there any possibility you can stick around awhile longer?"

"What did you have in mind?"

"A week? Several days? Overnight?"

He frowned. "I meant why?"

"Well, I do believe I've changed my mind about buying Lion, and there's this big horse show coming up in November. I've been trying to win a class there for a decade, but something unexpected always happens and I end up unseated, disgraced, humiliated...."

"Like what happens?"

"Like my pony, Pippin, eating the brush jump, or like me taking a dive into the water jump, or like my horse bolting at the screech of the loudspeaker...."

"Doesn't sound so bad. Those things happen at every show."

She groaned. "Like having my girth break in the middle of an equitation class so the saddle slowly slides sideways with me still clinging to it until I'm practically perpendicular to the ground...." She held up her hands to demonstrate, the fingertips of one angled into the vertical palm of the other. "And Dulcie's so well trained, she just kept cantering along...." Her fingers galloped up her palm and then made the leap onto Shane's denim jacket, dancing along the line of his shoulder. Using her left hand, too, she straightened his worn suede collar with an affectionate tug, unaware of the soft puckering of her lips until she saw his deep swallow.

The air thickened between them as the current of mutual attraction began to flow. She touched a wondering fingertip to his Adam's apple, smiling a little when it bobbed. The intimacy of the tiny movement caused a light shiver to skate along her spine.

"I need you," she said, her throat growing tight. "I need..."

Her gaze bounced to her ring finger, resting so glaringly unbejeweled on his chest.

"A coach," she blurted, withering inside. Why did she lose her daring when it mattered most? "And a magnificent horse like Lion. Think what a splash we'd make."

Shane stepped back, carelessly brushing her hands away. "If you intend to compete on Lion so soon, I can guarantee that the only splash you make will involve the water obstacle."

"That's why I need you as my coach. Even if it's only for a little while. You know the horse, you can give me the sort of valuable pointers that will speed up my learning process."

"I'm a rancher, Grace. I don't have any business being involved in your type of fancy-dress, silver-cup competitions."

"But *Vermilion* does."

With one jerk, Shane released the girth. The hollows in his cheeks deepened as he set his jaw, apparently determined not to respond.

Grace insisted. "At least we ought to give him the chance."

"We?"

"Yes." She nodded. "You and me and Lion. A team."

Shane stared at the stable wall as if he were counting its bricks. "Sounds like a screwy idea to me."

"I'm rather well known for my screwy ideas."

He shook his head. "Is that supposed to make me agree?"

She smoothed Lion's forelock. "Hey, it'll be a story to tell the boys back home."

"I've already seen more than enough of New York to entertain the fellas at the Thunderhead Saloon."

She whooped. "The Thunderhead Saloon! I love it! Promise me you'll take me there someday, huh, cowboy?" She gave Shane an impulsive hug, lassoing him with her linked arms. He looked rather rattled beneath his Stetson, probably because he'd realized that she'd decided he was going to stay and there was nothing he could do but give in. His innate sense of chivalry had him hog-tied...and at her mercy.

6

TWO MORNINGS LATER, Grace walked gingerly into the kitchen with her hands over her ears. Shane was on the telephone. She didn't mean to eavesdrop, but she was starving. And almost late for work.

He nodded hello, his gaze lingering on her short skirt, nude panty hose and the Manolo Blahnik heels that had cost a small fortune but were apparently worth it. "Tell Hank we'll bring the rest of the herd down from the high pasture when I get back," he said into the phone, sounding distracted. Little wonder. They'd spent Sunday on horseback, so not only had he never seen her bare legs before, he'd never seen them in a skirt that was Ally McBeal short. "No, the thigh—the *high* pasture," he said. "Yeah, he knows what to do. The yearlings will be sold."

His gaze followed Grace as she opened a plastic sack of bagels and began inserting them into her nifty bagel-slicing machine one by one. She walked to the refrigerator, every move slow and deliberate, but not because she was showing off her legs. Tugging the fridge door open made her wince; bending to reach inside prompted a soft moan.

"No," Shane said. The telephone receiver emitted squawky, high-pitched tones that were not quite discernible as words. "Not yet." He closed his eyes briefly. "Don't push it, Mom."

Grace set containers of lox, cream cheese, butter-

flavored spread and Zabar's wild gooseberry jam—
twenty bucks a pop—on the tiled island countertop.
All day yesterday Shane had been a no-nonsense
horse trainer, putting her and Lion through their paces
as if the fate of the free world depended on them
taking a set of rails in stride. As a result, her evening
had been spent in a hot bath working the kinks out
instead of showing Shane the city in all its nighttime
splendor as she'd intended. The missed opportunity
hadn't seemed to bother him. She even suspected that
he'd planned it that way.

Another blow to her ego, along with her spectacular double somersault off Lion's left shoulder when
the horse had refused a small oxer at the last possible
second. She'd completed the jump—independent of
her mount. Ergo the bruises on her butt.

"A few more days, I'd say." Shane moved his
head closer to the hook of the wall phone as if desperate to hang up. "Hank can handle it...."

From steely trainer to put-upon son in one fell
swoop, Grace thought. She rubbed her sore rump.
Served him right.

"Yes. No. Goodbye," he said firmly, and hung up
midsquawk. He saw Grace watching and shrugged.
"Mothers."

"Mine's been in Africa for three weeks." She
smiled. "That's why I'm smiling."

He drew his stool over to the island, where a cup
of the dense black motor-oil glunk he'd taken to
brewing in her high-tech espresso machine was trying
to eat its way through Gran's bone china. "Is that
so?"

She shook her head. "Not really. I get along quite
well with my parents, as long as I'm not engaging in
scandalous behavior and am meeting their expecta-

tions at least halfway. Even when I go renegade, like dropping out of law school, they're not into imposing guilt trips. I do that to myself." She shrugged. "My father's the stone-cold-stare-of-disapproval type. Mom only sighs—maintaining composure is important to her."

"Then you must be an alien baby, 'cause…" He gestured, palms up, as if the very fact of her was incomprehensible.

"Alien baby? That's a hoot!" She frowned instead of smiling. "I suppose you're right, though. I'm frequently not as Farrow as I should be."

"Hmm, I don't know." Shane sipped the motor oil. "Your parents are in Africa, your grandmother eloped and this apartment is sort of eccentric.…"

"Farrows are traditionally adventurers. Unfortunately my tastes run opposed to the family-approved itinerary." She thought of all the cowboy movies, holiday brochures and travel-channel documentaries she'd ingested over time. "Although I've yet to completely indulge myself." Her eyes went to Shane. *Even when my best chance is six feet tall and sitting across from me, big as life.*

She concentrated on spreading cream cheese on a bagel. "But how did we wind up talking about the Farrows again? I wanted to ask about your family."

He shifted. "I thought I told you—"

"Umm, let's see." She licked a dab of cheese off her pinkie. "You said it's just you and your mom and sister, right?"

"Since I was seventeen." Shane glanced at the morning edition of the *New York Express* he'd retrieved from her doormat, but he was obviously too polite to pick it up and hide behind the finance section the way Michael did whenever she geared up for a probing emotional discussion—which was not too often since she'd learned that her fiancé's opinions were remarkably similar to her dad's.

"What happened when you were seventeen?" she asked, slicing and toasting enough bagels to supply a chuckwagon.

"My father was killed in a lightning storm."

"Struck?" she squeaked, rising up off her stool.

"Not exactly. He was caught out in the high open country we lease from the BLM—Bureau of Land Management—and he used the only tree in sight for shelter. When a wicked lightning strike split it in two, he was pinned by one of the fallen branches. Died of injuries and exposure. We didn't find him till the next morning."

"Oh, gosh. I'm so sorry—"

Shane waved his hand to forestall her sympathy. "Do you see what I mean about the danger of your Hollywood-fed Wild West fantasies? Reality isn't so pretty. My father had lived in Wyoming for more than a decade by then and he still hadn't learned—" He cut himself off.

She sank back onto the stool. "I understand." He was saying that pretend cowgirls weren't welcome on the McHenry ranch.

"Stick to dude ranches, Grace. If my father had recognized his limitations and done the same he'd probably be sitting in an easy chair right now, watching a John Wayne movie."

She offered him half a toasted bagel. "Nothing like *tsuris* for breakfast, hmm?"

His eyebrows cocked.

"Anxiety," she said, nibbling as though her stomach wasn't knotted up with it. He had a point. But what good was staying safe if you weren't living your dreams? That day in the park, riding Lion, she'd had the merest sip of how life with Shane could be and it had intoxicated her beyond even her most fantastic expectations. She wasn't ready to give up just because he insisted on acting unresponsive.

"So then you took over the ranch and made a go of it," she continued. "What's your mother's story?"

"Why do you need to know?"

"Call me curious."

"Nosy," he said, but his eyes were smiling.

"I'm not nosy, I'm interested. I like people and I like to talk. I know the life stories of everyone in the Castle. Starting at the top," she said, pointing upward. "Charlotte Colfax, in the tower penthouse. Dr. Mrs. Colfax-Quinn, I should say—she just got her Ph.D. *and* a new husband. One floor down are the Applebaums, married fifty-two years. He started a button company out of nothing and she was his secretary. Across from them are Queenie and George, who've been divorced for three years, but neither will give up the apartment so they've split it into his and hers sections. Then there's Eddie, from the elevator. His hobby is taxidermy. I've had him in to see the trophy room and now he covets Granddaddy's wildebeest, Zanzibar. Asks after it every time I see him." She paused to take a breath. "Shall I go on?"

"You'd really tell me about everyone in the building, wouldn't you?"

"I'd rather listen. Remember, I've never met a real cowboy before...."

Shane reached for the gooseberry jam, as she'd known he would. Twenty bucks was a small price to pay to satisfy a cowboy's sweet tooth. "Okay, you win," he said reluctantly. "My mother was a small-town girl dying to get out of the Midwest. She thought marrying Ray McHenry would do it, but she miscalculated. By turn, my father thought he was marrying a sensible girl with homespun values. He miscalculated, too.''

''Were they unhappy?''

''They were…dissatisfied. The marriage survived, but they weren't cut out for ranching. Not for the long haul. If their finances and the real-estate market hadn't taken a downturn and left them stuck at Goldstream, they probably would have cashed out and moved on.''

''And so you grew up a cowboy,'' Grace mused. ''Hey,'' she exclaimed, ''who are you calling an alien baby?''

''Not me. I'm at home on the ranch. It's where I've always known I belonged.''

''How do you know for sure?'' She spread her hands. ''You haven't tried anything else!''

He looked uncomfortable. ''I've tried New York City.''

''Not yet you haven't.'' She leaned over the kitchen island, fired with enthusiasm. ''Listen, why don't I show you the sights? You haven't seen New York if you haven't seen it from the Statue of Liberty and the Rainbow Room. I can show you the Frick and Tribeca and my favorite French bistro.…''

''What about your job? For that matter, what about your fiancé?''

''Um,'' she mumbled, stalling. Michael had called Friday night to square their schedules for the weekend; she'd said she was busy with the arrival of her new horse, and he'd been relieved because that way he could work all day Saturday and on Sunday accompany his buddies to a game at the Meadowlands without suffering any residual relationship guilt. ''Michael and I often have conflicting schedules. We spend time together when we can.''

Shane frowned. ''And you two are supposed to be in love?''

''Supposed to be,'' she said, turning away to put the food back in the fridge.

He watched her in silence, then said, ''I think it's better if I'm on my own today. I have things to do.''

''Such as?''

''Laundry. I didn't pack many clothes and I've run out.'' He was wearing a white cotton undershirt tucked into faded blue jeans; she'd already noticed how very nicely both garments defined his muscles and brought out the toasty hue of his weathered skin.

''Oh.'' She peered over the island to examine him more closely, catching her lower lip between her teeth at the sight of the faded jeans that fit him tight as the hide on a cow. *Oh.* ''Boxers or briefs?''

Shane hesitated. ''Neither...at the moment.''

Oh my... She arched her brows. ''Going commando?''

He stood. ''I'm just going, period.''

''Wait! I could take you on a shopping spree.'' She was flustered enough to lose track of what she was saying. ''There's a Hugo Boss—'' Shane was shaking his head. ''No, you're right, you're not the three-piece-suit type. But I'm sure we can find jeans and, and, er, unmentionables at—'' He was still shaking his head. ''Right,'' she said, and jerked her thumb over her shoulder. ''The laundry room's down the hall and to the left. Feel free.''

''Thanks.''

She had to leave for work. She didn't want to go; she had a sneaking suspicion Shane might take off for good if she let him out of her sight. ''Are you sure you'll be okay in the city on your own? Maybe you ought to avoid the subway—you're bound to attract unwanted attention if you wear that cowboy hat. And don't be taken in by the panhandlers—some of them are professionals.'' She snapped her fingers. ''I hear that taxi drivers swindle tourists—you'd better not take a cab, either.''

''Then I guess I'll have to saddle up Lion if I want to get anywhere.''

''Are you positive you don't want me—''

''Go,'' he said.

He was positive. Just her luck!

''THERE'S A COWBOY in my house,'' Grace said to her boss, Troy Kazjakian, producer-director of the cable station's *The Johnny Jump-up Show,* among others. Troy was fifty, but so trim and impeccably hip that he could pass for thirty. Grace and he had been fast friends ever since he'd wangled her some killer reservations at Balthazar for Michael's birthday. Today they'd taken fifteen minutes away from the madhouse of the studio to go over the day's scripts and production schedule. The show wouldn't begin taping for another half hour and the public school studio audience was getting cranky with the wait.

Troy's fountain pen didn't so much as hesitate at her offhand announcement. ''Grace, Grace, Grace,'' he said, making rapid check marks. ''You and your cowboys. What is it this time? A Texas redneck with bad fashion sense or merely a life-size movie poster of Clint Eastwood?''

''Shane's a genuine cowboy. A rancher.''

''Shane?'' Troy echoed with a give-a-boy-a-break expression.

''Shane McHenry from Treetop, Wyoming. And

get this…'' She lowered her voice. "He's in my house as we speak and *he's not wearing any underwear.*"

"Why, you bad girl!" Troy flicked a paper clip at her. "Let me guess. You've finally deep-sixed your stuffy fiancé and called 1-800-FANTASY for relief."

She rolled her eyes. "It's not like that."

"Then woe is you."

"It's *better* than that."

"Meaning?"

"I told you. Shane's the real deal. He's the cowboy of my dreams. He's six feet of muscle and brawn, all wrapped up in denim and leather and macho pride. He's somewhat closemouthed, maybe even shy, but he's also straightforward, honest and kind. He even has a sneaky sense of humor. Plus…" She paused, her moony expression reflecting her drifting thoughts.

"Plus?"

She nearly purred. "Okay, so he's also the closest thing to paradise I've ever seen. He makes my mouth water. He sends my cowboy fantasies into overdrive. Even 1-800-FANTASY couldn't have done better."

"Really." Troy leaned back in his swivel chair and stroked his blond highlighted goatee in thoughtful Sigmund Freud style, which, as he often pointed out, was the entire purpose of having a goatee. "Veddy interesting," he said in a bad Viennese accent, one neat eyebrow forming a diabolical peak. "And is zee missing diamond as obvious a clue as one vould assume…?"

"Zee missing diamond." Grace looked down at her hand. Right. She'd never taken the ring back from Shane; it must be buttoned into his shirt pocket, utterly neglected. She rolled her eyes. No Freudian symbolism there, folks!

"I'm still engaged," she said. And maybe around sixty percent sure that marrying Michael was the right thing to do. "The ring is being...cleaned." She hoped it survived the spin cycle.

"Then this 'cowboy' of yours—" Troy made little quotation marks in the air "—is just a weekend fling?"

Grace jumped up and tossed away the plastic dish of congealed Thai noodles that was supposed to have been her lunch. The shows they were taping all this week would carry them through next month's schedule; traditionally, the hectic pace meant that she survived on coffee and adrenaline and snatched bites of cold burritos or stale sandwiches. Skimping on lunch didn't normally make her feel so hollow inside.

"He's not a fling," she said. Her voice was low-pitched and slightly tremulous; she'd recognized exactly how important Shane had become to her.

"Grace, sweetie, sometimes you gotta ride the buckin' bronco," Troy said, missing her gravity altogether. "As long as I've known you, you've had this thing for cowboys. If you've actually roped one—" the director's tone of voice said he was still skeptical on that point, but he was willing to use up all his cowboy colloquialisms anyway "—then sure as shootin' it's time to strap on the spurs and climb aboard. What does the Cowgirl Club say?"

Molly and Laramie had hung out at the riding stable all of yesterday afternoon, ostensibly watching Grace's training session. They were as gaga over Shane as she; they hadn't said much besides an awestruck "Holy cowboy!" now and then.

Grace turned. "Why is everyone ignoring the fact that I have a fiancé? And a family who expects my June wedding to proceed as scheduled?"

Elbows on his desk, Troy flipped his palms toward the ceiling. "You tell me, sweetie."

"There's no forgetting I'm a Farrow." She bit her lip. "Not for me."

She might have said more, but the door opened and Jenny Price, the go-getting Columbia intern who had serious designs on Grace's job, poked her surgically snubbed nose inside. "You guys have to see this." She waved her clipboard, a perfect match for Troy's. "C'mon, quick."

Grace cocked her head. By the sound of it, their studio audience had fallen asleep. She checked her wristwatch. Nap time? Not the optimal situation for taping a children's comedy show.

"Johnny was warming up the audience, but the kids weren't responding too well," Jenny whispered as they hurried out to the studio. The actor who played the clownish Johnny Jump-Up wore an eye-ball-zapping purple suit with electric yellow checks, polka dots and stripes; usually he had no problem warming up an audience. "Then he spotted this guy dressed as a cowboy standing off to one side, so he called the cowboy over and, well...see for yourself."

"*Shane,*" Grace said, stunned by the sight of him.

Troy's eyes bugged out. "This is Shane?"

The eight-year-olds that made up a typical Johnny Jump-up audience were rapt with attention, which took some mighty strong mojo, in Grace's experience. Shane, in his boots and hat and the worn denim jacket with the suede collar, was standing beside the actor who played Johnny, telling the kids what it was like to be a cowboy in Wyoming. Grace would have thought he'd be ill at ease, but he wasn't. He was captivating.

"Up in the Rockies, there are bull elk with antlers

this long." He extended his arms. "There're golden eagles, coyote, mountain lions. Bighorn sheep. Snowshoe rabbits white as a blizzard and quicker than a blink."

Troy silently signaled to one of the cameramen to begin taping. In response to a question from a little boy in the first row, Shane talked about famous cowboys, both real and not-so-real. He told a tale about the legendary Blue-Eyed Slim, who was the best cowboy in the Wyoming territories even though he'd lost an eye and half an ear to the claws of a grizzly bear when he was ten years old. Blue-Eyed Slim had once lassoed a bobcat just to prove that he could rope anything that moved. "But the toughest part about ropin' a bobcat," Shane told the kids with a charming grin, "is lettin' him go again."

Grace watched, mesmerized by her custom-built cowboy all over again. Pretty quickly she was imagining Shane with children of his own. He'd be one of those strict but loving dads, the kind who demanded hard work and discipline, but was really just a big old softie inside. Sometimes way deep inside, she acknowledged, thinking of her own father, Judge Arthur Farrow.

If she hadn't known that ultimately her dad would forgive her, she would never have dared quit law school. So…could she risk disappointing him and her mother again by choosing not to marry Michael?

Because suddenly, as she looked at Shane with starry eyes, feeling her heart swell with overwhelming emotion, the odds that her Farrow-approved marriage would take place were no better than even.

THE RING.

The engagement ring popped into Grace's mind

sometime after midnight, when she was tucked in bed but still wide awake. Seeing as how she couldn't sleep anyway, and since it was possible she'd forget again by morning, why not get the ring now, while she was thinking about it? If retrieving her six-carat-commitment-to-Farrowhood meant that she had to sneak into Shane's bedroom and maybe wake him up, well, then, so be it.

She really had to have that man—er, that *ring*. She really had to have that ring.

She slid out of bed, recoiling when her bare feet touched the cold marble floor. When she'd moved into Gran's apartment, she'd taken up the venerable Oriental carpet in the bedroom and replaced it with an inadequate scattering of Navajo rugs. Using her toes, she felt around in the dark for her favorite fuzzy slippers. Going on a midnight foray through a darkened apartment to retrieve her engagement ring from a man who wasn't her fiancé was a very, very bad idea. She'd better do it quickly.

With her hands tucked into her armpits, she tiptoed through the hallway to the guest-room door, which she inched open. A light, pleasantly masculine snore told her that Shane was asleep. Hormonal *tsuris* didn't have *him* tossing and turning.

Shuffling like Mr. Snuffalupagus, she moved to the bed, unable to resist a peek. Shane's face was turned toward the window. Its curtains had been left open and the city lights played like moonlight across his pillow, casting his profile in silver. The bedclothes were drawn up to his chin, but one bare arm emerged to curl around his head, his fingertips resting lightly near his temple. Grace yearned to crawl up beside him and wind her arms around his waist and feel his skin warm against hers, and his hands, and, oh, yes, his mouth, too....

Hey, cowboy, wake up and kiss me. She placed a hand on the bedding, depressing the mattress slightly. Shane muttered unintelligibly and turned, making her hop backward, away from the bed, away from him.

She pressed her fists against her face. *I can't do it.* Much as she wanted to take advantage of the situation, she couldn't—she was bound by the obligatory Farrowlike decorum. And there was no easy way out of it.

Think about the ring.

Earlier, she'd forgotten to ask Shane about the ring. He'd stayed at the television studio all afternoon, assuring her that he was enjoying watching her run around like a beheaded chicken trying to keep Johnny, the audience and the cameras all rolling in the right direction. Afterward they'd gone out to dinner with Troy. Despite an uneasy introduction to sushi, Shane had been as relaxed as Grace had ever seen him. Under Troy's slick direction, bantering conversation (Shane said if he could eat raw fish, they could eat Rocky Mountain oysters, which she'd been alarmed to learn were not oysters at all) and amusing anecdotes had flowed like a hundred-dollar bottle of wine. By dessert, she was liking Shane more than ever, all but positive that they'd reached a new level of understanding in their fledgling relationship.

Not so. Mr. Custom-Built had ended the evening by declining her offer of a nightcap and abruptly closing himself up in the guest room as if they had no relationship at all, fledgling or otherwise. As if they hadn't been exchanging hot, bothered, scorching looks during the cab ride home. As if she hadn't felt her lips tingling just thinking about kissing him.

Think of the ring instead, Grace. Where's the ring?

Dutifully resolute, she crossed to the walnut bureau and opened the top drawer. Socks and white cotton briefs, all freshly laundered. No ring.

Next drawer. By touch, she identified clean, folded jeans and a couple of soft T-shirts from Shane's scant wardrobe. A handkerchief—no, a blue bandanna, she realized, pulling it out. She tied it around her neck, squinting at her reflection in the dark mirror to get the knot right. Not bad. Very Dale Evans jaunty. But still no ring.

The third drawer was empty except for a floral liner paper that smelled faintly of clove cigarettes and Juicy Fruit chewing gum. Grace glanced at Shane. He was breathing evenly, his arm wound beneath his head. It was safe for her to continue her search, darn it.

When she opened the closet, the first thing she spotted was his gray felt cowboy hat, set on an upper shelf beside stacks of her grandmother's hat boxes. She took it down and ran a curious finger around the leather band before popping the hat on her head. The brim slid down to her nose. She shoved it back up, pulling the clump of her ponytail out the back to give the hat something to rest on. If she couldn't try out Shane, at least she could give his hat a whirl. *Whoopee.*

Another glance toward the bed reassured her that he still wasn't sitting up, rubbing his eyes, gaping at her as if she were part of a carnival sideshow. She ran her hands over the shirts he'd hung from the rod, but failed to discover the diamond ring in any of the pockets on the first pass.

No ring? Hard to be certain in the dark.

She stepped inside the closet and closed the door

behind her with the smallest of thuds; she pulled the chain for the overhead lightbulb with the quietest of clicks. The sudden bright light hurt her eyes. Reaching blindly, she buried her face in Shane's lined denim jacket, knocking his hat to the back of her head.

Oh, wow. The jacket smelled so, well, not exactly good, but so...so enticing. She breathed deeply, identifying horses and horse feed, the salty musk of male perspiration, the wild, clean scent of the great outdoors. *This is Shane,* she thought. *This is Wyoming. This is freedom.*

Nothing at all to do with a six-carat diamond engagement ring from Tiffany's.

Grace's eyes welled. What was she going to do? How could she stay a proper Farrow in the city when every part of her that mattered was yearning for another life altogether?

Needing comfort, she pulled the jacket off its hanger and slipped her arms into the sleeves. It was big on her, no surprise there. She wrapped her arms around herself, hugging the heavy worn denim, breathing it in, transported. There had to be a way for her and Shane to be together. He wanted it, she knew he did. He wouldn't be so definite about avoiding her otherwise.

When the closet door opened, her eyes were closed. For a few blissful seconds she'd forgotten herself, but when Shane said "Grace?" with a horrified, quizzical, absolute dumbfoundedness, it all came rushing back: she was in his closet in the middle of the night, wearing fuzzy green slippers and a cartoon nightshirt, plus his cowboy hat, bandanna and jacket. Talk about sideshows! All she lacked was the ring.

"What are you doing?"

She scrunched up her face. Gestured with the flapping sleeves. "Trying on your jacket?" she squeaked.

Shane gave a short, disbelieving laugh. "In the closet with the door closed?"

"I didn't want the light to wake you."

"Why?" he asked, clearly flabbergasted by her moxie.

"Because you were sleeping," she said, squinting at his face. "Obviously."

"Grace..."

"Uh-huh?"

"Give it another try."

She sagged. "Okay. I was looking for my ring. I was in bed, kinda not sleeping...er, definitely not sleeping, and I just happened to remember that you hadn't returned it and so I got worried that you'd *laundered* it and maybe it had gone down the drain or something, which is why I'm wearing your clothes."

He blinked at the light. "You were checking the pockets, right?"

"Right!"

He scratched his head, his face all muzzy with sleep and confusion.

"Which makes perfect sense, doesn't it?" she asked hopefully.

"It makes perfect Grace Farrow turn-the-world-upside-down sense," he said, his gaze sliding over the jacket to her nightshirt and exposed bare legs. Suddenly he looked wide awake. Grace tried not to grin. Must be that the sight of her fuzzy-wuzzy slippers packed quite a wallop.

She was feeling okay, slightly embarrassed but basically okay, until she took a closer look at Shane. What she saw was a lotta skin covering a whole lotta muscle, but very little else, save some cute chest and leg fuzz that fairly called out to be stroked. His hair was adorably tousled, and she'd bet her diamond that he was naked under the sheet clutched to his groin, giving a new throat-clenching meaning to the phrase *going commando.*

Trying to keep cool in spite of her growing warmth, she crossed one leg over the other and tamped the cowboy hat lower on her forehead—but not so low it blocked her view. "Say," she ventured, her throat Mojave dry and her palms Amazon moist, "are we gonna stand here all night staring at each other or are you gonna kiss me?"

Shane backed off, one hand clutching the sheet, the other waving in the air as if she'd leveled a six-shooter at him. "Hey. No. Sorry. I'm not kissing anybody."

It wasn't supposed to happen this way. "Look," she said, shrugging out of the jacket because suddenly she was melting with heat, "I know your intentions are honorable, but here's the plot. Whenever the winsome heroine and the studly hero run into each other in the middle of the night, they have to kiss. That's the way it goes." She shrugged to show him that it wasn't her idea, after all, even though she ached inside from the sheer rightness of it. "There's simply got to be a kiss."

Something—perhaps a mutual awareness that their kiss had been inevitable from the outset—had supercharged the energy pulsating between them. Shane's eyes were as dark as a pine forest at midnight, deep with emotion. His knuckles were white where they clutched the sheet, and his chest rose and fell as if breathing was something he had to concentrate on to achieve. He didn't say yes, but then again, neither did he say no.

One hundred percent sure of herself—and, suddenly, equally sure of Shane—Grace moved toward him, her slippers scuffing on the needlepoint carpets. He seemed to be struggling with the temptation, whereas she'd already surrendered, her skin burning hot as a branding iron.

She put out her hand. At the same time, he extended his.

A spark of electricity leapt between their fingertips.

7
_____

"Ouch!" Grace yipped, pulling back. Not easily deterred, she reached for Shane again, hands still extended. Another shock of static electricity sparked between them. "Hey," she said, as if surprised. *"Ow."* She licked the tip of her finger.

"It's your slippers," he declared, though in truth she seemed suffused with electricity. Her staticky cartoon sleep shirt clung to every curve, outlining her small breasts, enticing belly and slender thighs. Except where it was mashed down by his hat, her hair fairly crackled around her head, sticking out in every direction like copper wire sizzling with surplus energy. Even her eyes were infused, glittering with a green fire that heated up the dangerous thoughts already lodged in his head. Just looking at her made his blood boil.

"It's your sheet." She grabbed up a loose, dragging corner of it and tugged. Electricity flashed across it like a miniaturized lightning storm, dramatic in the darkened room. Her breath caught. "Cool!"

Shane was losing his grip. He clutched at the sheet when she tried to snap it, a reflex that reeled her in closer so the electricity forked between them in tiny slashes of light that made their flimsy fabric coverings crackle against each other. "Ooh." Grace shimmied her nylon-clad hips against his wadded-up sheet, producing another shower of static electricity. "Kinky!"

He was stuck. He couldn't let go of the sheet, so he couldn't push her away, or even maintain much separation. Neither could he step away; she was standing on the section of sheeting she'd unwound and he couldn't seem to work it free. Those gigantic furry slippers of hers were planted like the hooves of a Clydesdale.

"It seems we're combustible." She lifted her hand, slowly moving it toward his bare chest as if expecting another lightning strike. With every hair on his body rising and prickling, he thought of junior high science experiments. If ever a couple were both magnet and steel *and* opposite poles, it was him and Grace.

Touchdown. Her palm rested easily at the center of his chest. "Aw," she sighed, apparently disappointed that they hadn't generated another spark.

At least not the kind she was expecting. Even though she'd begun to pet him like a stuffed animal, he was oddly stimulated. Or maybe not so oddly, he thought, devouring her uplifted gaze and parted lips. There was a glistening patch of moisture on her lower lip, from when she'd licked at her finger. *Hold on,* he told himself, and he wasn't referring only to his sheet.

"Shane." Grace's voice was husky. "There's got to be a kiss."

As if from a great distance he heard himself say yes, and then darned if he wasn't kissing her. Kissing her like there was no tomorrow…which was too true and too awful to think about at the moment.

She leaned into him, both palms pressed to his chest, her mouth opening so her warm velvety tongue could unfurl against his. As the kiss deepened, he had to—*had* to—wrap his arms tightly around her, lifting her up onto her toes, bending her backward, knocking off the hat, one hand clasping her buttock, a firm curve of flesh beneath the thin nightshirt. He was taking liberties, but she just hummed in her throat, generous to a fault.

Their lips fused as if the kiss never had to end. *A grand idea,* he agreed almost stupidly, lost in the sweet heat of Grace's mouth, in the subtle sway of her hips against his burgeoning erection. The sheet he'd wrapped around his naked body was trapped between them, listing badly, baring more than it covered. Wrenching one hand off Grace, he fumbled for it, finding more soft silken thigh than crisp white percale. He lingered, brushing his fingertips over her yielding skin, sensing with a deep quaking need the melting feminine core only a touch away.

He wanted to be inside her, feeling the tight, hot burn of her flesh clasping his. And that wasn't right.

Man, oh, man, it felt right. *She* felt right, her nipples pressed like hard buttons against his ribs and her soft lips plucking at his, murmuring throaty little assents....

But damn if it wasn't wrong.

He gathered a handful of the sheet near his hipbone and stepped back toward the bed, intending to sink onto it so his impromptu toga would be at least partly anchored in place. Grace wasn't ready to end their kiss, though. Following him with her lips but not her feet, she fell against him, knocking them both off balance. Teetering, twisting, turning, they became hopelessly tangled in the sheet, until at last he fell supine upon the bed with her sprawled on top of him, giggling and saying things like, "Oopsy daisy," with remarkably good cheer. She raised her head, beaming at him like a half-drunk millennium reveler, her dishonorable intentions clearly focused on his mouth. "Heyah, cowboy, whaddya say we—"

Shane put his hand up. "No, Grace."

Her eyes had been shimmering with anticipation. They changed instantly, going the sharp green of an old broken bottle. The knowledge that he'd hurt her sent a rock-hard fist of regret slamming into his gut.

Frozen atop him, she started to protest, saying, "But it's obvious we were meant to—" until he rolled out from beneath her, abandoning the sheet and reaching instead for a pillow. Leaning back against the carved headboard, he tried not to look at her, because then he'd weaken for sure. A woman like Grace was hard to say no to even when you weren't naked and working with brain cells depleted of their normal blood supply.

"Shane, I—I know what you're thinking." Her voice shook as she unwound the sheet and pushed herself up to a sitting position, bare legs coiled beneath her. "And I'm willing to—"

"I'm not." He held on to the pillow in his lap as if it were a life preserver, battling the urge to pull her close and touch her creamy thighs and confess all the truths of his aching heart.

"We can just—"

He interrupted again; he didn't want to hear her argument, he didn't want to look at her and he really didn't want to think about how shockingly good their kiss had been. "Nope, Grace, we can't."

This time, she didn't argue. After a while she even took a deep, shuddering breath and nodded. But when he dared a glance he could still see the sharp hurt of his rejection in her eyes.

It was too much for him. He had to explain, even if that meant exposing the depth of his feelings for her and then as a result facing a future filled with both loneliness *and* misery. But he'd rather suffer forever himself than cause her even a fleeting pain.

"You see, Grace…" he started, then stopped. His voice sounded like a rusty hinge. He cleared his throat, not looking at her. "Grace. I don't want to be your fantasy. Making love has to be a beginning, not a one-shot deal. I won't do that. Not with you."

She sniffed. "What are you, some kind of saint?"

"Just a man," he said. *Hurting as bad as you.*

She slipped off the bed, not looking at him. "You're going to regret this."

He groaned. "You think I don't know that?"

Somehow, he'd have to find a way to live with the regret of not knowing what kind of Fourth-of-July-firecracker love they could have made together. And he would…because giving up what he'd never really had would be easier than losing her after she'd found her way into his heart.

Too bad every instinct was telling him that it was already too late.

"IN THAT CASE, I've got something to think about."

Grace couldn't believe she'd said it so calmly. Or that it was all she'd said, when a thousand words and just as many emotions were ripe and swollen inside her, on the brink of torrential release. Maybe it was because she knew that Shane was right. For once in her life she had to think before she leapt.

Frustrated with inaction, she bounced her bottom on the bed. She tore his bandanna from her neck. Rational thought was no fun. Not when there was such a diverting occupation only doors away. Of course, the occupation wanted to be more than diverting, and already was if only he knew it, but *that* was what she had to think about.

She drew up her sheets and patchwork quilt, trying her darnedest to remember the many reasons for marrying Michael that she'd once accounted so responsibly. It was no good. Whether or not she had a relationship with Shane, she couldn't marry Michael. She didn't love him in all the wonderful ways that she now realized it was possible—and absolutely crucial—to love the man you were going to commit to sharing your life with, in sickness and health, good times and bad, forever on end, amen and thank you very much, Shane McHenry, for turning her world upside down!

"Mm-hmm," she murmured after another moment of deep thought, fingertips pressed to lips branded by his kiss, "thank you, Shane McHenry."

He knocked on her bedroom door, pushing it open with a soft-spoken, "Grace? You awake?"

She sat up, poker straight. "Wide awake!"

He hesitated in the doorway, all rumpled hair and bare, golden-brown chest, his eyes glowing like a wolf's in the low light cast by her small bedside lamp. "Talking to yourself?"

"Only because you kicked me out of your room."

"Not exactly." He gestured. "I brought you the ring."

She stared unblinkingly.

"I, uh, found it in my shirt pocket before I washed it, so it's fine, it didn't go through the spin cycle or anything. I put it away for safekeeping. Then I guess I forgot to tell you where it was." He winced. "I wasn't intentionally keeping it from you...."

Grace clutched the white flannel sheet in her lap. "I don't want it," she said, enunciating deliberately.

Shane pinched the diamond ring between his thumb

and index finger, holding it away from himself. "Well, hell, Grace, I sure don't want it."

"I don't want it way more than you don't want it!"

Shaking his head at her vehemence, he came into the room and put the ring on her nightstand, a chunky pine table. "You might change your mind, come morning."

She grabbed his wrist so he couldn't retreat. "I won't change my mind. Before, you wouldn't let me finish what I wanted to tell you." She hesitated, her heart racing, but it needed to be said to be true. "As of tonight, I'm no longer engaged."

Shane closed his eyes for a moment and swallowed, his jaw set, the cords in his throat pulled taut as barbed wire. "Talk is easy at this time of night," he said, his hard stare probably meant to intimidate her, shake her resolve. Although he turned his wrist, he didn't try to pull away. She clasped his hand, hopes leaping.

"What's in my heart matters most. And in here—" she clasped his hand between her breasts "—it's official. I promise you."

"Grace," he groaned, like a man touching land after a shipwreck at sea. "Don't do this to me."

"Too late," she whispered. Too late for both of them.

"Hey, I just wanted to return the ring. I didn't come in here looking for—for…"

Her eyes connected with his, the current between them running hot and strong. "Yes, you did."

When he reached over to lightly cup her breast, she pressed his fingers against her puckered nipple. Her need had grown way beyond the merely physical, but it was clear that making love would at least temporarily soothe her itches and aches.

"Yeah, you're right," he said hoarsely, dropping onto the bed beside her with an astonishing suddenness. "Again." She slumped against the pillows, awed by his intensity. Kneeling above her, he took her face in his hands and covered her mouth with his in a way that told her more than pretty compliments or fevered confessions ever could.

He'd seemed so positive, only minutes ago, but now it was she who knew for sure. Shane wanted her as much as she wanted him—and he was a man who preferred action to words.

Just when she was getting really focused, her mouth ablaze and her tongue dancing in the fiery heat of their kiss, every nerve ending flickering in the spill-over of sensations, Shane said, "Wait a minute," and settled back on his heels, straddling her in nothing but a pair of unsnapped blue jeans that left very little to the imagination. "Last chance," he murmured, touching a gentle fingertip to her trembling chin. Her breath was coming in gasps. "Your choice, Grace. All or nothing."

She was half out of her head, but not so far gone she couldn't run a fascinated hand down the washboard ripples of his abdomen. He was rock hard...everywhere. "I want the fire," she said as a hot flush of daring crept over every inch of her. Delicately she took the tab of his zipper between her fingertips. "I want you, Shane. All of you."

With a sharp tug she released him, *all* of him, and that was the last conscious decision she made for a very long time. Shane was a cowboy possessed and she was a woman living her fantasy; they were too far gone for sweet and gentle lovemaking. He took

her with a swiftness and surety that thrilled her more
than she would have believed possible. Within
minutes, the world had burned into oblivion and they
along with it, two bodies coupled in the heat, all spark
and flame and scorching instinct.

Afterward, she remembered kisses that blazed upon
her naked body like coals. She remembered raw desire and deep, gorging thrusts and even a hazy blue
streak where she yelled *"Shane! Shane! Shane! Oh,
yes, Shane!"* at the top of her lungs, but that might
have been only in her mind, because without a doubt
her brain was in a screaming delirium. After her cli-
maxes—plural, the first time ever—and after his—
one was enough to rattle the windowpanes—they fell
into the kind of sleep that was next door to uncon-
sciousness. And stayed that way till morning.

When Grace awoke there was no confusion; she
knew instantly that her life had changed forever. She
grinned into the pillow, glad of it. There were lots of
details to work out, talking to Michael and returning
the ring chief among them, but she could deal with
anything now. Even the Farrows. At that, a pesky
little something nagged at the back of her brain, but
she wasn't one to let small inconsistencies ruin the
big picture.

Falling in love with Shane was a masterpiece.

She slipped from bed and hurried to the bathroom,
was struck dumb that her inner transformation didn't
reflect itself in the medicine cabinet mirror, not even
in the accordion-armed magnifying mirror, and after
a quick pee returned to her rightful place in Shane's
arms. The sheets hadn't even cooled. Nor had his
skin. Pressing her backside into the curve of his body,
she discovered that neither had his desire.

"G'morning." His voice was gravelly, as though

he'd licked sand off her skin during the night instead of just the sexual moisture that had risen from her pores like dew.

She rocked her hips, feeling wanton. And feeling want. "Make that a mighty fine morning, cowboy."

His slow chuckle prickled the hairs at the back of her neck. "If you insist, Miss Farrow." Reaching around, he sought her left breast and tweaked the crest into a small hard knot.

"I didn't mean..." She sucked in a breath. He'd pulled aside the loose neckline of her nightshirt and was sliding his tongue along her shoulder. "Well, okay, we'll do it your way."

"Then let's get rid of these," he said, sweeping the patchwork quilt and rumpled sheets off her. "I've been dying to find out if you're freckled all over."

"You mean after last night you don't already know?"

He slid his hand up her thigh. "It was dark. And I think at some point in the proceedings I might've lost my vision."

"So that explains my double vision—oh, my goodness, do that again, please." His fingers were accomplishing amazing things beneath the cartoon nightshirt. Yosemite Sam had never seen such action.

"Think you can handle two of me?"

She giggled. "I don't have enough body parts to occupy four of your hands."

"What about two of my..." Fortunately, the rest of his teasing question was lost in her sudden squeal of laughter; he was tickling her in places she hadn't thought were ticklish. Making love to Shane was a wondrously novel experience.

"Found any freckles?" she gasped, squirming

away from him because she didn't want to lose her marbles this early in the morning...did she?

"I can't feel any," he muttered, hell-bent on getting her back. He scooped her up and pressed her down onto the mattress so forcefully her legs flew up, pale and lightly freckled in the early morning light.

"Hah! My freckles aren't so big you can actually *feel* them."

"Big enough," he said, lifting her nightshirt off over her head and closing his hands over her breasts. He drew the tip of his tongue along her breastbone, going slow enough to lick every one of her freckles. "Mmm, usually you smell like a cinnamon bun, but not this morning." Looking up, he flashed his most unsaintly smile. "Wonder why?"

She threaded her fingers through his hair as his mouth lowered to her breast. "I should have taken a shower."

"Nmmph." When his tongue flicked her nipple, a tiny bolt of electricity shocked her system. Static had nothing on Shane. "I like you this way."

"Male animals," she groaned, arching into the delicious tingling heat of his mouth, her eyes rolling back until all she could see was the paisley swirls of the papered ceiling. "I've heard about this sort of thing. Male animals...marking their territory."

Shane spread her thighs and settled between them, his arousal pressed hard against her belly. "I don't want any mistake about whose woman you are."

The words elated her. "No mistake," she promised, and patted one hand across the surface of the bedside table, hoping to find the strip of condoms they'd tossed aside only a few hours ago. They hadn't used them all, not if she remembered correctly.

Instead of helping her, Shane eased his hand between her legs, which was more of a hindrance—an inspired, fabulously tantalizing hindrance, but a hindrance all the same. While he did his best to distract her, she scrabbled through a tangle of unmatched earrings, an alarm clock, a dog-eared paperback—*The Groom Wore Spurs*—a box of tissues and a horse magazine, knocking everything willy-nilly until finally she upended a small quill basket filled with ribbons, barrettes, bobby pins and the strip of leftover condoms.

With a skillfully soft touch, Shane parted the tender petals of her cleft and dipped inside; swooning, Grace ripped open one of the packets posthaste. "Here, here, here," she said, all jittery, "use this, quick!"

He rolled off her, a corner of his mouth quirked with amusement. "Well, now, Miss Farrow, I thought we'd take it nice and slow and easy this morning...."

She grabbed him by the scruff so he'd look at her and see how seriously hot she was. "Once you're inside me you can go as slow as you want."

"Might be too late by then."

He shifted toward her again and she sighed deeply at the weight of him, her legs wrapping around his. *So good.* She slid her palms to his firm buttocks. *So fine.*

Shane drew back slightly. "Hold on—"

"I am!"

"Slow down, then." His lips pursed. "Remember? There's got to be a kiss."

She found that amusing. "You've kissed me, Shane. I might have lost my mind regarding a few of the other details, but I definitely remember you kissing me."

"Not this morning," he said, and did a double whammy on her, his mouth landing squarely on hers as he entered her body with a slow, filling thrust that shocked her nonetheless, like a sudden blast of fire from a blowtorch. After a millisecond of adjustment, she opened fully to him, her mouth ardent, her fingers clenched in reflex, nails biting into his flesh, urging him to drive his hips just a little bit stronger, sink his shaft just the little bit extra that would make her believe they would be joined this way forever. Her heart expanded at the possibility, and the kiss they shared became an intimate exchange of emotion as well as sensation, ebbing and flowing with the easy rhythm of their bodies.

"You are my love," Shane murmured between slow panting thrusts, breathing a patch of moisture onto her arched throat as he nuzzled it.

"Yes…" She had relaxed, her muscles soft, her insides liquid and warm. It seemed this pleasure was infinite. And why not? Ever since he'd walked up to her table in the riding club lounge, she'd known that miracles happen.

"Grace," he said, shifting his weight off his arms so he could squeeze her breasts. The throaty timbre of his voice sent shivers down her spine. "Sweetheart."

"Umm." Incredibly, her desire intensified. She spanned his lean hips with her hands, pressing him on. Their rocking motion quickened. "Oh, Shane, yes…" What had been languorous was growing urgent. She couldn't quite catch her breath.

As her hands coasted upward over his back in a long, slow caress, his raw tension and primal need radiated through every nerve ending in her palms. She responded provocatively, tilting her hips with a womanly allure she didn't recognize. His shoulder blades shifted and his buttocks flexed and he drove harder into her, his breathing harsh and hurried, sounding like a freight train in her ears. "Shh," she said to soothe him, but the effort was token. She wanted the completion. She wanted to know exactly how much pleasure she had given him. Before the thought had evolved, he reached his climax with a guttural shout, his arms wrapped so tightly around her that she felt every shocking pulse of it reverberate through herself. And as naturally as sunrise and rainfall and spring-time, his satisfaction became her own. Under normal circumstances, she wouldn't have thought she was ready, but suddenly she was crying, "Oh, yes, touch me right there!" her detonation helped along by his devastating caress and a kiss that kept her anchored even as all her senses spun riotously out of control.

They stayed twined together until their breathing slowed and they could no longer feel each other's heartbeats. "Too fast," Shane said regretfully, mov-ing to shift his weight off her. "It's over already." He smiled his sexy, crooked, cowboy smile, the one that made her thoughts sputter like drops of water on a hot griddle.

"S'okay." She pushed her tangled hair out of her eyes. "We've got a lifetime to get it right."

"Do we?"

Her eyes widened. She became very still. After ev-erything, he couldn't possibly be one of those guys who quailed at the first mention of commitment!

"Sounds good," he said after a moment, and she relaxed. Of course he wasn't one of those guys. His every action up to now had been the antithesis of those guys.

"But..." He was staring up at the ceiling as if the answer to the world's problems could be found in the busy patterns of Gran's paisley wallpaper.

She tried not to hold her breath. "But?"

"I'm wondering how this is going to work."

Again, relief washed through her. "Don't worry." She cuddled against him. "We'll think of a way."

He put his arm around her, warning mildly, "I've had about as much of New York City as I can take."

"And here I thought you were considering Troy's job offer."

Shane grunted. "Johnny Jump-Up's country cousin, Cowboy Shane? No way, sweetheart."

"Yes, well, there are other options," she murmured, hoping he'd pick up on the hint. Was it anti-feminist of her to use a man as an excuse to escape her stifling life? She frowned, not wanting to be weak or dependent, but then the answer came to her. It was okay as long as she really loved the man and wasn't just using him. And that was the case.

Right?

"Grace Farrow in Wyoming," Shane mused, smiling indulgently at the prospect. His gaze flicked over her, taking in her absorbed expression.

She tried to smile away the worry, wanting to appear superconfident, ready for anything. Fortunately, living in Wyoming wasn't her concern. She just needed to be sure that she got there the right way. "I've done enough damage here," she said brightly. "I need new horizons. *Viva la cowgirl!*"

His wary eyes warmed at her enthusiasm. "You wouldn't miss the city?"

"What's to miss? Status invitations to dinner parties that bore my socks off? Face peels and leg waxes? Interoffice e-mail? Bumper-to-bumper traffic?" She delivered a karate-chop to his midsection. "*Art News?* Face-lifts? Designer sunglasses, designer perfume, designer divorce attorneys? I don't want any of it!''

''Hey, now, wait. What about your job and your friends and family?''

''Jenny Price can have my job. Molly and Laramie would be thrilled to visit me in Wyoming. And my family...'' She shrugged, not wanting to tell him that the Farrows would take awhile to recover from her defection.

Shane let it slide. ''And the change wouldn't be too much for you? This isn't happening too fast?''

''Yes, it's happening too fast! That's what I like about it...about us. I did the proper thing with Michael and how wrong was that? It took me awhile to figure it out, but the socially correct, family-approved way isn't necessarily the *right* way. Not for the me I've been waiting forever to become, anyway.''

Shane shook his head. ''It still sounds kind of... flimsy. We need to be absolutely sure.''

She sat up. ''Look around you, cowboy.''

''Um-hmm.''

With a roll of her eyes, she spread the flannel sheet across her breasts and tucked it into her armpits. ''Okay, now look.''

He propped himself up on his elbows and gazed at the bedroom, taking in her brass bed, country pine furnishings, Indian rugs and the colorful serape hung beneath her Georgia O'Keeffe-style steer skull. None of it suited the Castle, but all of it suited her. Every time she'd been pressured to accept Michael's proposal, she'd bought another piece of Southwestern pottery or another turquoise necklace and had gone home to think about her escape.

''It's a tourist trap,'' said Shane, not unkindly.

"It's where my heart is. I'm absolutely, positively one hundred percent sure."

He kissed her softly, touching his lips to her cheeks and eyelids and forehead and hair. "I guess we don't have to decide anything right now."

It was not a totally satisfying way to conclude their first postcoital talk, but then she was the one with the fiancé in limbo and the parents expecting a lavish wedding—

Her stomach dropped. Omigawd, her parents!

Missing Grace's sudden dismay, Shane asked if she wanted to shower first. She waved him off, waiting until he'd disappeared into the bathroom before letting out a small shriek of horror and falling face first into the bedclothes. Her parents were the bothersome detail niggling at the back of her mind. Her parents, due back from Africa late yesterday, and oh, jeez, she'd forgotten to call or even check her messages. Her parents, and the welcome-home cocktail party she'd promised to throw for them this very evening. In the Castle. With Victor and The Lemon-Sucker and the Howards, the Seaborgs and pushy Bunny Urquhart, a notorious Upper East Side gossip.

Grace groaned. The only guest she dreaded more was Michael. Nice, respectable, unbendable Michael Lynden, erstwhile fiancé, who, unless she could contrive a way to catch him beforehand, would arrive unaware that he was now her ex-fiancé.

Canceling was out of the question. Farrows didn't cancel at the last minute, especially Farrows who were on the verge of canceling out on their very Farrowhood.

It was going to be a heckuva bad party. There was only one way she could think to save it.

"COWGIRL CLUB TO THE rescue!" said Molly as she breezed through the door Grace held open. Dressed in jeans and a bulky sweater, she toted two net bags filled with produce and a backpack with several loaves of Italian bread sticking out the flap. "Don't fret, Grace. We shopped on the way to save time."

"The woman's a demon at the market. She squeezes things that were never meant to be squeezed." Laramie's arms were loaded with paper bags stuffed with assorted party supplies and lots more food. "I'm never buying vegetables with her again."

Molly made for the kitchen. "Those tomatoes were overripe!"

Grace grabbed one of the bags and followed her friends. "I owe you guys big-time. My mother's usual caterer laughed in my ear when I called and said 'same-day emergency.' But she was prepared to pencil me in for *next* October." She hefted the paper sack onto the counter and peered inside. "I don't know how I let myself forget about this cocktail thing. Didn't you overshop, Mol? What are we going to do with all this food? My mother's friends are all on perpetual diets."

Molly and Laramie exchanged a look. "Leave everything up to me," Molly said, shifting the provisions out of Grace's reach. She gave Laramie a nudge.

"I think I can guess how you got so distracted." Laramie slid her Hollywood glamour-puss sunglasses up her forehead and arched her brows suggestively. "Where's the cowboy?"

"I sent Shane to the stable. I'm not sure what he'd do if he knew about the cocktail party. Probably take off for Wyoming like a bull out of a rodeo chute."

"So you're just going to spring it on him?" Molly

pulled an economy-size box of water crackers from one of the bags. Grace figured she'd be scarfing leftover hors d'oeuvres for weeks.

Unless she was in Wyoming. Yes, of course—she'd be in Wyoming!

Well, maybe. Seeing as how Shane hadn't actually invited her yet, she tried to scale back her enthusiasm. If need be, she'd invite herself, but surely he'd get around to it. The sooner the better. Once she sprang her decision on Michael and her parents, getting out of town would be a priority. But it was best not to bother with that now, or with Molly's excessive menu. There were other, more urgent concerns.

"Difficult to keep it from him," Laramie murmured, unloading the groceries.

"I'm afraid Michael's the one in for a shock," Grace said, checking her watch. "Listen, I hate to leave, but I have to get to work. The cleaning service will be in this afternoon, so preparing the food's the worst of it. Are you sure you two can handle all this on your own?"

"What's a few nibbles and schmears to a professional party planner?" Molly shooed her. "Go on, go on. I can put this party together in a snap."

"You're a lifesaver, Mol. You, too, Laramie." Grace edged toward the doorway, distracted by the etiquette of jilting your fiancé by phone. "Thanks don't suffice, but thank you so, so much for helping me out of another jam." Michael lived on the phone; why not break up on it, too?

"Just a minute, cowgirl." Seated on one of the stools, Laramie leaned her elbows on the island and crossed one long stocking-clad leg over the other. She'd shifted around her appointments at the travel agency so she could be Molly's scullery slave for the morning. "You haven't given us the official Cowgirl Club update. Since Shane's still here in Manhattan, I take it things are going well?"

"Pretty well."

Laramie's eyes narrowed. "I know a ride-'em-cowboy smile when I see one."

Molly dropped a bundle of asparagus. *"What?"*

"Plus there's a love bite on your neck."

Grace slapped a hand over her throat. She hadn't noticed.

"Gotcha," said Laramie.

Grace's expression was sheepish. "Okay, yes, I confess...."

Her friends' reaction to the news was a little subdued. Normally Molly would have squealed and jumped up and down like a game show contestant and Laramie would have celebrated the Cowgirl Club victory. Instead they just stared in astonishment, their mouths open and no words coming out.

"Details?" Laramie said at last, rather faintly.

"I don't have time for details. But let me just say that The Lemon-Sucker was wrong."

"About...?"

Grace's smile was the teensiest bit smug. "Cowboys do love scenes. Expertly."

While her friends were exchanging another look, this one of serious concern, Grace departed. By the time Molly and Laramie had recovered their wits, they were alone.

"I didn't realize things had gone so far," said Molly. "Oh, boy, the party. What do we do about the party?"

"If the party goes through, Grace is really in for it." Laramie frowned. "We've got to tell her."

"But we promised her mother we'd keep it a surprise."

"Tough tamale. We have to clue her in."

Molly nodded. "You're right. Come what may, Grace must be told that she's been tricked into throwing her own surprise engagement party."

8

HER LIFE RARELY proceeded smoothly. Why should today be any different, just because for once she had something to be sure of? Loving Shane wasn't a cure-all. It transported her, yes, but as revealed that morning in the reflection of her bathroom mirror, it hadn't transformed her.

She was the same screw-up she'd always been.

Grace let herself into the apartment, expecting to find Molly busy in the kitchen and maybe Shane, too, but the place was deserted—clean, silent and empty, except for several foil-covered pans of party food. Molly had left a note that consisted mostly of heating instructions for the hors d'oeuvres, though written at the bottom in heavy black ink were the words *CALL ME IMMEDIATELY!!!*

Grace checked the clock. Scarcely time to turn on the oven and change her clothes before the guests started to arrive. Molly would have to wait. She was sure to arrive soon, anyway, if only to prevent Grace from charring the *crostini* or overspicing the bean dip.

Grace slid two of the cooking sheets into the oven and set the timer. No smoke alarms tonight.

Earlier in the day, she'd left messages at Michael's office and on his beeper. When he'd finally called, her voice had seized up, so she'd decided he deserved the courtesy of a face-to-face breakup. As soon as Troy had wrapped the day's taping, she'd raced downtown to Michael's office. Too late—he'd already gone. She'd tried to catch Shane at the stable, just because, but had also missed him. And all that futile chasing around had put her in a serious time crunch.

She pinned up her hair and dashed in and out of the shower, then went to her bedroom and opened the closet, ignoring the blinking light on her answering machine. Helen Farrow always called before a party, hoping to talk her daughter into an appropriate little black dress. Wondering why, Grace pulled out a cheerful, long-sleeved, lime-green number, utterly simple except for the fluff of marabou trim around the hem and wrists. The dress was made of the kind of stretchy, clingy fabric that precluded all underwear except a G-string; since the only place she cared to put dental floss was between her teeth, she went without but for a pair of panty hose. A glance in the mirror as she tugged down the dress gave her pause, but then the oven timer buzzed and she decided that her figure wasn't bountiful enough to attract much notice. She snatched up a pair of shoes and ran for the kitchen.

Shane was there, trying to figure out which oven knob to turn, a bouquet of colorful autumn flowers cradled in his left arm. Grace skidded to a stop. "When—what—how—?"

"I just got here." He silenced the buzzer. "You gave me a spare key, remember?"

"Right. I did. You're here. With flowers." Time to warn him about the party.

"Looks like you read my mind," he said, taking in her dress and the party preparations and mistaking them for something else. He offered her the bouquet. She said thanks, eyeing him as though he was a piece of cheesecake and she was on a diet. He was lean and handsome in sharp black jeans and what must be a new shirt, a soft, silky, pearly-white button-down that clung to his wide shoulders and flat abdomen as though it had been tailored to Wyoming cowboy specifications.

The cowboy discovers designer labels, she thought, feeling rather otherworldly. Impending disaster often made her as skittish as the cockroaches that predicted earthquakes, but she never seemed to learn to get out of the way of falling houses.

"I thought we'd have a cozy supper, just us. To celebrate…just us. Sound good?" Shane smiled at her unblinking reaction. "Nod if you agree."

Sentiment spiraled through her like the swirl in a peppermint. His expression was one part shy, two parts loving, and wholly, incredibly, heartbreakingly sweet. "I would like nothing more," she said, floating. "Unfortunately—"

The doorbell gonged, two deep, mellifluous notes. The doorman had the guest list, so he was letting everyone straight up to the apartment. Not such a good idea, in retrospect. *Let it be the Cowgirl Club,* Grace prayed as she gave Shane an apologetic smile and rushed to the door, crushing the paper tissue cone of his bouquet in one hand. *Bing.* She unclipped her hair and let it tumble across her shoulders. *Bong.* She dropped her sling-backs to the stone floor and stepped into them as she cautiously opened the door. "Molly! Thank heaven, it's you…."

Wait a minute. Molly didn't look right. Grace's gaze skipped to Laramie, frowning in a classic black cocktail dress; frowning. Michael's face appeared over her shoulder, which meant he was standing on tiptoe. "Traffic jam," he said, belligerent because he didn't care for situations that exhibited his lack of height. "Care to let me by, ladies, so I can kiss my fiancée? The one I haven't seen in nearly a week?"

Even though Molly and Laramie seemed reluctant, they stepped aside so Michael could buss Grace's cheek. He went for her lips, but she turned away at the last moment, keenly aware that Shane was hovering at the other end of the foyer. "You're early, Michael."

He smirked. "I wanted to be in on the surprise."

She wouldn't exactly call this evening a surprise, at least not a good one. *Duty* was a more appropriate word, as in the sort one dreaded.

Lacing her fingers around the bundle of flower stems, Grace realized that she hadn't bothered with her engagement ring since what felt like forever. Putting it on again seemed like a step in the wrong direction.

Michael embraced her. "It's our night, Grace, darling."

She returned the hug with her upper arms, thrusting her bare ring finger behind his back and wiggling it at Molly and Laramie. *The ring,* she mouthed, saying aloud to Michael, "And here I thought this party was for my parents."

"That's where you're wrong." He drew back, grinning. A becoming shade of pink had tinged his cheeks. He was all spiffed up in a matching ice-blue shirt and tie and his prized Saville Row suit with a silk square poking artistically from the breast pocket. His Italian shoes were buffed and his beach-boy blond hair was freshly molded into an undulant wave over his unlined brow. Michael was rather conceited about his well-groomed good looks.

Grace frowned. After four days of exposure to Shane's natural, rugged virility, Michael seemed like a fusspot. He was still a nice enough fellow, she sup-posed, but that was all. She had no romantic feelings left for him whatsoever. In fact, now that she'd fallen for Shane, she had to wonder if she'd ever had any, beyond an excitable initial attraction that now seemed superficial and fleeting. The difference between lov-ing Shane and feeling that she *should* love Michael was so immense that she was actually reassured.

She was on the right track at last. All she had to do was stick to it.

"Surprise, surprise," said several people at once as they crowded into the foyer. "Congratulations on your engagement!" Perplexed, Grace smiled and bur-bled nonsense and waved her flowers, hoping that the guests would be too distracted to ask to see her en-gagement ring. Out of the corner of her eye, she spied Shane, Laramie and Molly consulting with their heads together. Hopefully they'd gotten the hint and would go looking for the diamond, although carrying on the charade of her engagement was no longer Grace's top priority.

At least it wasn't until her parents arrived, brown and sleek as otters after three weeks of African sun and the deluxe pampering of a Butterfield & Robinson photo safari. "Surprise, Grace, surprise," they also said after dispensing with the initial hellos. Wearing their most doting expressions, they turned to their chosen son-in-law. Arthur Farrow shook Michael's hand. "Congratulations, Son."

Helen Farrow hugged him. "Arthur and I were so pleased when you two called us in Africa to let us know that Grace had accepted your proposal." An unspoken *finally* hung heavily in the air.

Grace's smile had faded. "I'm really not getting this."

"Darling, forgive me," Helen said in the dulcet tones that meant mothers with their daughter's best interests at heart needed no forgiveness. "I've been conniving behind your back, all the way from the veld."

"Grace." Laramie made her way through the crowded foyer as another group of guests arrived, laughing and chattering. She lifted Grace's hair and whispered into her ear. "We were trying to warn you…"

Helen Farrow threw out her arms in an extravagant gesture. "Surprise! This is your and Michael's engagement party, darling. Aren't you pleased?"

"Ecstatic." Grace looked around her, realizing for the first time that the Howards and the Seaborgs had arrived, but so had a lot of other people, some of them her parents' friends, many of them hers. There was Charlotte and Quinn, from one of the tower penthouses, along with the Applebaums, Queenie and George, and the entire second floor. People from work, including Jenny and Troy and their mix-and-match dates. Molly and Laramie must have had a hand in the invites—Eddie and a couple of the other off-shift doormen hovered near the open doorway, making googly eyes at the women in their abbreviated cocktail dresses.

"This is my engagement party?" Grace felt as though she'd been bonked over the head with a mallet like a cartoon character. *Boing.* She turned to Laramie, details ricocheting inside her skull. "That's what all the extra food was for."

"It was your mother's idea. But after Molly and I found out about—" Laramie leaned in, lowering her voice "—you-know-who, we intended to warn you."

She gripped Grace's shoulders. *"You were supposed to call one of us."*

Grace's eyes skimmed the guests as her mother took charge and directed everyone toward the open rooms. "And where did you-know-who go?"

"Don't know. We told him what was happening and then..." Laramie shrugged.

Grace spotted a beaming Michael heading toward her, eager to have her by his side while he collected his congratulations. Fortunately, the still-in-character actor who played Johnny Jump-Up stepped in the way for an enthusiastic handshake, the silk pansies attached to his purple top hat bobbing above the milling guests. Grace thrust her bouquet at Laramie. "Try to stall Michael from looking for me. I need to explain to Shane."

Explain what? she wondered in despair, casting about for the sight of him. Explain that she was too much a Farrow to stage an embarrassing public breakup?

"He already knows," Laramie said, referring to the party's—and engagement's—bad timing.

"All the same..."

"What about your ring?"

"Oh, yeah." Grace looked down at her left hand, deringed yet again. "Guess I'd better go look for it, huh?"

Laramie gave her a gentle shove. "Don't worry, kiddo, the Cowgirl Club's on the job. Between me and Molly, we'll find the ring before anyone even notices it's missing. Do you have any idea where you left it?"

Grace waved distractedly. All she could remember of the past night was Shane, barefoot, bare chested and sexy as sin in unsnapped jeans, his eyes hot on hers as he tried to get her to take back the ring.

Forget the stupid ring, she wanted to say as she left the party. *Forget Michael,* she wanted to shout, loud enough for everyone to hear. *I want Shane!*

He wasn't in his bedroom. She checked the closet. Surely a cowboy wouldn't boot-scoot out of Manhattan without his hat. It was probably a code of the West, on a par with dying with your boots on.

The hat was there.

But where was the cowboy?

A DUSTY HAIR CLIP, a striped sock and a discarded Men of Texas calendar was all that Shane found under Grace's brass bed. No sign of the diamond engagement ring, either above or below. Wiggling his ticklish nose, he tried to think of what else she might have done with it, but aside from a creased, full-color shot of a half-naked steroid stud wearing fancy fringed chaps with silver conchas, the only picture that came to mind was an erotic mental snapshot of how Grace's cinnamon-sprinkled skin had glowed in the early morning light when he'd peeled off her nightshirt.

Shane sneezed on Mr. August. Time to move, even though it was blissfully quiet under the bed. A cocktail party with several dozen sharp-tongued, flinty-eyed New Yorkers was not his idea of a good way to spend his last evening with Grace. He'd intended to sweet-talk her into taking a Wyoming vacation as soon as possible, but it appeared now that she'd have to straighten out her social life first. Fiancés were not invited.

Definitely not invited.

Inching his way out from beneath the bed, Shane

bumped into a pair of solidly planted shoes. He twisted sideways to get a better look. The shoes were attached to a man.

He slid out all the way, dropped the bed skirts and sat with his back against the bed. *Hellfire.* The man in the tasseled leather loafers was Grace's slick fiancé, Golden Boy.

Golden Boy's nostrils flared. "Who are you and what are you doing under Grace's bed?"

Shane planted his boots and pushed himself up off the floor. He dusted his shirtfront, deliberately delaying the testosterone-driven response that had caused his instant dislike of Golden Boy. Something about the man's pompous, proprietary attitude toward Grace made Shane want to let loose with the kind of roundhouse right that would clear the decks from here to Wyoming. Normally he wasn't the kind of guy who went around spoiling for a fight, but in this case...

"He's Shane McHenry from Treetop, Wyoming."

Both men turned. Grace stood in the doorway, her color high, her hands clasped behind her back. There was a certain look of defiance about her. Shane sensed that Golden Boy was wary of it. He supposed that with a spitfire like Grace, a pompous prig would tend to worry about her behavior, but damned if he, personally, hadn't come to crave the headiness of a racing, rousing, chest-thumping pulse. Not to mention the woman who could always provide it, one way or another.

"Shane," she said softly, "this is Michael Lynden."

"Grace's fiancé," Golden Boy supplied, with emphasis.

Shane looked at Grace.

Grace looked at the floor.

Secure again, Golden Boy turned to offer his hand. They shook. "You're the cowboy Caroline was telling me about. I thought you'd gone back to Wisconsin days ago."

"Wyoming."

Golden Boy passed off the majority of the country with a flick of his hand. "Same difference."

"I run cattle, not milk cows."

"As I said, same difference."

Shane flexed his fingers. Hastily Grace stepped between the two men. "Michael, I need to speak to Shane for a minute. About, ah, his horse. Could you be a trooper and supervise the party for me? Please? I won't be long."

She'd shoved Golden Boy toward the door as she spoke, but when she tried to prod him over the threshold, he dug in his heels, obviously sensing a brush-off. "Just a moment, Grace. I want to know what this stranger was doing under your bed. I demand to know."

"Oh, that." She nibbled her lower lip, obviously gearing up for one of her garbled explanations. "Well, see…"

"What is he—some kind of pervert?" Golden Boy thrust out his chest and stabbed a finger toward Shane, who slid his hands into his pockets and tried to remember that *he* was the one who'd stolen another man's fiancé. *He* was the jackass who deserved a punch in the nose.

"Shane was looking for his bandanna." Grace scooped the wrinkled square of patterned cotton off the floor, waving it like the proverbial white flag. "I borrowed it from him when we were riding and then I got busy with the show—we're taping this week, you know—and so I guess I forgot to return the bandanna, but here it is. No worse for wear!''

To Shane's ears, her high-pitched patter sounded as fake as a player piano, but Golden Boy was either easily fooled or not as possessive as assumed. He let her nudge him out the door with a few sisterly pats and another flurry of reassurances. While he looked affronted when she closed the door in his face, he knocked only a couple of times and didn't even try the knob. Some devotion.

With a grim satisfaction, Shane decided that Golden Boy's bluster was mostly for effect. The chance that Grace's hollow engagement was not all that it should be on her fiancé's part, either, was a conscience lightener. Even if Shane still had a primal urge to uppercut the guy's teeth into his skull.

Grace was leaning against the door, watching him. ''I'm sorry,'' she said.

''Don't waste our time on apologies.''

She swallowed. ''But everything's a mess.''

His attitude softened; it looked like she was holding back tears. ''Won't take much to clean it up,'' he said, going toward her with a swiftness that made her eyes widen. He reached behind her back to snap the lock.

Her eyes glistened. ''I know I promised, but I can't do it, Shane...not tonight.''

''Do what?'' He slid a finger inside the neckline of her dress and followed it to where it scooped low across her breasts. Her racing heartbeat was fascinating, reminding him of how he'd once cupped a frightened bird in his hand and felt the wild beat of its fragile life throbbing against his fingertips.

She glanced at his hand. ''I can't tell Michael it's over. In front of everyone. Mother's party. Gossip. Scandal.''

Shane had discovered that there were ways to distract Grace from her chatterbox tendencies. Skin-to-skin contact worked best. So when she began blurting out her string of excuses, his response was to touch her—fingertip to cheek, palm to breast, thumb to nipple, thigh to thigh—until she ran out of words altogether and became silent, staring up at him with her eyes brimming and her lips slightly pouted.

"Tell him tonight," Shane said.

She nodded.

"After the party if you insist," he added, conceding that much before he took her into his arms and kissed away any lingering doubts she might have. He suckled her bottom lip, kissing her mouth open until he felt the hot velvet tickle of her tongue licking against his own. His scalp tingled, his jeans tightened. She squirmed against him. Her body was both soft and firm, tight and pliant, every curve shrink-wrapped in a dress designed to drive men wild. After a minute that stretched into five, he took his hands off her, peppering her lax mouth with a dozen quick, soft kisses in compensation.

"Tell him." He removed the bandanna wadded up in her fist and slipped it around her nape, lifting the heavy mass of her rippled curls with his other hand. Clutching a handful of it at the roots, he kissed her once more, hard, and then knotted the kerchief in a few quick motions. "You tell him and then you come back to me."

She blinked. "That's all you have to say?"

"All that matters."

"Yes," she said, and turned and rattled the doorknob until she remembered it was locked. "Yes, I'll tell him," she said, opening the door to a wave of noise that momentarily rocked her back on her heels.

She squared her shoulders and walked toward her engagement party like an inmate on death row, saying beneath her breath, all the way down the length of the hall, "Yes, yes, yes, yes..."

"WHAT'S OUR STATUS?" Molly asked as she drizzled olive oil over squares of focaccia.

Laramie returned from her lookout station midway between the kitchen—a.k.a. Cowgirl Club Central—and the ongoing engagement party. "Charlotte and Quinn are searching Grace's bathroom. Eddie's scouring the hallway, just in case. I sent Troy to the laundry room. Shane already did the bedroom." She paused, gauging just how well Shane could have checked the bedroom. Going by the frazzled but blissed-out state in which Grace was fulfilling her social duty, a second reconnaisance might be in order. "Maybe I'd better search the bedroom again."

Molly dimpled. "Good idea."

Before refilling it, Laramie picked over the nuts left at the bottom of a sterling silver dish. "What we need is a Tiffany-trained bloodhound."

"Or a special guest appearance by Zsa Zsa Gabor. She could sniff out a diamond at a thousand paces." Molly grew serious. "How's Grace holding up?"

"Remarkably well, considering the way her parents are going on and on about how thrilled they are with the brilliant addition to their family. Instead of freaking and doing something nuts like she normally would, Grace just keeps glancing at Shane and smiling. Somebody's bound to notice."

"They're all too busy watching Caroline fawn over Michael. Victor's the only one who hasn't noticed that The Lemon-Sucker has a hankering to squeeze her lemons with another man."

"Sheesh." Laramie popped a cashew into her mouth. "There's enough drama going on out there to fill a soap opera. Makes me glad I've never had to worry about family reunions."

Molly glanced up. "Now, Laramie," she gently chided, knowing her friend's flippancy was a cover for a deep chasm of hurt. "The Farrows believe they want what's best for Grace."

"Why not want what *Grace* thinks is best?" asked a masculine voice.

Molly winced. Shane stood in the doorway, listening to them. "Good point," she agreed. "But if you have a family, you know that it's not so easy."

Laramie arched her brows at Shane. "And are you what's best for Grace?"

"Maybe. You'd have to ask her."

"Just because you happen to suit her cowboy fantasy doesn't mean that you two are built to last."

"Laramie," Molly said. "Hold your tongue."

"No, she's right." Shane came into the kitchen. "That's what I've been trying to tell Grace. Tomorrow I'm leaving for home, and who knows if—"

"You're leaving?" Grace stood in the doorway behind Shane, holding a stack of dirty plates and crushed napkins. She thought she sounded pretty calm, considering.

He nodded. "It's time."

"Does your abrupt departure have something to do with this being my engagement party?" Her losing-its-calm voice rose until the word *party* came out in a squeak.

Shane shrugged. "You knew I couldn't stay."

They stared at each other, their silence weighing on her chest like a block of stone. *Let me run away with you*, she pleaded without saying a word, and she could have sworn he responded, *I can't be your fantasy forever.*

She shut out his searching gaze and heard herself ask distantly, "Has anyone found the ring yet?"

Molly shook her head.

"I have to have it. My father wants to make the official announcement."

Laramie eased toward the second exit, a shortcut to the bedrooms. "I was going to double-check your room. You remember putting the ring on the bedside table, was that right?"

"At some point. It may have…fallen off." Grace shivered at the memory of Shane's hands on her breasts. Of his saying "sweetheart" in her ear. She had no intention of giving him up, just of stalling for a few hours longer. Was that too much to ask of a man?

Yes, she thought, studying his still face. It was.

Her brother, Victor, joined them in the kitchen, explaining with a shrug, "Michael sent me to retrieve his fiancée." He glanced at Shane, whom he'd been briefly introduced to, then took off his wire-frame glasses and polished the lenses, disconcerted by the tension in the room. Older than Grace by eight years, he was protective of her even as an adult and had often acted as the family peacemaker, though he usually deferred to their parents before their conflicts became too contentious. His studies and medical training had always been his refuge, just as the Cowgirl Club was Grace's.

"They want to make the announcement," he said, squinting.

No one spoke. No one moved.

Victor replaced his glasses and took a good look

at his sister's face. "You don't have to go through with it, Grace."

Her hard stare cut his. "Just like you didn't have to marry Caroline."

"It's not the same thing," Victor said, but clearly he was uncomfortable with the comparison.

Helen Farrow entered the kitchen, dainty heels tapping on the stone floor. A well-preserved fifty-six, she was chic as always in a form-fitting black skirt, ivory silk poet's blouse and a magnificent ethnic choker purchased in Africa. Her hair was as curly as Grace's, but cut short and sculpted into submission; an emergency color rinse at her favorite salon had brightened the reddish highlights. Although her expression was pleasant as she glanced around the room, skimming unblinkingly past Shane, she wore it like a shield.

"There you are, Grace." A raised eyebrow was Helen's only response to her daughter's feathered dress and odd neckwear. She extended a hand, always one to choose her battles judiciously. Tonight's was to see Grace safely engaged. "Come along now. It's time. Arthur and Michael are waiting."

"I wish I had been consulted." Grace strained to keep her voice level. The rest of the Farrows were so sure of themselves and their place in the world. Her mild instances of resistance usually came off as fractious and trivial. "Mother, have you ever considered that I might not want—"

"Nonsense." Helen's smile held as she looked toward the others. "If we hadn't sprung a proper engagement party on this girl, heaven knows what theme she'd have come up with on her own. Trapeze artists and fireworks, I imagine."

Worse than that, Grace thought, realizing that despite her true feelings, she couldn't wreck the evening for her parents and Michael.

Her mother gestured with a game-show hostess flourish. ''After you, darling.''

Grace went with a brief sigh, all that, as a Farrow, she'd *ever* be allowed. And how repressed was that?

To a degree, the others were all aware of the full import of the situation. Laramie sniffed and said, ''Like a lamb to the slaughter,'' before leaving the kitchen in the other direction. Molly wrung her hands, muttering her concern. Victor watched in mute futility.

Shane stared after Grace, momentarily rooted in place. With a clarity as sharp as a bobcat's teeth, he understood that the next move would have to be his.

9

SHOULD HE STEAL her hand or should he force it?

Shane stood at the back of the large Gothic living room where the guests had congregated, feeling sure that Grace would appreciate a grand gesture. He could ride Lion up Fifth Avenue, spinning a lariat, and she would come to him gratefully, roped or not. He could be both her savior and her escape.

Was that what he wanted?

Laramie sidled over to him. "Found the ring." The diamond winked in her palm. "It was in a little quill basket beside the bed, mixed up in a tangle of junk jewelry."

"Too late now," Shane said. Grace stood near the massive granite fireplace, flanked by her parents and a puffed-up Golden Boy. Arthur Farrow, a stocky, muscular man with silver brows and a matching fringe circling his suntanned bald head, was pontificating about the value of a good match and how impressed he'd been when Michael had asked for his daughter's hand in marriage. Helen Farrow smiled in agreement, her approval evident.

Grace looked pained.

"Judge Farrow's used to making long speeches," Laramie whispered. "We might have time to slip Grace the ring." Her glance slanted toward Shane's face. He couldn't imagine what she saw there, because to him it felt like a mask. "That is, if you want to…?"

He didn't. But Grace had said she did. And as much as it gnawed at his pride, and *his* possessiveness of her, he could see her point. It was a damned if you do, damned if you don't situation.

"Give me the ring," he said.

Laramie pressed it into his palm unquestioningly.

He hesitated, searching the crowd, unsure whether or not he should just bull his way forward and hand over the ring so Grace could make her sham engagement official. But would she think he was coming for her?

Should he be?

"Pass it on to Charlotte," Laramie suggested.

"Right." He threaded his way toward the woman from the penthouse, easy to identify because she had long blond hair like a fairy tale princess. She turned at his touch. "The ring," he murmured.

She nodded and passed the ring to her burly husband, who handed it forward to Troy Kazjakian. Troy glanced back as Shane rejoined Laramie, gave them a thumbs-up, and slipped through the narrow gap between Victor and Caroline like mercury in a thermometer. Several staunch upper-middle-class couples formed an unbreachable barrier between him and the Farrows. Fortunately, Johnny Jump-Up, the goofy TV character dressed in loud purple and yellow checks and polka dots, had snagged a ringside position. While Grace's father continued his lecture, Johnny and Troy consulted in urgent whispers.

"And so," Arthur Farrow said, "without further delay…"

The guests chuckled obligingly. Troy plucked the phony pansies off Johnny's top hat.

"I am happy to announce the engagement of my daughter, Grace…"

A few of the female guests oohed as Johnny stepped up to Grace in his wacky suit and zigzag tie, offering her the pansies with a sweeping bow. Shane saw the change in her expression when she realized that Johnny was also handing her the missing ring, but she managed to maintain her smile. It was not the wide, million-dollar, exclamation-point smile that Shane loved. His relief at that was painfully raw—little comfort.

"…to Mr. Michael Lynden," Arthur Farrow continued smoothly. He reached for Grace's hand.

After a fumbling moment of hesitation, she let her father take it. He passed her hand on to Michael, patted her knuckles and let out a hearty, "Congratulations!" as he enfolded the young couple in a big bear hug. The guests applauded.

To a chorus of cheers, Michael kissed his fiancée's hand. He held it up like a trophy, showing off the large sparkling diamond that decorated her third finger. Grace was accommodating, even indulgent, but despite her socially correct exterior she was searching the crowd for Shane.

He knew it. Her silent longing tugged at his heart, but the distance between them seemed immense.

Laramie tucked her arm around his and said something consoling. Molly appeared on his other side, her chocolate eyes gone bittersweet. She leaned her cheek against his shoulder.

Nevertheless, Shane felt totally alone. Here he was, hundreds, thousands of miles from home, odd man out, cut loose in a horribly fascinating city, and it was only now, in the instant of losing Grace, that his entire world seemed to drop away from beneath his feet.

BUNNY URQUHART WAS the kind of middle-aged busybody who gave middle-aged busybodies a bad name. She was sixty trying to appear forty, dark brunette gone a brassy New Yawk blond, every inch of her snipped, tucked and liposucked until all the life had been drained out of her. Only her eyes had retained their vitality. They were beady and mean as a ferret's, and they were trained on Grace Farrow and her new fiancé. That being the case, Grace was forced to smile brilliantly as she agreed to Michael's invitation to dance.

Their engagement party had picked up momentum, a by-product of Grace's half of the guest list. The fireplace had been lit and the rug rolled back, with lively music pouring from the hidden speakers of the stereo system so the entire room pulsed with sound. Her grandmother's classical piano recordings had come first, in keeping with the cocktail hour, but as alcohol was consumed and the atmosphere heated up, a variety of Grace's music was played, selections spanning from Patsy Cline to Aerosmith to Ricky Martin.

Michael danced well, in the way that he did most everything well. But there was no passion about it. Grace decided that dancing with Michael was like dancing with an uncle—pleasant at best. But dancing with Shane…ah, that would be an experience!

She wondered where he'd gone. There had been no sign of him since the official announcement.

"This is not a bad party," Michael said, occupied with rating the social value of the guest list instead of gazing into his beloved fiancée's eyes. "But who asked the doormen in? And couldn't you have hired a professional caterer?"

"Michael! Molly's been slaving in the kitchen all evening, and all as a favor. Give her some credit."

He swayed to the music, his expression as bland as vanilla pudding. "It was only a comment." He squeezed her waist. "We deserve the best, darling."

Guilt painted her cheeks crimson. Even though she was prolonging the engagement for his benefit, an argument could be made that she was treating him shabbily all the same. And it was true…he did deserve better than a temporary fiancée.

She took a deep breath. "Michael, we must talk— oh, ugh, *ptooey*." With a fingertip she removed a wet, lime-green feather from her mouth. Michael winced at the gauche display. "Pardon me," she murmured dutifully. "But as I was saying…"

The beat of the music accelerated. Michael swung her in a half circle—for him, an extravagant display of fervor. Quite a few of the tiny feathers from the trimmings on her dress wafted through the air. Perhaps there was a reason why marabou wasn't big on Madison Avenue.

Grace laid both hands heavily on Michael's shoulders and tried to appear serious even though one of the feathers had drifted onto the top of his head and was swaying back and forth in sync with the rest of him. "Can we go somewhere to talk?"

He made a face. "Do we have to talk *now?*"

"It would be best, I think…." She stopped, distracted by the phenomenon of her molting feathers. Apparently the glue that held them in place had softened in the warmth from the fire and accumulated bodies. When she took her hand off Michael's shoulder, the fine green dust she left behind made his suit look like it had grown moss. She shook her head in amazement; several feathers took flight, set free from the trap of her rampant curls.

"I hope that you realize now what a mistake that dress was," Michael said, screwing up his nose at the sight of her. Or maybe not. He sneezed, sending feathers spiraling through the air. Laughing, Troy caught one in his palm and blew it into the face of his date as they danced by.

Michael clenched his jaw. "After we're married, it might be smart if I help choose your wardrobe."

It was Grace's turn to make a face. "You do have very good taste," she conceded.

Michael evaluated her rather objectively. "Darker colors and more makeup would tone down your hair and freckles."

She thought of how Shane couldn't look at her without desire igniting the depths of his primeval-green eyes. "Can we talk about something more important than my appearance?"

Michael averted his face to discreetly snort a feather out of one nostril, then turned back and stared. "What is wrong with that dress?"

The dress, again. Who cared about her dress? "Whew, it's warm in here," she said. "Perhaps we should open the French doors." Maybe the cold air would coagulate her feathers. And once she got Michael alone out on the balcony, she could tell him the truth. It might be politic to wait for tomorrow, but she didn't want to go another night knowing that she'd let Shane down.

They brushed past another couple. When Grace looked back she saw that Bunny Urquhart—who'd finagled Quinn onto the dance floor so she could pump him about his recent marriage to Charlotte, no doubt—was left wearing a poufy tail of lime-green feathers across her rear end like a squirrel gone punk. In fact, tiny shreds of marabou were wafting through the high-ceilinged room like dandelion fluff. Many of the guests were amused, but others were glaring at her as if she'd begun molting on purpose.

"Grace!" Her mother's voice rose above the crowd. "Really, Grace—your dress. It's shedding."

Michael had released her to open one of the glass doors to the balcony, so Grace did an experimental twirl. She was enveloped in a flurry of green feathers, but only momentarily. A gust of wind swept inside and sent them swirling into the upper reaches of the vaulted ceiling.

"Look!" someone said. The scattered feathers slowly wafted downward, landing on guests' uplifted faces, in their drinks, on their plates of sticky marinated mushrooms. They landed on their expensive salon hairdos and glossed lips and cashmere sweaters. Inside their starched collars. Even in their exposed cleavages. With a debonair glint in his eye, George approached Queenie and plucked a lime-green feather from the depths of her overfilled, deep V neckline.

Grace started to giggle.

"Grace?" Apparently Michael couldn't see the humor. "Stop that," he said beneath his breath.

"Stop what?" She snorted with laughter. "Stop molting, or stop thinking it's funny?"

"Both!"

"But I can't," she said, a serious awareness growing through her gulps of laughter. "I've tried to be good and proper and boring, and I simply can't do it, Michael. Don't you see?" She rose on her toes, flapping her arms and wiggling her hips in her own unique Fifth Avenue version of the funky chicken, making more and more of the feathers fly off her dress. "I can't do it!" she sang jubilantly. "I can't be your fiancée!"

"*What?*"

She slapped a hand over her mouth, then took it away just as fast. "I'm sorry. I meant to tell you in private. It just kind of slipped out." She said it again, for good measure. "Michael, please don't hate me, but I can't be your fiancée!"

His brows drew together in a frown. "You sound…happy."

"I know. And I want you to be happy, too."

"I thought I was."

"Not in the way that really counts. You'll know what I mean when you fall in love." *Like me!*

A choked gasp signaled Helen Farrow's arrival. "Grace—oh, dear, Grace, what have you done now?" she wailed, her usual cool demeanor cracking.

The instant of spontaneous reaction gave Grace a glimpse of a woman she hardly knew, but recognized all the same. And that made what she was about to do a little bit easier. Perhaps, buried beneath her mother's easy confidence, were remnants of a girl very much like herself, a girl whose thirst for passion and adventure had matured into a strong marriage and a taste for travel. Perhaps Helen would come to understand Grace's choice sooner than expected, and would explain it to her husband.

"Mom," Grace said. Arthur Farrow bulled his way through the guests, looking thunderous. "And Dad. I didn't mean for this to happen tonight, but I—I guess there's no avoiding it now." *Spit it out,* she commanded herself, trying to steady her teetering conviction. "Mom, Dad…I'm not going to marry Michael."

"Yes, you are, Grace. It's all settled." Her father scowled ferociously. "We'll have no more of your shenanigans, my girl. It's time you lived up to the family name."

Grace met his eyes bravely. "You're right. And that's why I'm going to Wyoming!"

The announcement stunned the room. Her parents looked at each other in alarm, momentarily incapable of putting their many objections into words.

Grace scanned the party guests. Bunny Urquhart was tittering with glee, already relishing the gossip-mongering to come. Caroline let out a watery exclamation and fell into Victor's arms as if the shock had rendered her incapable of standing upright. Several of the older guests were whispering among themselves, denouncing her behavior, but in the scheme of larger crimes, Grace figured her small scandal wasn't really so bad. She'd broken no laws or caused any pain— not even to Michael. He did look upset, but she'd wager it was because of the ignominy rather than any great heartbreak over losing her.

Definite sounds of support came from the rest of the gathering, including Troy's sassy "Yee-haw!" and the glorious sight of Molly and Laramie rushing toward her, their arms open to welcome her back to full-fledged membership in the Cowgirl Club, no further forfeit necessary. They laughed and hugged like giddy schoolgirls.

"Where's Shane?" Grace asked, mopping her damp face with her sleeve. She spat out a couple of feathers, leery of Molly's sobering expression.

Laramie spoke first. "He was here for the engagement. I lost track of him once the dancing began."

"He didn't leave?"

Molly put her arm around Grace's shoulders for comfort. "If the positions were reversed, would you stay?"

Grace knew that she'd asked too much of him. He might even be counting himself lucky to be rid of a troublesome pest such as herself. Too bad—she was gonna stick to him like a burr under a saddle!

Caroline stepped out of Victor's arms. "How could you, Grace?" she demanded, spitting nails instead of feathers. "You're a disgrace to the family name. And what about Michael?" Her pinched-lemon face softened when she looked at him, talking in harried tones to the elder Farrows. Her hands went out. "Oh, Michael, you poor thing." Cooing in sympathy, she took him to her meager bosom. Victor stood apart, eyeing them curiously.

The Farrows approached. "Now, Grace..." her father began.

"Tell us you didn't really mean it," her mother said.

"I meant it more than I can ever say." Grace took Molly and Laramie's hands and squeezed them tightly. "It's a shock, I suppose, but you know about the Cowgirl Club—"

Her mother gestured dismissively. "Oh, that."

"I've always wanted another life. I just didn't know how to go about getting it."

"This is that cowboy's fault," Michael accused, tearing himself away from Caroline's ministrations. "You fancy him, don't you?"

"I think I love him," Grace said, "but that's not why—"

"Running off with a cowboy," Caroline sneered. "How very tacky!"

Helen hushed her. "Is this true, Grace? Are you planning to leave with—with—"

"Shane McHenry," Laramie said.

"From Treetop, Wyoming," Molly added exultantly.

Grace's smile was as wide as the prairies. "It's not true yet, Mom. But I have to say that I'm going to do my best to see that Shane doesn't get out of the city without me." Before any further objections could be raised, she turned to go.

Molly and Laramie accompanied her to the door. She stopped there to remove her ring. "Give this to Michael," she told Molly, dropping the diamond into her friend's cupped palm. "Tell him it never did fit me right."

Molly sniffled as she hugged Grace goodbye. "Remember the mantra."

"You've already done the hard part," Laramie said, joining the hug. "Straight talk is hard work when you've got the Farrows breathing down your neck."

Molly broke away, grinning. "But at least that leaves the good part…"

"Open skies and tight jeans," Grace murmured, knowing where she could find both.

Laramie held the door. "Go get 'em, cowgirl."

DEEP POOLS OF SHADOW had turned the enclosed stable yard into a spooky landscape of mysterious shapes and sounds that gave Grace the willies. Shivering, she pressed herself against the redbrick wall, welcoming the recognizable snort of one of the horses within. The night air was chilly. She should have grabbed a jacket and boots, but one didn't think about such practical matters when one was in the grip of a grand romantic gesture.

Parked near the arched exit was Shane's horse

trailer, hitched to his pickup, battened down for the trip to Wyoming. There was no sign of Shane.

Grace knew where he was. She scurried across the paved yard in her flimsy sling-back shoes and entered the stable, slinking unnoticed along the wall where the shadows were darkest.

Shane's voice carried. "You'll like her, Lion. She's a good rider. A good person..."

Grace stopped. He was leaving her the horse. Was that on a par with leaving her his heart?

For a cowboy, yes.

She slid into a nook and peered toward Lion's stall. Shane leaned against the stall's half door, one hand sliding back and forth beneath the horse's mane as he said goodbye. "As for the city..." His chuckle was brief. "Lion, I don't envy you the city. But you'll survive." There was a long pause. "So will I." He slapped the horse's shoulder. "Too bad neither of us will thrive."

Grace tilted her head against the wall, her eyelids closed to hold back tears. She would find a way to make everything right.

When she looked again, Shane's head was close to his horse's, his hand cupped beneath the stallion's nose. "Make my father proud," he murmured as Lion lipped at his palm. He stroked the horse's muzzle, bending even closer. His final goodbye was spoken in a voice pitched too low for Grace to hear.

He moved briskly to the tack room, stepping past her without a sideways glance. She kept still. Because she had impinged on such a private moment, she didn't want to show herself...yet.

While Shane gathered his saddle and other gear, she tiptoed to Lion's stall and opened the door just wide enough to slip inside. The stallion swung around to greet her, churning the fresh straw Shane must have put down. Trying not to think about her unprotected toes being squashed under one of Lion's heavy metal horseshoes, she reached for his halter, belatedly realizing that she didn't have a lead rope.

Shane was tucking his saddle into the trailer's tack compartment when she arrived, leading Lion by the short length of blue bandanna she'd tied to the halter. "Grace," he said. Just that.

"Don't *Grace* me. People are always *Grace*ing me. Well, I say get over it already. My name might be Grace Farrow, but from now on out, I'm doing as I please!"

Shane dropped his hands. He wagged his head. "Oh, Grace…"

"You might take this horse of yours before he crunches my tootsies."

She reached for the hasp on the door of the horse trailer as soon as he grabbed hold of Lion's halter. "What are you doing?" Shane asked, though it was obvious.

"Like I need a stallion." She scoffed to cover up the rawness of her throat. "Especially one as unmanageable as Lion."

"You've been managing just fine and you know it."

She swung open the upper wings of the trailer door. "Lion's going back with you. No arguments allowed."

Shane hesitated. "What about my sister's chance at music school? Have you forgotten why I needed to sell Lion in the first place?"

"We'll think of something else. There's got to be a way."

"*We'll* think of something?"

"We're a team, aren't we?"

Shane lowered his hat brim. "Not after tonight."

She turned so fast a few of her remaining feathers tore loose. She caught one, a symbol of her emancipation. "Tonight was a big night for me. It was the night I told Michael I couldn't marry him," she said. Her spirits soared. "It's the night I told *everyone* that I was going to Wyoming. With you." She uncurled her fingers and let the tiny feather go free, waving as it floated away on the night air. "Bye-bye."

"Listen," Shane said roughly, "that's all well and good. I applaud you. But it doesn't mean that you and I are..."

She fixed him with her most brilliant smile.

"We're not..." He shook his head helplessly.

She set her hands on her hips. "Why not?"

"Because it's too fast." With a clang, Shane let down the ramp and walked Lion into the trailer. His voice rang hollowly from the interior as he made quick work of securing the horse. "Fast doesn't last. Slow and easy's the thing. You need to take the time to think about what you really want. Now that all your options are open."

Open skies, she thought. *That's what I want.*

"But I like it fast," she said as he closed up the trailer doors. She was starting to feel just the teensiest bit worried. Shane couldn't possibly intend to leave without her, could he, when from the first it was obvious that they were meant to be together? How could any man be so gosh-darned foolish as to turn down a featherbrained, chicken-plucked cinnamon bun?

"Yeah, you would like it fast," he said, watching as she hugged herself for warmth. He took off his denim jacket and draped it over her shoulders. Then he just stood there, staring as if memorizing her, his face obscured by shadow so she couldn't quite tell what he meant, what he thought. If he still wanted her.

Abruptly, he turned on his heel and strode to the driver's side of the pickup. Grace panicked. She ran to the opposite side as fast as her heels could carry her, wrenched open the door and more or less flung herself into the cab. "I'm coming with you," she panted, wiggling up onto the seat. "There's no way you can stop me."

He got out of the truck. He walked around to her side. And he lifted her down, slinging her over his shoulder when she tried to squirm from his arms. She only had time to let out one lame squawk of protest and then he was dropping her onto a stack of straw bales outside the stable door. The breath went out of her at the jolt, even though she was only stunned at the expedience of his manhandling, not hurt.

"Don't move." Shane straightened the jacket around her, snapping a few of the snaps, making sure that she was all tucked inside. For a moment, his gaze lingered on her exposed thighs. She warmed with an answering desire, realizing that she could always *seduce* her way to Wyoming. Before she could attempt it, though, he gave her dress a good tug, covering as much leg as possible, which wasn't very much if the molten look in his eyes was any indication.

She curled one leg beneath her, making the defeathered hem rise again. "You moved," he accused.

"So sue me. I don't take orders well."

"Grace..."

"There you go again."

The corners of his mouth twitched. "I won't take you with me."

"But I'm no longer engaged! I'm totally unencumbered! There's absolutely nothing to stop me from living as I please!''

"Like I said, that's great. When I get home and call to invite you out for a visit, it'll be a simple matter for you to arrange time off, book a flight, pack a suitcase—''

"I'm not coming for some piddling little visit, Shane. You might as well send me to a dude ranch for all the good a vacation will do me.''

"A one- or two-week visit would be the right way for us to begin...if we mean to go on.''

Well, that sounded *slightly* better. "I still don't see why I can't come with you right now.''

He plucked a few of the remaining feathers off her dress and let them float away. "Seems to me that now's a good time for you to use your head instead of following your impulses. Goldstream's not the place for this kind of getup.'' He put his face close to hers and spoke low enough to raise goose bumps on her goose bumps. "Even though you do look pretty darn sexy.''

She stuck out her lower lip. "Then don't go without me.''

He kissed her. No more than a peck, really, but for Grace it was enough. Not enough to make her accept his leaving—enough to make her certain that she wouldn't let him leave alone.

"Let's do this the right way, sweetheart.'' He gave her a pat on the head and walked quickly to the truck, his boot heels clacking against the bricks. He waved. "See you soon.''

Grace waited for the slam of his door before she scrambled off the straw bales. Crouching low so Shane wouldn't spot her in the truck's rearview mirrors, she trotted to the horse trailer and popped the skinny side door open. When he started the engine, she clambered aboard, hoisting herself up over the side and shutting the door behind her so fast it nearly clipped her bare heels.

Startled by the intrusion, Lion tossed his head and whickered, shifting his bulk from side to side. The double trailer rocked on its wheels. She stroked the stallion's neck until he calmed, then moved shakily to the empty side of the partitioned interior as the rig rolled out of the stable yard.

She put her eye to one of the louvers that served as ventilation. In minutes, they were coasting past the acres of darkened parkland, probably on their way to the Lincoln Tunnel and New Jersey. "Goodbye, Central Park," she said, poking her fingers through the louvers until the cold, streaming air numbed the tips. "Goodbye, New York."

Hello, Wyoming? Astonished at what she'd done, she slumped onto one of the hay bales that half filled her side of the trailer. Lion had settled down for the long ride; he was pulling at the hay net hung near his head, swishing his tail contentedly. Suddenly, Grace was the nervous one. The entire trailer seemed to vibrate around her, its various parts rattling like dice in a cup. Already it smelled rather ripe. It was cold, too, and bound to get colder.

Despite the blaring sirens and traffic sounds of a typical evening in Manhattan, she could hear the powerful hum of Shane's truck engine, taking her away from all that was familiar. She huddled inside his jacket. Sooner or later, he'd stop, discover his stowaway and then...well, she didn't know what would happen then.

But she'd bet her entire life on a happy ending.

10

THE PROBLEM WITH driving the interstate at night was that it was dull. Staring mesmerized as the road unspooled beneath his wheels gave Shane far too much time to think.

For the first hundred miles, only momentum kept him going. He was sure it had been a mistake to leave Grace. The way she'd disappeared so quickly made him wonder if she'd run into the stable for cover, upset, maybe crying. The thought of Grace crying was not a good one. It ate at his resolve until he was on the verge of turning his rig around to go back for her.

On the other hand...

His decision to use caution had been wise. Grace herself had owned up to her impulsive nature. She had a lot to come to terms with, primarily the end of her engagement—*Way to go,* he couldn't help gloating—and her parents' disappointment. If he forced her to take it slow, to learn that reality was better than fantasy, thus keeping their already unlikely relationship in perspective, maybe they had a chance of lasting.

Where he came from, merely lasting out the winter was a challenge. Lasting a lifetime when you were as different as he and Grace would be an out-and-out miracle.

Then again...

Every time she smiled, he believed in miracles.

When his resolve weakened at the mere thought of her, he slapped the steering wheel to distract himself. He hummed along with a country-and-western radio station, and when that didn't work, he cussed a rare blue streak. Finally he grew silent, staring dully at the road until the broken white line blurred into one long arrow taking him away from Grace.

Figuring that crossing two states ought to have put enough acreage between them, he pulled over near the western border of Pennsylvania. It was too far and too late to return to New York. After sitting for five minutes with his hands clenched on the wheel, visions of Grace dancing through his head, he shook himself, put on a thick sweatshirt to replace the jacket he'd left behind, and stepped outside to check on Lion. God bless Grace for giving him the horse, even though that put him back at square one.

The night air was brisk and refreshing, its darkness cut by the neon lights of a twenty-four-hour gas station–diner–convenience store complex. Shane thought that if he tried he could probably convince himself that it was a good night to be alive and on the road— just a man and his horse.

Right. A tall tale, if ever he'd heard one.

Grace was with him. It didn't matter how many miles separated them.

Lion had zoned out, nodding in the kind of standing-on-all-four-legs-eyes-half-shut sleep that horses do so well. As Shane closed the side door, he saw that the hay net was empty. Knowing that Lion was liable to kick a dent in the trailer if he had nothing to occupy him during the ride, Shane climbed aboard to fill the net. And that's when he saw Grace.

Her eyes were open, but she didn't seem to be fully awake. Or at least not what he'd call cognizant. She was huddled in a nest made from the rearranged hay bales, her mouth working soundlessly as if her voice box was all frozen up. It probably was. His stock trailer was not built for human occupancy.

"Grace!" Kneeling on the bales, he scooped her into his lap. Her face was so white its freckles stood out like sprinkles of paprika. She was shaking all over. Her legs felt like Popsicles when he tried to chafe some life back into them, the panty hose covering them no better than a skim of ice. Stomach lurching, he mentally ran through the warning signs of hypothermia, which had contributed to his father's death fourteen years ago. Damn all if he'd let such a tragedy happen again!

"C-c-cold," Grace said, burrowing her face into his chest. He gathered her up in his arms, willing his body heat to rise enough to envelope her in its warmth. The truck heater would surely work better, but he didn't want to move her just yet.

"Grace," he murmured, hugging her. "Grace," he said, over and over again, as if her name was a hosanna.

She whispered; he had to lower his head to hers so he could hear. "D-d-don't Grace m-me," she said through chattering teeth.

"Stay awake, stay with me," he pleaded, but her response had elated him. She would be okay. He kissed her icy lips and cheeks, the reddened tip of her nose. For warmth, he told himself, not from the overwhelming joy at having her in his arms again. Such a purely impulsive reaction was Grace's territory.

He cradled her like a baby, saying, "Grace, what were you thinking?" For the moment, it was better than asking himself the same question.

"N-nobody ever t-told me t-trailers were such a wretched ride."

He stroked her cheek. "Next time, stick to first class."

She wrapped her arms around his shoulders, her eyes closing. "You bet."

To keep her awake, he started talking. He explained the difference between a heifer and a cow, between a steer and a bull. He talked about cattle prices, auctions, feedlots, relying on what he knew best until he got worried that he'd bore her back to sleep. Finally, he wrapped her in a horse blanket and carried her to the cab of the pickup, where the heater took away the last of her chill. He helped her dress in his sweatshirt and a pair of jeans, insisting she keep his denim jacket as well. While she reclined across the seat, warming her hands by the heater vents, he took her feet into his lap.

"What did I tell you about this getup?" He took off her girly shoes and warmed her poor frozen feet in his hands before sliding on a pair of his thick woolen socks. "And you haven't gotten even halfway to Wyoming yet."

With a wan smile, she tucked her hands into the jacket sleeves. "Make one little miscalculation and it's a federal offense."

"Hitching a ride in a horse trailer," he scoffed, finally able to swallow the lump in his throat. "What did you think you were doing?"

She gave a not-quite-apologetic shrug. "I was getting to Wyoming any way I could."

He gripped her feet. "What am I going to do with you?"

Her eyes narrowed. "Marry me?" she suggested in

a small voice, staring fixedly at the dome light in the ceiling.

"If that's what it takes."

Her blink came slowly. "Huh?"

"You heard me." *Love's an everyday miracle,* he thought. *It's Grace who's unbelievable.* Amazing how wonderful it felt to have her back where she belonged. The truth of it was, if they were together it didn't matter where they lived...as long as it was Treetop, Wyoming. He nearly laughed out loud at that, plumb crazy in love from his hat to his heels, but apparently not so far gone he'd give up the ranch.

Grace's lips were flirting with a smile. "Hmm...I guess that's good enough. For now." She crawled toward him, smile expanding. "You gonna take me home to Wyoming, cowboy?"

"Reckon so."

She nestled against his chest, making herself comfy as a kitten. "I couldn't go back, you know. I had to be with you."

He angled his face to look through the windshield, squinting as though he were staring into a stinging rainstorm. A semi rumbled across the blacktop parking lot on its way to the ramp. From not far off came the humming sounds of traffic on the freeway, heading west, into the open spaces that he craved.

"Hitching a ride in the trailer was a dumb thing to do," he said, keenly aware of the tenderness that underlay his gruff tone. "But at least it saved me from coming back for you." There were a million other things he wanted to say to her, words that would welcome her to Goldstream and keep her there for the rest of her life, words about love and commitment and raising a whole passel of pesky little cowpokes.

But he was a man who spoke more often of bulls

and barbed wire, so instead of putting his feelings into words, he simply held her in his arms and silently thanked the gods and powers and awesome, mystifying forces of New York City for giving him such a woman.

And after a good long while, his amazing Grace lifted her head off his chest and smiled at him with such eloquence that he knew no words were necessary.

Epilogue

IT TOOK THEM three days to reach Wyoming. Shane swore he could have made the trip faster if Grace hadn't insisted on stopping at motels along the way, but she hadn't heard any complaints when they shared a good dinner, hot shower and real bed. Nope, he'd stretched out on the bed like the king of the prairies, every pillow stacked beneath his head, a low chuckle rumbling in his chest while she did the dance of the seven towels to seduce the cowboy custom-built for her pleasure....

They also talked along the way. About everything. When she revealed the Cowgirl Club mantra, he laughed and shook his head, but then, after a few seconds of silence, surreptitiously adjusted himself inside his tight jeans as if maybe the mantra had hit a little too close for comfort. She looked out the window at the flatlands of Ohio, pretending not to see.

By the second day, he worked his way around to telling her about the wear and tear of living with his mother's complaints about the ranch. Answering to Grace's unending curiosity, he came to see that he'd been afraid of repeating his parents' mistakes with her. Since there was no quick way for her to convince him that though she might be a flibbertigibbet, she was a flibbertigibbet with gumption, she finally agreed to keep the option of wintering elsewhere open. Privately, Grace thought that being snowed-in with Shane sounded like a darned good honeymoon. And after the first winter, she'd be adjusted to ranch life and he'd be thoroughly accustomed to having a warm, willing woman in his bed, so there you go!

On the third day, they built castles in the air, eventually coming up with a not entirely far-fetched plan to put Lion out to stud. Shane owned a few good broodmares, too, so in a few years they could sell Lion's progeny back East, where prices were high and Grace had many well-connected connections. Ellie would get her music school, later if not sooner. And Shane's mother could do as she pleased, though Grace decided—still in private—that she would see to it there was a gift certificate from a travel agency tucked in her mother-in-law's Christmas stocking.

It wasn't until late on the third day that she ran out of talk and turned to word games. They tried the trick about making up your drag queen persona out of the names of your first pet and the street you grew up on. Grace's—Pumpkin Madison—worked, but Shane's turned out to be Inky Rural Route #1, which was dead-on for his present lifestyle, but not really suitable for wigs, makeup and heels. After she quit giggling over his reaction to that picture, she started doing anagrams with the letters in their names. The best she came up with for Shane was Seen My Ranch, with a leftover *H*. However, adding punctuation to her own anagram was a revelation. Grace Farrow could be rearranged into Race Far—Grow! And that was what she'd finally found the courage to do.

The sun was setting when they arrived in Treetop. It was a dinky little town, nothing special except for the majesty of the Rockies that framed it. Although Grace was dying to stop at the Thunderhead Saloon—she was picturing brass spittoons, a player piano and endless rounds of poker—Shane was focused on introducing her to his ranch in what he called the "right way."

They took a road that wound high up into the mountains, to an elevation of eight thousand feet. The air had grown thin enough for Grace to notice, but most of her attention was focused on the magnificent view. She got out of the pickup, an urban cowgirl in a trance.

Even this high up, they were surrounded by much taller mountains, the snow-capped peaks soaring into the sky like the spires of cathedrals. It was too much for Grace to take in.

She looked across the pine-laden valley, its autumn-brown pastures slashed by silver streams. Here and there leaves on slender aspen trees glimmered like gold and copper coins in the setting sun.

"There's Goldstream." Shane pointed, squinting as he gazed into the distance. She squinted, too, but couldn't really tell what she was looking for—there was too much land, too much sky, too much breathtaking beauty.

"I see it," she said, and that was the truth.

Shane's ranch was already in her heart.

HARLEQUIN

Duets™

When they were twelve, it was horses.

At fifteen it was boys…and horses.

At eighteen it was cowboys…
in tight jeans…and horses.

And *now*…look out, Cowboy!

Talented **Carrie Alexander** brings you

The Cowgirl Club

three smartly funny stories about love
between three most improbable couples.

April 2000 **Custom-Built Cowboy**
July 2000 **Counterfeit Cowboy**
October 2000 **Keepsake Cowboy**

Available at your favorite retail outlet.

HARLEQUIN®
Makes any time special.™

Visit us at www.romance.net   HDTCC

Looking For More Romance?

Visit Romance.net

Look us up on-line at: http://www.romance.net

Check in daily for these and other exciting features:

Hot off the press — View all current titles, and purchase them on-line.

What do the stars have in store for you?

Horoscope

Hot deals — Exclusive offers available only at Romance.net

Plus, don't miss our interactive quizzes, contests and bonus gifts.

PWEB

HEART OF THE WEST

Every Man Has His Price!

Lost Springs Ranch was
famous for turning young
mavericks into good men.
So word that the ranch was
in financial trouble sent
a herd of loyal bachelors
stampeding back to
Wyoming to put themselves
on the auction block!

July 1999	*Husband for Hire* Susan Wiggs	January 2000	*The Rancher and the Rich Girl* Heather MacAllister
August	*Courting Callie* Lynn Erickson	February	*Shane's Last Stand* Ruth Jean Dale
September	*Bachelor Father* Vicki Lewis Thompson	March	*A Baby by Chance* Cathy Gillen Thacker
October	*His Bodyguard* Muriel Jensen	April	*The Perfect Solution* Day Leclaire
November	*It Takes a Cowboy* Gina Wilkins	May	*Rent-a-Dad* Judy Christenberry
December	*Hitched by Christmas* Jule McBride	June	*Best Man in Wyoming* Margot Dalton

HARLEQUIN®
Makes any time special ™

Visit us at www.romance.net

PHHOWGEN

Love and GLORY
by LINDSAY McKENNA

Morgan's Mercenaries have captured the hearts
of millions of readers. Now, in this special
3-in-1 volume, discover the bestselling series
that began it all!

**Meet the Trayhern family—bound
by a tradition of honor…and
nearly ripped apart by the
tragic accusations that
shadow their lives and loves.**

"When it comes to action and romance,
nobody does it better than Ms. McKenna."
—*Romantic Times Magazine*

On sale April 2000 at your favorite retail outlet.

Silhouette®
Where love comes alive™

Visit us at www.romance.net

PSBR3500

ATTENTION ALL
ROMANCE READERS—

There's an
incredible offer
waiting for you!

For a limited time only, Harlequin will mail you
your **Free Guide** to the World of Romance

inside
romance

Get to know your **Favorite Authors,** such as
Diana Palmer and **Nora Roberts**
through in-depth biographies

Be the first to know about **New Titles**

Read Highlights from your
Favorite Romance Series

And take advantage of
Special Offers and **Contests**

Act now by visiting us online at
www.eHarlequin.com/rtlnewsletter

**Where all your romance news
is waiting for you!**

PNEWS

HARLEQUIN
Duets™

Ever wondered what would happen if you could change the way you look? Explore the pluses—and minuses!—of being transformed as we enter the topsy-turvy world of

Makeover Madness!

The Cinderella Solution
#23
Cathy Yardley
On sale
March 2000

Beauty and the Bet
#26
Isabel Sharpe
On sale April 2000

New and...Improved?
#28
Jill Shalvis
On sale May 2000

HARLEQUIN®
Makes any time special.™

Available at your favorite retail outlet.

Visit us at www.romance.net

HDMM